C000165689

BAD BLOOD

GUY YOUNG

Ordering Information:

For orders and inquiries, please contact:
1-888-375-9818
www.toplinkpublishing.com
bookorder@toplinkpublishing.com

Printed in the United States of America

PROLOGUE

S he died. She didn't need to die. She shouldn't have died, but she did. Her mother collapsed to the ground in shock. Her father, tears welled up in his eyes like a cup filled to the brim, dropped to the floor to console his wife. Her older brother cupped his hands over his face, perhaps too embarrassed to let the strangers in the room see him weeping like a baby, while her younger sister just stared straight ahead, mouth slightly agape, not able to fully comprehend what had transpired. The strangers in the room were the medical staff: nurses, doctors, social workers. They were all there to support the family, yet what could they do? The doctors had done what they could to save her, but they can't save everyone. It was the most helpless feeling a health-care provider could ever have. The chaplain was there too, but the arrival of the chaplain to a hospital room is rarely a welcome sight, and this case was no different. The chaplain's arrival, like that of vultures, meant death was nearby. His role now was to console and to aid in initiating the gut-wrenching grieving process.

She had doctors who were among the best specialists in the world working in one of the best hospitals in the world. They had the knowledge required, the supporting staff of nurses and other health-care professionals, and particularly, in this case, a family that did everything they could to care for their beloved. But she still died. How could this happen? How could this happen in a nation of such wealth and prosperity? Sometimes there are no explanations. Sometimes, we must simply accept that we and our loved ones are mortal and that to all their day will come. However, one never expects to have to bury a child—not ever and especially not as the child is just beginning to blossom into adulthood. Parents should never have to bury their child, but our health and the health of our loved ones is not entirely in our control.

Still, she shouldn't have died. Her doctors had the knowledge and experience but did not have all the tools at their disposal. It was like a firefighter arriving to the scene of a house ablaze with his brigade, his trucks, his axes, and ladders, only to find there is no water anywhere. In the case of the girl who died, it wasn't quite so random. Her doctors were soldiers with the best strategy yet without the best weapons. It shouldn't have been this way. She really shouldn't have died. But she did.

CHAPTER 1

NOVEMBER 22

NEW YORK CITY

lthough Thanksgiving was just around the corner, Manhattan was bathed in the unexpected warm sunshine of Indian summer. With a temperature around sixty-five degrees, Central Park was full of people enjoying what would likely be the last warm day for many months. Under the specter of climate change, the winters were colder and snowier than ever, and the summers were hotter, a combination that often wreaked havoc across the United States, and felt acutely in the largest city in the country. There had been many cases of children and spouses waiting additional days for their loved ones to return home from business trips, ruining many well-planned vacations. For all of man's ingenious inventions, it takes but a few inches of snow on the tarmacs, streets, and driveways to halt humanity's comings and goings as if they were a colony of marching ants frozen in time.

Could this Indian summer day be the harbinger of a warmer winter to come? Detective Sean O'Reilly pondered just that as he was sitting outside Foley's Irish Pub on Thirty-Third Street in the shadow of the Empire State Building. Although he hated the cold, snowy weather, it had one odd bonus—a lower crime rate. It seemed even the activities of criminals bowed to harsh weather. The weathermen were predicting a warmer than usual winter, but O'Reilly knew better than to believe them. *How wrong they were—and so many times*, he thought. If only he had a job where being wrong with infinite regularity was accepted, he would entertain far fewer of the commissioner of police's rants. The irony that meteorology was a science and detective work an art was not lost on him. The early-afternoon crowd at Foley's was a mixture of off-duty firefighters in jeans and T-shirts enjoying a late afternoon Guinness and well-dressed young men in suits and loosened ties drinking scotch on the rocks, McCallan or the like, and probably discussing their business dealings. Foley's had a very long, beautiful dark-wood bar on one side and cocktail tables lining the opposite wall.

The walls were painted black and hung with pictures of the motherland, Ireland: Trinity College and Grafton Street in Dublin, the Connemara coastline, and others. O'Reilly recognized the iconic Cliffs of Moher on the picture just above his table.

As he sat sipping his club soda and lemon—no alcohol was allowed while on duty—he wondered how his Irish ancestors had lived. He'd been told by his father that they had left during the horrendous potato famine, which peaked in 1847, and his family has remained in New York ever since. O'Reilly had grown up in a typical, blue-collar Irish American family in Queens, just over the bridge from Manhattan. His parents were caring and loving but also taskmasters when it came to school and homework. After all, his dad, a policeman for thirty years in the New York Police Department, and his mother, a public-school teacher, expected their children to achieve even loftier careers, if not equally noble ones, and while they were proud of their professions, they also realized that in the current culture of America they were both undervalued and underpaid. O'Reilly was a good son and took great pride in his parents' jobs, often reminding them that they had two of the most noble professions one could find. He had been fourteen years old when his grades first started to falter. His parents had sat him down and recounted in great detail how his great-grandfather had come to New York during the great Irish wave of immigration in the latter half of the nineteenth century. They'd gone on to explain how each successive generation had had better jobs, longer careers, and more money, and that he and his two sisters were expected to do the same.

While his sisters did achieve his parents' dreams, O'Reilly truly wanted to work in law enforcement, and though he went to great lengths to convince his parents of this, they surmised that he simply did not have the determination it took to finish college and go to a professional school. His oldest sister, Mary, was a lawyer working for Cravath, one of the most prestigious law firms in the world. His other sister, Kelly, had toiled through medical school for four years and was now a celebrated obstetrician with a million-dollar practice on Fifth Avenue, catering to the wealthy and donating twenty percent of her time to the poor who could not dream of affording her high-end services. She was one of the only physicians in New York who still paid house calls.

O'Reilly's grades eventually improved, but he was always fascinated by the crime-drama television shows of his teenage years—*Law & Order* was his favorite—and he was enthralled by the role the detectives played. He would dream he was Jerry Orbach playing Detective Lenny Briscoe and solving the crime. He was convinced, or at least he convinced himself, that the lawyers had it too easy, what with the detectives essentially handing them a slam-dunk case each time. Of course, that wasn't always true, neither on the show nor in real life, he would learn years later. Although his parents were disappointed at first, his father eventually reconciled himself with the fact that his only son, Sean, was not a beat cop but a detective, and eventually he grew proud that his son had indeed surpassed his achievements, as he had always hoped.

Sitting outside Foley's and sipping his club soda with his partner, Detective Jose Alvarez, he couldn't help but feel happy today—that is what Indian summer does. He had been partnered for nearly two years now with Detective Alvarez, who at thirty years of age was fifteen years his junior. Over the past two years, O'Reilly had gained a healthy amount of respect for Detective Alvarez, though at first he had balked at being partnered with him, considering that all of O'Reilly's associations with Hispanics to this point in his life had been with gangs, drugs, and assorted other crimes. When Alvarez showed up in his office announcing that he was his new partner, he had been utterly lost for words, not unlike the feeling he'd had when being asked to give a toast to his sisters and their grooms at their weddings. He'd never felt that he had harbored any bigotry toward any race or ethnic group, but the sense of shame that engulfed him like the swirling debris from a tornado had unearthed his hidden prejudice like an uprooted tree. After the initial discomfort and awkwardness, however, he grew to learn that he and Alvarez were more similar than different. Both had grown up in Queens in close-knit Catholic families, and both had high-achieving sisters that they simultaneously loved and hated. They were even both ardent fans of the New York Yankees and New York Giants, and once those facts surfaced, any last vestige of awkwardness disappeared, and it was as if they were cut from the same New York Yankees jersey.

The last few weeks had been quite slow. Crime had been falling in New York City for the past three decades, to the point that fewer detectives were being hired and those that were retiring were no longer being replaced. They had both unwittingly entered a field where their success could make them obsolete, and they feared falling victim to their department's success. As they sat inside Foley's, they pondered what they would do with their lives if that fate befell them. As the warm air caressed their faces, they felt content, despite the boredom. An Indian summer breeze transported the smiles and joy from one New Yorker's face to another. It was contagious. Then, Detective O'Reilly's phone rang.

"Hi, Sarge. What are we doing? Not much. Uh, we're just sitting outside, enjoying a perfect afternoon of Indian summer."

"Not perfect anymore," came the booming voice of Sergeant David Andrews, so loud that Alvarez could easily hear the conversation bursting forth from the tiny speakers of O'Reilly's mobile phone.

"What is it?"

"I'm not sure, but I want you and Alvarez to check it out. They told me that there is a lot of blood, but no sign of foul play."

"Uh, I don't get it. Blood, even a lot of it, doesn't mean a crime was committed," responded O'Reilly.

"Well, apparently this guy is dead *and* he's still bleeding. I've never heard of such a fucking thing, so I want you to check it out. Weren't you telling me recently you were bored and worried about losing your job?"

"Yeah."

"Well, maybe this will bring you some job security," Andrews continued. "Okay, Sarge. Where are we headed?" asked O'Reilly.

"The Plaza Hotel. Ask for a Mr. Ridgewell, the manager. He'll take you to the room."

As O'Reilly hung up and he and Alvarez stepped onto the concrete canyon that was Sixth Avenue, a stiff and cold wind began blowing from the west, pushing away the warm soft breezes they had both been enjoying. A swath of foreboding, dark-gray clouds with a leading edge of bright white clouds arcing toward the sky was heading in over the Hudson River like a gigantic upside down crashing wave. Indian summer was going to come to an abrupt end just as the weathermen had predicted. O'Reilly had to concede that their predictions were correct at least once in a while.

Upon arriving at the Plaza Hotel, they met Mr. Ridgewell. His calm demeanor in the lobby could not hide the look of terror in his eyes. It was as if he were staring down one of New York's broad avenues about to be hit by a bus. His eyes were bulging out of his head like those of a fish. It was clear that his pupils were dilated, and his lids flickered up and down at a maddening pace. Clearly he was trying to keep his emotions together in the lobby of this famous hotel with its expensive clientele all around and was exerting great effort to keep anyone from suspecting that anything unusual was happening. As O'Reilly reached for his badge, Ridgewell pushed his hand back down into his pocket and asked him to keep it in his jacket. For the clientele of the Plaza, everything was normal, and he wanted to keep it that way.

Ridgewell escorted them to the service elevator so as not to mix with the rich and chic tourists and business people. Once in the elevator, he became more agitated, and it became quite clear he was a rather good actor, because he entered a state of agitation and anxiety that would have clearly aroused the hotel guests, not to mention the employees.

His face had become distorted with terror, raising both O'Reilly's and Alvarez's pulse and blood pressure to the point that they could feel their hearts beating in their chests as they watched this display. After an interminable elevator ride, they finally reached the eighteenth floor and proceeded to room 1812. Ridgewell unlocked the door and stepped back. Now that he had escorted them to the room, he was in a full panic.

"I c-c-c-can't go in there again," Ridgewell stuttered.

"Okay, you don't have to, but tell us how you found the …" O'Reilly realized that besides finding blood, he didn't know what to expect. *Has Andrews forgot to tell us there was a body, too, or is there just blood?* he thought to himself.

"I got a call from one of our maids. She was frantic and could barely speak. When she finally did speak, she just kept saying '*sangre, sangre, sangre*' over and over again while hysterically crying," Ridgewell stated.

"What the hell does that mean?" asked O'Reilly.

"*Sangre* is *blood* in Spanish," Alvarez clarified. "You really didn't have any Hispanic people around you growing up," he added. He had thought that most Americans would know what *sangre* meant. "Then what?" O'Reilly asked.

"We got one of our bilingual employees to talk to the maid, and she stated that she walked in to clean the room and saw a huge puddle of blood and ran out crying. I wasn't sure what to think, so I went up there myself. I took one step into the room, and I saw a large puddle of blood. I took another step, making sure not to step in it, and saw the legs of what I am guessing is a man. I just saw the gray trousers and black shoes, and that was enough for me. Then I ran out and called the police."

Alvarez went in first, taking slow, deliberate steps. He had withdrawn his pistol and was followed closely by O'Reilly.

"Holy mother of God," exclaimed Alvarez suddenly.

"What the fuck!" added O'Reilly, not one to hold back on expletives.

"This can't be. Hey, Ridgewell," Alvarez yelled to the hallway, "what time did the maid find the blood?"

"It was at around 1:30." Ridgewell's distant voice came through the door. "Jose, it's 3:30—that's two fuckin' hours ago," O'Reilly said.

"It can't ... it just can't be," Alvarez replied. "Uh, are you sure he's dead?" O'Reilly asked. "He must be dead," Alvarez replied.

"Do you want to check?"

"Uh, why don't you do it—you're the more experienced detective," Alvarez skillfully deferred this gruesome task to his partner.

O'Reilly laughed. "Are you kidding me—what are you afraid of, man? Don't think you can tell a dead man from a living one?"

"Just ... I don't know ... it's too weird."

"All right. Move over a bit."

O'Reilly walked as gingerly as if there were a sleeping baby nearby toward the man's body. It was lying face up on the hardwood floor near the entrance area of the room. He made sure not to step on him or on the large, slowly expanding, pool of blood. He managed to gently grab the man's wrist. It was cold—quite cold. The coldness of his skin meant just one thing, and though O'Reilly was sure the man was dead, he nevertheless proceeded to check for a pulse just to be 100 percent sure, because what he and Alvarez saw defied all the logic that they could muster.

"He's dead, for sure," O'Reilly stated bluntly, looking up at his partner. "Okay, then, how can this be happening? This—it makes no sense," Alvarez wondered aloud.

"Let's call the crime scene unit. I'm sure there is a perfectly logical explanation."

"So you're sure he was murdered, then?"

"No, but we still need CSU here. Meanwhile, we need to find out who the stiff is. Hey, Ridgewell," O'Reilly shouted toward the hallway, "we need to know everything you have on this guy. Name, address, everything—got it?"

O'Reilly remained calm. He was the senior detective, after all, but he nevertheless felt the same discomfort and consternation that Alvarez was so avidly displaying. If this guy was dead—and he was, indeed, very dead—how could he still be bleeding? Dead people don't move. Dead people don't talk. And dead people don't bleed—at least not until today. With Alvarez now waiting in the hallway with Ridgewell, O'Reilly's morbid curiosity brought him back to the room for a closer inspection of the body. The closest he could get now was about two feet, due to the continuously enlarging pool of blood around the man. The body was fully dressed with a white—apparently starched—dress shirt with the top button undone, gray slacks, and shoes. The shirt was heavily stained with patches of bright-red blood. O'Reilly carefully bent down to take a close look at his face, and it was clear that blood was still slowly oozing from his nose and the corner of his mouth. It was trickling out slowly, the way milk leaks out from a half-empty carton turned on its side.

Having calmed Ridgewell down to some extent, Alvarez also returned to the room. Taking in the scene, he decided to pull out his iPhone and shoot some video, because he knew no one would believe them. The man had dark hair with some gray flecks behind the temples and looked well to do in O'Reilly's mind.

He did have a suite at the Plaza Hotel, after all, so he must be well off. He had no facial hair, and O'Reilly thought he looked almost presidential, but he did not recognize him as anyone famous. Then he stepped back and examined the room. There were no signs of a struggle, and Ridgewell assured him there had been no forced entry. The room was tidy—the bed was still made, the bathroom towels still hung neatly on their racks as if the man had just checked in. The only unusual aspect was the drops of blood in the sink, on the bathroom floor, and on the carpet near the bed. Even more bizarre was the fact that these drops appeared to have just landed, as they were still liquid. He then returned to the body and looked at the puddle of blood, which had expanded just a bit more in the five minutes he took to survey the room, bit by bloody bit. While he could not understand how a dead man could bleed, he also could not comprehend how this could be a crime. From what he could see, there were no marks on his body to suggest a struggle, no gunshot or stab wounds, nor any signs of blows to the head or body. Nothing. *How could this be, indeed?* he wondered to himself.

The Crime Scene Unit arrived within the hour. By then, the man had finally stopped bleeding, and O'Reilly was concerned that the CSU team wouldn't believe him, just as when he'd taken his car to the mechanic to evaluate a strange sound only for the sound to disappear at the most inopportune moment. He explained to the lead technologist that the dead man had just stopped bleeding a few minutes ago.

"Maybe it's the heat," the technologist said sarcastically. "You know, Indian summer."

O'Reilly, not sensing the sarcasm, replied, "I'm no expert in this, but that doesn't make any fuckin' sense. Besides, it's much hotter in the summer. It can't be the heat, and it's not that hot. Sixty-five degrees is not hot."

"I was kidding. Are you sure he was still bleeding when he was dead?"

"Yes, I am sure—do you think I'm an idiot? It doesn't take a fuckin' medical degree or your CSU certificate to know what bleeding looks like," O'Reilly retorted, now catching on to the technologist's tone.

"Then, are you sure he was dead?"

"Are you sure you're a crime scene investigator, asshole? Yes, I am sure—I'm damn sure. No pulse, and he was cold. Really cold," O'Reilly replied.

"We'll see about that," the technologist said pulling out a thermometer and taking the victim's body temperature in various locations. After a minute, he looked up at O'Reilly, his face taking on a decidedly different and more serious tone, and nodded his head, implying that the victim was indeed cold and had been dead for at least a few hours.

"Well, I can't explain it, then. I've been to hundreds of crime scenes, and I can tell you, dead people don't bleed," replied the CSU technologist as he gazed intently at the dead man and the large pool of purple blood surrounding him.

"Hey, is this some kind of fuckin' joke, detective?"

"What are you talking about?"

"Uh, the blood on the floor … well, I don't know. It's—it's weird."

"Weird. How?" asked O'Reilly.

"Well, it's still liquid. I mean, the blood should have dried up by now."

"Just make sure you get a lot of samples. God only knows what tests we might need to do on it."

"Yeah, okay. Fuck, this is weird. Who is the stiff anyway?" asked the technologist.

"We don't know yet."

The CSU team stayed in the room while O'Reilly went down to the lobby to meet up with Alvarez and Ridgewell, who had long since left the floor. On his way down, he tried to put together how this could be a crime, and he could not come up with even the most remote idea. Maybe the guy had some weird disease. He remembered watching some show on the Discovery Channel about Ebola virus and how people would bleed to death. But did they keep bleeding after they died? He couldn't remember that or whether it was even discussed on the show. He began to sweat as his thoughts turned to the possibility that he could have caught something being so close to the stiff. *No, I couldn't have*, he thought. *I'm just freaking myself out for no reason.* He could go for a drink about now—a real one, not another club soda. He only had those while on duty and always in a glass, so people would think he was having a real drink. *No self-respecting New York City detective drinks fuckin' sparkling water. Hell, no.*

O'Reilly had enough respect for the job that he'd never drink on duty, but his shift would soon be over—at least he hoped it would—so he could get a real drink.

Down in the lobby, he saw Alvarez and a now-calmer Ridgewell speaking behind the reception counter. They motioned to him, and the three of them settled into Ridgewell's office in the back room behind the reception desk.

"All right, what can you tell us about the dead guy?" asked Alvarez.

Ridgewell had pulled the man's information from the computer on his desk. "His name is Robert Anderson. He paid for the room with a Visa card, was staying alone, and has an address listed as 62 East Eighty-Sixth Street in the City. That's about it," offered Ridgewell.

"How much does his suite cost?" asked Alvarez.

"$1090 per night."

"Seriously? That's half my monthly rent," Alvarez exclaimed, not holding back his exasperation. "What does this guy do, I wonder?"

"I hate to tell you, Detective Alvarez, but there's lots of filthy-rich people around here, and they like to spend their money on lavish hotel rooms. If not, we'd be out of business," Ridgewell responded, noting that Alvarez didn't probably know the extent to which guests of the Plaza Hotel flaunted their money.

"Do we know if he's married? I mean, we need to notify his wife, you know, if he has one," O'Reilly put in. "I don't remember seeing a wedding ring, but I didn't look for one, either."

Just then, one of the hotel receptionists knocked on the Ridgewell's office door.

"Cindy, I asked that we not be disturbed," Ridgewell stated, clearly irritated.

"I know, Mr. Ridgewell. I am sorry, but—well—I'm not sure what to do."

"Well then, what is it?" he pleaded, now even more irritated.

"There is a woman at the desk, and she asked us to call Mr. Anderson's room—the one you said was not to be disturbed under any circumstance."

All three men stared at each other, each waiting for one or the other to figure out what to do. This was not expected—not so soon, anyway. Given that they had no idea whether Mr. Anderson was married or not, they couldn't be sure whether this was his wife or sister or daughter. In the confusion, they forgot to even ask Cindy how old the woman appeared to be. They summoned her back, and she suggested that the woman was probably in her thirties. O'Reilly figured Anderson to be around sixty years old, give or take, but this being America, and in particular New York, a thirty-something woman could be his daughter or his wife.

"What should we do?" asked an increasingly agitated Ridgewell.

They quickly put a plan together. It probably wouldn't work, but was worth a try, anyway. Ridgewell, clearly panicked, could not be counted on if the plan were to succeed, so Alvarez decided he would impersonate a hotel receptionist.

"Half the people working here are Hispanic anyway. I am the one most suited to get away with it."

He quickly donned a hotel uniform Ridgewell supplied him and went to the reception counter, where Cindy pointed out the woman to him.

"Hello, I am Jose; how can I help you, Ms., uh … what shall I call you?" Alvarez asked.

The woman was probably around thirty-five and strikingly beautiful. If this were Los Angeles, he was sure she would be a movie star. She was tall at five foot ten, with thick auburn hair flowing past her shoulders and a pair of Gucci sunglasses on top of her head holding her bangs back. Her eyes were green—so green that Alvarez thought they must be contacts, but looking carefully, he didn't see any. She was wearing hip-hugging tight-fitting jeans, showing off slender legs, shapely hips and bottom; and a snug cotton tank top with a light jacket over it. He could see her breasts were large—too large for her frame and presumably surgically enhanced. No question about it, this woman was beautiful, but more than that, she exuded a sexuality that eluded most women.

"You can call me Alexa, and you have all wasted too much of my time already," she answered in a way only rich and famous people can get away with—as if she deserved to be treated in a special way just because she was beautiful. "Sure, Alexa. I'm really sorry, but our guests expect a high degree of privacy and, well, I will be happy to call his room, but I would need your last name as well."

"Listen, Jose—is that your name?" she said in a demeaning and condescending tone, "either give me his room number or dial his room now. He is expecting me. Besides, how would I know he was staying here, anyway?"

"I understand, ma'am, but that is our hotel policy, and I am not at liberty to violate it."

"Well, who can violate it?"

"May I ask if you tried contacting him yourself? Surely he must have a cell phone?" Jose asked, trying to pry as much information as he could from the irritated beauty queen.

"Of course I tried, you idiot! Why would I ask you to contact him if I was able to? Jesus, you hotel workers aren't too bright. Well, I suppose if you were, you wouldn't be working here for minimum wage, would you?"

Clearly, she was reaching a boiling point, with each sentence more insulting than the one prior. Surely an ethnic slur was on its way, Jose thought, and surely this woman was capable and more than happy to deliver it, if it came to that. He kept his cool nonetheless, as any good hotel receptionist would, so as not to insult the rich guests.

"Okay, let me see what I can do. I'll be right back."

O'Reilly and Ridgewell were able to watch, though not hear, the exchange on closed-circuit television from the hotel security cameras. Ridgewell complemented Detective Alvarez on his hotel receptionist skills, particularly in light of Alexa's attitude and demands.

"Now what?" Alvarez asked O'Reilly.

"Call the room and let her have the phone. Obviously, there will be no answer, and let's see what she does. She's already pretty pissed off, so who knows? She might say something that will give us a clue about who she is."

Alvarez, or Jose now, returned to the reception desk. "I'm truly sorry, ma'am, for the delay. I have been given clearance to call the room. I can't give you the room number, as you know, so let me dial, and I'll give you the phone."

He dialed room 1812 and handed the phone to Alexa. She grasped the handle, held it to her ear, and waited ... and waited. The irritation on her face grew with each passing second and each ring. This was clearly a woman who was used to getting exactly what she wanted when she wanted it. Another second, another ring. Her face contorted to a scowl. Her eyes grew closer together, her eyebrows furrowed and now nearly touching each other. Her lips were pursed, and if it were possible, surely smoke would be coming out of her ears like a cartoon character that had had all it could take. Finally, rolling her eyes, she slammed the phone down.

"No fucking answer! He didn't answer my text messages or phone calls for the last two hours, and now this. Who the fuck does this asshole think he is?"

Alvarez was thinking of what he could say to irritate her just that little bit more so she might give something away about who she was and why she was meeting the bleeding dead guy.

"Ah, ma'am, perhaps he's just taking a nap." Knowing patience was not her strength, he then added, "If you like, you can have a seat in the lobby, and we can try again in half an hour or so."

She bit on the bait. "Yeah right, a nap. Not when he and I have a rendezvous, I can assure you. The fucking pussy probably started feeling guilty and went home to his useless wife."

Yes! thought Alvarez, that one line just provided the detectives with the first important piece of information about Mr. Anderson—if that was even his real name—that they had been able to gather so far. Unfortunately, following that display of anger, not to mention a healthy dose of humiliation, which Alexa was probably not used to, she bolted out the front door of the hotel.

Alvarez joined O'Reilly in the back office again, removed the hotel uniform, and got back into his work clothes as the three men thought about their next step.

"Well, he's got a wife," Alvarez said. "Let's start trying to track her down."

"Fine, see what you can do."

"Uh, detectives, what about the body? How long is he going to be here?" Ridgewell asked.

"Why, you want to get someone else in there and get a two-for-one special, Ridgewell?" O'Reilly asked, not withholding his cynicism.

"No, not at all. I just want to know when we can get the room cleaned up.

We'll probably need to replace the carpet, you know," he replied.

"Don't let anyone in there until we give you the all-clear. As for the body, once CSU is done, the stiff needs to go to the morgue."

"Maybe an autopsy will help," Alvarez said hopefully.

Just then the phone rang in the back office. Ridgewell answered. "Ridgewell here. What! Really! Okay, patch her through."

"Detective Alvarez, it's Alexa. She wants to talk to you. Maybe she would like a room with you," he said jokingly. He was clearly more relaxed than he had been before.

Alvarez, making a snarling face at Ridgewell's poor choice of humor, picked up the phone. After speaking into it, he quickly changed back into the hotel clothes and headed to the reception desk.

"Yes, Ms. Alexa, what can I do for you?"

"I think the bitch followed me. Is she here?"

"Uh, I am sorry, but who are you referring to?"

"The bitch—the wife, you moron."

"Oh, well, how would I recognize her, and what do you want me to tell her?"

"I don't want you to tell her anything, I just want to know if she is here—like I said, I think she followed me. I thought I saw her walk into the lobby as I was walking out."

"Well, how would I recognize her?"

"God, you're stupid. You don't need to recognize her. Just overhead-page her."

"Okay, but then what shall I say if she comes to the desk?"

"Tell her there was a call for her, and then hand her a phone with a dial tone and tell her the person hung up and did not identify himself."

"I am not sure she'll buy that."

"She will; she's not very, uh ... sophisticated."

"What's her name?"

"Julie Millbank."

"Oh, she has a different last name from her husband then?" queried Alvarez. "Were you born yesterday? Jesus! Her husband doesn't use his real name when he checks in here. He can't; he's too important—not to mention that cheating husbands have to be discreet."

"Sorry, you know, I'm not really … well, I don't know these things," Alvarez answered hesitatingly, as he was afraid he might be giving away that he was not really a "simple" hotel employee as Alexa believed him to be.

"Can you page her then and see if she responds? There's a nice tip in it for you. You know what bill Ben Franklin is on, I hope."

"Yes, I do. Thanks, ma'am."

He did as Alexa asked and had Julie Millbank paged to the reception desk. Just then, a woman Alvarez assumed to be in her late forties came to reception. He asked if she was Julie Millbank, and upon her confirmation, he handed her the phone. She picked it up, held it to her face, and then handed it to Alvarez. He pretended to be surprised at hearing just a dial tone, apologized, and stated that he didn't know whom it was that called for her. Mrs. Millbank then left the hotel.

Alexa returned, and Jose told her that a Julie Millbank had answered his call. He described her, and Alexa immediately knew it was the right person. *She must have figured out he's cheating on her again*, she thought.

"Thanks, Jose, and sorry that I was so impatient before and, well, you know, also for what I said to you."

That was as close to an apology as he was going to get. She handed him a hundred-dollar bill and left her cell-phone number. She asked him to call her if Mr. Anderson—well, Creighton Millbank—came to the hotel or called in.

"Creighton Millbank, is that really his name?"

"Yes, that's his real name. Ridiculous, isn't it?"

What neither Alexa nor Mrs. Millbank knew was that Creighton Millbank was lying in a pool of his own blood and that he wouldn't be coming in or calling—ever again.

O'Reilly and Alvarez were still unsure whether they were dealing with a criminal act or not; however, taking into consideration the unusual manner of Mr. Millbank's death, combined with the almost-bizarre encounter with Alexa and Mrs. Millbank at the hotel, they felt they needed to keep digging. They decided to split the work, with O'Reilly following up with Mrs. Millbank while Alvarez tried to find

Alexa and touch base with the coroner to see if there could be an explanation for what they had witnessed in room 1812.

O'Reilly tracked down Mrs. Millbank at her residence on Park Avenue, and she invited the detective inside based on his pretext that he needed to discuss something about her husband with her. To his surprise and concern, she had no questions for him before requesting that the doorman show him to their private elevator and up to her home. The apartment, if you can call it an apartment, covered three floors and twelve thousand square feet. There were six bedrooms, eight bathrooms, and an enormous great room with floor-to-ceiling windows and a mesmerizing view arcing from the north end of Queens nearly 270 degrees to Staten Island. The view encompassed a number of New York's bridges, from the Queensboro Bridge in the northeast to the Verrazano Bridge in the south. The air was clear despite the fact that it had become quite cloudy, and the view to the east over the flat plain of Long Island was endless. The apartment was lavishly furnished and had many works of art adorning the walls of the vestibule and the hallway that led to the sitting room. O'Reilly assumed they were very expensive, though his knowledge of art was nonexistent, so he really didn't know.

Mrs. Millbank's live-in maid brought a tray with coffee, tea, and water, as well as some biscuits that O'Reilly had never seen before. Mrs. Millbank was an attractive woman of about forty-five years old. It was clear that she took great pride in her appearance and was as fit as a thirty-year-old. The only thing that gave away her age were the wrinkles around her eyes and corners of her mouth. She was wearing nicely fitted khaki slacks and a thin blue sweater unbuttoned to just above her breasts, revealing a hint of cleavage. She had a gold watch around her wrist and what was probably an expensive double pearl choker caressing her neck. She was clearly a woman to be reckoned with, not only as a result of what she was wearing but also by the manner that she carried herself. This woman had self-confidence; there was no doubting that.

"So, detective, what is it that brings you here today?" asked Mrs. Millbank.

O'Reilly had thought to call and have a counselor come with him but at the end had decided not to. He felt comfortable and experienced enough to break the awful news to Mrs. Millbank himself.

"Mrs. Millbank—" he started.

"Please call me Julie."

"I'm afraid I have some terrible news," O'Reilly continued despite Mrs. Millbank's brief interruption. "Ah, I don't know quite how to say this, so I will just come out with it. Your husband is dead. We found him in a room in the Plaza Hotel."

"Oh, really. You don't say?" came her almost matter-of-fact response. It was as if she wasn't all that surprised.

"I'm very sorry, ma'am."

"I'm not," came her terse and cold reply.

"I, uh ... don't understand, Mrs. Millbank, I ... I thought you would be upset."

"Well, let me explain, then. You see, Creighton was—well, like you said 'I don't know quite how to say this, so I will just come out with it'—an asshole."

O'Reilly did not expect that word to come out of this seemingly highly refined lady.

"Creighton has been cheating on me for years. I confronted him about it finally last year, and he admitted it and asked me what I was going to do. He asked if I wanted a divorce. That's when I realized that he didn't want to be with me anymore," she continued. "I told him that if he wanted a divorce, he would have to be the one to push for it."

"But why?" asked a perplexed O'Reilly. "Our prenuptial agreement, that's why."

"I don't get it."

"We made an agreement that whoever demanded a divorce would only keep twenty percent of our assets. We figured that it would force us to work hard to keep our relationship strong and to not give up on our marriage easily. In other words, whoever wanted out would have to pay dearly."

"Money is more powerful than vows, I guess," suggested O'Reilly. "So, you're not upset at all."

"Well, let's see. He was rarely home. He cheated on me relentlessly. He didn't love me, and I get to collect on his life insurance—five million dollars—not to mention I get everything since, as his spouse, I will be the sole beneficiary. So, Detective O'Reilly, why *should* I be upset? I should be jumping up and down with joy, don't you think?"

"I came here to give you the terrible news of your husband's death and now I feel like perhaps I should be congratulating you. Regardless, I do need to ask you some questions about your husband, if that's okay."

"Go ahead."

For the next hour, Mrs. Millbank responded openly and, in O'Reilly's estimation, honestly about her husband's life. Creighton Millbank was born to a wealthy family in Brookline, Massachusetts, just outside of Boston. He went to Harvard University for undergraduate education, majoring in economics, and then to the Wharton School of Business at the University of Pennsylvania, graduating at the top of his class. He and Julie met in New York about ten years ago at a charity fundraiser event for the Museum of Modern Art. They began dating, fell in love, and got married less than a year after meeting. She explained that at their respective ages at the time, there had been no need to waste any time playing games. She went on to explain how Mr. Millbank had become so wealthy, stating that his first job after graduate school was at the Metropolitan Life Insurance Company (Met Life). He was initially in their annuities division but later moved into the risk-management division. During those years, he developed an interest in health insurance and became well known in the field for his novel methods for increasing profits. Mrs. Millbank didn't quite understand the nuances of his work, but she knew that he was highly regarded. Then, in 2001, he was recruited to be the CEO of Empire Health Insurance, one of the smaller players in the health-insurance industry at the time. Over the course of the last twelve years, Empire Health grew to become the second-largest health-insurance company in the United States. Their profits grew year after year with Mr. Millbank in charge. He was such a success that he was even featured on the cover of several business magazines. With the rising profits came an ever-increasing salary and even bigger bonuses, leading to an extravagant lifestyle for the two of them.

"Thank you for being so cooperative and for all that helpful information," said O'Reilly.

"Anything I can do to help you," she replied with a smile.

"There's a good chance I'll be contacting you again. I'm pretty sure we're going to have more questions for you."

"Certainly."

And with that, O'Reilly left. He had thought to ask Mrs. Millbank why she hadn't asked him about Creighton Millbank's manner of death, but then he decided not to in the end. He did find it rather curious, though, that she didn't inquire about it. Any rational, innocent human being would at least have the morbid curiosity to ask—this wife hadn't even offered a hint of curiosity.

CHAPTER 2

NOVEMBER 22

BASEL, SWITZERLAND

A silver sky hung over this border city in the northwest section of Switzerland. The Germans call it Basel, pronounced Ba-zel, while the French omit the *S* sound and simply pronounce it *Bahl* with the "ah" pronounced like the *A* in father. With both France and Germany just a short drive away, this city has embraced the best of both: the culture and cuisine of France with the industry and efficiency of Germany. Though a relatively small city, Basel houses the headquarters of some of the largest pharmaceutical companies in the world, including Novartis, Actelion, and Roche. Otherwise, it is fairly nondescript, lying between rolling hills in a valley split by the Rhine River.

Crime is not a common occurrence in Basel, which boasts an exceptionally low rate of violent crime. The Kantonspolizei, as the city police are called, mostly deal with petty, nonviolent crimes such as shoplifting, drug sales, and the odd burglary. It was not only for this reason, however, that Inspector Felix de Ville called for help. Inspector de Ville was not unlike many Swiss in the regions where the French and German influence overlapped. He had a German first name as the result of an agreement his Swiss German mother had made with his father before getting married. In fact, she had made it a condition for marrying

Henri de Ville, a Swiss businessman from the French-speaking part of Switzerland. Inspector de Ville spoke French, German, and English, as did many Swiss people, and he took pride in his ability to communicate freely in any of those languages. He was forty-eight years old, six feet tall, with a slim, muscular build, and at least according to his account, he was an excellent tennis player—just not quite good enough to make a career out of it. Despite his size and his position as the lead inspector in the Basel region, he was soft-spoken and exuded a gentle demeanor. Inspector de Ville was an intelligent man—intelligent enough to know that in this case he needed to get help.

He called his old childhood friend, Marco Kupfer, who had risen through the ranks of the Basel Kantonspolizei and, following a brief time working for an international security firm, found his way to Interpol. This was the multinational police organization based in Lyon, France, which lay just 180 miles from Basel. Although there was no evidence a crime had even been committed, much less one that would be under the jurisdiction of Interpol, Inspector de Ville could not think of a better place to seek guidance than from his old friend Marco.

"Hello, Marco, it's been a long time. How are you?"

"I am very well, thank you, and you?"

"I am quite fine. Still playing tennis. Teaching the kids to play now. Maybe one of them can be the next Roger Federer if they're lucky," de Ville said with a chuckle.

"Sure, if they're very lucky," responded Kupfer with a tone suggesting they had no chance of achieving that feat.

The small talk continued for several minutes as they caught up with each other's lives; they had not spoken in a few years. Marco's children were also twelve and nine years old, though they would rather play football (soccer), as many kids in France do. His oldest would be trying out with the local club in Lyon. Both had reached a point in their lives where they were quite settled, not bored, but much more settled than their younger years when nights had been composed of going to the clubs, drinking, and chasing women. Neither missed it, though.

Although their challenges were different now, there were still enough of them to keep life interesting.

"So, what's going on, Felix, that prompted this most unexpected call?"

"I need your help, but it would be best if you could come to Basel and see for yourself."

"How about at least a hint?" asked Kupfer.

"Okay. I know you've seen lots of dead bodies in your time, but have you ever seen one that was bleeding?" replied de Ville.

"I'm sorry; I don't understand."

"A dead person—their heart has stopped ... dead as dead can be, but ... still bleeding," answered de Ville haltingly. He was getting the sense his friend thought he was out of his mind—the local policeman with the wild story that he might embellish when there had not been any interesting cases for a long time.

"Uh, dead people don't bleed, Felix," came the terse response de Ville expected.

"That's why I need you to come here ... to see the pictures, the body, well, everything. A man died here, and I know it sounds crazy, but ... he was still bleeding even after he died. I can't explain it and, well, we don't get cases like this in Basel."

"Nobody gets these cases, Felix. There must be some simple explanation."

De Ville was getting the sense his old friend either didn't believe him or didn't want to bother with it, as if coming back to Basel was too petty for him now that his cases involved multibillion-dollar money laundering, terrorism, and multinational organized crime. He needed to find a way to convince Marco to come. He remembered that Kupfer had a favorite restaurant in Basel and that he was a lover of gourmet food.

"Marco, if you can come down just for the afternoon—a couple of hours, just to give me your thoughts—I'll take you to Cheval Blanc. Remember it? It's still here, and it's still ranked the best restaurant in Switzerland."

"Cheval Blanc, huh? Wow, I miss that place. I haven't found any restaurant like that in Lyon. Okay, since you seem quite desperate for my help, I'll come down, but please let me pay for dinner."

De Ville sensed a measure of condescension from that answer—desperate *and* he'll pay—but he needed the help, so he was willing to swallow his pride in this situation. He didn't want to feel foolish in front of the Swiss national police, so he would take Kupfer's help with whatever dose of humility was required.

Kupfer told his wife and kids he was going to help his old friend Felix and would be back either later in the evening or the next afternoon. During the two-hour train trip from Lyon to Basel, Kupfer was thinking about Cheval Blanc and what he would eat. He could not have anticipated how surprising this simple, short visit would end up being.

Felix, in the meantime, phoned the morgue and asked them to have the body ready for viewing. He realized that, with all the small talk with Kupfer and the time it had taken to convince him to come, they never even discussed anything about the case other than the peculiar finding of post-mortem bleeding. He figured Kupfer was really just coming for a memorable meal, since he hadn't even cared to ask any questions about the case. Felix also called his wife and told her he wouldn't be home for dinner. He could not have anticipated how much this case would change his life as he headed to the central train station to pick up his childhood friend.

"Felix, so good to see you! You look well."

"As do you, but if it is okay with you, we need to dispense with the pleasantries so that I can brief you."

"Go ahead," replied Kupfer.

"This morning I got a call from Terrapharma's main office here in Basel, asking me to come and give my opinion on a man who died there this morning. Since you left, Terrapharma has become one of the largest pharmaceutical companies in the world, with one blockbuster drug after another. They've developed various technologies to prolong the effect of drugs and have made billions selling drugs for everything from high cholesterol to cancer to erectile dysfunction."

"Prolonging the effects of an erectile-dysfunction drug—sounds like a recipe for disaster, if you ask me. I'm sure they didn't ask any women their opinion on that," Kupfer said cynically, and they both laughed.

"Have you ever seen the commercials for this drug on TV? The man and woman look so happy and are giving each other quite the look," de Ville added.

"Yeah, I've seen them. How long does this erection last, and who needs an erection to last for, what—days, weeks?" Kupfer continued.

"It's not like that. It just means men can have an erection whenever— uh, enough of that and, uh—" de Ville interrupted himself. "We don't need to discuss that. In any case, this once-small Swiss firm is now a multinational, multibillion-dollar company of tremendous proportions and has also become an important player in philanthropy in Switzerland and abroad. It is not just very financially successful but also highly respected in the business and medical world and even in the charity world. Before I went there, I asked them why they needed a policeman. They asked that I just come and have a look and didn't explain any further. I got there in fifteen minutes and was escorted to the offices of the chief executive officer, a Mr. Andreas Stern, and found him on the floor in a large puddle of blood. The paramedics were still there and just shook their heads when I looked at them. I asked them how long they thought he'd been dead, and they said he was still warm, so not more than thirty minutes. They happened to be in the building for another reason and were summoned to the office when Mr. Stern's executive assistant found him after he did not respond to his intercom."

"Was there any sign of foul play? Why did they call you? I mean, on what basis do they think this is criminal?" inquired Kupfer.

"Well, they said that they decided to call me because Mr. Stern was dead but was still bleeding, and they couldn't explain it, so they decided they ought to call the police. So I took the short drive down, and when I arrived, I asked them if they were sure he was dead, and they gave me a look, the 'we-are-not-idiots' look. So I stepped into his office to have a closer look, and all I can say is that he was still bleeding from his mouth and nose, and not a little either. It was as if he got punched—except there were no signs of trauma. I couldn't understand it and just stared at him, and he kept bleeding. It continued while I surveyed the office and spoke to the staff. I am telling you, it went on for an hour before it finally slowed down and eventually stopped. None of us knew what to do. He was dead—do you have to stop the bleeding in someone who is dead?"

"So, no signs of trauma, you said. Any forced entry into the building?

Anything out of the ordinary at all?" asked Kupfer. "No. Nothing. Strange, huh?"

"Yes, but what do you think I can do?"

"I don't know. I just felt that I should tell someone, and I felt most comfortable asking you. You know the Federal Criminal Police—they'll just swoop in and take over, or more likely, they'll just dismiss it," added de Ville.

"I'll tell you what. Let's conduct some interviews and see if it leads anywhere and go from there."

"Thanks, Marco. It will just make me feel better that it's not a crime if together we find nothing."

It was already three o'clock in the afternoon at this point, and the two men went directly to the Terrapharma offices, where de Ville pulled his car into the parking garage next to a gleaming ten-story glass-and-steel office building. They were greeted by an attendant who pointed them in the direction of visitor parking, to which de Ville proceeded. Kupfer was astonished at the size and modernity of this beautiful building. It was like a giant diamond jutting out from the drab stone it was embedded in. At the top of the building was a giant clock, with golden hands on a black background and enormous silver letters looking like a shiny, monogrammed necklace spelling out Terrapharma. Kupfer asked de Ville whether the whole building was solely for Terrapharma, to which de Ville replied that the building had been built and was owned by Terrapharma. After parking the car, they walked into the stunning lobby, which had a marble floor and beautifully adorned, lightly stained wood panels of various shapes jutting from the walls, supported from behind by short metal rods. The centerpiece of the lobby was a giant aquarium the size of a small swimming pool, filled with fish and corals of varying shapes and colors. In front of the elevator bank was a security desk with three guards sitting behind the rounded wooden partition.

De Ville introduced himself, and he and Kupfer flashed their badges, after which they were given a key card for the elevators.

They reached the top floor where Mr. Stern's office was located, and upon exiting the elevator were greeted by his executive secretary. She had gathered the list that de Ville had requested of all the employees who had regular contact with Mr. Stern during a typical week. De Ville and Kupfer spoke to as many of these employees as they could find. In addition, his executive secretary went through his calendar with the two policemen. It was all quite routine, including meetings with the senior staff and conferences calls. She stated that she always brought him his breakfast and lunch from the building cafeteria, which he took in his office alone, as was his modus operandi. He had arrived and left at his usual times. There was simply nothing out of the ordinary. They then met with the chief financial officer, Philippe Boudreaux, who went over the finances in simple terms and without revealing any company confidentiality, essentially telling the men that the company was doing very well.

"Could anyone want Mr. Stern dead for any financial reasons as it relates to the company? Has he had any deals fall through or any that took significant advantage of another company or another person?" asked Kupfer.

"Well, yes, everyone knows about the technology we bought from Sami Innovations, and surely they are not happy about it, but it was a fair deal," replied Boudreaux.

"I'm sorry, maybe we are not as worldly as you think—can you enlighten us about this?" asked de Ville.

"I take it you've heard of Provitax, yes?"

"That's the erectile dysfunction drug I was telling you about," added de Ville. "The one that lasts—how long *does* it last?" asked Kupfer.

"You just take one pill, and you can have normal erections for a month without having to worry about, you know, your performance," responded Boudreaux. "It has made us over ten billion dollars in just two years. You wouldn't think it was such a common problem, but apparently it is."

"How much does it cost?" asked Kupfer.

"It depends on the country, but more or less $150 per pill."

"Holy shit, are you kidding me!" exclaimed Kupfer. "Men are willing to pay this amount?"

"How often do you have sex, officer?" replied Boudreaux.

"That's none of your fucking business—no pun intended! And I don't need a pill to help me, by the way. Anyway, get on with this deal, would you?" replied Kupfer with obvious irritation.

"As I was saying, we bought the technology for the prolonged drug action three years ago from a small firm in Tromsø, Norway. We paid them 100 million dollars for it, fair and square, and now they're rather upset with us, since we have made one hundred times that in just two years, and that's just from sales of Provitax. We will keep making that much for the next ten years, until our patent runs out. We have also employed the technology in several other drugs. It was a great business deal for us," Boudreaux concluded.

"I see. Who is 'them'?"

"Ah, yes; that would be Sami Innovations and their founder and senior scientist. He is really quite upset, as he had spent ten years in the laboratory at the University of Tromsø developing this technology, essentially his life's work. Then, and apparently without his prior knowledge, the CEO of his company sold the patent to us. Apparently, the senior scientist hired some supposedly savvy Swedish businessman to help the company with their business arrangements and contracts, and his vision was that scientists belonged in the lab, not the boardroom. Anyway, he is pissed off, but we did nothing wrong, I swear."

"Fair enough, but could this scientist be pissed off enough to want to kill Mr. Stern?" asked Kupfer.

"Oh my God, Mr. Stern was killed! I thought he died of natural causes," a suddenly panicked Mr. Boudreaux fretted. "Do you think he'll come after me?"

"Hey, get a hold of yourself. First, no one said Mr. Stern was killed, and—"

"You said he was killed," a still anxious Boudreaux responded, with sweat beading on his forehead.

"No, I didn't. I just asked if this scientist was so pissed off that he would consider killing Mr. Stern. Anyway, you probably wouldn't know the answer to that," Kupfer said.

"Look," Boudreaux replied, slowly calming down, "this scientist did send us lots of e-mails claiming he didn't know about the sale and that he didn't get his fair share. He kept telling us how this was his life's work, etc., etc., and that we owed him more money."

"When did that start?" asked de Ville.

"Right after we closed the deal," replied Boudreaux.

"So, he's been after you for three years now?" Kupfer asked.

"Well, actually not that long, but the past year, when he realized how much we were making from the sales of Provitax."

"Did you offer him anything as compensation? I mean, you've got to feel for the guy, and you're making billions," added de Ville.

"No, we didn't. Look, business is business. It's not our fault this scientist hired a CEO who wasn't sufficiently experienced and who didn't realize the potential value of this invention. This is business, and it was a fair transaction," Boudreaux stated with the cold, calculating language of a CFO.

"What's this scientist's name, anyway?" asked Kupfer.

"Why? Do you think he did something to Mr. Stern?" asked Boudreaux, the panic and sweat returning.

"We don't know. It's just the way Mr. Stern died that makes us wonder if there was some foul play, that's all," added Kupfer.

"How did he die—I mean, what is it about how he died that makes you wonder?" More sweat.

"When we found him—" de Ville began to reply.

"We'll get to that later if we have time. What was the scientist's name?" interjected Kupfer, glancing at de Ville with a 'what-the-hell-are-you-doing?' look.

"Jan Erik Bergeland."

"And do you know where he lives?" asked Kupfer. "I assume he still lives in Tromsø."

"Where is Tromsø? I am embarrassed to ask," admitted de Ville.

"It's known as the Paris of the North," replied Kupfer, "and claims to have the northernmost university on earth."

"Thanks for the hint, but I need a little more than that," replied de Ville. Kupfer went on to explain that Tromsø was a small city in northern Norway, north of the Arctic circle at seventy degrees north latitude, which was well known for having both an excellent university with a strong research pedigree and as one of the best places on earth to see the aurora borealis, the Northern Lights. He went on tell him about a trip he had taken there with his wife in the summer—when the sun doesn't set and the bars don't close. He explained that the city was actually set on an island in the middle of a fjord and was connected to the mainland by two bridges.

"Must be cold as hell up there," de Ville assumed given its very northerly location not far from the northernmost point on the European continent.

"Actually, it's not much colder than Germany in the winter, due to the strong influence of the Gulf Stream. Even though it is the same latitude as parts of Siberia and Alaska, it is considerably warmer in the winter. You should visit it one day—it's quite a beautiful city. Take the kids; there's lots of nice hiking, boating, and they even have an aquarium," Kupfer suggested.

"Perhaps, but for now we need to get back to what, if anything, Jan Erik Bergeland has to do with the death of Mr. Stern," de Ville stated.

"Boudreaux, we'll need to see the e-mails Bergeland sent. For now, that will be all, but we may be back to ask you more questions," stated Kupfer. "Actually, one more thing, what happens now that Stern is dead? Who takes over?"

"The board has to decide that."

"And who is on the board?" Kupfer went on.

"Most of the senior leadership and some patient and doctor representatives from the community," responded Boudreaux.

"Does senior leadership include you?"

"What are you implying?"

"I didn't imply anything—I merely asked if you were on the board."

"Yes, I am," replied Boudreaux curtly, sensing he was under suspicion suddenly.

"Very well," Kupfer responded, "we'll need a list of the board members as well. Thanks."

Boudreaux had finally stopped sweating, when the beads began to form again. He thought Kupfer noticed too, which didn't make him feel particularly comfortable. He could not help but feel this out-of-town policeman had suspicions about him. *And he works for Interpol,* he thought, *so he must not be a complete idiot like the local policeman.*

"Sure, no problem."

Kupfer left his card with his e-mail and mobile number, as did de Ville, and they left the CFO's office.

They interviewed several other Terrapharma employees; however, none of the others offered up anything they considered interesting or useful, and none of them started sweating either, unlike Boudreaux, who had started and stopped sweating several times during their interview. They left Terrapharma with plans to return to view Bergeland's e-mails.

They then drove the wide, clean avenues of Basel, heading for the police station, which was right next to the morgue and the coroner's office. It was past five o'clock, and Kupfer couldn't stop thinking about Cheval Blanc, but it would have to wait for now. The fifteen-minute drive through the downtown area of Basel brought back many memories for Kupfer. While passing bars and restaurants he had frequented, he recalled the days of his youth, when he had just joined the police force and felt invincible. Police work had been, after all, his second choice for a career, and he was perfectly happy with that, knowing that his first choice—a professional footballer for Basel Football Club—was never going to happen. Passing St. Jakob-Park, FC Basel's beautiful and relatively new stadium, reminded him of his childhood dream, but it would never have been, as Kupfer had not come from a sporting family and was not much of an athlete growing up. That realization had come at the age of eleven, when he first tried out for his local football team but didn't even pass the first round of cuts. After crying and feeling sorry for himself the rest of that day and night, he woke up the next morning thinking he never wanted to feel that sense of worthlessness ever again and vowed to find a career in which he would excel.

Over lunch at school one day, sitting with de Ville, Kupfer had told him to look at the lady cleaning tables for a minute and to watch her carefully. De Ville had shrugged and said he didn't really notice anything. Marco had merely looked at him, sighed, and given him one more chance, telling him to watch even more carefully as she cleaned the tables—and that's when he noticed it too. As she used the rag to wash the table off, she "washed off" all the money on the table: coins and bills. *Ingenious*, thought Felix and smiled at Marco, who merely looked sternly at the woman.

A petty thief, is what Kupfer had thought. De Ville had remarked how observant Marco was and told him he should be a detective when he grew up. And that was it. From that day forward, all Marco thought about was a career in law enforcement. It was something he most certainly did excel in, and that is why de Ville had called him now. He needed his keen powers of observation and his skill at sniffing out a crime. After all, de Ville wasn't sure whether this dead man had died naturally or been killed. He knew calling Kupfer had been the right decision.

"Almost there," said de Ville. "We built a new police headquarters—very modern and technologically advanced, only we rarely rely on it. Who needs all this to catch stupid petty thieves and drug dealers?"

"Don't complain. You should see the shithole that is the Interpol office in Lyon. We have no money."

"So, why work there?"

"It's the cases—the crazy, tangled maze of information that we have to sift through. It's really challenging, and I love it. That's what keeps me going. I'm sorry, I probably sound so arrogant about that, but I just couldn't stay here in Basel and work these simple cases, like you. No offense."

"None taken," said de Ville and he smiled. "You always had ambition, and I am happy for you. And that is why I called you. I need your help to sort this out. It's probably nothing—the coroner will probably tell us that he died of natural causes and then we can have dinner at Cheval Blanc and you can go home."

They arrived at police headquarters, Kupfer dropped off his briefcase in de Ville's office, and they walked over to the morgue next door. Upon arrival, they were greeted by the receptionist, who told them Dr. Angelina Costa was waiting for them and led them to her office.

"Felix, hello! I am so glad you found time to come. I have already conducted the autopsy and have some interesting and, I think, good news for you," she said.

Dr. Costa was a well-respected pathologist who had completed her specialty training in forensic pathology at New York Hospital, in a program only the most highly regarded young pathologists were accepted to. Although she had been offered a position in New York, she'd always wanted to return to her Swiss roots and raise a family in Switzerland. Although she considered returning to Lugano, in the Italian part of southern Switzerland (or Svizzera to her), she couldn't envision an interesting life there as a pathologist. She spoke five languages fluently, having added Spanish to the French, German, English, and Italian that she'd learned growing up.

"Who did you bring with you today?" she asked with a smile, eyeing Kupfer as if he were an intruder.

"This is Inspector Kupfer, from Interpol," replied de Ville.

"Interpol," she said, laughing, "you must be kidding! What's this all about?"

"Marco is actually from Basel, a childhood friend, and I asked him to come and help me with this case."

"What case?" Costa said, surprise furrowing her eyebrows a bit. "Mr. Stern, of course."

"Well, there is no *case*, as you call it. There is no sign of foul play—no external injuries or wounds of any kind."

"I understand, but you did hear about how he was found, right?" de Ville asked.

"You mean the part that he was still bleeding even after he died—yes, I know about that, and now that I've completed the autopsy, it makes sense," Costa stated confidently.

"Uh, explain, please," de Ville requested impatiently.

"He bled to death. I found evidence of internal hemorrhage in many of his organs—liver, intestines, stomach, and brain. That's what killed him—the bleeding in the brain, that is. It increased his intracranial pressure, which compressed his brainstem against his skull, causing his vital functions to cease. So, I don't see any so-called case here. Felix, I think you're bored. Maybe *you* should go work for Interpol."

De Ville suddenly had a feeling of shame engulf him and sensed he was blushing; a sense of heat encircled him as if he had just stepped into a sauna. *What was I thinking, calling Marco here?* he thought. *I got all worked up over nothing. He must think I'm an idiot, not to mention what Angelina thinks of me now—she will keep laughing at me for years over this.*

"It just seemed so weird that someone could be bleeding after they died, so the paramedics suggested that I get called, just to make sure we weren't missing anything, you know, criminal—but I feel really stupid now," de Ville said as he put his hand on his forehead and scratched his head.

"I'm sorry, Felix; I didn't mean to make you feel stupid. It's just that I don't see how this could be criminal. He probably had an undiagnosed bleeding problem—you've heard of hemophilia, haven't you?"

"Yes, that's the disease where people can bleed anywhere, anytime, and can bleed to death, right?" he inquired.

"More or less. There are excellent treatments these days, and most boys—it affects males primarily—can lead a nearly normal life with treatment."

"Wouldn't Mr. Stern have known if he had hemophilia, though?" asked Kupfer.

"Some cases are not diagnosed until adulthood, and there are rare bleeding disorders like hemophilia that can be silent for years before some event leads to catastrophic bleeding," Costa answered.

"What kind of events?" Kupfer pressed.

"Another illness, medication—even just taking an aspirin could do it. Look, I am sure that is the explanation—a bleeding disorder. Unfortunately, now that his blood has finally clotted, we can't do the usual tests, but I can order some genetic tests, although none of those could ever fully rule out the possibility of a bleeding disorder. As the forensic pathologist, that will be my explanation—unless you come to me with some other information that might suggest a crime. But for the life of me, I can't imagine you will find anything. This is eminently and scientifically explainable."

"All right; thanks, and thanks for getting to the autopsy so quickly. I was worried we might be dealing with something, er ... criminal, but I am comfortable with your explanation," de Ville stated simply.

"Well then, Felix, I suppose we are off to dinner, then.

No more worries. Let's just relax and have a great meal," Kupfer said.

"Where are you going?" asked Costa.

"Cheval Blanc!" the two policeman said in unison, like children about to go to their favorite amusement park.

"Would you like to join us?" Kupfer offered.

"Sure, is that okay? Or perhaps I would be interfering with your catching up with each other."

"Nonsense; please join us. My treat," added Kupfer.

"Well, in that case, sure," Costa responded sarcastically. "Us locals can't afford to eat there, so we might as well take you up on this incredible opportunity."

Then she laughed. They all laughed. Felix felt relief; the laughter worked to unwind the uncomfortable tension he had been feeling since he got the call about Mr. Stern the previous day.

"When are you going?" asked Costa.

"Soon. We're going back to my office to get Marco's things, and we'll drive over in thirty minutes. We have a reservation set for 7:00. Shall we meet you there?" asked de Ville.

"Sure, that'll give me time to do one last check of my e-mail in my office. I'll walk over when I'm through in fifteen minutes or so."

Kupfer and de Ville left, discussing Costa's explanation regarding Mr. Stern. They trusted her and figured that there was no case after all. All the suspicions they'd fostered, Kupfer of Boudreaux and de Ville of Bergeland, vanished now. They laughed at how easily people could fall under suspicion for saying something that turned out to be totally innocent, and even how their behavior, Mr. Boudreaux's sweating, for example, could place a cloud of suspicion over someone who was entirely innocent. Kupfer explained to de Ville that at Interpol they constantly had to sift through the noise of so many suspicious people to find just one who was indeed hiding something. It reminded them of their days chasing young women in the bars of Basel, trying to pick out the one girl whose behavior showed genuine interest in them among the many whose flirtations were just that, flirtations. As they got back to de Ville's office, his phone was ringing. He picked it up.

"Yes, Felix here. What? You must be joking. Haven't you had your laugh at me today already? You're not joking? Seriously, now—okay, we'll be right over."

Felix marched over to Kupfer, pointed to the door, and told him to grab his briefcase. Kupfer looked surprised, but de Ville decided not to say anything. He had already looked like a fool today on more than one occasion, and he didn't want to have that feeling again. He just kept walking, heading back to Costa's office. They marched in and found her in front of her computer, staring at the screen with a worried, if not anxious, look on her face.

"Well, what is it, Angelina?" Felix asked.

"Why don't you read it for yourself? It's an e-mail from a pathologist friend from New York; we trained together."

They walked around to her computer screen and read the e-mail:

Hi Angelina,

I hope you are well. I just wanted to run something by you—I always trusted your opinions. You are the smartest and most intuitive pathologist I know. I'm warning you, though, it's going to sound weird. I just got a stiff who the police told me was bleeding for around two hours after he died. I laughed at them and told them they had a wild imagination; only then one of them produced a video he recorded on his iPhone showing a quite dead middle-aged man bleeding from his mouth and nose. Anyway, I autopsied him and well, I have to tell you I was surprised. He had hemorrhaged in most of his organs. Weird, huh? Anyway, if you have any thoughts, let me know. The asshole New York detectives, you know how aggressive they can be, are pressing me to tell them if I think this could be a criminal act. So far, I told them it appears natural—the stiff had no signs of trauma or any wounds of any kind. If you have any thoughts, let me know.

Thanks
Jennifer

"Can we still go to Cheval Blanc?" asked Costa.

Chapter 3

"If I was still in New York, they would call this Indian summer," remarked Dr. Andrew Friedman to no one in particular. He was sitting in his office, listening to *The King of Limbs*, the latest offering by Radiohead. "This is crap," he said. *What was Thom Yorke and company thinking*, he said to himself. *Sure, "Lotus Flower" is great, but the rest of this CD is virtually unlistenable.* Dr. Friedman loved Radiohead and other bands that explored at the edges of what was alternative music, but as much as he loved *In Rainbows*, one of the best collections of alternative music ever, he felt that Radiohead's latest work was just a bit too out there. After *Lotus Flower* ended, he turned off Radiohead and put on Sigur Ros, the innovative, unique, and incredibly talented band from tiny Iceland. He often mused how most people had heard their music either in movies or on television commercials and didn't even know. *Let them listen to Lady Gaga all they want; I'll keep listening to what I like,* he thought.

Dr. Friedman was forty years old and happily single. Well, mostly happily. He loved being around children—that is what had led him to him to pursue a career in pediatrics. He'd always thought he would one day want to have his own children, though he had recently wondered if he was getting too old for that. He was certainly hoping to one day meet a woman whom he would fall madly in love with; however, he had set quite a high standard for women he would be willing to even date. He felt that if there was no hope for a long-term relationship, then what was the point? He had had relationships with several women over the past ten years but none that he had stuck with—or rather, none that would stick with him. This was in part due to his career, a mixture of taking care of patients and research that kept him working through weekday evenings and weekends. His career was like a deep chasm between two cliffs, with just a flimsy wooden bridge connecting his work persona with his social persona. The women he did have brief relationships with only saw the chasm and sensed no hope to bridge the gap. The only real way to close the gap would be to build a sturdy bridge, and he had yet to figure out how to do that. Whether he used his career to put distance between himself and the women he dated, he wasn't sure.

After switching his iPhone from Radiohead to Sigur Ros, he returned to his desk at Children's Hospital Los Angeles (CHLA), not far from downtown, and began reading his e-mail. It was Thursday, and he had the morning to himself before heading down to the clinic to see patients. Thursday happened to be the thrombosis clinic, patients with blood clots, and the list for that day was long. That never bothered him, though, since he was at his happiest working with his team of health-care providers, taking care of children and their families with these unusual and complex medical problems. He truly enjoyed seeing patients. Some of his colleagues at other hospitals were getting burnt out, but Dr. Friedman's best guess was that it was because they didn't also pursue or participate in research. It was the research that provided the balance to his work. Seeing patients every day in the current era of medical bureaucracy took its toll, what with the seemingly endless amount of paperwork, or these days computer work, necessary to see patients and provide them with the best possible care.

He lamented how medicine had changed in over the last fifteen years. In the past, taking care of patients had involved spending time with them, their parents, and his team in developing the best treatment plan. But now more than half of his patient-care time involved documenting visits in the ever-more-complicated electronic medical record system, filling out overly complex billing forms, and dealing with health-insurance company denials of his recommended treatment plans. Since Dr. Friedman still loved the patient interactions, he accepted the drudgery of the other work, though reluctantly, and often complained about it to anyone who would listen. And he loved hematology and, in particular, coagulation disorders—diseases where a patient's blood either clotted too little or too much. He also loved the complexities and intricacies of the coagulation system, which is built from a series of many proteins that work together to prevent the body from bleeding to death if a wound or cut occurs but also are perfectly balanced so as not to clot too much. To him it was like an orchestra—many parts working together to perform a beautiful symphony. For those unfortunate patients who, either through a genetic error or an acquired medical condition, had an imbalance in their coagulation system leading to either too much bleeding or too much clotting, the symphony was terribly out of tune. This was Dr. Friedman's career; it was what he'd spent many years training for, and he always found joy in helping patients with these types of medical problems.

There was no joy and much frustration in the rest of the patient-related work. *I must sign my name a hundred fucking times a day, and that's not counting electronic signatures on the computer,* he would often say. Insurance forms, prescriptions, school notes, consultation notes, letters, more insurance forms, more prescriptions, and more insurance forms. *How did the American medical system get so fucked up,* he would ponder, *and how will it ever get fixed?* Besides the forms, there were all those training sessions, some in person and some online—and as soon as he finished one, another one was required. It was like looking at a freight train bending a curve in the tracks—just as you think you see the last car, another twenty begin to appear. Leadership training, sexual-harassment training, electronic medical record training, medico-legal training, and on and on. In med school no one had ever thought to mention that this would be part of the job. But back then it hadn't been part of an academic physician's routine, so perhaps he really couldn't blame those professors of days gone by.

He didn't mind some of it, and rather appreciated that some was required, such as the sexual-harassment training, for example. He had seen enough asshole men in supervisory positions abuse their power over the women who worked with them—or, as they saw it, *for* them—and were on a lower hierarchical rung. Oh, there was no shortage of hierarchy in medicine. Instead of generals, lieutenants, and sergeants, there were professors, associate professors, assistant professors, and if that weren't enough, the pyramid continued with medical trainees, from fellows to residents to medical students. And all of that was just the physicians' ladder. There were similar, if somewhat less complex, hierarchies for nurses, administrators, and even the security guards.

Sexual-harassment training was definitely necessary, and while he never felt that he learned anything that to him wasn't intuitively obvious, clearly there were men who, for reasons Dr. Friedman never quite understood, lacked such intuition. So, without a doubt, sexual harassment training was necessary. Perhaps, the reason Dr. Friedman had always held women in high esteem was related to the strong female figures he had come across throughout his life. Because of them, he had a tremendous amount of respect for women, regardless of whether they were his supervisors, colleagues, or assistants. There were strong and accomplished women both in his family and his profession. In fact, his two main early career mentors had been women. He would often say, "If the world were run by women, we wouldn't have wars, and the world would be a kinder and better place." As for the rest of all those training sessions, well, they were in his view mostly a waste of time. *A way for administrators to justify their jobs,* he would say.

Another area of deep frustration and one that often belittled the years of training he had was dealing with health-insurance companies. *The problem in the United States is that medicine is treated like any other business,* he thought. The goal of an insurance company is like that of any other company: make a profit while providing something humanity needs or wants. Dr. Friedman found this to be a conflict of interest. An insurance company takes in money through premiums paid by employers and the people they cover, as well as individuals who purchase extraordinarily complex policies on their own. The insurance company will then cover the costs of the medical care of those people by paying the providers—doctors, hospitals, pharmacies, etc. The more claims an insurance company denies, the less they pay out to providers and the more money they make. For this reason it is in their financial interest to deny the very service they are supposed to be providing. While Dr. Friedman recognized that all insurance works in such a manner, he hated the fact that with health insurance, the companies were gambling with the very lives and health of the people they were tasked with servicing. This was not the same as haggling with a car-insurance adjustor about the degree of damage to the front bumper of a car. Regardless, he was resigned to the fact that there was no way he could change the system, and so long as he wanted to take care of patients, dealing with insurance companies was a necessary evil.

After going through his e-mails, Dr. Friedman began working on a presentation he was due to give at an upcoming medical conference. His research had led to several important publications in prestigious medical journals, which in turn had led to invitations to discuss not only his research but patient care as well. He became a so-called expert in bleeding and clotting problems in children. While he was proud of that fact, he always claimed there were lots of other doctors who were more accomplished and more knowledgeable than he was, and he remained relatively humble. He was really looking forward to this presentation, as it was back in New York, where he had grown up, and he always loved visits to New York. He still had family and friends there, and of course, there was the pizza. He essentially refused to eat pizza anywhere other than New York. "The pizza in Los Angeles is shit," he would say.

The morning quickly passed, and it was time to head off to the clinic to see the patients in the thrombosis clinic. All the patients today had had a blood clot of some kind, and many were still receiving medication to prevent their blood clots from growing or returning. He was greeted in the clinic by members of his team, including a nurse, Andrea Carter, a physical therapist, Karen Jacobsen, and a young physician who had a strong interest in taking care of patients and performing research in coagulation disorders. Her name was Leila Baker, and her family had fled Iraq after the first Gulf War. Her family was Kurdish, and they rightly feared reprisals targeting the Kurds by Saddam Hussein after the war wound down and the American army had left. Once in the United States, the family changed its name from Bakir to Baker to make their children's lives easier. They wanted to change Leila's name to Linda, but she staunchly refused, telling her parents to let her keep something from her childhood. Everything else—toys, books, home, and friends—were lost.

"Good afternoon, boss," she said with a playful grin.

"You know I hate that. How many times am I going to tell you to call me Andy—not boss, Dr. Friedman, sir, or anything resembling that?"

"I know, but I love to hear you complain about it, uh … sir," she added, raising her eyebrows while maintaining her grin.

Leila had a healthy sense of humor, which Dr. Friedman appreciated.

"Don't you always say 'We need to have fun and laugh in this job, or we'll get burnt out'?" she added.

"Yes, you seem to be learning that part really well, but have I taught you any medicine as well or just my philosophies of life?"

"Both," she replied.

Leila had been just twelve when she'd left Iraq in 1991. Her family had first moved to Dearborn, Michigan, a haven for Iraqi refugees in the United States, but then had moved to Los Angeles a few years later, as Leila was entering high school. Her father wanted her to live in a more integrated community and while *he* missed being around other Iraqis, he felt it would be best for Leila and her two younger brothers to grow up, in his words, more American. That didn't sit well with his family, but that didn't stop him. Her father was an engineer. He'd found a job with an aerospace company in Redondo Beach and moved the family to California in 1994. They'd settled in El Segundo and began living the American (and California) dream.

Leila was an excellent student and had graduated at the top of her high-school class. She'd then gone to University of California Los Angeles, better known as UCLA, graduating with a 3.9 grade point average, and been accepted to the University of Southern California (USC) for medical school. She'd completed a three-year pediatrics residency followed by a three-year fellowship in pediatric hematology/oncology at Denver Children's Hospital, but she'd missed California and thus returned to Los Angeles after completing her training. She had accepted a position at Children's Hospital Los Angeles and joined Dr. Friedman in the Hemostasis and Thrombosis Center, the group in the Division of Pediatric Hematology/Oncology that focused on the patients with bleeding and clotting problems. She had developed this particular interest during her training years at Denver Children's Hospital, a center known for their expertise in that area. Dr. Friedman was delighted to have a young physician join his team who shared his interest and passion to care for patients and pursue research in this field. He always complained that not enough young physicians were entering the field of coagulation. In fact, Leila had been the first one to do so at CHLA in more than ten years.

"So, which patients are here?" Dr. Friedman asked.

"Lets' see," answered Andrea, the nurse. "Steven Findley, Jessica Espinosa, and Diana Vasquez."

"Great, let's start seeing them."

Andrea went to see Steven, a sixteen-year-old who'd developed a blood clot in his leg after being injured playing football. Leila went to see Jessica, an eleven-year-old with leukemia, who had a blood clot in her arm related to her leukemia treatment. And Dr. Friedman went to see Diana, a fifteen-year-old cheerleader and star student who had a pulmonary embolism, a dangerous blood clot in the lungs that is one of the leading causes of death in the developed world. In fact, Diana's older sister, Vanessa, had died a year ago from a pulmonary embolism. Her family was, as expected, devastated, and had not yet recovered from the shock and the loss. Dr. Friedman had recommended grief counseling, which the family had eagerly accepted and even a year later was still receiving. It turned out that Diana and her late sister had a genetic condition they were not aware of that increased the risk for developing blood clots. A little over a year ago, after returning from a trip to their native Costa Rica, both daughters had developed severe shortness of breath the day after the flight home. They'd come to the emergency room at Children's Hospital Los Angeles and been properly diagnosed and admitted to the hospital. Dr. Friedman had been consulted and taken over their care. They had been placed on blood thinners, first enoxaparin and then warfarin, also known as Coumadin, and been sent home in stable condition.

Unfortunately, Vanessa had developed another clot in her leg while on warfarin, an unusual situation that Dr. Friedman had rarely encountered, and she continued to develop blood clots despite the usual treatments. Eventually she was prescribed a blood thinner that had just been approved, called Lyzanda. It was very expensive and was not covered by the family's health insurance. The family could not afford to pay for the Lyzanda, so they opted to have Vanessa remain on the warfarin despite Dr. Friedman's concerns. Two weeks later, she had been at the movies with friends when she began coughing and having severe shortness of breath. Paramedics were summoned, but by the time they arrived it had been too late. She'd stopped breathing and could not be revived. Her autopsy demonstrated that a massive pulmonary embolism, a blood clot in the lungs, had killed her. Her family were beside themselves with grief and an insurmountable degree of guilt, which had not abated to this day.

"Hello, Diana, how are you?" Dr. Friedman asked.

"I'm fine, thank you. I feel really good, actually."

"No pain in your legs then, I presume, and no episodes of shortness of breath?"

"No, I feel great," she responded.

"How is the Coumadin going? Are you still losing some hair? I've got to admit I don't see it."

"My hair isn't falling out anymore, but how can you not tell? You're a doctor.

Aren't you supposed to have keen powers of observation?"

Clearly she had a good relationship with Dr. Friedman. Most patients didn't make fun of their doctors, though Dr. Friedman found it endearing.

"And how is your brother?"

"He's doing great. Would you believe, he just got hired by ExxonMobil and he is going to be helping them with international oil exploration? He is really excited about his work. He is going to get to travel a lot, which he is looking forward to, though I am going to miss him if he's gone too long," Diana said proudly.

Bryan Vasquez, her twenty-eight-year-old brother, was the first in the family to go to college, getting accepted to California Polytechnic University at San Luis Obispo, or Cal Poly SLO, as it's known. He had always been a stellar student and had a steely determination to succeed. He was the pride of the entire family, including those still back in Costa Rica. He had also been tested for the genetic clotting abnormality that his sisters had, but fortunately he did not have it.

Dr. Friedman then explained his thinking to Diana's parents, who were primarily Spanish-speaking, as were about fifty percent of the patients at Children's Hospital Los Angeles. There were interpreters always available to help. Dr. Friedman enjoyed caring for the Latino patients and their families. Although he was opposed to stereotyping groups, even if it was a positive stereotype, he nevertheless felt that the Latino families were unquestionably the most grateful patients. It was not that the Caucasian, African American, or Asian Americans weren't; it was just that the Latino patients and their parents seemed to be just that much *more* grateful as a group. The visit was one of many for this family and for Diana, and this office visit was quite routine. At the end of the visit, the father vigorously shook Dr. Friedman's hand and her mother gave him a gentle embrace. *What a great family,* Dr. Friedman thought, *and how sad that they lost a daughter and in such a sudden an awful manner.*

Next he went in to see Steven, the football player that Andrea was already seeing. Dr. Friedman liked the way they worked as a team. Andrea was a uniquely qualified nurse with a passion for taking care of patients with complicated problems, the ones most nurses, and doctors for that matter, preferred to avoid. Steven's main concern was when he could go back to playing football. He was two months into his treatment but needed at least one more month of his blood thinner,

Coumadin, as well, before he could stop, and it was far too dangerous to play a violent sport like football while on blood thinners.

"Doc, football season will be over by then. C'mon, let me stop now," he pleaded.

"It's not safe," Andrea responded. "You'll be fine for next season."

Andrea's attempt at consolation wasn't well received. "Next season" for a teenager is an eternity away. Steven was an excellent linebacker with the potential for a scholarship to a major university, and while he was only a sophomore, he worried that not playing this season could jeopardize a college career.

"I was reading about these new blood thinners that are supposed to be safer than Coumadin. Can't Steven go on one of those?" his mother asked.

"You've been doing your research, Mrs. Findley, I see," replied Friedman. "Look, they are really new and are not approved for children. Not yet, anyway."

"Children? Surely you are kidding! Steven may be sixteen, but he is six foot two and 230 pounds—he's bigger than ninety-five percent of adults. Isn't that what matters?"

"Good point, and yes, he is definitely adult-sized, but still ..." Dr. Friedman was searching for a reason not to prescribe Lyzanda to Steven.

All the studies clearly showed that the risk for bleeding was far less than for Coumadin, and if he did switch to Lyzanda, though he still could not officially allow him to play football, he thought he could tacitly suggest to him that it might be okay. *Ah, the insurance issues,* the thought and excuse came to him.

"I assume you are referring to Lyzanda. There is no way your insurance company will approve it anyway, since Coumadin is much cheaper."

"How much is it? If I can play football with that medicine instead, I'll pay for it myself," Steven said.

"It's ten dollars per pill, and at your size you'd need two per day, so that's twenty bucks a day," Dr. Friedman stated in a matter-of-fact manner.

"Jesus Christ, you've got to be kidding me," Steven added, incredulous.

"Steven, watch your language and be respectful," his mother said. "Doctor, how can that be? How can pharmacies charge that much for it? It's obscene. We're talking about medicine, not video games. People need medicines."

"Mrs. Findley, you're right. It is obscene, but what you have to understand is that drug companies spend many years and hundreds of millions of dollars developing these drugs, and they have to then recoup the costs of the drug development. And, of course, being companies, they have to make a profit, as well. I hate to say it, but at the end of the day making drugs is a business like making video games."

Steven was dejected. He worked hard at his weekend job at the sporting goods store and made some money, but there was no way he could pay twenty dollars a day for Lyzanda. Nor could his mother, who was raising him herself after her husband had died in a car accident several years ago. While they'd received a large payout from his life insurance, she'd needed to save that money for Steven's college education. There was no guarantee he would land a scholarship.

"Could you check with our insurance company, Doctor?" asked Mrs. Findley.

"Sure thing. I'll look into it and do my best," Andrea responded.

"Thanks," Steven said in a defeated tone.

After the visit, Andrea told Dr. Friedman that there was no chance the insurance company would pay for the Lyzanda, since one dose of Lyzanda cost more than a month's worth of Coumadin. He knew she was right. After all, Andrea was the one who made most of those calls on behalf of their patients. She'd once calculated the amount of time she spent on the phone with insurance companies, pharmacies, and financial counselors in private doctor's offices, and she'd found that for every thirty minutes she spent seeing patients, she spent an additional two hours dealing with that most annoying task. "I have to go and deal with my two hours of bullshit," she liked to say. Well, it would bullshit if it were not such an impediment to taking good care of patients. It was, in fact, all too real a problem. Dr. Friedman was not completely immune from dealing with such issues. He often helped Andrea, as she really did not have enough time to deal with the sheer volume of this irritating and frustrating work. He would deal with particularly difficult situations, like the Vanessa Vasquez case. He'd pleaded with the insurance company multiple times on her behalf, because she had needed an alternative to Coumadin, unlike Steven, for whom it was more of a luxury, just so he might play football.

After spending nearly an hour with the first two patients, Dr. Friedman caught up with Leila, who had been seeing Jessica, the girl with leukemia and the clot in her arm. She was doing quite well, with her leukemia in remission and her clot no longer present; her last ultrasound had demonstrated that. Leila spent a lot of time counseling the family about her blood thinner, Lovenox, and told her she just needed to stay on it for two more weeks and then she would be able to stop.

"Thank God," her mom stated. "She hates those shots."

Lovenox is given as a somewhat painful injection under the skin, and while the patients hate receiving it, even more so the parents hate having to inject their own children. When Dr. Friedman caught up with Leila, she told him how well Jessica was doing. He was pleased that at least one of the patients that day would be fairly straightforward. The rest of the afternoon proceeded uneventfully with six additional patients, none of whom posed any particular problem or unique challenge. All that was left was the paperwork, some on actual paper and much of it on the computer, though that didn't make it any easier. First they had to record the vital information from every visit, then complete the prescriptions and call the pharmacies, and then order all the laboratory tests and ultrasounds for the next visits. It was truly a Sisyphean effort with the incessant and redundant paperwork representing the rock Sisyphus was condemned to roll up the hill forever. This tedious task had to be completed for each patient during each clinic and then repeated again the following clinic and so on.

"I could use a drink this evening—who's up for it?" asked Andrea. "I'll go," said Leila.

While her family clearly wanted their children to integrate into the American lifestyle, they were still getting used to the bit about happy hour when alcohol was generally forbidden in their culture. Leila was indeed as much American as she was Iraqi at this point, and while she hated the second Gulf War and the American Imperialism, as she called it, she preferred not to dwell on it, instead focusing on living out her American dream. And that dream included having a Mojito now and then, especially after clinic.

"What about you, doc?" Leila asked.

"Not tonight, I have too much shit to do."

"What shit could be more important than hanging out with us?" Andrea asked in her typical teasing style.

"I'm sorry, but I have to finish a presentation I started working on this morning."

"That's lame," said Leila.

"Sorry. I'll tell you what—I'll meet you later on and we can get a bite to eat."

"Yeah, right. I'll believe it when I see it," Leila responded, clearly having heard that unfulfilled promise several times before.

With that, Dr. Friedman went back to his office to work on his presentation. He plugged his iPhone back into its dock and, scrolling through his choices, decided a good early-evening choice would be Death Cab for Cutie, the great Seattle Indie band. He put on "Soul Meets Body" and began working on his presentation. After thirty minutes, he had pieced together the last few slides, and he sat back in his chair to the soothing cello of Death Cab's "Bend to Squares." The fusion of rock music with classical instruments had remained one of Dr. Friedman's favorite styles of music since the time he'd discovered Electric Light Orchestra as a ten-year-old on Long Island.

He decided to check his e-mail before leaving to meet Andrea and Leila for dinner. He resolved to go if for no other reason than to prove Leila wrong.

When he checked his screen, he thought, *How could I have fifty e-mails in the last four hours?* He quickly scrolled through one after the other, deleting most without even opening them. *Why do so many people feel the need to "Reply to All" for e-mails that don't even need a response?*

He was about to leave when he saw an e-mail from a colleague in New York, Dr. Lisa Goldberg. He had known Dr. Goldberg from many meetings they'd attended together over the past ten years, but he had never actually worked with her. She was a pediatric hematologist at New York Hospital, and since she rarely e-mailed him, he decided to read it before heading out to meet Andrea and Leila.

Hi Andy,

Hope all is well with you. I'd like to pick your brain. One of my friends is a pathologist here at New York Hospital and she did an autopsy today on a middle-aged man who apparently bled to death. I didn't get a lot of detail, but she was asking me how common hemophilia is and at what age do the symptoms start and what kind of bleeding do patients get, etc. I had lunch with her, and she told me that this poor guy that died had bled into many of his organs and basically that he bled to death. I told her that it seems strange that a man that had no apparent bleeding symptoms would suddenly bleed so extensively internally and seemingly without provocation. So, I was fine answering all her questions but then she asked me a really strange one. She asked me: "When hemophiliacs die, can they still bleed?" Well, I didn't know what to say to that. I asked her why she was asking, and she told me that the dead guy apparently was still bleeding after he died. Have you ever heard of such a thing? Any thoughts? Thanks.

Lisa

Interesting, he thought. And with that, he headed out to meet Andrea and Leila.

CHAPTER 4

I t had been two days since the discovery of Creighton Millbank's body at the Plaza Hotel. His autopsy, which the coroner initiated the day he died and had completed yesterday, revealed the cause of death to be massive internal bleeding in many of his organs, including his brain, which was where the pathologist reported the fatal bleed had occurred. Over the past forty-eight hours, Detectives O'Reilly and Alvarez had been working virtually nonstop, and still they were no closer to determining whether he had died of a natural cause or was the victim of a crime. They decided to meet at police headquarters to go over what they had discovered so far. O'Reilly briefed Alvarez on his meeting with Mrs. Millbank and how he had grown ever more suspicious about her, particularly when thinking about the life insurance and the inheritance.

The building housing police headquarters, situated in Lower Manhattan at One Police Plaza, was a stark, red-brick, rectangular building constructed in 1973 that housed among other divisions the Homicide Analysis Unit, where Detectives O'Reilly and Alvarez worked. The building had identically shaped windows on every floor, lending a monotony belying the incredible stories that were discussed inside. Aside from the windows, the building otherwise had no character—in direct contradistinction to its inhabitants, an eclectic group of detectives, inspectors, and patrolmen from every ethnic group that New York City had to offer. The north wing of the sixth floor housed the offices of Detectives O'Reilly and Alvarez. The hallway was long and narrow, with a low ceiling and a series of doors opening off both sides. Detective O'Reilly's office had a window overlooking the square below, while the lower-ranked Alvarez still had to contend with a windowless office. Actually, he didn't mind, as it offered him more space to post pictures of the family he was so proud to be a part of. Alvarez made his way to O'Reilly's office to discuss their progress and sat on a chair across the desk from him.

"This guy really was an asshole, as Mrs. Millbank put it, but that doesn't mean he deserved to die," O'Reilly stated. "Assuming we are talking about a crime here, for sure his wife had a motive—he cheated on her, well, at least that's what she says—and she definitely had a financial motive, too—collecting the life insurance and inheriting their fortune. But either she is a really stupid criminal, more or less telling me she was happy he's dead, or she really had nothing to do with it. My gut tells me she had nothing to do with his death. I hope you've had more luck than I have trying to sort his out."

"Well, yes and no, I would say," replied Alvarez.

Detective Alvarez decided that a good news/bad news approach would work the best. For the bad news, which he elected to describe first, he explained that he hadn't been able to find Alexa, and that he was quite convinced that Alexa was not her real name, regardless. For the good news, Alvarez reported on his meeting with the coroner. He told O'Reilly that Mr. Millbank had bled to death and that while this could be explained by natural causes, the coroner was leaning toward something she could only describe as "unnatural." She had gone on to say that she had e-mailed a colleague in Switzerland, whom she described as the most brilliant pathologist she knew, and that was when he'd discovered what he called "the great coincidence."

"Holy shit! You've got to be kidding me. They have a stiff who died the same fuckin' way in Switzerland?" said a startled O'Reilly as he pondered the shocking information. "That—that can't just be a coincidence!"

His heart began to pound in his chest when he came to the realization that they were in all likelihood dealing with a crime.

"Yeah, it kind of reminded me of 9/11 a bit," Alvarez said as he continued his explanation. "You know, when the first plane hit the tower, everyone was like 'What a horrible plane crash,' but when the second plane hit, everyone—and I mean everyone—knew it was deliberate. One bleeding stiff, who knows what happened? But two on the same day dying the same way—it's got to be related, and almost without a doubt, it's got to be criminal. So, what are you thinking, Sean?"

"I don't know," replied a dumbfounded O'Reilly, "but there's got to be some explanation. I think we need to find out more about Mr. Millbank. Let's interview his employees, get some sense about his work and his business, and let's find out more about his personal life, including finding Alexa or whoever the fuck she is and any other mistresses he had. We need to find out everything we can about this asshole. Then, once we have all of that, we may need to take a trip to Switzerland—you think the boss will cover it?"

"Why are you calling him an asshole?" Alvarez questioned.

"I figure if his wife can call him an asshole, so can I. And I'm willing to bet we find a harem of mistresses and that his employees think he's an asshole."

The headquarters of Empire Health Insurance was located in a giant office building on West Thirty-Fourth Street, not far from the Empire State Building. It was a fifty-six-story structure owned entirely by the company, and they occupied most of the office space, though they leased several floors out to a pharmacy benefit-management company, Empire Prescriptions. Despite the similar name, they were in fact two separate companies. O'Reilly and Alvarez arrived shortly after lunch for a series of meetings, which their secretary had hastily arranged for them that morning. The chief operating officer, James Felton, at first resisted allowing the detectives on site, until threatened with a subpoena, at which point he relented. The detectives requested to meet with a variety of employees, ranging from upper management to the secretaries, from those with many years of experience to those with just a few, and in particular, they wanted to meet with a number of women—and specifically, young, attractive women. They began with Mr. Millbank's secretary, Susan Jenkins. She was an average-looking approximately fifty-year-old woman with a conservative hairstyle and glasses. After meeting the director of security in the lobby, they were escorted to Ms. Jenkins's office.

"Ms. Jenkins, my name is Detective O'Reilly, and this is Detective Alvarez. We need to ask you some questions about your former boss, whom I assume you know by now is deceased. Is that okay?" asked O'Reilly.

"Yes, I know. How tragic. Of course, I would like to help in any way I can, but why are you involved—I heard that Mr. Millbank died of natural causes," she replied.

"To be honest, we are not sure whether his death was natural or not, and we are simply trying to gather some information," O'Reilly answered, using his "polite policeman" tone that he had honed over years of doing interviews. He found witnesses to be more forthcoming if he was polite. It wasn't easy for him to speak that way. "How would you describe Mr. Millbank? Oh, and please be frank and honest."

"I'm not sure what I can tell you that would be of interest. He was very nice at times and very stern at other times. He wasn't in the office very much. He traveled a lot, and even when he was in town, he was often in meetings either here or off-site."

"I understand you kept his calendar—is that right?" Alvarez asked. "Yes, I did."

"So you always knew where he was, then. Is that correct?" continued Alvarez. "Well, more or less."

"I'm not sure what you mean by more or less."

"Um, well, I am … uh, not really sure I should say," Jenkins answered haltingly, clearly hesitating with her response.

Alvarez gave her a look, with his eyes cajoling her to continue.

"He, uh, sometimes left the office in the early afternoon and would not tell me where he was going. He just said he had an important meeting that came up and that he would not be returning the rest of the day. All I can say is that it seemed he was hiding something," she added.

"Go on," Alvarez pressed.

"I also would get strange phone calls—from women, well, recently from one woman in particular. She identified herself as Alexa, and she was very demanding, asking me where Mr. Millbank was and what he was doing. She called very often, you know, like she was checking on him."

"Do you have her last name?" Alvarez asked.

"No. I asked her several times, but she wouldn't give it to me."

"Did you ever meet her?"

"No. Never."

"When did this behavior begin?" O'Reilly chimed in. "I mean the disappearing for the afternoon and the calls from Alexa."

"About six months ago."

The meeting lasted another fifteen minutes; however, Ms. Jenkins had no additional noteworthy information. There was little doubt left that Mr. Millbank was having an affair with the so-called Alexa.

Next they met with several account managers, most of whom were nurses and one of whom was even a doctor from Vietnam. Their job was to review cases in order to determine whether a particular surgical procedure, test, or medication should be authorized, based on the patient's condition and their specific benefits—Empire Health offered numerous different insurance plans for employers to provide their employees, as well as individual plans. The permutations of benefits available with these plans were virtually infinite, making it essentially impossible for consumers to fully comprehend the plans they were choosing.

The nurses and the one doctor spent their entire days making decisions that would impact the lives of individuals they would never meet and for whom all they knew was what they read in their medical records. They also would review the appeals letters from the few with the fortitude to dispute their rulings. The nurses were all older women in their fifties and sixties, who had worked in hospitals and doctors' offices for many years before moving into the insurance industry. The three nurses the detectives interviewed that morning had never met Mr. Millbank.

Next they met Tran Vinh the doctor from Vietnam who, after several attempts, had failed to pass the United States medical licensing exam, a prerequisite to practicing medicine regardless of one's experience abroad. Thus he had given up any hope of ever being able to take care of patients. He'd answered an advertisement for physicians to review cases for an insurance company and had jumped at the opportunity. He'd felt this would allow him to utilize his medical skills and in some way he would have a positive impact on people's lives.

"Dr. Tran, have you ever met Mr. Millbank?" O'Reilly asked.

"Yes, a few time," he stated with his broken, heavily accented English catching the detectives by surprise.

"What was the nature of your meetings?" asked Alvarez.

"He ask me why I not deny more. I say I just do what I think is right," Tran continued, "but, he get very mad. He say my job is to deny, not approve. I say I don't understand, I think you want me to do what is right for the patient. He say no, you job is to do what is right for the company. He say, if I don't deny more, I get fired."

"So, what did you do?"

"Sir, I need job; I need take care of my family here and I need send money to my family in Hanoi. So, I deny approvals and write letters to say why procedure or medicine is not covered by insurance. I feel bad, but I need job, you know."

"We understand. Thank you," O'Reilly replied.

The rest of the day was spent meeting various other employees, but other than Dr. Tran, with his interesting insights into Mr. Millbank's business approach, none of the others had ever met Mr. Millbank and did not have any useful information. O'Reilly and Alvarez chose to meet with the chief operating officer and the chief financial officer together as their last meeting.

"Detectives, this is Patrick McFarlane, our chief financial officer. Please tell us how we can help," James Felton, the COO, started.

Alvarez began the questioning. "How would you characterize Mr. Millbank as a CEO?"

"He was a brilliant businessman. He took this company from a small regional player to one of the biggest health-insurance companies in the United States. He was an inspirational leader, charismatic, and really got his employees to believe in what we were doing and how we were helping millions of people. And the workers rallied," answered Felton in a manner befitting a long-term corporate executive.

"What made him so successful? I mean, how did he get you guys to get so big?" asked O'Reilly.

"Well, I would say getting the big accounts from the largest companies. From 2001 to 2010, we became the insurer for some of the biggest companies in the United States, including Ford, Honeywell, Disney, and others. These were enormous accounts and propelled us to the top," answered Felton.

"How did he convince these companies to switch to your company from their previous insurer?" Alvarez continued the interrogation.

"Business is sometimes complicated, but when you boil it down, it really all comes down to the bottom line—money. He offered the best rates for the companies. If one insurer would charge the company eight thousand dollars a year to cover one employee, Mr. Millbank would offer to provide the same coverage for seven thousand, or even less. Then, after we added one large company after another, suddenly companies would come to us," added the chief financial officer, McFarlane.

"And … you were able to provide the same level of service for less money? How were you able to do that?" Alvarez pressed harder. He sensed a problem, though he couldn't quite figure out what it might be.

"Look, detectives, the health-insurance business is very complicated. There are many plans, with different levels of benefits and many providers—doctors, hospitals, pharmacies, radiology services, etc. It would take hours to really explain how we were able to contain costs better than other insurers. I am happy to spend that time with you, but it is getting late, so we would need to set up another time," Felton answered cautiously.

"Very well; we may take you up on that, Mr. Felton," Alvarez responded politely.

Mr. Felton left, and the detectives were getting ready to leave when Mr. McFarlane invited them to his office.

"What is it, Mr. McFarlane?" asked a curious O'Reilly.

"Look, I've been here for the past few years and have been looking after the accounting very carefully, and well, something interesting happened two years ago. After winning all those contracts and becoming the number-one insurer in the US, we did initially begin collecting a lot of money from these companies, but, uh … then, the claims started coming in … and coming in … and coming in. We started to pay out huge sums in claims for all the patients we were now covering, and well, those great accounts we'd acquired were now beginning to cost us. We were heading to bankruptcy. I reviewed this with Mr. Millbank a couple of years ago, and not long after that, things started turning around, and we were making money again."

"Do you have an explanation?" asked Alvarez. He sensed more and more that something wasn't quite right.

"Not really. I mean, Mr. Felton was right in saying that this is a very complicated business."

Alvarez sensed Mr. McFarlane had something important he wanted to say but was afraid to say it. He decided to gently coax him along.

"But you think something fundamentally changed about the way business was done here, correct?"

"Yes."

With that, the interviews for the day ended. Neither O'Reilly nor Alvarez could quite figure out what, if anything, was wrong nor if there could be any connection to Mr. Millbank's death. On their way out of the building, they ran into Dr. Tran again, which triggered Alvarez to lob one more question at him.

"Dr. Tran, when did your meetings with Mr. Millbank start— you know, the ones where he told you to deny more procedures and medications?"

"Well, I start here three years ago, and he talked to me to have more denials about two years ago."

"Thanks," responded Alvarez, feeling more confident about his sense of a "problem"—perhaps even the one that had cost Mr. Millbank his life.

CHAPTER 5

Felix de Ville, Marco Kupfer, and Angelina Costa enjoyed their meal at Cheval Blanc—although they would have enjoyed it more had they not sensed they were becoming embroiled in a very serious situation. While Angelina continued to suggest theory after theory on how this could be a natural occurrence, however odd, both de Ville and Kupfer knew that two such occurrences couldn't be explained away as natural. Two deaths, by the same apparent cause, two continents apart on the same day, could only be explained by a deliberate act. In their minds, a crime had been committed. They spent the rest of the evening discussing their next step and agreed they needed to learn more about the death of the man in the United States. They decided to make contact with the police in New York and exchange information. Kupfer had to return to Lyon for two days to attend to Interpol matters; meanwhile, de Ville researched all he could about Terrapharma and the business of pharmaceutical companies. He decided to wait for Kupfer to return before delving further into the investigation in earnest.

When Kupfer returned two days later, de Ville picked him up from the train station and they proceeded to Del Mundo Café near downtown, each ordering an illy coffee and a croissant. There was nothing like a great Italian coffee with a warm French pastry for breakfast. They revisited the previous events step by step, just to be sure they agreed and were convinced that they were dealing with was in all likelihood a criminal act. As it was just 10:00 a.m. and Switzerland was six time zones ahead of New York, they realized it would several hours more before they could contact the New York City Police Department. Fortunately, Kupfer had contacts, through Interpol, directly to the commissioner's office, which would facilitate finding out who in New York was investigating the case. As they had at least four hours before they could realistically expect to make contact, they elected to return to Terrapharma to review the e-mail records of Mr. Stern. In particular, they were interested in reading the exchanges between Mr. Stern and the Norwegian scientist, Jan Erik Bergeland.

After making a quick stop at the police station to review the case with de Ville's superiors, Kupfer and de Ville headed back to Terrapharma's office building. They called ahead, requesting that Mr. Boudreaux meet them and bring their information-technology expert with him. When they arrived, Mr. Boudreaux took them to the board conference room, where they were greeted by Terrapharma's IT specialist, Reto Ingler, who claimed to be thirty-three years old but looked more like twenty-three. Reto had set up several screens, all linked to the same computer, so that they could quickly and easily read through the e-mails together.

"Well, detectives, where shall we start?" began Boudreaux.

Kupfer noted that Boudreaux seemed agitated again, just as the day before when they'd first questioned him.

"At the beginning," offered Kupfer in his usual commanding style.

"Reto, can you search Mr. Stern's e-mail correspondence with Mr. Bergeland, and can you search by date, please?" said Boudreaux.

"Sure, but don't you want to know how many e-mails there are first and the dates they span? Also, are you sure that it was only through these e-mail addresses that they communicated?" asked Reto. De Ville was impressed with Reto's thinking—he hadn't expected him to offer suggestions.

"We don't know, Reto, but we need to start somewhere," Boudreaux went on.

"That is fine, but I am not sure Mr. Bergeland would necessarily use this e-mail account to threaten Mr. Stern," said Reto.

"Do you know if by any chance he would know Mr. Stern's private e-mail account? I mean, he probably wouldn't know that," Alvarez offered.

"I agree, but you never know," Reto replied.

"You may be right, but let's start with the work e-mail account. So, how many e-mails are there between Stern and Bergeland, and when do they start?" asked Kupfer.

"Give me a minute." Reto feverishly typed at his keyboard, and after several minutes Reto gave them the answers. "The first correspondence is in 2003. There are 2113 e-mails between them over the past eight years, split nearly 50/50 between those to and from Mr. Stern. I can put them all on a flash drive and you can read them all if you wish, but is there something specific you are looking for?"

"Please put them all on a flash drive so we can go over them later, but for now we are looking for anything that might indicate a threat directed at Mr. Stern. Any suggestions?" asked Kupfer.

"We can search by keywords, if you like," responded Reto.

"Sure, let's do that. Let's see, what words shall we start with? How about *kill, threat, money, owe*? Any other suggestions, Felix?" asked Kupfer.

"How about *patent, idea*, and ... I can't think of any others right now."

"All right, Reto, what do we get with that?" Kupfer inquired.

"Give me a minute." Again they waited. "All right, well, there are none with the words *kill* or *death*, and as for the others, there are 412 e-mails that contain any of those words."

The group spent several hours perusing those 412 e-mails and additional ones that were linked to those they had read. Unfortunately, most of the e-mails were bland and strictly business related, and there was only one that could possibly suggest that Bergeland might seek revenge. It was dated March 23, 2009—one year after Lyzanda was marketed.

> *Andreas, for the last time, I am requesting that you renegotiate our deal. I have told you many times that my invention is worth much more than you have given me. You are making money hand over fist. You owe me more. The idiots that made the deal with you—well, you took advantage of them. You know it. I am asking you one last time, or else I will have to take drastic action.*

"What was Stern's response?" asked de Ville. "Just a short reply the next day," said Reto.

> *Bergeland, we have a signed contract. You signed it. I signed it. That's it.*
>
> *There will be no renegotiation.*

"Marco, what do you think?" asked de Ville.

"I think we need to speak to Mr. Bergeland. This could be interpreted many ways—a threat to harm or just a threat to pursue legal action or some other kind of nonviolent action. It certainly would not hold up in any court, or could it even be used to get a search warrant. It's too vague," replied Kupfer.

"So, what's our next step?"

"The New York detectives must be awake by now. We need to talk to them, and then we may need to pay them a visit. And … we definitely need to pay Mr. Bergeland a visit, as well."

"What is Tromsø like this time of year?" wondered de Ville.

"Dark, wet, and cold. Should be fun," answered Kupfer, making no attempt to hide his sarcasm.

CHAPTER 6

After a couple of busy days, Dr. Friedman finally got hold of Dr. Goldberg regarding the "bleeding dead man" case, as he called it. He always loved getting calls from colleagues asking him his opinion about difficult cases, and he was particularly intrigued by this bizarre case. He had never heard of someone bleeding after they had died, but then again, he wasn't often involved in cases where someone was dead. He also enjoyed talking about tough cases with colleagues, and so he invited Leila Baker to his office for the conference call he'd set up with Dr. Goldberg and the pathologist in New York, Jennifer Carmichael. With her interest in bleeding disorders, he figured this might be a good learning opportunity for her though he wasn't sure exactly how this particular case would unfold. Nevertheless, Dr. Friedman missed having a colleague as passionate and interested as he was in this field of medicine and as such made every effort to involved Dr. Baker in all of his work. He was happy that she agreed to come to to his office to help with this unusual situation.

"Hi, boss."

"Leila, how many times am I going to have to tell you to stop calling me that?

Please, just Andy," Dr. Friedman demanded.

"Until you learn to ignore me ... ah, sir," she said to needle him some more.

Leila knew Andy had a great sense of humor, but she enjoyed playing a game of one-upmanship, particularly when they were in the presence of the rest of their team. They would often compete to get the biggest laugh during their meetings.

Dr. Friedman in fact liked it when Leila teased him, but he couldn't tell whether she was just trying to be funny or if she was flirting with him. While he ordinarily despised it when women flirted with him, he somehow didn't mind when Leila did it. Perhaps it was because he found her to be not only attractive but also his intellectual peer. Leila had thick, raven-colored, wavy hair that flowed down past her shoulders, and large, round brown eyes with dark, curved eyebrows. She had a wide mouth with upturned corners and thick maroon-colored lips covering bright white teeth. She was always quick to smile, and her big, bright smile reminded him of Julia Roberts' beautiful, full-face, perfect smile. Leila was five foot four and generally dressed conservatively, hiding what Dr. Friedman sensed was a shapely figure underneath her loosely fitted clothes. Regardless of what he thought, any chance at a relationship beyond their working relationship was off-limits as far as he was concerned. First, she was someone he was supposed to be mentoring, and such relationships were not considered appropriate within the hospital system, and second and even more important, he was Jewish and she was Muslim. He was, in fact, glad there was no chance at a sexual relationship, since he felt that would interfere with their working relationship. Besides, he was sure she was not attracted to him.

Leila entered the Dr. Friedman's office and sat next to him, facing his large computer screen. He showed her the e-mail from Dr. Goldberg.

Hi Andy,

Hope all is well with you. I'd like to pick your brain.
One of my friends is a pathologist here at New York

Hospital and she did an autopsy today on a middle–aged man who apparently bled to death. I didn't get a lot of detail, but she was asking me how common hemophilia is and at what age do the symptoms start and what kind of bleeding do patients get, etc. I had lunch with her and she told me that this poor guy that died had bled into many of his organs and basically that he bled to death. I told her that it seems strange that a man that had no apparent bleeding symptoms would suddenly bleed so extensively internally and seemingly without provocation. So, I was fine answering all her questions but then she asked me a really strange one. She asked me: "When hemophiliacs die, can they still bleed?" Well, I didn't know what to say to that. I asked her why she was asking, and she told me that the dead guy apparently was still bleeding after he died. Have you ever heard of such a thing? Any thoughts? Thanks.

Lisa

"Andy, that's ridiculous. Seriously, we don't have time for this BS," Leila said firmly.

"Don't be so quick to judge, Leila. First, I trust my colleague, Lisa, and second—*hey*! You called me Andy. I think that's a first. Thank you."

"And second, *what?*"

"It's important to listen to people, be it our nurses, physical therapists, parents of patients and, of course, the patients themselves. You just never know what piece of information might solve your mystery or answer a key question. *Listen.* That is an important piece of advice."

"Fair enough, but don't you think this is beyond odd—even impossible?"

"It is bizarre, but let's see what Lisa has to say and go from there. Let's approach it as a mystery we need to solve and with open minds—it will make it more interesting and enjoyable that way," Andy suggested.

Lisa had sent Andy a series of pictures from the crime scene and the autopsy report, which she had asked him to have available for the conference call. He opened the e-mail with the link to all the pictures and was ready to view them. He then dialed the conference line.

"Hello, this is Dr. Andy Friedman. Anyone there?"

"Hi, Andy. Lisa here."

"Hi, Lisa and Andy, this is Jennifer. Can you hear me okay?" she asked.

A round of affirmative responses and "how are yous" followed. Andy introduced Leila to the hematologist and pathologist from New York.

"So, how can I help you?" Andy began the discussion.

"Can you give us a brief summary of hemophilia, Dr. Friedman?" asked the pathologist, Dr. Carmichael.

"I am going to let Leila tell you about hemophilia," he replied. Leila looked at Andy in surprise, and he gave her a "go-ahead" nod.

"Hemophilia is a genetic condition that occurs almost exclusively in males, because the gene defect is on the X chromosome and males have only one X chromosome. So, if they inherit an X chromosome from their mother that has a hemophilia mutation, they will be affected. Basically, people with hemophilia are much more prone to bleeding than others. There are three forms of the disease: severe, moderate, and mild. Severe hemophiliacs usual manifest bleeding symptoms from a very young age and untreated would have very frequent bleeding episodes, mostly in their joints, which can result in permanent damage that can be crippling. The moderate and mild forms have less-frequent bleeding episodes, and these are often associated with some kind of trauma. Patients with hemophilia are lacking an important protein in their blood, called *factor*, and they can be deficient in one of two factors: factor eight or factor nine. Treatment consists of replacing the missing factor with a medicine administered directly into the vein. Today, these medicines, called factors, are synthetically made and can be given regularly, say two or three times per week, in such a manner as to prevent bleeding. One important point is that these factors are very expensive—thousands of dollars for each dose, if you can believe that. So, to prevent bleeding, which would require 100-150 doses per year, you are talking about several hundred thousand dollars *each* year. In the developed world, patients with health insurance, Medicare or Medicaid, can receive this treatment with little out-of-pocket expense. In the developing world, most patients never get factor and die in their teens and twenties from bleeding. Anyway, that is a very brief overview," concluded Leila.

Andy put his lips together, raised his eyebrows, and gave a forward nod, an expression that indicated he was impressed with Leila's concise explanation.

"So, let me get to the point," followed Dr. Carmichael. "By all accounts, the deceased never had any bleeding symptoms in his life. We even uncovered that he had had three surgeries—a hernia repair and a tonsillectomy when he was a child, and an arthroscopy of his knee as a young adult—and didn't have any bleeding complications. Does that sound like someone who has hemophilia?"

"Extremely unlikely," Andy said.

"Is there a way we can test him for hemophilia?"

"You would need a fresh blood sample, and then it's a simple laboratory test," advised Leila.

"Well, that's not going to happen. Mr. Millbank gave his last blood sample on the floor of his hotel room a couple of days ago," came the blunt, if not ironic, response from Dr. Carmichael.

"Any chance there might be a blood sample from one of those old surgeries or a doctor's office visit?" asked Leila.

"No. We looked into that already, at Lisa's suggestion."

"The other option is to test his DNA. Many hemophilia mutations are well known, and a DNA lab can look for those. I have to say, though, that the chances of finding anything are slim, as it is extremely unlikely, given his medical history, that he has hemophilia," Andy chimed in.

"And even if you don't find any mutations, it cannot rule out hemophilia for a certainty, anyway," Leila added.

"Andy, Lisa here. So, can I sum things up by saying that Mr. Millbank in all likelihood does not have hemophilia?"

"Yes, that would be fair."

"So then, just out of curiosity, when hemophiliacs die, do they keep bleeding—let's say if they bled to death?" Lisa asked, changing the line of questioning.

"I don't see how that could happen. When a person dies, their blood stops flowing and it clots within minutes, so I don't see how anyone can bleed after they die," stated Andy matter-of-factly.

"Well, this guy did. The officers were very clear about that, and they even have a short video of the dead guy still bleeding."

"Video?" asked Andy.

"Yes, video. As you well know, everyone's mobile phone has video capability now. Detective Alvarez whipped out his iPhone and shot some video of Mr. Millbank—dead and bleeding," continued Carmichael.

"Andy, what could be the cause of this? You are the superstar hematologist and bleeding disorder expert. Give us some ideas—we are totally at a loss here," Lisa implored.

"I … I can't think of anything. I've seen lots of weird cases, but nothing like this. I would just chalk it up to some bizarre fluke."

"Well, we can't do that," Dr. Carmichael stated emphatically.

"What do you mean, you can't do that?" asked Andy bluntly.

"Because you can't have two bizarre flukes in one day," answered Carmichael.

"*What?* What do you mean, two?" asked a bewildered Dr. Friedman.

"There's another one. A man in his fifties in Basel, Switzerland, turned up dead a couple of days ago. And guess what?" Carmichael continued.

"No way!" Leila exclaimed.

"Yes way! He was bleeding for a couple of hours after he died, too. All over the floor of his office."

"Andy." Lisa spoke softly and with a hint of desperation in her voice. "Can you come to New York and help us out? We really need your expertise. The police are stumped. We're stumped. The New York press are crazy all over this. You remember what they're like, right? I am sure you can help us. Please."

Andy glanced at Leila, who held two thumbs up and smiled broadly.

"Okay, we'll work on the logistics and head over there in the next few days," he said, looking at Leila, who flashed that big Julia Roberts smile on her face. He could tell she was excited.

"Thanks so much," Lisa exclaimed.

The call ended, and Leila was still wearing that big smile on her face.

"What's with the giddy smile, Leila?"

"I've never been to New York. Are you really going to take me with you?" she said with the excitement of a young child.

"Yes, I certainly planned to, and now with that big smile, how can I say no? By the way, this is not a vacation or sightseeing trip. We've got a really interesting case to pursue, and we'll have lots of work to do over there."

"Yeah, but we have to eat sometime, and I heard New York has great restaurants."

Andy couldn't get over how excited Leila was, and it made him more excited about this trip. He wasn't sure what they would have to offer the investigation, but he never tired of trying to unravel a mystery. After all, that is why he'd chosen hematology as his field of study and patient care—there were lots of mysteries to unravel. What he and Leila did not know was that this trip to New York would only be the first part of what would become a long and fascinating adventure. In the coming weeks they would be logging many miles on many airplanes. They also didn't know that they would come across some familiar and entirely unexpected faces on this journey.

CHAPTER 7

NOVEMBER 25
BASEL, SWITZERLAND;
NEW YORK CITY

I t was early afternoon in Basel, the gray skies of the previous days
had parted, and glorious winter sunshine bathed the Rhine River
Valley. The air was dry and crisp, and the spectacularly blue sky
was dotted with small, impossibly white, fluffy clouds. Perhaps this
was a sign that some clarity would come to this perplexing case—at
least Detective de Ville hoped so. It was nearly three in the afternoon
by the time he and Kupfer had completed their review of the e-mails at
Terrapharma. They decided to pick up some lunch at a Turkish kebab
takeout place. They returned to the police station and settled into de
Ville's office with their food and drinks. De Ville asked his assistant
to get hold of the New York Police Department and find out who was
handling the mysterious "case of the bleeding dead man," as they had
begun calling it. In the meantime, they enjoyed their doner kebabs
and sparkling water. Unfortunately, his assistant was not having much
success in contacting the detectives involved in the case.

"Marco, any suggestions?" de Ville asked with a wink.

"Okay, I guess it's time to get some Interpol help," Kupfer responded.

Interpol headquarters could usually find out in a matter of minutes who was investigating any particular case worldwide—at least in countries that participated in the organization. Kupfer made two phone calls, turned to de Ville, and told him to be patient. After about five minutes, de Ville's phone rang.

"Hello, Detective Felix de Ville speaking."

"Yes, Detective, this is Commissioner Garret Williams speaking from the New York City Police Department. I understand you are looking to speak to a couple of our detectives about an unusual case."

"Yes, Commissioner, we understand that you have a victim who … well, had a bit of an unusual finding following his death."

"A bit unusual!" Commissioner Williams followed with a loud laugh. "A bit of an understatement, wouldn't you say?"

Commissioner Williams was a tall, well-built African American man who had risen through the ranks of the New York Police Department. He had exemplified outstanding leadership on 9/11 and been immediately noticed not only by his superiors but also by Mayor Rudolph Giuliani himself. He became New York City's first African American police commissioner and by all accounts their most effective one in many years. He commanded respect not for his size or booming voice but for his intelligence, charisma, and leadership skills. Political pundits suggested he had a bright future in politics should he choose that path.

"I take it you wish to speak to the detectives on the case here in New York. I will patch you through to them; however, I wanted to personally assure you that you have the full support of the New York City Police Department to help you figure this case out."

"Well, thank you very much, sir," responded an astonished de Ville. His experience in Europe was that such a high-ranking officer would never speak to a local detective, so he welcomed Commissioner Williams kind and heartfelt offer. Moments later, he and Kupfer were on a conference call with Detectives O'Reilly and Alvarez. They began by reviewing the basics of what they had each found at the crime scene, and they were all quite shocked at the similarities.

"This cannot be a coincidence," Alvarez firmly stated.

"No, not at all. We agree," added de Ville.

"So, could you guys tell us what the fuck happened over there? Sorry about the language—I can't help it," O'Reilly apologized.

"Yes, of course. Well …" de Ville began, a bit taken aback by O'Reilly's bluntness. "Let me begin with our side. We have the victim, Mr. Andreas Stern, a wealthy pharmaceutical company executive who had worked at Terrapharma for many years. At Terrapharma, we also have the following people who we met and interviewed: Philippe Boudreaux, the chief financial officer, and Reto Ingler, the head of IT."

"That's it. No one else is aware of this situation, then?" O'Reilly asked.

"Well, the staff at Terrapharma are aware that Mr. Stern has died."

"What I mean is, how many people know that he died, you know, and was still fuckin' bleeding?"

"I'm not entirely sure," de Ville replied politely. "His executive assistant found him, so she is aware, at least, that he was bleeding after he died. I don't know who she may have told."

"Seriously, then, you should just assume everyone at the company knows, unless you Swiss know how to keep quiet. I mean, if she's like all those blabbermouth New York secretaries, she would have told everyone she knows. Anyone else in Basel know the way your guy died?" O'Reilly went on.

"No one outside of police headquarters," Kupfer answered.

"Well, Angelina knows," de Ville corrected Kupfer.

"Who is Angelina, if I may ask?" Alvarez questioned in an overly polite tone, as if trying to compensate for his partner's behavior.

"Angelina Costa is our pathologist and coroner. She did the autopsy, so of course she knows about Mr. Stern and the manner of his death," de Ville replied.

"All right then. Anyone else?" O'Reilly asked again.

"No, that's it as far as we are aware," Kupfer added. "How about on your end?"

"How much time have you got?" O'Reilly sharply stated.

Alvarez, hearing the silence, chimed in. "Things are quite a bit more complicated on our end, you see. That is what Sean meant. Sean, shall I?" Alvarez followed up.

"Sure, if you can keep it all straight. Good luck."

"Our victim is a Mr. Creighton Millbank, CEO of a large health-insurance company. He was found dead in the same fashion as your Mr. Stern. Only instead of dying in his office, he was found in a hotel room, presumably waiting for a mistress of his named Alexa. We don't know who this Alexa is, but it seems she was at least one of his mistresses. Of course, where there is a mistress, there is also a wife. Mrs. Julie Millbank. She is, as a matter of fact, nothing short of delighted that her husband is dead. We'll get to that later. We also have a Mr. Ridgewell—never got his first name—and the maid who found the body. I think it is safe to say they had nothing to do with Mr. Millbank's unfortunate end. Then we have several interesting people we met at Empire Health, Mr. Millbank's insurance company. We interviewed a number of the employees, but only a few had much to say that could be of any help. There was his secretary, Mrs. Susan Jenkins; the COO, James Felton; and the CFO, Patrick McFarlane. Lastly we met a Vietnamese doctor named Vinh Tran who had some, well, how shall I put it, uh … interesting insights."

"Wow, you've had your hands full," Kupfer observed. "Anyone else aware of the case, outside of your superiors?"

"Of course the coroner, Jennifer Carmichael, who e-mailed your pathologist, Dr. Costa, which is what brought this coincidence to light. How fortunate was that?" Alvarez suggested. "I have to admit that we probably wouldn't have even considered this to be a crime if she hadn't sent that e-mail. Let's see … I think that's it."

"Jose, you're forgetting about the hematologist, Lisa Goldberg, that Dr. Carmichael consulted with. And then there's that doctor from LA, I forgot his name," O'Reilly added.

"Yes, sorry—forgot about them," Alvarez said. "Dr. Carmichael sought some help from a hematologist because she wasn't sure how Millbank could have had all this bleeding when he apparently had never had a bleeding problem before in his life. Anyway, Dr. Goldberg didn't have a good answer, so she contacted a hematologist she knows in LA, who is apparently some kind of expert in this area. His name is Andrew Friedman."

"Well, where do we start?" asked de Ville.

"Let's start with the similarities. Both men died by bleeding to death—and both continued to bleed after they died. Both were in their fifties and apparently in good health, and both were the CEOs of their respective companies and clearly wealthy and powerful men," Alvarez began.

"We know one cheated on his wife, and it wouldn't surprise me if your guy did too. You know how these business types live. I am sure they all cheat on their wives. You should investigate Mr. Stern's family—and his fidelity," added O'Reilly.

"What strikes me is that they both died on the same day. This was either a carefully executed plan or an unbelievable coincidence," de Ville said.

"This is no coincidence, my dear Felix. This seems to be a very carefully coordinated plan, and one with the intent of making a point. Someone is clearly trying to make a statement here. That's my take on it," Kupfer confidently stated.

"Agreed," added O'Reilly, "so what else could the two stiffs have in common?"

There was silence for nearly ten seconds before Alvarez broke it. "Let me suggest that we each get back to investigating our own cases, but let's agree to share any findings. We need to look for any links the two men might have had. You know, like if they ever met, spoke to each other, e-mailed, etc. Did they share anything at all in their past—a disgruntled employee, a woman?"

"Oh, you just reminded me of something," Kupfer said. "Speaking of disgruntled, there is one other player, Jan Erik Bergeland, a Norwegian scientist who developed some technology he sold to Terrapharma. Apparently, he was trying to renegotiate his deal with Terrapharma, claiming he was taken advantage of. Some of his e-mails were pretty threatening, but not in a physical way, necessarily. The threats could be construed as taking legal action, for example. I think the words that he used were something like, 'I'll take drastic action' or something like that. The problem is, we don't even know if he had ever met Mr. Stern, let alone killed him."

"Interesting possibility," said Alvarez.

O'Reilly interjected and suggested they all further explore the two victims' lives to see where their two paths might have crossed. He advised that he and Alvarez would keep searching for the mysterious Alexa and would revisit Mrs. Millbank to determine whether there might be some connection with Terrapharma, Mr. Stern, or even just Switzerland in general. He asked de Ville and Kupfer to garner more information about Mr. Stern's personal life, given that Mr. Millbank had an active social life; perhaps there would be a connection there. He also asked the Swiss team to look further into the Norwegian scientist and see whether the threats were idle or if there was some possibility that he could have acted on them.

"Let's plan on catching up with each other in a couple of days, unless you come across a good lead," Alvarez stated.

"One more thing, Detective. You were going to tell us why Mrs. Millbank is apparently quite pleased her husband is dead," Kupfer requested.

"Oh, yes; I nearly forgot," O'Reilly responded. "Well, let's see, he cheated on her, they didn't spend much time together, and apparently she will not only inherit a shitload of money but she is also the sole beneficiary of a life-insurance policy Mr. Millbank has, which will take her from filthy rich to filthy fuckin' rich, if you know what I mean."

"And you don't find that suspicious? I mean, clearly she has a motive—a few motives in fact," Kupfer pondered.

"That she does, but you know, she is so up-front about it that it's hard to believe that she is involved. You would think she would at least pretend she was unhappy if she'd actually killed him or got someone to kill him for her," O'Reilly replied.

"May I suggest, perhaps, that you still consider her a suspect," Kupfer said with suspicion in his voice. "I have come across a few criminals in my career who used such reverse psychology, acting so stupidly suspicious that the police discounted them."

"Sure thing. We'll keep an eye on her and keep investigating her," O'Reilly responded, and with that the conference call ended.

Kupfer and de Ville looked at each other and smiled. "I have never met a detective from New York, but that Detective O'Reilly sounds like he could have come right out of one of those police dramas set in that city," said Kupfer.

"Detective Lennie Briscoe from *Law & Order* would be my vote."

"Agreed." American culture in Europe was best exemplified by the imported television shows. European television, particularly in Switzerland, had little to offer, leaving the majority of Europeans quite familiar with American television characters.

"It's getting late; shall we call it a day?" asked Kupfer.

"Sure. Are you going to go back to Lyon?" de Ville followed.

"I think so. It's not too late to catch the last train. I'll call ahead and ask one of my colleagues to look into the travels of Mr. Bergeland. Perhaps he has seen fit to visit Switzerland in the recent past."

"Sounds good. I'll find out what I can about Mr. Stern's private life. I guess we were a bit overwhelmed by the whole ordeal that we didn't even look into that. I'm not even sure who informed his next of kin—whoever that might be."

"Very well; let's regroup by phone in the next day or two," Kupfer said.

Felix drove his colleague and friend back to the train station and then went home. He felt the need to find an old episode of *Law & Order* to watch—one with Jerry Orbach playing Detective Briscoe.

Following the conference call, O'Reilly and Alvarez decided to get straight back to their investigation. It wasn't yet noon in New York, and the discussion with their Swiss counterparts had added a sense of urgency to their investigation. They realized there was much work to do, but with the various characters they had already encountered, they were struggling to determine the best way for them to proceed.

"I think we need to find this Alexa woman, Sean. She was coming to the hotel to meet the victim. How do we know she wasn't in the room with him, killed him, and then came in playing dumb?"

"Okay, then do you have a clue how the hell she could have killed him?"

"No. I ... I don't, but we can figure that out later. The question at hand is this: Was she in the hotel room with the victim or not? We can try to find that out by asking the hotel staff, and maybe we can get some fingerprints from the room or the victim."

"The first idea is a good one, but forget the second—a hotel room is going to have so many prints. I can assure you, my young partner, that's a dead end."

"Maybe the maid cleaned it really well before Millbank checked in. You never know," Alvarez stated hopefully.

"I think I know who can tell us more about Alexa."

"Who?"

"Mrs. Millbank. After all, she followed her down to the Plaza, didn't she? Why don't you go to the hotel and see what else you can find out about Alexa, and I'll go have another chat with Mrs. Millbank," O'Reilly suggested.

Detective O'Reilly, as the more senior and more experienced detective, took the lead role in the decision-making and determined that, considering the scope of work at hand, it would be best for him and Alvarez to divide and conquer.

Alvarez returned to the Plaza Hotel and met up with Mr. Ridgewell again. This time, both out of courtesy and curiosity, he asked him his first name and found out it was Bartholomew, though Mr. Ridgewell clearly preferred Bart. At the same time, O'Reilly called Mrs. Millbank to see if she would be interested in getting together to have a chat, which is precisely how he put it. He didn't want her to get the sense it would be another interrogation. She agreed and suggested they meet at Daniel, a swanky French restaurant the rich and famous lunched at —she said it would be her treat.

Alvarez met Ridgewell in his office behind the front desk and asked him if he had ever seen Alexa before.

"Detective, many beautiful woman walk in here every day," Ridgewell replied.

Alvarez then asked Ridgewell to send an IT expert in and to provide him with a list of all the front-desk staff. He explained that he wanted the IT expert to search whatever databases they had for the name *Alexa* to see if they could find a connection. Then he asked Ridgewell to summon all the front-desk staff one by one to his office so he could question them.

O'Reilly found the restaurant Daniel quite easily, as it was just off Park Avenue on Sixty-Second Street near Central Park. It had a polished white exterior with large bay windows covered with delicate, intricately designed curtains, and a large door with shiny bronze door handles. He stepped in to find the maître d', who apparently recognized him and brought him to a private table toward the back of the large main room, where he found Mrs. Millbank sitting facing him and smiling as he approached. What was she up to, he wondered, bringing him to this highbrow and probably high-priced restaurant. She was dressed in a tight black V-neck top with the neckline plunging below what were surely enhanced breasts. She had a white wool button-down sweater that was opened and mostly just covered her shoulders. He saw her in a completely different light than just a few days ago when she had been at once angry and thrilled and her face had kept contorting from a scowl to what he could best describe as a "shit-eating grin." It was the same look Sylvester, the cartoon cat, would have had after he'd cornered Tweety Bird and was ready to pounce. And today, well, she looked like a model just slightly past her prime. Neither look was attractive.

O'Reilly felt quite out of place. What was an Irish American policeman doing in this swanky restaurant? He only hoped he wouldn't be recognized. This would certainly make for some good-natured ribbing by his colleagues and friends. As he got closer, he felt a lump in his throat and butterflies in his stomach. *Why am I feeling like this?* he thought. *Get a grip.* It was moments like this he wished he were married, like all his friends. Then he wouldn't have the feeling that was suddenly taking hold of him—like a teenager about to ask a girl out for the first time. He felt a combination of excitement and fear that he worried his face could not contain. *Get a grip*, he thought again. He was meeting this woman, a widow barely three days, to interview her in regard to a serious crime, but how could he do it under these circumstances?

"Hello, Mrs. Millbank," he said as he reached the table; he was fighting to remain matter-of-fact despite this sudden wave of emotion that had come upon him so unexpectedly.

"Please call me Julie, Detective."

"Sure, okay. I am going to go wash up. I'll be right back."

Good thinking, he said to himself. *Go compose yourself.* O'Reilly walked slowly to the bathroom, which was all the way in the back of the restaurant down a long and narrow corridor, and quite a ways from the table where Mrs. Millbank was sitting. As a policeman, he often had to control his emotions and was well trained for what he had to do now. He walked into the bathroom, stood at the sink, and looked at himself in the mirror. He grabbed a washcloth; there were no paper towels in such a fancy place. He wiped the bit of sweat that had formed on his brow and above his upper lip. He took a deep breath and reminded himself of the purpose of this meeting that *he*, in fact, had set up. *I am here to interrogate a potential suspect of a murder.* And that was all it took to get his mind back on task. He still couldn't quite understand how this woman, attractive though she was, could have made him so ill at ease and with nothing more than a sexy outfit and a smile. When he headed back to the table he was composed and confident.

"Sorry to keep you waiting," O'Reilly stated.

"No problem, Detective," came the reply, with yet another smile.

"I appreciate you taking the time to meet with me. To be honest, I would have preferred meeting at the police station or your house, rather than in a public place such as this."

"Public? There's no one here but us right now."

"And the maître d', waiters, busboys. Look, feel free to get yourself some lunch while we talk, but you need to understand that this is serious and you have not been ruled out as a suspect," O'Reilly stated sternly.

"Oh, Detective, please. If I killed my husband, I would not be meeting with you, nor would I tell you that I am glad he is dead. Come on, your experience surely should tell you that," retorted Mrs. Millbank.

"I suppose, but still, we don't exclude any suspects until the evidence excludes them," O'Reilly said.

"Do I need a lawyer?"

"Well, I am not arresting you, so I don't need to read you your Miranda rights; however, I will say that you are under no obligation to talk to me."

"I had nothing to do with my husband's death," Mrs. Millbank stated confidently. "You should check out his mistresses, though. I have no doubt he pissed many of them off."

"Well, as a matter of fact, I came here to discuss Alexa with you, though if you have information about other mistresses, I am open to hearing about them," O'Reilly continued, again refraining from the profanities he usually threw around liberally and maintaining his "polite" self.

"I honestly don't know who else he might have been fucking," Mrs. Millbank said, almost sensing that O'Reilly would feel more comfortable with a more profanity-laced discussion. "So you will need to figure that out on your own, but Alexa, well, I do have some information about her. Not much, mind you."

"Go on."

"I went to meet Creighton at his office one day, and while he was finishing a meeting in the conference room down the hall, his phone rang. Normally his secretary would pick it up, but she was taking minutes at the meeting and wasn't available. Anyway, I don't know what possessed me to pick up the phone, but I did and pretended I was his secretary. I figured I could just take a message. A woman spoke, asking for Creighton, and when I asked who it was, she replied in a playful tone, 'You know—tell him to call me as soon as he is free.' I said, 'Can

I take your number?' and she replied, 'Uh, he has it, remember?' as if I were an idiot. Well, that was it. That could not have been anyone but a mistress. So that's how I found out."

"How did you know this was Alexa?"

"Well, at the time I didn't, to be honest. In retrospect, though, I can tell you it was definitely her, because the woman on the phone that day had the same voice and tone as the woman who made a scene at the Plaza Hotel the day Creighton died. By the way, did you know that I was there that day? Well, anyway, I followed her to the Plaza Hotel and saw her making a fuss about needing to see him—so I know it was her."

"And what is it that you know about this woman?" O'Reilly asked.

"Well, after that call, I began to do a little detective work on my own. I would stand outside the Empire Health building, waiting to see if he met her there. While that didn't happen, I did start to notice a pattern where he would leave early every Wednesday—those just happened to be the nights I would go play cards with my friends. So I tried following him, but his limousine would be hard to follow on foot, and by the time I hailed a cab, it was usually too late. But one day I managed to get a cab right away and followed him to the infamous, now anyway, Plaza Hotel. So it seemed that I found his little afternoon hideaway, though still no sight of Alexa. But I'm a persistent woman, Detective, so I kept at it, and eventually it paid off. About two months ago, once again in the Plaza Hotel, I saw them together in a corner of the lobby bar. At first they were very discreet, but a few drinks later they were all over each other. I took some pictures with my phone— unfortunately, I was too far away to get a clear shot."

Mrs. Millbank ordered her lunch and insisted Detective O'Reilly share the foie gras with her. He nodded just to get the order out of the way.

"Mrs. Millbank, you said you had some useful information for me about Alexa."

"I said I have *some* information, and I said that it was not much."

"Well, what is it, if you don't mind?"

"Do you promise to have a nice lunch with me if I tell you and not just run out and leave me by myself?"

O'Reilly relented. "Sure," he told her.

"Well, one Wednesday, they're at the bar like usual, and then she reaches down and grabs her phone, talks for maybe a minute, and then leaves quickly. I decided to follow her. To be honest, I don't even know why. I probably should have just gone straight to Creighton and told him I'd caught him red-handed, but, uh, I was curious."

"So, I saw her get into a cab and hopped the cab right behind her and followed her. She got out at New York Hospital and rushed in, and that was the last I saw her that day. Since then, I've staked out the hospital several other times—*stake out*, that's what you call it, right?"

"Yes, very good," O'Reilly complimented her with wry smile.

"Well, I have seen her go there on a couple of other occasions as well."

"Interesting, but I don't know what to make of it. Maybe she has a sick relative or … I don't know. Interesting. Anything else?"

"I told you I didn't have much. Now then, you promised we could have a nice lunch, so shall we order … and let's not talk about my dead husband, okay?"

"Okay."

CHAPTER 8

While New York City took on a festive feel during the Thanksgiving holiday, Los Angeles was typically blasé about the holiday season. After all, a holiday signifying the bounty of the fall harvest doesn't make much sense in a region where the year-round growing season provides a year-round harvest. While in New York families gather and eat the traditional feast of turkey, stuffing, and seasonal fall vegetables as well as pies made from everything from pecans to apples to sweet potatoes, Los Angelinos are more likely to celebrate with surfing, hiking, and sushi. And while New York is festooned with holiday decorations on storefronts and Christmas lights adorning naked trees bared of their leaves, Los Angeles this time of year is better known for Santa Ana winds, hot temperatures, and brush fires. After the spate of Indian summer, New York had turned considerably colder, with temperatures in the high forties, more typical of this time of year, while in Los Angeles the Santa Ana winds were indeed blowing, and temperatures soared to the eighties. Thankfully, there were no forest fires as yet.

So, typically, both Detectives O'Reilly and Alvarez took a few days off to celebrate Thanksgiving with their families. It was a welcome respite following the hectic pace of the past few days, chasing down whomever they thought could possibly help solve the case they had decided to call "the bleeder." It was clear at this point that they were now investigating a murder. O'Reilly spent the weekend shuttling between his sisters' houses and playing uncle to their kids. Detective Alvarez hosted Thanksgiving at his house and had invited his extended family of nearly forty relatives for the day. While the traditional American Thanksgiving cuisine was served at the Alvarez residence, there was also a healthy mixture of Latino foods from his native Mexico, including tamales and, for dessert, the smooth, rich, and deliciously sweet custard known as flan.

In Los Angeles, Dr. Friedman spent Thanksgiving weekend mostly outside, either biking or hiking. He was invited to the home of one of the other physicians for "traditional" Thanksgiving, but as one who had grown up in New York with authentic traditional Thanksgiving, he could not truly accept this meal of tofu turkey (affectionately called "tofurkey"), southwestern salad with jicama, and green beans almandine as traditional. It was, in fact, very far from his notion of authentic Thanksgiving dinner. Nevertheless, while he complained passionately about the meal, he enjoyed being in the company of many of his colleagues away from the hectic pace of the hospital. There was just one person missing whom he wished could have been there, and that was Leila.

While the Baker family shunned some American traditions, they very much embraced Thanksgiving. They were thankful to this country that had accepted them when their own country, or at least its leaders, had considered them outcasts, and been hell-bent on destroying their culture and even killing them. Kurds were outsiders in Iraq—and Turkey, for that matter, but in the United States, and in particular in Los Angeles, they were like many others: immigrants seeking a place where they could flourish. What they appreciated most was the ability to both maintain their Kurdish traditions while simultaneously adopting new American ones, and Thanksgiving was the new tradition the Bakers most enjoyed. For this was the one day in the year when the smell of turkey and stuffing would emanate from the kitchen, rather than eggplant, garlic, and lamb. Leila enjoyed having a few days off and the quality time with her parents and two younger brothers. One brother was an engineering student at the University of Southern California, and the other was a physician currently in his residency in anesthesiology at UCLA. While this break from work was welcome, she couldn't help thinking about the case and the upcoming trip to New York. To her surprise, she also found herself thinking about Andy. She wondered what he was doing during this holiday weekend, but after contemplating the idea briefly, she ultimately decided not to bother him and so resisted the urge to call and invite him to her house.

Thanksgiving was not celebrated in Europe; thus there was no time off for de Ville or Kupfer. As the events of the past several days had been so hectic, and since the case of Mr. Stern had occupied most of their time, both fell behind in their many other tasks. They were aware that it was a holiday weekend in the United States, making it unlikely any further news would come from New York, and so both attended to other cases that were being neglected. Kupfer returned to Lyon while de Ville dealt with the more typical cases of car theft and drug-dealing in Basel. Certainly none of the other cases were as intriguing as that of Mr. Stern, but there was other work to do, nonetheless. Prior to parting, they had agreed to each look into part of the case they had not yet dealt with. De Ville would work on finding out more about Mr. Stern's family and fidelity, while Kupfer would try to find out about Bergeland, in particular looking into his travels. Interpol had access to passport information, and he would search that database in case anything interesting turned up in Bergeland's itinerary. They agreed to regroup in one week, with Kupfer returning to Basel so they could go over their findings together.

CHAPTER 9

DECEMBER 2–4
LOS ANGELES

The Monday after Thanksgiving was a quiet day at CHLA, particularly for the Hemostasis and Thrombosis Center. Many of the staff extended their holiday weekend, and patients were not seen on Mondays. Thus Andy or Leila each spent valuable office time catching up on e-mails from the weekend and on other work, including research papers they were writing, in various stages of readiness for submission to medical journals. There seemed to be no break from communication anymore. Andy had toyed with the idea of writing an e-mail etiquette book, sensing the ones that had been written were largely ignored due, in his opinion, to the tedious style in which they had been written. He wondered whether he could write a guide with sufficient humor that it would be a hit. Perhaps all he needed to do was put together a list of the many absurd e-mails he had received, many unintentionally humorous, with cautionary notes on how to avoid doing the same. How had the medical profession and the rest of the world gotten by without e-mail, he often pondered, seeing that now the typical weekday brought with it a barrage of 120 or so e-mails. Weekends were slower—but only marginally. After four days of purposely ignoring his e-mails, he saw they had piled up like rocks blocking his only path forward. In addition to the four days' worth of e-mails, living in the Pacific time zone, three hours behind the east coast and eight to nine hours behind Europe, meant that the e-mails from Europe that had been sent during their day were already waiting for his reply, while e-mails from the rest of the United States had started coming in fast and furious.

Ignoring his usual pattern of going through them in time-sequential order, he curiously scrolled through them looking in particular for anything regarding the "bleeder" case. He came upon an e-mail from Lisa Goldberg asking—in fact, pleading—to know when he was going to come to New York. This led him to pull up the patient schedule for the upcoming week, and considering where his mind had wandered, he fortunately found it to be quite small. He called Leila and requested that she come to his office. Upon reviewing a printout of the patients scheduled for the week, they marked which ones could be rescheduled and were left with just two. They could see them the next day, or if they couldn't make it, have Andrea, their nurse, see them with one of the other physicians. Both were simple follow-ups that Andy and Leila felt wouldn't miss them. And with that, they planned to take an early flight to New York on Wednesday to arrive there in the late afternoon.

"What about the boss?" Leila asked, referring to their division chief. "Can we just leave to take care of this case?"

"I'll talk to him. He's pretty reasonable. I'll just need to sell it to him—tell him this could bring CHLA and the Division a lot of notoriety, at least, potentially."

"Will he go for that?"

"Yes, he will, but if we don't see any way that this will bring good publicity to our program or the hospital, we'll need to stop and come back, you know, to our regular jobs."

"I've never been to New York, Andy—promise me we can have at least a little fun."

"I won't promise, but we can try."

Andy suddenly began feeling excited and uncomfortable all at the same time. He had never travelled with a colleague before for anything other than a medical conference, which was obviously work-related, had a clear mission, and was for a finite length of time—and even that had been an infrequent occurrence. He preferred traveling alone. This was different, but not only because the underlying reason for this trip was different. *Fun*, he said to himself. They were not going to New York to have *fun*—but what if they did? He had never even considered Leila as a potential girlfriend and really never had paid much attention to her looks. But, now that they were going to New York together, albeit on a pseudo-work mission, he noticed for the first time how attractive he found her. Her black hair and deep-set big, dark eyes gave her a truly exotic look. Well, she *was* exotic, after all. Andy had never known a Kurdish person before; he thought, *A Jew and a Muslim, that could never happen*—and that was his refrain every time his thoughts had wandered toward considering Leila as a potential girlfriend. And as he said to himself *A Jew and a Muslim*, it had the effect of abating some of the excitement that he felt and put to rest the butterflies that were swarming in his stomach. *Snap out of it*, he said to himself. *She doesn't like you anyway, you idiot.*

"Come on, at least a nice dinner and a show at night—I mean, we are not expected to work day and night, are we? We wouldn't be if we were at home." Leila was working toward persuading Andy.

"Sure, we should be able to do that," Andy replied slowly, making no effort to hide his hesitation at the idea. With that, Leila left his office, and he decided to call the division chief, "the boss," as they all called him, and let him know what he was planning. *I hope I catch him in a good mood*, he thought. To his surprise, when the boss's secretary picked up the phone, she told him to head on down to the boss's office. Usually one had to wait a week or more to get to talk to the boss. Maybe he had heard about this already, which led to a different kind of worry in Andy's mind. His emotions just went from that of a seventh grader with his first crush, to those of a seventh grader suddenly and unexpectedly summoned to the principal's office.

"Hi, Candice," Andy addressed the secretary. "Just wait a second; let me see if he is ready."

Inevitably you would wait at least five and sometimes twenty minutes in the hallway before being told the boss was ready and you could proceed to his office. At least this gave him a few minutes to get poised and decide on the talking points that would hopefully convince him they should go and investigate this bizarre mystery. *Talk up the potential for positive publicity for CHLA and the Division of Pediatric Hematology/Oncology*, he thought, *and that should work.* The minutes passed by slowly, but Andy did not complain this time, as he would be more composed once he'd rehearsed what he was going to say.

"You can go in now." Candice was calling for him to come in from the hallway. After greeting the boss in his office, he sat down facing him across his large desk, which served as not just a literal but also a figurative barrier.

"So, what is this about?" their chief asked bluntly.

"I got an interesting e-mail last week, asking for my help in what appears to be a murder case."

"Go on," the boss said, the subject piquing his interest.

Andy explained the e-mail and the request and the little else he knew about the case.

"So, what's in it for you and, more importantly, our division and CHLA?" Andy had known this was coming and was prepared.

"Well, sir, this is such an unusual case that it is making headlines back east. *The New York Post* is calling it the 'Cheater and Bleeder' case so, for one thing, CHLA will get publicity if I get involved. I'll be sure to invoke the name of CHLA as often as I can," Andy replied with his carefully rehearsed answer.

"CHLA, sure, but make sure you mention the Children's Center for Cancer and Blood Diseases as well, and the Division of Pediatric Hematology/Oncology."

"Yes, of course."

"One question, though. Don't they have someone like you in New York who could help them with the case?"

"Yeah, I was surprised by the call, and sure, they have hematologists like me in New York, but the e-mail requesting my assistance actually came from one of those hematologists, who is stumped. Anyway, now that I have been asked to help them, I am really intrigued. In fact, there may be some good research to come from this," Andy followed, dangling another carrot in front of the boss, who was always looking for a research angle in any endeavor.

"How about money? Are you getting paid? Who's paying for your trip? Are we getting compensation for you being away?" interrogated the boss.

Shit, I didn't think of that, Andy thought. *Quick—think of something.* "Isn't publicity another kind of currency?"

"Yes, it is. Or, it can be."

"And I am paying my own way for now—and, uh, for Leila Baker, as well."

"Why is Leila going?"

"This is really quite an unusual situation. I am quite sure I will need some help, and Leila would be the best choice for that. Besides, it will be a good experience for her."

Then one of those long—painfully long—pauses occurred. *What is he thinking about*, Andy wondered. The pause seemed to last for an hour, though it was probably only ten to fifteen seconds.

"Okay, go ahead—but remember, something positive for our Center and CHLA must come from this, or you need to come right back. Is that clear?"

"Yes, crystal clear, and thanks for your support."

"I am not supporting you—I am merely letting you go."

"Yes, I know—I didn't mean financial support," Andy replied, forgetting momentarily that the boss was always concerned about finances.

Andy was so excited that he ran straight over to Leila's office, which was just down the hall from his, and told her the news. With that, the Julia Roberts smile appeared, adorning Leila's face. The sheer excitement that was so obviously displayed on her face was priceless. Her enthusiasm mirrored Andy's. Her first trip to New York, a medical mystery involving a criminal case, and some social time with the man she had grown to like over the past six months—what could be better?

"Who is paying for this trip, by the way?" Leila asked.

"For now, I am, but if we help the New York City Police Department, I am sure they will cover our costs."

"How do you know?"

"Okay, I'm not sure, but let's just get there and see what happens. I have some money saved away, so don't worry about that part for now. By the way, what do your parents think of you going?" Andy asked.

No sooner had the words escaped his mouth, like the fog of exhaled warm air on a cold day, than he wished he could inhaled them back into his larynx. He wished there was a "recall words" function, like recalling an e-mail. He swallowed hard and hoped Leila hadn't inferred anything from what he'd said.

"Excuse me!" Leila said feistily, with a glare that brought Andy a huge sense of embarrassment.

Andy tried to recover. "What I meant was, do they know you are going?"

"Oh, really," Leila responded as her glare morphed into a smile.

"Well, uh … uh, yeah," Andy stuttered, still trying to recover from the question he wished he hadn't asked.

"Well, uh … uh, Andy," Leila responded, mocking his uncertainty, "I don't *need* to tell my parents *anything!*"

"Look …" Andy began, but he was immediately interrupted.

"But out of courtesy, I did. And as for what they think—well, they think I am going there for work—and isn't that *why* I am going?" she replied.

"Yes, of course." *Phew*, Andy thought, *I got away with that.*

"So, why did you ask me to go? It's not like your friend Lisa asked me to go."

Shit, I thought this part of the conversation was over, Andy muttered to himself. "The truth is I am not sure what I am getting into here, and I have a feeling I will need some help," he told her. "Also, I think this could be a great learning experience for both of us. Who knows what we might discover—maybe a new disease," Andy stated as matter-of-factly as he could while trying to shift this uncomfortable conversation back to a purely work-related discussion.

"Okay," Leila acceded. "I do agree it will be a great learning experience." Andy couldn't tell whether Leila's statement carried a double meaning or not, and just returned to his earlier thoughts: *A Jew and a Muslim, a Jew and a Muslim.*

Andy told Leila he would make the travel arrangements, and with that they parted ways. Andy returned to his work—answering e-mails, reviewing a paper submitted to a peer-reviewed medical journal, and finishing work on a paper he was writing on the potential changes in the treatment of hemophilia patients in the coming five years. Just then, his phone rang.

"Hi, Andy." It was his secretary. "I have Mrs. Vasquez on the line— she said it was urgent."

"Put her through."

"*Hola*, Dr. Andy," Mrs. Vasquez greeted him in heavily accented English.

"*Como estas, señora?*" Andy replied in Spanish. He had picked up Spanish since moving to Los Angeles and was reasonably conversational.

"Since our appointment with Diana last week, I have seen commercials for Lyzanda, and I keep thinking about our poor Vanessa," she continued, clearly trying to keep from crying. "Don't you think Diana should be on it instead of warfarin? I can't lose another daughter."

"Señora, please understand that Vanessa could have passed even if she had been on the Lyzanda." Andy would often tell the family this to spare them any more guilty feelings, though he didn't necessarily believe it, since Lyzanda has proven to be a far better drug than warfarin.

He continued, "Besides, we discussed how expensive it is and how we have tried to have your insurance pay for it, but they won't because it has not been studied in children."

"But my daughter is not a child! She is bigger than me and fully mature now—you know, physically. She is like an adult."

"I agree with you, but she is fifteen years old, so as far as the insurance company goes, she is a child. I am sorry."

"*Bueno*, I understand. I am just so worried. I can't lose another beautiful daughter."

"I know, but the warfarin is working well for Diana—remember that before Vanessa passed, she had a new blood clot while she was taking warfarin, and Diana has not had that happen."

"Yes, I remember, Dr. Andy. When will this new medicine cost less money, Doctor?"

"I don't know, but not for a long time, señora. I am sorry; I know it's not fair."

"Yes, it's not fair that rich people can get better medicines. Medicines should not be like selling jewelry or shoes or cars," continued an exasperated mother clearly still living the nightmare of losing a daughter for reasons she could not accept.

"I agree with you, but this is the way our health-care system works right now. It is not entirely fair, and I hope it will change and be more fair in the future," Andy agreed.

He wasn't concurring just for the sake of appeasing an upset parent; he genuinely felt that the health-care system was in complete disarray, with skewed incentives and conflicts of interest for all the parties involved: payers, hospitals, doctors, pharmaceutical companies, and especially the government. His view was that the payers'—insurance companies and the federal and local governments—incentives were to deny care to any extent possible while the hospitals' incentives were solely cost-saving and had nothing to do with the best patient care. If they got paid on a per-diem basis—a per-day sum from payers to cover all their expenses—then that was their incentive to keep their beds full and not discharge patients. On the other hand, if they got paid a lump sum for each patient depending on their diagnosis, no matter how long their stay in the hospital (known cryptically as diagnostic-related groups or DRGs), then they had the exact opposite incentive—get the patients out as quickly as possible. It was even possible for patients in the same room, admitted for the same problem, with one on a per-diem contract with his payer and the other on a DRG-payment system, to have planners insist that one stayed while coaxing the doctors to quickly discharge the other. Hospitals hired employees, often nurses, under euphemistic titles such as "discharge planner," whose main role was to identify those patients the hospital was losing money on and hasten their discharge. It was a perverse system that dealt each day with the health and very lives of patients.

Andy was acutely aware of the conflicts that doctors faced each day as a result of the bizarre system of health-care reimbursement. For one thing, doctors were subtly encouraged to order various imaging tests and laboratory tests for their hospitalized patients. The hospital made significant profits by having a laboratory on site and charging obscene fees for tests that might cost them a few dollars to run. Ordering lots of imaging studies, such as CT scans and MRIs, served several purposes. For one thing, an MRI scanner installed cost millions of dollars, and the hospital had to recoup the cost of such a large investment by having the machines operate nearly twenty-four hours a day scanning patients.

In addition, ordering these tests provided revenue for the radiologists, often among the highest-paid physicians in a hospital. Doctors were also not shy about requesting consultations from other doctors. Whether this was done in excess, Andy was not entirely sure. A consult, such as a pediatrician requesting Andy to provide advice on a patient with a possible hematologic problem, was a common and important aspect of medical care. With the highly specialized nature of medicine in the twenty-first century, consulting a specialist could uncover an unusual diagnosis and improve the outcome for a patient. Thus, it was an indispensable part of medicine. However, did physicians consult other physicians unnecessarily and with an economic incentive? Would a cardiologist request a consult from a surgeon who then in turn would request consults on other patients from that cardiologist, in a financial game of *quid pro quo*? Lastly, how much of this excessive laboratory testing, imaging, and consulting was done as part of what is called "defensive medicine"—in a cover-your-ass approach—to enable defense of any lawsuits that might arise from an overzealous lawyer using a patient's misfortune to line his or her own pockets from the roughly forty percent commission they charged for any settlements or verdicts? It was something Andy pondered from time to time, but more as a rhetorical question, as it was impossible to know for sure.

Regardless, the perverse and insanely complex payment systems currently in place were beyond anyone's full understanding, and the American health-care system was surely in need of a major overhaul, well beyond what the Affordable Care Act, known as "Obamacare" would be able to accomplish. What Andy most wanted was a system that was more fair.

"Why do new medicines cost so much money, but warfarin does not? I don't understand," Mrs. Vasquez continued lamenting.

"It is very complicated to explain, señora, but let's just say that when drug companies spend many millions of dollars to discover and research new medicines, they need to then make that money back—otherwise they won't spend money to try to develop new medicines. So the government gives them something called "exclusivity," which means they have a period of time where they are the only ones who can make this medicine and sell it, and so they can charge a lot of money."

"So, the poor people suffer so the drug companies can become rich."

"Well, it's not meant to be that way, but yes, this is what happens."

"And why won't my insurance pay for it? My husband and I both work and both have health insurance for us and our family. Shouldn't they pay for medicines we need?"

"Well, again, it's not that simple. If we put every patient who is now on warfarin on Lyzanda, it would cost billions of dollars to the insurance companies, and they might decide then not to offer health insurance. Then there would be fewer companies offering health insurance, and the insurance would get very expensive. Look, I am not trying to defend the insurance companies or the drug companies, but that is the system we have. I agree it needs to be fixed so that I can give all of my patients the medicines I think they should take, but it is very complicated."

"Okay; thank you for taking the time to talk to me, Dr. Andy. You are very kind. Thank you for caring for our other daughter—we really appreciate all that you do for her and all that you did for Vanessa. *Muchas gracias.*"

"It's my pleasure."

The conversation took Andy away from his other tasks, and after he hung up, he couldn't refocus. He decided instead to begin planning the trip to New York. He went onto Kayak to begin searching for flights to New York. Since this was coming out of his own pocket, he needed to find a decent fare and, of course, he was not only going to be paying for two airline tickets but two hotel rooms in New York, which didn't come cheap, even for a modest hotel. He thought about the inherent unfairness of the health-care system while shopping for airline tickets and realized that, on a lesser scale and without gambling with people's lives, the airline industry was also inherently unfair. How could the two hundred or so people on a flight from Los Angeles to New York pay dozens of different fares for the same flight? *This is the law of supply and demand taken to the extreme*, he thought. He found a nonstop flight for $427, which was not a bad price to New York, so he purchased the two tickets and then spent some time finding a hotel. He ended up settling on the Marriott Marquis in Times Square, although it was far more than he had intended to spend. But since it was Leila's first time to his hometown, rather home city, he wanted her to have a very positive impression, and so he splurged.

The next two days passed with no further news from New York or Basel. It seemed the investigation was losing steam. When Wednesday morning came, Andy again got butterflies in his stomach and quickly suppressed them by repeating his refrain, *A Jew and a Muslim* to himself several times. Leila met him at the gate in Terminal 4 at LAX for their American Airlines flight. He was nervous. What would they talk about? Work? The case? Their families? All of that? Andy checked to be sure his iPhone was fully charged; maybe he could get away with listening to music. Maybe Leila would sleep—it was a 6:30 a.m. flight, after all. Following boarding, they found their seats, a window and a middle. Leila insisted on sitting by the window so she could look at New York as they were landing. As Andy settled into his seat, he pulled out a manila envelope with about thirty pages of papers.

"What's that?" Leila asked.

"The detectives in New York sent this over. It is a summary of what they have so far on the two victims and the little bit they have on the crime scenes. I read through it a couple of times already, so I figured I would have you read it on the plane, and we can start to figure out how we want to approach the case."

"Uh, I know you're a genius, but our job is not to solve the case— just to try to figure out if there is some medical issue with the victims," Leila responded sarcastically.

"I suggest we keep our minds open and see how we can help. Why can't we solve the case? We solve cases at work every time we see a new patient and not infrequently when we encounter problems with our current patients. Remember, we have the type of analytical skills that could help solve the case—don't sell us short," Andy replied.

"Okay, fair enough. Let me have the papers and I'll let you know what I think once I'm done."

Andy was thankful about this turn of events. *Let's keep the conversation to the case and away from anything personal*, he thought. After takeoff, Leila was reading intently, so Andy scrolled through his iPhone for some music and stumbled upon the excellent Wallflowers album *Bringing Down the Horse*. The title of one of the songs caught his attention; it was called "Bleeders" and started with "Once upon a time they called me the Bleeder." Another song caught his attention as well—"6th Avenue Heartache"—and he hummed the refrain in his head. There would be no Sixth Avenue Heartache during this trip; he was sure of that. After the Wallflowers, as Andy scrolled through the selections on his iPhone, he decided that a trip to New York needed some New York music. So he settled on Pat Benatar, the strong-voiced but diminutive rocker who was born in Brooklyn but found her early fame on Long Island. Leila read the case files while Andy immersed himself in *USA Today*. *Where would this paper be without business travelers?* he thought. Time passed quickly, and when Leila had finished reading the case files, she was deep in thought and decided to look out the window for what must have been ten minutes.

"Can you see anything?" Andy finally asked.

"Snow-capped peaks—must be the Rocky Mountains," replied Leila. "What are you listening to?"

"A variety of stuff," Andy answered, not willing to risk telling her he was listening to a 1980s rock diva. He quickly thought of an answer that was less vague but not Pat Benatar. "Did you know that the Wallflowers have a song called 'Bleeders'?"

"No. Maybe we can make a mix for this trip. Let's see, how about we add 'Sunday, Bloody Sunday' by U2 and ..." Leila was thinking of another song, but Andy interrupted.

"'Blood and Roses' by the Smithereens. Hey, they made their name in New York City."

"No, I was thinking more like 'New York State of Mind,' by Billy Joel and 'In a New York Minute,' by Don Henley. I think two songs with blood in the names is quite enough," Leila responded, laughing.

"So, what do you think about the case?"

"It's weird, isn't it? Two men with seemingly no connection who die the same day and in the same bizarre manner—really strange. Did the Swiss guy have a mistress?"

"I don't think we know that yet," Andy replied.

"Still, how could one spurned wife or mistress kill both men on the same day continents apart? It's not possible. Any chance both men visited the same country and contracted some weird virus that caused them to bleed to death?"

"But on the same day?" Andy questioned her logic.

"You're right. The same day. Do you want to know what I think? Someone or several someones must be trying to send a message with these killings. Believe me, I unfortunately know all about killing to send a message—sadly, these kind of 'honor killings' are not uncommon in my culture. What do you think?" Leila continued.

"Hey, I'm glad you're thinking like that—forget just focusing on the medical facts. We need to look at every aspect of the case and research every angle."

"Okay, but we're not detectives," Leila stated bluntly.

"Yes we are. Leila—didn't we just discuss that? We are as much mystery-solvers as are the detectives," Andy reassured her.

They continued the discussion, touching mostly on the New York piece—Alexa, Mrs. Millbank, and Vinh Tran, the Vietnamese doctor forced to deny medical procedures and medications.

"I don't want to shift our discussion, but since you brought up medication denials, I forgot to tell you that Mrs. Vasquez called again to ask about putting Diana on Lyzanda," Andy said.

"Again. That poor woman—she just can't get over losing her older daughter. She is wracked with guilt. There is no way they could have afforded the Lyzanda, and we tried to get authorizations from their insurance company at least ten times. How many letters did you write to the medical director of their HMO?" Leila questioned.

"I don't know. A lot. And I called and spoke to him, and he said it was out of his hands because the insurance carrier denied it and he couldn't overturn it as just the local guy."

"These new drugs are so expensive, and insurance companies don't want to—hold on!" Leila stopped in midsentence. She shuffled through the papers regarding the case.

"What is it, Leila?" Andy asked impatiently.

"Just wait a second," she responded sharply, continuing to rapidly turn the pages.

"What are you looking for?" Andy asked again.

"Would you just ... please, just wait," Leila was more and more animated in her responses.

Andy, looking over her shoulder, was becoming more and more impatient, when suddenly Leila blurted out, "Aha!"

"Aha *what*?" asked Andy.

"As you were talking about Mrs. Vasquez, I had this slowly growing feeling of familiarity, like a smell that you know but can't quite make out. And just like that eureka moment when you figure out what you were smelling, I figured out what was familiar. It was something I had just read."

"Yeah, so? You're killing me—what is it?"

"Hey, I gotta go to the bathroom first," Leila said with a wide Cheshire grin. "Well, you can pee in your pants—you're not leaving until you tell me," Andy insisted.

"I'm just toying with you—I love getting you all riled up because it almost never happens. Hmm, how long should I keep you in suspense?"

The Cheshire grin shifted to a Julia Roberts smile. Leila finally continued. "Okay, seriously. Your conversation with Mrs. Vasquez revolved around an expensive new drug and an insurance company's denying the request to cover the prescription, right?"

"Yeah."

"So, what did Mr. Millbank do for a living?" Leila asked. She was giddy with excitement.

"He was the CEO of a health-insurance company," Andy responded matter-of-factly.

"And what did Mr. Stern, the Swiss 'bleeder' do for a living?"

"He was the CEO of a pharmaceutical company." A pause.

Andy continued, "So, you think that is the connection between the two victims?"

"Yeah. Don't you think that is just a bit too much of a coincidence?"

"Well, I suppose," Andy answered slowly and without much confidence. "What are you saying?"

"Okay, maybe I got a bit too excited about this, but I still think it is quite a coincidence. Don't insurance companies and drug companies squabble over the price of the drugs?" Leila asked.

"I suppose."

"Think about it: some new blockbuster drug comes along that can cure, say, Parkinson's disease, but only one company has it, and they are charging a fortune for it. The insurance company would have to pay—they can't deny a drug to patients with Parkinson's disease—a disease which currently has no cure, right?" Leila suggested.

"I'm not so sure. In my experience, insurance companies try to deny anything expensive, even if the patient does need it. Take the example of Vanessa Vasquez. She got blood clots on every blood thinner we tried, and yet when we explained it to the insurance company, they just said that they wouldn't pay for it because it's not approved in kids—even though we explained to them that most drugs are not approved for use in children and that she really needed this new drug. So, they can often find a way out of paying."

"Fine, but still, I think it's weird that they were both tied to the health-care industry—one more coincidence in this case of coincidences."

"Well, we can keep it in mind, but I'm not sure that it's not just a plain old coincidence."

Leila couldn't let go of the thought that this was somehow related to the case. She sat in thought while Andy went back to his *USA Today* and his music. Time for some Waterboys, another one of his musical discoveries—and in his opinion the most underrated band ever. It was not so much a band as one musician, Mike Scott, from Scotland, and whichever group of musicians he chose to surround himself with at any particular moment in his career. Andy settled on the album *A Pagan Place* to get his mind off the case and Leila until they got to New York. Why did he keep thinking about Leila? As the staccato acoustic guitar and triumphant trumpet sounds of the first song, "Church Not Made with Hands," came on, he lost himself in the music.

CHAPTER 10

DECEMBER 5

BASEL

"Hello again, Simon," de Ville greeted Kupfer at the main Basel train station. Winter had come early to Switzerland, and though it was just four in the afternoon, darkness had already made its appearance. The streets glistened with moisture, reflecting the headlights up toward the sky like an upside-down world with lighting on the ground and the flat gray cement of the clouds above. Kupfer and de Ville closed their umbrellas and stepped into the car, making their initial stop at the first café they found to review the "bleeder" case. It had been over a week since they had discussed the case or sought any new evidence.

The café was busy with people, many of whom were there to avoid walking or standing in the steady rain. Kupfer motioned to de Ville that there was an empty table for two toward the back; they snaked their way toward it between the mass of humanity gathered near the counter for takeout orders. It was a small café, with ivory-colored walls adorned with photographs of the city of Basel. Kupfer particularly liked the one showing a full St. Jakob-Park, packed with tens of thousands of soccer fans holding the dark-blue and maroon scarves of the home team, FC Basel. No sooner had they sat down than a waitress arrived to take their order. Kupfer requested a cappuccino, while de Ville opted for a hot chocolate.

"Any news from New York?" Kupfer asked.

"No, nothing new. Well, except that they have invited an expert, a hematologist, and specifically one who specializes in diseases where people bleed too much, to see if he can provide some valuable insight," de Ville replied.

"Okay, interesting. Where are we on our end of things?"

"It turns out Mr. Millbank was quite the ladies' man—at least a few mistresses according to our colleagues in New York, so they've asked us to explore that angle with Mr. Stern. Maybe we have an unhappy mistress or her unhappy husband—boyfriend, whatever—that might be responsible," de Ville replied. "So I went back to Terrapharma and interrogated several of his co-workers, mostly the ones you had already met."

"I understand, but I am not sure that is the right angle to take. Are they thinking that there is some connection between them in terms of lovers, mistresses? I think it would be pretty unusual for something like that to emerge, considering the distance between the two men. Anyway, did you find anything interesting?" responded a skeptical Kupfer.

"I spoke to Stern's wife. According to her, they are happily married and they have two adult children—two boys. I also spoke to his secretary, Mr. Boudreaux, and a few other employees at Terrapharma. At first they all said what a good and devoted husband he was and how he would always bring gifts back to his wife from far-off destinations whenever he travelled for work. He seemed like the last man to cheat on his wife. But then, unsolicited and totally out of the blue, I got a call," de Ville explained.

"Go on."

"It was a woman who refused to identify herself. I told her I couldn't use anything she said, but she insisted on giving me the information she had. So I reluctantly agreed, but I told her she would eventually need to come forward, and she said she would think about it."

"Did you recognize the voice?" Kupfer asked.

"Well, that's the weird part. She was using some kind of device to disguise her voice. I didn't get it. Why would an anonymous caller feel the need to disguise her voice?" de Ville pondered.

"Are you sure it was a woman?" Kupfer asked.

"It wasn't that disguised. It was definitely a woman."

"What did she say?"

"She said that she knows about an incident between a woman she would not name and a person that she believes to be Mr. Stern. She added that she had met this mystery woman coincidentally when they were doing a group hike in the Alps last summer. She went on to say that they had spent much of the weekend talking together and had become fast friends—something about they both grew up in the Alps and had a similar childhood. Anyway, the anonymous woman told me that the woman asked if she could confide in her about something personal. Anyway, the woman told her she had met a very wealthy man from Basel who worked for a drug company," de Ville explained.

"How does she know it was Stern?"

"Apparently, she said the man was the CEO of the company that made that very successful erectile-dysfunction drug, Provitax, but—and here's the part that makes it all a bit unclear—she said the man was single."

"That doesn't mean anything," Kupfer responded with a chuckle. "But Mr. Stern was married," replied a confused de Ville.

"Felix, really. Are you joking?"

"No, Mr. Stern was married," de Ville replied naïvely.

"Of course he was married, but he probably lied to this woman and said he was single. You know, some, maybe most, women would not betray a family by having an affair. Maybe he sensed this woman had integrity and would not be with him if he were married. So, off with the ring and on with the lies," responded Kupfer confidently.

"I see now. Sorry; pretty naïve, huh?" de Ville was embarrassed and Kupfer noticed.

"Let's chalk it up to you've lived in Switzerland your whole life. I, on the other hand, live in France, where if a man doesn't cheat on his wife, he is hardly considered a real man. So, what else did this woman say?" Kupfer pressed on, intrigued.

"She said that the woman started crying when discussing the man, but the caller would not elaborate on why or what might have happened between the two of them," de Ville said.

"Anything else?"

"No. That's it. It was a short conversation. She seemed pretty anxious to get off the phone."

"Did you get her number?"

"No."

"No name. No number. What about caller ID?" Kupfer pressed. "Blocked."

"Surely you can trace it with the phone company," Kupfer insisted. "I did. It was from a pay phone from the Basel airport."

"For real. So, we have no name, no number, nothing to follow up on. So, this really was an anonymous tip."

"Should we believe it?" de Ville asked.

"Well, what would this woman gain by making this up? I mean, Stern is dead, so it's not like she could blackmail him or anything like that. My gut says that this is true, but we need to confirm it. Did you speak to Stern's wife about this?"

"No, the call came after I had spoken to her. I did ask her if she thought her husband had ever had an affair."

"What did she say?"

"It wasn't her words, but her glare that convinced me she was sure he never had strayed. That, by the way, was the last question of the interview. I was quickly sent out. She was pretty upset I would even bring it up."

"So, she was convinced he was faithful," Kupfer added. "In her mind, yes he was."

De Ville reviewed with Kupfer all the people he had spoken to and asked about Mr. Stern's fidelity, aside from his wife. He'd asked his children, Max, a thirty-year-old attorney, and Philippe, a thirty-five-year-old pilot for Swiss International Airlines. Both of them seemed more open to the idea that it was possible but told de Ville that they had no knowledge or even suggestion that their father was being unfaithful. He also spoke at length with Stern's secretary, Sandrine LeClair, who was quite adamant that he had not had an affair. She stated that she kept Mr. Stern's calendar and that she would surely know if he had been cheating. He also spoke with Mr. Boudreaux and Reto, the IT specialist. De Ville also had asked Reto to sweep Mr. Stern's e-mails again, but this time looking for any sign of an affair. Reto had searched numerous words such as *date, dinner,* and other words that might signal an affair, but to no avail.

He also asked him to review every outside e-mail from women. Reto told him that would take an inordinate amount of time, but he would try to do so with some filters and would let them know if he found any e-mails with even a remote reference to an affair. Again, no leads were produced from this search, at least to the extent that Reto performed it.

"What do you think, Felix? Did he have an affair?"

"From what we have, it's impossible to know. Let's keep in mind this mystery woman's call, but for now, we should focus on leads we can actually follow."

"What other leads? I have nothing else," de Ville stated bluntly.

"Well, I do," Kupfer answered with a smile. "Remember our man in Norway, Jan Erik Bergeland? It turns out he has been to Switzerland several times, most recently just a month ago."

"And? You think he could be involved, then?" de Ville asked. "Remember the threatening e-mails he sent Stern?"

"Yes, sure."

"So, he has been to Switzerland eight times in the past two years. He came through Zurich four times, Geneva twice, and Basel twice. He came through the Basel airport just a month ago."

"Interesting, but he has not been here any more recently than that?" de Ville queried.

"Passport control has him leaving Basel on October 29. I checked with the airlines, and he flew from Basel to London and then London to Oslo. I confirmed with Oslo Immigration that he entered Gardermoen

Airport on October 29, and they were further able to tell me that he then boarded a flight to Tromso."

"I'm not sure how he could have anything to do with this if he'd left nearly a month before Mr. Stern died," de Ville said in a dejected tone.

"Me neither, but this is our best lead, and I think we need to follow it up. Are you up for a trip to Norway?" Kupfer asked. Just then his mobile phone rang.

"Yes. Yes. You must be kidding! Oh, for God's sake. Yes, I'll return at once."

"What is that all about?" de Ville asked.

"For fuck's sake, one of our key witnesses in a case against a homegrown terrorist from Marseille was killed. They need me to come back and lead the investigation. This is a matter of national, even international, security. I'm afraid you'll need to work on this case on your own, at least for a little while," Kupfer said dryly.

"But I can't leave Basel. We are short on policemen right now."

"I don't know what to tell you."

"I'll see what I can do. You need to go right back to the train station, don't you?"

"Yes, do you mind?"

"Of course not."

De Ville drove his friend back to the Basel central train station. He felt a note of sadness, and helplessness as well. He was convinced that he was not capable of solving this case without help, and furthermore, he knew that even if he could go to Norway to track down Jan Erik Bergeland, he wasn't the man to interrogate him. He was not experienced in handling a case he quickly had come to appreciate as being quite complicated. He asked Kupfer about trying to call Bergeland on the phone in order to interrogate him remotely, but Kupfer strongly admonished de Ville not do that. Kupfer explained that it was much too easy to lie on the phone and that a detective could not as easily pick up on cues of deception without an in-person interrogation. De Ville asked about using Skype, Kupfer just laughed, and while he thought it was not a bad suggestion, he didn't think that it would work either. Kupfer went on to say that the only effective way he knew to interrogate someone—especially a potential suspect—was in person. And with that, Kupfer stepped out of the car and into the train station. He peered into the passenger window once he had all his bags and told de Ville one last thing.

"I really think you need to find the woman who knows about Stern's affair.

Figure something out. Good luck."

CHAPTER 11

D etectives O'Reilly and Alvarez gathered in the conference
room at New York City Police Department headquarters with
their superiors to review the bleeder case. O'Reilly informed
them about his lunch with Mrs. Millbank and her own detective work
in finding that the mysterious Alexa had gone into New York Hospital
on several occasions in October and November; however, he also had
to confess to his superiors that this trail had grown cold. In fact, there
had been no more sightings of Alexa at all, but O'Reilly said that he was
not surprised, given that Mr. Millbank was dead. While O'Reilly had
been having lunch with Mrs. Millbank last week, Alvarez had returned
to the Plaza Hotel and met with Ridgewell, along with as many of the
hotel staff as he could. Several remembered Alexa by her description but
not by name and stated that she would come to the Plaza once or twice
a week and spend some of her time at the lobby bar, but other times
she would go straight to the elevator. He also explained how they had
searched the Plaza Hotel database for guests with the name Alexa going
back to the beginning of this year, but that among the small percentage
of guests with that name, none had fit the description of the Alexa they
were looking for in terms of age. The few that did all lived in Europe.

"Look, there is no way that Alexa is her real name. Shit, I can't believe we let her slip out that day," O'Reilly mused.

"Sean, we didn't even know if we were dealing with a crime at that point. We couldn't have held her, and I doubt she would have answered questions even if we knew it was a crime."

"So what now?" asked the commissioner sternly and succinctly. "The mayor is on my ass about this case. Give me something. You must have some kind of lead, don't you?"

"Not really," O'Reilly responded meekly, which was quite out of character for him.

"If I may, sir," Alvarez politely interrupted. "We have a hematologist from Los Angeles who will be trying to help us out."

"What the hell is he gonna do? Whose idea was this?" the commissioner asked, quite surprised by this suggestion.

"Dr. Lisa Goldberg, the hematologist who our pathologist consulted with on the case, asked him to come to New York to see if he could shed some light on the case. Apparently, he's a real expert on bleeding, and she thought he could provide some insight into how Millbank might have died."

"Who's paying for this?" the commissioner asked. "He is," Alvarez answered quickly.

"Really. Who's *he*, and what's in it for him?"

"Oh, uh, sorry sir," Alvarez continued. "*He* is the hematologist. I guess he is so intrigued, he's coming on his own dollar."

"Very well. Since you have nothing else at this point, go ahead then, but no NYPD money is to be spent on the hematologist without my approval, okay? When is he arriving?"

"He arrived yesterday evening. We have a meeting scheduled with him this afternoon," O'Reilly answered.

"Fine. Keep me posted," the commissioner demanded and briskly left the conference room.

Andy and Leila had arrived late the previous afternoon, checked in to their hotel, and at Leila's request had immediately gone sightseeing, since that might have been their only free day. She asked to go to the

Statue of Liberty—an excursion for which Andy had no particular enthusiasm. He actually hated going to one of New York's most famous and most-visited landmarks. He recalled visiting there as a child and teenager whenever out-of-town family or friends visited New York. They seemed to always come around Thanksgiving or Christmas, and the most indelible memories he had were the interminably long lines and bone-chilling freezing wind. And all for a statue you could see quite easily from Battery Park at the southern tip of Manhattan Island. What his family and friends often overlooked was the much more interesting and historically relevant Ellis Island—the gateway for America-bound European immigrants in the first half of the twentieth century. He loved to say that New Yorkers never went to Liberty Island unless accompanied by overzealous tourists. Regardless, he couldn't deny Leila this opportunity, and off they went. Thankfully it was sunny and not terribly cold.

Following the visit to Liberty Island, they had dinner in Little Italy, per Leila's request. This was another iconic New York City landmark, but one that Andy always enjoyed, not just for the food but also the fascinating character and history of what had once been an Italian mafia-controlled neighborhood. Finally, after an exhausting day, they went back to the hotel. Andy felt he had fulfilled his duty as a tour guide for the day. He wondered if he would have done it for anyone else. Leila thanked him, and they retired to their separate hotel rooms. She left him with a smile that left him wondering if, just maybe, she did like him.

It was Thursday morning, and Andy and Leila were going to meet Drs. Goldberg and Carmichael at 10:00 to talk about the findings of the autopsy and to examine in general terms the highly unusual case. Following that meeting, they were expected at police headquarters to review their findings and discuss their opinions at 1:30. Andy and Leila had slept in, though given the time difference of three hours, waking up at 9:00 a.m. was really more like waking up at 6:00 a.m., at least until their internal biological clocks became adjusted. They met in the lobby of their hotel and headed straight to Starbucks. Leila ordered her usual, a vanilla latte, while Andy settled for a bottle of water. Leila also had an egg-white wrap and Andy a bagel and cream cheese, and after eating their breakfast, they headed over to Dr. Goldberg's office at New York Presbyterian Hospital. New York Hospital, as it was known for years, was arguably the most famous and well-respected hospital among the many outstanding health-care facilities in Manhattan, and the fact that Dr. Goldberg and Dr. Carmichael worked there instantly earned them a high level of respect and credibility.

After they had made their way through security at the hospital's main entrance, Andy immediately recognized Dr. Goldberg just beyond the main entrance, in the hospital lobby. Dr. Lisa Goldberg was just a couple of years younger than Andy and had met him at the American Society of Pediatric Hematology/Oncology annual meeting eight years ago when the meeting was held in Toronto. They got into a discussion about a case that was presented at one of the workshops, and though they had disagreed about the proper approach in the management of the patient, they'd instantly developed mutual respect. Dr. Goldberg had shoulder-length dark, wavy hair and wore stylish glasses with a black frame surrounding rectangular lenses. She had smooth, pale skin that contrasted sharply with her dark hair. She wore a knee-length black skirt and white blouse, which was mostly hidden by her long white lab coat.

"Hi, Andy," she said and gave him a warm embrace and kiss on the cheek. "Who did you bring with you?"

"This is Leila Baker, one of our recent recruits. This case gave me enough of the creeps that I figured I would need some help. Leila is exceptionally well trained, intelligent, and intuitive and might have some insights neither one of us would think about. We were so pleased to be able to recruit her to our center." Andy said matter-of-factly and professionally, without a hint of warmth.

"Wow! Leila, you should be proud. Andy almost never says that about anybody. He's a tough critic. Believe me, I know. I have been on the receiving end of his criticisms more than once—all very professional, I assure you—but still," Lisa stated with a smile. "Shall we?"

They walked through the enormous lobby and into an elevator. Moments later, they found themselves in a rectangular conference room with a large screen at one end and an LCD projector illuminating it brightly with the New York Hospital logo in clear view. There were two individuals seated at the far side of the table, one of whom had a laptop computer in front of her.

"Andy and Leila, this is Jennifer Carmichael, the pathologist who conducted the autopsy, along with her colleague, Stephan Moser."

They exchanged handshakes. Leila noticed Stephan had an accent. "So, Stephan, where are you from?" Leila asked.

"I am from Switzerland—I came here to train for several years with the esteemed Dr. Carmichael," he stated proudly.

"Switzerland, huh? Does he know about the other victim?" Leila asked.

"Yes, this is one reason I have asked him to get involved. He is actually from Basel, if you can believe that," Dr. Carmichael responded.

"Yet another coincidence—will they ever end in this crazy case?" Andy chimed in. "By the way, I thought potential criminal cases went to the coroner's office for autopsy?"

Lisa and Dr. Carmichael looked at each other and then at Andy and smiled.

"What?" Andy said, surprised and feeling as if he was supposed to know something he did not know.

"She is the coroner," Leila said.

"Oh, well, doesn't the coroner usually work in or near the police station?"

"They don't pay me enough to just be the coroner, so I work here, too."

"You must be good," Leila said.

"I am that good," replied Dr. Carmichael with an air of arrogance usually espoused by other types of physicians, in particular, surgeons.

"Shall we start then?" Lisa interjected.

Dr. Carmichael adjusted the focus on the LCD projector while Stephan dimmed the light in the room. She then displayed a series of slides, moving deliberately from one to the next, beginning with the pictures from the Plaza Hotel room of Mr. Millbank's body. She then played the short video from Detective Alvarez's iPhone. Following that set of pictures, for which she only provided brief comments, she began displaying the images from the autopsy. As she moved from slide to slide, she was showing microscopic sections of each of Mr. Millbank's organs, explaining and demonstrating using a pointer that each one was engorged with blood. She provided more detailed descriptions, explaining in anatomical terms precisely which organ and which part of the organ was in view. She pointed out where the hemorrhages were and described how damaging they would be to each organ. Finally, she showed several slides of Mr. Millbank's brain, only instead of microscopic sections, she showed the actual brain, so-called gross sections, in which the brain was sliced as if it were a loaf of bread. In the first slice, Andy and Leila could easily identify, the light tan outer part of the brain called the cortex and the white interior section known simply as the white matter. In addition, there was a large purple-to-black irregular collection of what they recognized to be blood occupying at least 50 percent of one side of the brain. In lieu of a detailed explanation, Dr. Carmichael simply looked at the two doctors from Los Angeles, who motioned for her to move on to the next slide. Doing this, she moved through several more pictures, all of which demonstrated more or less the same finding in different parts of the brain. She then showed another picture, stating that this was the bleed that had caused Mr. Millbank's death. In that picture, one could see an oval ivory-colored piece of tissue with a brown central area; it looked like a freshly peeled hard-boiled egg sliced in half, in which the yolk had turned from yellow to brown. Dr. Carmichael explained that what they were looking at was the midbrain and medulla, the part of the brain that controlled the body's vital functions, and that the damage caused by the blood in this area was fatal. She then went through all the toxicology reports, essentially telling them that other than finding some alcohol in his blood, there were no illicit drugs present nor any prescription drugs. The only drugs found in the toxicology report were aspirin and Tylenol.

"So, that's it," Dr. Carmichael concluded. "Lisa tells me you're quite the genius when it comes to people with bleeding disorders. So, what do you think? Could he have something like hemophilia? Keep in mind, we couldn't do any tests of his coagulation system because by the time he got to me, ironically, his blood had clotted."

"This can't be hemophilia," Andy stated firmly.

"How can you be so sure—without any blood tests?" responded Carmichael. "Because, patients with hemophilia, while they do bleed, only bleed in one place a time usually, and I have never seen a hemophiliac with this extent of bleeding—you know, in so many organs all at once. In fact, bleeding into even just one organ is quite rare in hemophilia."

"You're pretty sure of yourself," Carmichael added with a hint of doubt in her voice.

"I'm quite sure."

"What about Leila—what do you think? Women sometimes have insight men don't," Dr. Carmichael added, making no attempt to hide her doubts about Andy's conclusion.

If a man said that, he would be branded a sexist, Andy thought. *Who does this woman think she is, insulting me like that?*

"Well, I have to agree with Andy. Hemophiliacs don't bleed like this. They... just don't," Leila stated with a bit of hesitation, trying to support Andy, though her tone lacked confidence and Dr. Carmichael picked up on this.

"Of course you agree. Is he your boss or something?" Carmichael asked, now insulting Leila with her insinuation.

"No, I am perfectly capable of making my own decisions," Leila responded sharply, stepping up to defend herself and Andy.

"Okay, let's try to keep this pleasant," Lisa broke in, recognizing that tensions had suddenly risen. "Jennifer, thanks for reviewing your findings. We all appreciate it. Andy, Leila, any questions for Jennifer before she leaves?"

Yeah, how about, 'Why are you such a bitch?' Andy thought but refrained from vocalizing what was going through his mind.

"I have one," said Leila. "Is there a reason you are being so rude?"

"I don't like my opinions being questioned, and I feel as if you and the police think that I should have some easy answer for you. But I don't. So, you will need to come back with more information for me before I can shed any further light on the reason for the extensive bleeding in this man. With *CSI* and those other shows, everyone seems to think you just go to the coroner and get all your answers," replied a woman who now seemed more frustrated, perhaps, than obnoxious. "Look, I didn't mean to be rude, but you have no idea how many times I have had to go over this case in just a couple of weeks and how annoying it is to have the cops, the mayor, and the press think I should tell them precisely what happened."

"Fair enough," Andy replied. "We won't bother you again with this unless we really have a question we think only you can answer. Thank you again for your time."

The two pathologists left the room, and Lisa invited Andy and Leila to lunch at a local deli that was well known for its great sandwiches. Over lunch they discussed Dr. Carmichael's rude behavior, which Lisa chalked up to the frustration she and the detectives were feeling over this case.

"She's actually usually a super nice person. I have never seen her like this, but then again, she's had everyone and their brother visit her recently to get her point of view on the case. So don't take it personally."

They then reviewed their collective opinions; all three strongly agreed that this man did not have had hemophilia or any other bleeding disorder—but they could not figure out what could have led to such extensive internal bleeding. The conversation then turned more casual and a bit more personal.

"Leila, I thought it was pretty funny for you to ask Stephan about his accent," Lisa mentioned.

"Why?" Leila asked, surprised.

"Well, you have an accent," Lisa replied.

"Oh, you know I don't even think of it—I've been in the US for over twenty years now."

"Where are you from?"

"I grew up in Iraq. My family left after the first Gulf War. We were refugees."

"Oh, wow. Andy never mentioned you before he told me he was bringing you with him," Lisa replied.

"I'm his little secret weapon," Leila responded with a smile.

"It's almost one o'clock. Should we head to police headquarters now?" Andy asked.

Both Leila and Lisa noticed how Andy had not-so-subtly changed the subject, though they both kept it to themselves. They finished their lunches quickly, and Lisa helped them hail a taxi to take them to police headquarters downtown. Upon arrival, they were escorted to a conference room, which they found to be much more glum than the one they had just left at the hospital. It reminded Andy of those interrogation rooms he'd seen on *Law & Order*, one of his favorite television shows. They were the first ones in the room, and they sat and waited for the detectives to arrive. Andy hated it when meetings didn't start on time. It was one of the harder things to get used to about Los Angeles. Punctuality, an important aspect of life in New York, particularly in the working environment, was an afterthought in Los Angeles. While in New York, he recalled, if you arrived to a meeting one minute late, it would already have started, whereas in Los Angeles, if you arrived five minutes late, you were frequently the first one there. Of course, he had no idea how things worked in a police station, where a prime tactic of interrogation was making the suspect just sit and wait—at least on television crime dramas. They sat in silence, as if they sensed someone was listening in to their conversation. About ten minutes passed before the door opened.

"Hello, I'm Detective O'Reilly and this is Detective Alvarez. Welcome to New York." They introduced themselves and then sat down to review the case. First, Detective O'Reilly briefed them on what they knew about Mr. Millbank with respect to his background, the alleged and now-confirmed affair he'd had with Alexa, and the information they had gathered from the hotel workers, employees at Empire Health, and, of course, from Mrs. Millbank. The statement regarding the increased denials of service by Empire Health Insurance that Dr. Tran had mentioned touched a nerve with Andy, who relayed briefly to the detectives that this was a common tactic used by insurance companies to increase their profits.

"Nice to know that we are not being singled out in California when it comes to insurance companies denying payment for necessary medications and procedures," Andy said. "Do you think that has anything to do with Millbank's death?"

"I don't know. You're the medical experts. What do you think?" O'Reilly asked.

"I can tell you that this is something that is really affecting the delivery of health care. Insurance companies are looking for more and more ways to deny service. I always thought health insurance would be different, because we're dealing with people's lives, but I guess not. Business is business," Andy went on.

"Hey, doc, speak in English. What the hell are you talking about?" O'Reilly asked, annoyed.

"Say you're in a car accident; your car-insurance company will first do what they can to blame the other driver so that person's insurance would have to pay the claim, and if that doesn't work, then they will pay the claim and increase your insurance payment. It's ridiculous," Andy explained.

"Spoken like a man with experience of car accidents," Alvarez said.

"Sadly, yes. But with health insurance, you would expect that things would be different. After all, a car is ... well, just a car, but a human life, that's different, or at least it should be."

"Are you saying that this could be a motive to kill, doc?" O'Reilly asked.

"It would depend on the situation, but if it was something egregious that cost someone's life, sure, I could see that happening," Andy replied.

"What about Mr. Millbank's autopsy. Any thoughts? Could he have had some kind of disease or infection that led to his death?" asked Alvarez.

"We don't think he had hemophilia or any other bleeding disorder. We reviewed the autopsy findings with Dr. Carmichael, and well,

I don't know what killed him, but I don't think it was any kind of inherited medical condition," Andy responded.

"What about something he caught, like a virus?" Alvarez queried.

"Unlikely; something like that would probably be contagious, and Mr. Millbank wouldn't be the only one," Andy answered. "He's not the only one, you know," said O'Reilly.

"Yes, of course. I know about the person in Basel, but I meant the only one in the city. Surely, someone else here in the city would have had the same thing happen to them."

"Actually, we don't know that, do we Sean?" Alvarez chimed in.

"You're right. Let's put a call in to the public-health office," O'Reilly suggested. "So, doc, do you think this is foul play? Do you think someone could have done something that led to the deaths of Mr. Millbank and the other stiff, the one in Switzerland?"

"Yes. I think it is too much of a coincidence. There are a lot of coincidences in this case, you know," Andy stated.

"What other coincidence are you referring to?" Alvarez asked. "Leila, explain what you put together for the detectives," Andy said.

"Oh, well, while I was reviewing the case on the flight from LA—five hours is a long time to be reading and thinking—I noticed that the two dead men both were involved in the health-care industry. One is a CEO of a health-insurance company, while the other is a CEO of a pharmaceutical company. I was thinking that this could somehow be related to the case," Leila explained.

"Clarification. They were CEOs not are CEOs. Interesting thought, but there is another coincidence that you should be aware of which, in my view, trumps this one," Alvarez said. "We spoke to our colleagues in Basel this morning and discovered that Mr. Stern, the dead CEO in Switzerland, also cheated on his wife. The detective there received an anonymous tip about his infidelity."

"In our world," O'Reilly stepped in, "this type of coincidence is more likely to be a key to the case. When there are murders and affairs, the fucking and the killing usually are related."

"Sean, easy with the language,'" Alvarez said.

"Yeah, sorry," O'Reilly said, though his tone was far from apologetic. "Dr. Baker, I am not trying to dismiss your suggestion, and feel free to follow up on it, but don't forget about this other coincidence."

"Who is—er, *was*—Mr. Stern's mistress?" Leila asked.

"We don't know. Like I said, it was an anonymous tip. The detective in Basel will be working that end of the case."

"Okay then, it seems as if we have answered your questions to the best of our knowledge. Should we plan to go back to Los Angeles?" Andy asked, looking over to Leila, who couldn't hide a look of disappointment.

"Not exactly. We … uh, want to ask the two of you to … well, do some more work on the case. We think you'd be the best ones to do this," O'Reilly stated slowly, as if the request would more likely be met with a yes if he asked slowly, like a child requesting a new toy or permission for something from his parent.

"What is this about?" asked a curious Andy.

"Jose, you want to explain?" asked O'Reilly, though it really wasn't a request, and the fact that he'd asked his junior partner to do it brought a sense of worry to both Andy and Leila, who looked at each other blankly.

"As we mentioned, we spoke to Detective de Ville from Basel this morning. In addition to mentioning the anonymous tip about the affair, they have another lead. They uncovered several threatening e-mails from a man named Jan Erik Bergeland. Apparently, he feels that he was taken advantage of, financially that is, by Terrapharma. He is the inventor of some technology that has gone into the production of medications by Terrapharma, and well, he seems quite pissed off at Mr. Stern, judging by his e-mails. Besides the e-mails, the Swiss detectives via Interpol found out that Mr. Bergeland has travelled to Switzerland eight times in the past few years, including a trip to Basel in October," Alvarez concluded.

"Okay, that's interesting, but what do you want us to do?" asked Andy.

"We want you to go to Norway and interview Mr. Bergeland," O'Reilly said bluntly.

"Norway. We can't just up and leave our jobs and our patients to do your work," Andy stated firmly. "Besides, why don't you two go?"

"Believe me, we'd love to, but we can't," O'Reilly answered. "We have too many fucking cases going on here in New York. Besides, we need to track down Alexa—she seems to have completely vanished. So that's what we're going to be working on."

"It's also outside our jurisdiction, so we'd need to work out some agreement with the authorities in Norway," Alvarez added.

"Regardless, this is not our business. We helped you, and we need to get back to our regular lives and jobs in LA," Andy said as he glanced over at Leila. Noting her disappointed face, he suddenly changed his tone. "Well, maybe we can. Let me make some calls."

Andy pulled out his iPhone and peered over to Leila, whose face transformed from that of a disappointed child to one full of happy anticipation. The detectives left the room and returned fifteen minutes later.

"Well?" O'Reilly asked brusquely.

"I got clearance for us to go, but after interviewing Bergeland, we're done. Is that clear?" Andy said firmly.

"Yes, no problem. Thanks so much," Alvarez added.

"By the way, even though I paid for the trip here myself, there is no way that I can pay for this trip. It will have to be on the NYPD."

"Oh shit! I—dammit—I should think of these things ahead of time. Wait here, please," O'Reilly said and quickly left the office.

Alvarez left the room as well. At that point, Andy found himself alone in the conference room with Leila. She told him that she thought they should accept the assignment so long as NYPD agreed to pay for their expenses. She was excited not only to travel to Norway but more so to try to figure out what had actually happened to Mr. Millbank and Mr. Stern.

"C'mon, Andy, you said this would be an adventure. And you also said we are detectives, in a manner of speaking. Why the sudden urge to go back home? I really think we can help figure this out. Detective Alvarez is right; with our medical knowledge we are probably better placed to interview this Bergeland person, anyway. And Norway. I've never been to Europe."

"Never been to New York. Never been to Europe. You haven't travelled much."

"No, I haven't, but it's not about that. This case is really intriguing. I'm telling you my gut tells me this insurance company and pharmaceutical company link is real."

"What about the affairs?"

"Maybe they're real too. Who knows? That's what makes this so interesting.

C'mon. Let's go," Leila urged.

Andy relented, though he was still trying to figure out how the trip would be paid for, especially since the part of the case involving Mr. Stern was not in the NYPD's jurisdiction. Then Detective O'Reilly returned.

"Fuckin' commissioner won't cover the trip. He says this part of the case is out of our jurisdiction anyway. Asshole! Sorry about my language, Dr. Baker," he apologized to the only lady in the room.

"It's all right, Detective; I have cable television," she replied, and they all had a good laugh.

"So, what now?" Andy asked.

"Dr. Friedman, have you had a change of heart?" O'Reilly asked.

"Yes, we'd like to go and try to figure this case out."

"Great. Wait here for a minute."

He stepped out and had a brief discussion with Alvarez outside the conference room before returning.

"I have an idea," O'Reilly said. "Why don't you two go back to your hotel, enjoy your night in the city, and I'll call you tomorrow with an answer about Norway."

Andy and Leila looked at each other and nodded toward O'Reilly.

They returned to the hotel and agreed to meet in the lobby at 7:00 p.m. Andy sat in his room, staring out of the window down toward Times Square; though the sun had set hours ago, it was never dark in Times Square. His feelings toward Leila were growing by the hour.

She was really funny, a quality he hadn't appreciated so much before. To make a New York City detective laugh the way she had with her comeback to his apology for cursing was no small feat—especially with the gruff Detective O'Reilly. It endeared her to him even more. Again, he started saying, *A Jew and a Muslim*, but this time, instead of repeating the refrain over and over again, he suppressed it and just thought of her as a woman instead of as a Muslim, Kurdish woman. But while he wasn't officially her boss, or for that matter her mentor, she was younger than him, and he wasn't completely comfortable with the idea of dating her—that is, if she even wanted that. He'd begun to sense that she might like him, but he had never been very good at reading the signs women gave him, so he wasn't sure, and this made him grow only more anxious about the situation he now found himself in. Norway. Shit. A quick trip to New York was one thing. A trip to Norway was something else altogether. *Wait! What about the patients and the clinic?* he thought to himself. He made a few phone calls and was able to rearrange a number of his and Leila's patients' appointments and, for those who needed to be seen, find one of the other hematologists to see them with Andrea. He had full confidence in Andrea to manage all of the patients; she would only need one of the other hematologists available in case she had a question. He also promised his secretary and Andrea to take calls on his cell phone at all times should questions arise, and to check his e-mail daily.

Leila lay on her bed, resting and staring at the ceiling. She was thinking about this crazy trip she was on. She was really intrigued by the case and thought about it incessantly. Mr. Millbank, the philanderer … and Mr. Stern, the maybe-philanderer. Their deaths on the same day. The way they'd died. Their jobs. It all had to be connected, she thought. The mysterious Jan Erik Bergeland. Why had he threatened Mr. Stern? She was consumed by the case. While her body rested, her mind could not. And what about Andy? *He's acting strange*, she thought to herself. He was probably worried about his patients and his research, and while she knew he wanted to help the detectives, she felt he was torn between continuing to pursue the case and going home. Or was it something else? She couldn't figure it out.

They met as planned at 7:00 p.m., hopped into a taxi, and headed to Greenwich Village, a community of artists, New York University college students, and former hippies reliving their youth. This part of the city was not known particularly for its restaurants but rather for the live music scene and the general bohemian atmosphere. Andy knew where he wanted to take Leila for dinner. It was not a fancy or expensive place but one where she could find food she was familiar with. After getting dropped off on Bleecker Street, the main street of the Village, as Greenwich Village was known, they went down a side street and found the Olive Tree Café and Restaurant.

"You're kidding! You're taking me to an Arabic restaurant? You are so funny.

I'll probably hate it, you know," Leila said.

"It's supposed to be good. By the way, aren't there different types of Arabic food?"

"Yeah, and none of it is as good as Kurdish food."

"Of course, but I wouldn't take you out for Kurdish food when you eat that at home all the time. Plus, I don't know if there are Kurdish restaurants in New York," Andy said.

"Are you kidding me? This is New York. I'll find a place on my phone in less than a minute."

"Okay, we can go to a Kurdish restaurant if you prefer."

"Oh my God!" Leila burst out laughing. "I am just giving you a hard time. You are too easy to make fun of. By the way, how come at work you are always the one poking fun at everyone, and you are so loose and relaxed all the time, but recently when you are with me ... well, you are almost like a different person. You are anxious and, I don't know—you're just not the same as the person I know at work."

"Because I like you?" he said in the tone of a question. *Shit, why did I say that*, he thought. While part of him wished he could retrieve the words out of the air, another part of him did not. A pendulum was swinging inside his head. At one moment he regretted professing his feelings, and a moment later he was happy he had let Leila know how he felt. It was as if his breath had been held under water for over a minute, and the carbon dioxide that had built up in his lungs had just had to come out.

"Oh, really?" Leila replied with a straight face, not giving anything way.

"I'm sorry; that was totally inappropriate. After all, I am your, well, you know, your …" Andy hesitated.

"You're my what?" Leila pressed firmly. "What? My boss, my superior, my mentor?"

"Yeah, kind of," Andy responded meekly—not in his normally self-confident manner.

"I am calling bullshit on that," Leila replied almost angrily. "You are not my boss, superior, mentor, or anything like that. Oh, please. Hey, where is that self-confidence you usually have, anyway? What is wrong with you?"

Andy became confused. Was she toying with him again? Was she serious? He didn't know what to say or do.

They were silent as the hostess seated them. They were both hungry, so the thought of leaving this awkward situation without eating was out of the question. Andy excused himself to go to the men's room. Leila got up and followed the waitress. When Andy came back, there were four shot glasses filled with a clear liquid on the table—two for each of them.

"What's this?" Andy asked, surprised. "*arak*—do you know what that is?"

"I think so," he replied.

"Bottoms up. That's the only way we're going to get through tonight," Leila said, quickly downing the first of her shots.

They finished their two shots of the anise-flavored liqueur. The waitress came back. They ordered dinner and Leila ordered more arak, and the previous discussion was not resurrected for the rest of the evening.

CHAPTER 12

O'Reilly got out of his car on Park Avenue and proceeded up to Mrs. Millbank's massive apartment. On the way up, he recalled their lunch the previous week, and he had to admit that beneath that tough exterior and the elitist tendencies lay a genuine, nice woman. They'd talked about her husband's philandering, and all the while she'd sworn that she'd always been faithful and devoted to him, and that while the money he'd made had helped them live a life of luxury, all she'd really wanted was his love and companionship. Once that was lost, she hadn't cared about all the money. She did admit to O'Reilly, though, that now that he was dead, she would in some odd form of revenge spend it all. They did not have children, and she therefore did not have to concern herself with heirs. She'd thought about what she could possibly do with the money and told the detective that she planned to donate much of it toward a good cause. She wanted to start a foundation and, in particular, wanted to help children in need, but she hadn't quite decided what form that would take.

"So nice to see you again, Detective O'Reilly. To what do I owe this wonderful surprise?" Julie Millbank was dressed in a more relaxed manner today—no cleavage or tight T-shirt, but she looked beautiful nonetheless, in her jeans and turtleneck sweater.

"It's nice to see you again as well, Mrs. Millbank," O'Reilly said in the most friendly tone he could muster, knowing he was coming to request a favor.

"It's Julie."

"Yes, I meant Julie. It's going to take some getting used to, calling you Julie. I want to thank you for that really nice lunch last week. I don't really ever eat food like that. I'm still not sure what I ate, but it was really good, I must say."

"The pleasure was all mine, Detective."

"Look, if I'm going to call you Julie, then you need to call me Sean—at least when we are not at the station or interviewing you, if you know what I mean."

"I understand, Sean. Are you here to take me down to the station? Haven't you already figured out that I am not involved? Surely you have gotten that far in your investigation, I hope."

"Well, to be honest, no one has been ruled out, but personally, I don't think you had anything to do with it," O'Reilly reassured her.

"So, why are you here? Is this a social call disguised as a professional call?" Julie Millbank asked playfully.

"No. Not at all," he replied firmly. "I am here to, well, to ask for a favor."

"Really. It will cost you, you know."

"What will it cost me?" O'Reilly asked nervously. "Let's see just how big a favor you are asking."

"Okay. The investigation into your husband's death has stalled. We have no new leads. No Alexa sightings and nothing new from his employees, or from you, for that matter."

"Well, I don't really care, to be honest. The coroner has ruled it a homicide and not a suicide, so I will be collecting his life insurance as well as inheriting his fortune, which my lawyer assured me won't be a problem so long as I am cleared."

"That's where you can help. I would like to clear you as well, but as I said, we are a bit stuck in the investigation. We do have one lead we would like to follow, but ... well, it's in Norway."

"Norway?" Mrs. Millbank replied with surprise and curiosity. "Explain, please."

"I can't. Again, until you are cleared, I can't divulge any aspect of the case, especially not any leads. I am sorry, Julie, but you are still a potential suspect, and those are the rules."

"Fine," Julie relented, "but what do you want from me, then?"

"It's a long story, and I can't get into it other than to say we would like to chase a lead in Norway, but—and here's where you come in. You see, the NYPD won't pay for the trip."

"Why not? Isn't it part of solving the case?" Julie asked.

"Yes, but ... uh, look, I can't explain it now, but I promise you I will when I can. I am here to ask you to support the investigation financially."

"You want money to help solve my husband's murder?" she laughed. "Didn't I tell you I don't care?"

"I know you don't care about him, but if it will help solve the case, then you will be cleared, and you'll collect your inheritance and the life insurance," O'Reilly stated as persuasively as he could.

"Hmm." Mrs. Milbank puffed. "I'd say that's a convincing argument. I'll tell you what, I'll put up a hundred thousand dollars, but you have to promise me this is only for the costs the NYPD won't cover," Julie said.

"Thank you so much—that is very generous of you."

"So, are you going to Norway then?"

"No. Actually, it's going to be two doctors from Los Angeles. They are pediatric hematologists—it means they take care of children with blood diseases," O'Reilly explained.

"I know that, Sean. I am not the dumb trophy wife you might think I am."

"I'm sorry. Yes, of course you know that. Anyway, they are not just hematologists, but in particular, they are experts in bleeding problems in people, so we think they can help figure out how your husband was killed."

"So, you're staying in town, then," Julie said with a smile that could not belie her thoughts.

"Yes."

"Good. Norway, huh? Do you think a hundred thousand dollars is enough?"

"For starters, yes, and I hope to not have to ask you again for money. I promise I will ensure it is not wasted."

"Well, I'll tell you what—you can't let those two doctors fly coach to Norway, so while I don't want the money wasted, I am ordering you to fly them in business or first class."

"Thank you, Julie. That is a very kind gesture. As for your price …"

"Forget it, no need. You can have the money—no charge," she said, smiling.

"Okay. Well, I was about to offer to take you to lunch, but … well, I, uh, I would like to take you to lunch on me. To my hangout."

"All right, a date then."

"No, we can't call it that. Remember, you're a suspect. Let's just have lunch and not call it anything."

"Very well. Thanks, Sean," she replied with a wide smile. "I'll call you."

And with that, Detective O'Reilly left.

Andy woke up with a wicked headache. How many shots of arak had they ended up downing? He could not remember. He did remember that he'd felt like a fool all night. *What the hell was I thinking telling her I like her?* he thought. *How am I even going to face her today?* He didn't know what had come over him to make him, without any lead-up or any warning, just blurt out that he liked her. He was worried it would affect their working relationship and their friendship. But his immediate concern was how he would face her today and what would they do with this increasingly complicated investigation. Were they actually going to go to Norway?

Leila woke up early and went to the gym to "sweat out" her hangover. She felt she had been too hard on Andy the previous evening, and she knew he had felt embarrassed most of the night. Thank God for the shots of arak, or it would have been an impossible night to get through. What Andy did not realize, however, was what specifically Leila was upset about. She was not upset that he'd told her he liked her. Rather, she was flattered. She was, however, dismayed that he viewed her as some kind of subordinate. That's what really bothered her. She was sweating profusely while going up and down the stair-climber, as if she were being chased up a hill by a wild animal. She thought more clearly this way—more oxygen to the brain was her rationale.

Andy called Leila's cell phone. No answer. *Fuck*, he thought, *what have I done? I am an idiot. She's not answering my calls now.* How was he going to face her? He called again. No answer. He went down to Starbucks, got his coffee and biscotti, and sat down with his laptop to check his e-mail. After an hour had passed, he sensed a presence in front of him, looked up, and there was Leila. No smile. No frown. She just stood there looking at Andy. Neither one knew what to say. Finally, Leila broke the silence.

"How's your head?" she asked. "Hurting, how about yours?"

"Fine now. Sweated it out in the gym."

"Oh, is that where you were? I tried calling," Andy said.

"I know. Caller ID, genius!" she retorted, trying to break the ice with a slight smile and a bit of humor.

"About last night, I—" Andy began.

"Not now," she interrupted. "We have work to do."

"Yeah, okay." Andy said.

"Now what?"

"We wait for the call from O'Reilly. That was the plan. Why don't you get your coffee and something to eat? I'll meet you back here."

Leila left Andy to his thoughts and headed out to the street to get a bagel for breakfast. One American treat she'd grown to love was bagels, and although New York bagels had the reputation for being the absolute best, she couldn't reconcile how such a simple food could be so drastically different from the ones she was used to in Los Angeles. She walked a few blocks before she found the Midtown Bagel Deli. As soon as she stepped in, the smell of freshly baked dough filled her nose, and she knew she was in for a treat. The line was quite long and filled with a combination of men and women in expensive suits and overcoats, policeman in their uniforms, and people dressed casually in jeans with New York Yankees jackets. Aside from the variety of outerwear, Leila also noted the variety of ethnicities represented on the line, with Latinos speaking Spanish, African Americans, and people she immediately recognized as being from the Middle East intermingled with "typical" Caucasians of European descent. Ironically, she felt at home, comfortable with the notion that everyone was a minority. The line moved swiftly. Clearly the deli workers had developed a highly efficient system of taking and delivering the orders. When Leila's turn came, she asked for a sesame seed bagel with vegetable cream cheese and an egg bagel with plain cream cheese and a cup of coffee. For that moment she felt like a New Yorker. She headed back to Starbucks and found Andy in the same seat. She offered him his choice of the two bagels like a peace offering. Andy gladly accepted and took the egg bagel.

Leila decided that she would not discuss with Andy what was bothering her until the right time, though she was not sure when that would be or how she would know it was the right time. Just then, Andy's cell phone rang.

"Hello."

"Andy, are you with Leila?" came O'Reilly's voice.

"Yes."

"Please come down to the station. I have some news about Norway."

"Okay. We'll head right over."

Upon arriving at the police station, they were escorted to the same conference room that they had been in the day before, where they were greeted by Detectives O'Reilly and Alvarez. Detective O'Reilly told them about his meeting with Julie Millbank, explaining that she had agreed to fund any part of the investigation the NYPD wouldn't cover, including the trip to Norway. Perplexed, Leila asked Detective O'Reilly why she would do that. He stated that she was anxious to clear her name and that the sooner the mystery was solved the sooner she could put in a claim for the life-insurance policy.

"We need to go back to Los Angeles for a few days, to see some of our patients, tie up some loose ends and, I assume, pack for some very cold weather," Andy stated.

"Andy, you called yesterday already and rearranged the patient schedules—don't you remember? And I don't know about you, but I don't even own any warm clothes," Leila responded.

"Sorry, I forgot. So much has gone on in the last couple of days that I am getting confused."

Leila shot him a look, including a tilt of the head, raised eyebrows, and pursed lips, affirming that she agreed he was confused—and not only about having made the call to their office.

"So, Andy, we need to *buy* some warm clothes. I haven't been in cold weather until this trip to New York. Do you think Mrs. Millbank will pay for some clothes, too?" Leila asked, the way a schoolgirl might ask her mom for a new dress.

"Yeah, go ahead, but be reasonable, and just get what you think you will need for your trip."

"Yay! Shopping trip," Leila cried out, "and in New York!"

"Be reasonable!" O'Reilly said, slowly enunciating each syllable clearly. "I will, I promise," Leila responded.

"Oh, one last thing, when Mrs. Millbank found out that we are sending the two of you—she seems to have a soft spot for children and for doctors who take care of them—she insisted that you fly in business class. Andy, can I have your bank account number? I'll arrange for the money to be transferred to your account. One last thing—receipts, for everything you spend. Clear?"

"Got it. I'm used to that. If you only knew how the bean counters in my hospital watch the money." And with that, Andy and Leila left. First on the agenda was a shopping trip in what could be considered the best city in the world to shop for clothes. Andy tapped on the face of his iPhone, exploring the Weather Channel app. *Just how cold is it in Norway in December?* he wondered. He added Oslo and Tromsø to his favorites in the app, and as he gazed at the page for each city, he was surprised to find that while it was indeed going to be cold, it wasn't quite as cold as he'd expected.

Andy hoped that both he and Leila could put yesterday evening behind them. He promised himself he would not bring up anything remotely resembling a relationship discussion again, but wondered whether he could he hold himself to that promise. He really did like Leila.

CHAPTER 13

L eila and Andy had spent the previous afternoon buying a variety of warm clothes, gloves, and hats, as well as luggage for the trip to Norway and then returned to the hotel in the early evening. They agreed, much to Andy's relief, not to go out to dinner but to spend the evening resting in their own hotel rooms and preparing for their trip the following day.

Andy, ever curious, spent much of the evening on the Internet learning all he could about Norway in general and Tromsø in particular. Through his research, he learned numerous facts about Norway that he hadn't know, such as that it had one of the most wealthy, educated, and civilized societies in the world. Rich in oil, the country had used that wealth to diversify its businesses and was now a leader in the sophisticated engineering and technology required to efficiently and safely extract oil from both the sea and the ground. In addition, the non-petroleum technology sector was very strong and was growing on the strength of a highly educated workforce, funded largely by wise investments of oil money. Norway had also marketed itself well, resulting in a thriving tourism sector. For a small country with a population of less than five million, it was well known for its artists, including Edvard Grieg (music) and Edvard Munch (painting). Finally, Norwegians were historically among the finest explorers, not only in Europe but also throughout the world. As an example, Fridtjof Nansen, aboard the ship *Fram*, was the first explorer to reach the South Pole, a quite surprising feat for someone from the country furthest from the Antarctic. The only aspect of Norwegian popular culture Andy had previously been familiar with was the one-hit-wonder band A-ha and their hit song, *Take on Me*, which had accompanied an amazing and groundbreaking video back in the 1980s heyday of MTV.

Andy also wanted to learn as much as he could about Sami Innovations, the company Jan Erik Bergeland owned and ran. However, their website was suspiciously limited in its information, and the little information available was vague. There were no pictures of the headquarters, the staff, nor any mission statements or tag lines, only some simple statements about their past successes. *Strange,* he thought. But it reduced the time he had anticipated needing to learn what he could about the company of the man he was going to meet. Thus he was able to go to sleep earlier than he'd expected.

Leila chose to limit her research to Tromsø, a city she had never heard of before this case began. She was curious to know how such a city, seemingly so far removed from the core of Europe, could be home to what she learned were several technology companies. This led her to look up the University of Tromsø, which laid unofficial claim to being the world's northernmost university, and that brought her to study the geography of Norway—which led to several more surprising findings. She hadn't realized quite how far north Norway was, with its southern population centers lying at the same latitude as the city of Anchorage, Alaska, while its northernmost points lay farther north than even the northern tip of Alaska. She found that Tromsø, at seventy degrees north latitude, lay equally as far from the equator as the city of Barrow on Alaska's north coast. With his newfound information, she became concerned that the cold-weather clothes she'd bought would not suffice. However, upon further reading, she learned that even the northern reaches of Norway were not nearly as cold as Alaska despite the fact that they lay in the same general latitude. The relatively mild weather was due mostly to the effect of the Gulf Stream. She found it hard to believe, yet fascinating, that water originating in the Gulf of Mexico was responsible for making winter in Tromsø more similar to winter in Boston than winter in northern Alaska. While she became less concerned that she would freeze to death, she did become concerned about how she would deal with the lack of daylight. Apparently, during this time of year, Tromsø was in perpetual darkness save for a few hours of twilight. *How do people deal with this darkness for so long?* she thought, noting that the sun wouldn't make its return appearance until about mid-January and even then only fleetingly.

Andy and Leila met in the lobby for breakfast and discussed how they had spent their evening learning all they could about Norway, Sami Innovations, and Jan Erik Bergeland. Typical of doctors, Andy thought, that in lieu of relaxing with a novel or a movie they'd each spent hours conducting research on the Internet. They reviewed their findings with each other, both remarking on the scant information they could find about Sami Innovations. The rest of the day they spent on e-mail and on a teleconference with Andrea, their nurse, to review the patients scheduled for the next week and to discuss their medical plans. She would be the primary person seeing the patients, as the other physicians were less familiar with them and would only provide a supervisory role. Andy and Leila also had a short teleconference with the division chief, persuading him that this investigation would likely lead to a lot of good publicity for the Children's Center and Children's Hospital. Andy knew he had to be convincing, since he was asking for an open-ended return date for both himself and Leila. By the time all of these calls were completed, it was time to head to the airport.

There was just one nonstop flight to Oslo from New York, and it was from Newark International Airport, just across the river from New York City in New Jersey. Neither Andy nor Leila had ever flown business class before, so they didn't know what to expect. Their flight left at 7:00 p.m., and they assumed they would be fed, so they skipped dinner and arrived early to go to the lounge and have a drink—just one drink. This time it was not to cover awkwardness; it seemed they had both managed to put the previous evening's discomfort behind them—at least for now.

At 6:30 p.m. they boarded their United Airlines flight and found their way to their seats. The seats were much larger than the coach seats they were used to, with a lot of legroom and plenty of width. They sat down and looked at each other and smiled.

"Not bad," Andy said.

"Yeah, we'll really need to thank Mrs. Millbank when we return. So nice of her to insist we be given seats in business class."

"The best way to thank her is to find the truth, which will exonerate her," Andy added.

The rest of the flight was uneventful—dinner and a movie (like a date with yourself) followed by sleep. Andy was thankful the flight left at night. He was worried the discussion he had ruefully started the other night at the Olive Tree Café would come up, and he desperately was hoping to avoid it, not only for the flight but for the entire trip.

Their plane landed at Oslo Gardermoen Airport just past nine o'clock in the morning local time. The sun had just risen, far off in the southeastern sky, and it was a clear day as far as Andy could tell as he looked out the small, oval window of the airplane. The pilot had just stated that it was minus fourteen degrees Celsius, which reminded Andy that they now needed to think in the metric system. Andy could never quite understand why the United States couldn't embrace the metric system. He and Leila were used to it, regardless, since all of the measurements in medicine were done in the metric system. Despite that, Andy had to do some math to calculate the temperature in Fahrenheit, since such cold temperatures were never encountered in medicine. As he thought about it some more, he realized that such temperatures were never encountered in Southern California weather, either. He quickly calculated in his head that it was seven degrees Fahrenheit.

Andy and Leila exited the plan into a beautiful terminal with a high, arched ceiling supported by enormous curved wooden beams. They proceeded to immigration side by side, and as soon as Leila was called to one immigration officer, Andy was called to the next window a few feet over to the left of hers. Andy showed his passport and, after a few perfunctory questions, whizzed through to the other side of the line of booths, having now officially entered Norway. After he'd proceeded past the booth, he looked for Leila but didn't see her. He gazed down toward the baggage-claim area but did not see her there, either. He decided to wait. As the minutes passed, he began to wonder whether Leila had proceeded to baggage claim without him. Just as he was ready to head in that direction, Leila emerged from between the booths with a chagrined smile, as if she had expected her passage through immigration to take that long.

"What the hell took so long?" Andy asked quietly so as not to draw any undesired attention.

"That's what I get for being born in Iraq, I guess," she said.

"What did they ask you?" Andy asked curiously.

"Where was I born? What is my religion? Do I have family there? How long will I be in Norway? When I said I wasn't sure, which is actually the truth—well, that just opened a Pandora's box of more questions. Let me tell you, that was probably not the best answer. Next thing you know, the officer called his supervisor, and then he had more seemingly irrelevant questions. Anyway, it doesn't matter, and I don't want to talk about it. I guess that is the treatment I should expect for being from a politically messed-up country."

"But—you have an American passport," Andy said haltingly.

"Yeah, you'd think that would help, but it, of course, says I was born in Kirkuk, Iraq."

"Okay. Let's get to our flight to Tromsø. It leaves pretty soon," Andy said. Norway is shaped roughly like a curved, upside down chicken drumstick, with the "meaty" southern section home to most of the population. Oslo, the largest city and the capital, lies in the eastern section, with Bergen, the second-largest city, situated on the west coast.

Norway narrows to a thin middle, with Trondheim being the major city in this central region. There are few cities and only a small number of people north of Trondheim. Tromsø lies about seven hundred miles north of Oslo, and the flight there is similar in distance and time to a flight from New York to Chicago. The quickest way to get from city to city in Norway is air travel, given the significant distances. The paucity of roads and numerous fjords necessitate either taking long, circuitous routes or hopping on a car ferry to take you across the fingers of the ocean that interdigitate Norway's long coastline. While east-west train travel is efficient across the populous "meaty" south, any south-north route requires traversing either mountains or fjords.

Andy and Leila boarded the SAS flight and pulled out the map in the airline magazine to get a better sense of where they were heading. Jan Erik Bergeland had agreed to meet them and asked that the hematologists contact him once they arrived in Tromsø. During takeoff at 11:00 in the morning, the sun, albeit fairly low in the sky, shone brightly on the tarmac. Norway's geography and the time of year conspired to provide Andy and Leila with a rather odd experience. Following the plane's ascent and a sharp turn northward, they saw the sun set in the southern sky despite the fact that it was just past noon. The further north the plane flew, the darker the sky became with each passing minute—it was like a late-winter's afternoon in Los Angeles—until the plane finally touched down in the rather dark twilight that hung over Tromsø.

"That was strange," Leila said referring to the midday nightfall. "Yeah, well, get used to it. No daylight while we are here."

"It's amazing people can live like this," Leila responded.

"At least in the summer they get paid back with continuous daylight in return."

"Not sure I would like that, either. Where does the sun go, though—it doesn't just stay in one place, surely?" Leila wondered aloud.

"Good question. I don't know."

The city of Tromsø lies on an island in the middle of a sliver of the Norwegian sea and rests like a fallen ash leaf floating in a large puddle.

As such, it has two shorelines, with the central eastern shore serving as the hub of its downtown area while the airport sits as the lone sign of civilization on the western shore.

Andy and Leila took a taxi to their hotel on the waterfront in the center of the business district. They'd chosen the SAS Radisson, figuring a Scandinavian brand made the most sense. The downtown area was beautifully lit with numerous streetlights and Christmas decorations everywhere as if Santa Claus could easily take a short ride at any time from the North Pole (which was, in fact, not all that far away!). Their hotel was clean and neat, and both Andy and Leila were pleased with their rooms. They were both tired, and the midday twilight served to heighten the fatigue that washed over them from their long journey. Thus, in short order they agreed it was a good time to take a nap. They planned to meet in the lobby at 6:00 for dinner.

Felix de Ville had exhausted every lead he could think of to trace the woman who had made the anonymous call regarding Mr. Stern having had an affair. When he sat in the chair of his office staring blankly at the ceiling and reviewed the call again in his head, he found a number of inconsistencies. First, he found it odd that the call had come just as he was investigating the possibility of Mr. Stern having an affair. It was as if the woman knew that this notion had just become part of the investigation—as if she had some inside knowledge. Second, the caller claimed that the person who had the affair was not actually herself but rather someone else she knew, and de Ville found that to be strange as well. Third, of course, was the use of a device to disguise her voice. If she really was just an anonymous informant, why would she go to such lengths to protect her identity? He came to the conclusion that perhaps the informant knew more than she let on, but alas, he had no way to communicate with her, as she left no contact information. Just then, he had an idea. He contacted his communications officer and asked him to see if the telephone company could provide any more information besides that the call had been placed from the Basel airport. Through their investigation, they were able to pinpoint which pay phone the call had been placed from. De Ville dispatched his crime-scene technician to retrieve fingerprints from the phone, only to find out that the phone was wiped with a disinfectant every twelve hours, which would remove any traces of fingerprints. Unfortunately, without additional information, it seemed impossible to find out who had placed the call. *Another dead end*, de Ville thought to himself. He wasn't sure where to even resume the investigation.

Leila arrived in the lobby before Andy and decided to take a quick walk outside to gauge whether or not the four layers of clothes she had donned would keep her from being cold. As she stepped through the revolving door, her face, the only part of her skin that was left exposed, was met by cold, yet not frigid, air such as she might feel upon opening her freezer at home. Her only recollection of such cold air was winter mornings in the suburbs of Detroit when she'd first moved to the United States; she had no idea how she might react to being in cold weather for the first time in many years. As she stood outside the hotel's revolving door, she was satisfied that she felt warm enough in her new winter clothes. Leila had taken some advice to dress in several layers, and had on a long-sleeved T-shirt covered by a turtleneck shirt, a wool sweater, and a wool overcoat. She had leather gloves and a wool hat, and as she stood outside, she oddly felt almost too warm. She returned to her room to peel off the sweater. Upon returning, she saw someone she thought might be Andy, but she couldn't be fully sure.

"Hello, Andy. Is that you?" she asked inquisitively.

"Oh, hey there. How was your nap?" Andy asked, oblivious to the fact that he was barely recognizable.

"You look ridiculous," Leila told him and she laughed out loud. "It's not even that cold outside. Seriously, I've been outside."

Andy had on a huge nylon parka with a fringe of fake fur on the brim of the hood, which hung over his face several inches in front of his forehead. The parka flowed down below his knees like a closed cape, revealing just the bottom of a pair of jeans. As if the hood of the parka, which was covering the top of his head, weren't enough, he was also wearing a balaclava covering his face to the extent that Leila could only make out his eyes.

"It was seven degrees in Oslo, and that was with some sunshine. You're going to freeze out there," Andy said confidently.

"I was outside already, I told you—and seriously, it's not that cold," she added. "You look like you are going to rob a bank, or climb Mount Everest—or rob a bank on Mount Everest. Take that stupid thing off your face, will you?"

"What, the balaclava?"

"Is that what it's called? Funny, sounds like *baklava*, but you couldn't even eat baklava, let alone anything else, with that thing on."

Leila went over to the lobby reception desk to inquire about the temperature and was told it was minus one degree Celsius.

"Hey, Sherpa Friedman," Leila teased, "it's minus one Celsius, which my math tells me is thirty degrees Fahrenheit. That's warmer than it was in New York."

The lobby receptionist, overhearing their conversation, explained to the American tourists that since it was not yet the middle of winter, and the Gulf Stream waters were still relatively mild, that Tromsø could be warmer than Oslo this time of year. Andy, feeling quite embarrassed, went back to his room, removed a few of the layers that Leila thankfully hadn't seen, and returned without the balaclava and with the hood of the parka draped on his back rather than over his head.

"That's much better. I can see your cute face now," Leila said.

Cute face? Why is she teasing me like that, just a few days after making feel like an idiot for telling her I like her? he thought. He decided he was not going to take the bait and respond to her compliment in any way.

They headed over to the Arctandria Restaurant, which had been recommended to them by the hotel staff. It was a short walk from the hotel and turned out to be a far more pleasant stroll than either one of them expected. Although the twilight that had greeted them upon landing had given way to a completely dark sky, the lights of the town, the relatively mild temperature, and the many people walking on the streets lent a sense of warmth to the town that belied the bleak darkness they'd expected. After being seated at their table, they were immediately spotted as foreigners by the couple sitting at the next table over.

"Where are you from?" the woman asked in perfect and virtually unaccented English.

"America. Los Angeles," Andy answered.

"Well, you've picked an odd time to come to Tromsø, unless you are here for our Christmas festival. I'd recommend coming in February to see the Northern Lights," she added.

"Oh. Well, believe it or not, we are here for work, actually," Leila answered which resulted in a stern and almost scolding glance from Andy.

"What kind of work?" the woman asked. Andy glanced at Leila with raised eyebrows as if to say, *How are you going to answer that one? We are investigating a crime.*

"We're here to do some research on the thriving technology industry in Norway. We are doctors and are interested to learn how Norwegians are so good at applying scientific advances to business," responded Leila, glancing back at Andy with a smile as if to answer his prior thought.

"Interesting," the woman answered.

"So, what should we order?" Leila asked, changing the subject.

"It depends on how adventurous you are. You can have beef or chicken, if that is what you are comfortable with, but I suggest either some of our local fish or the reindeer. You can even eat seal or whale, if you like."

"Seal and whale—isn't that against international law?" Andy asked.

"Norway is allowed to hunt a small number of whale and seal, as it is part of our native diet, especially up here in the northern areas," the woman answered.

"What about the reindeer?" Leila asked. "In terms of taste or legality?"

"Both," Leila answered.

"Reindeer are a staple of the Sami diet—the Sami being our native people. Besides, it's too cold for cows up here. So it is perfectly legal and quite delicious, I would say. I've been told it tastes like venison, which I imagine living in America you must have had before."

"Thanks for the suggestions," Andy answered. "Sure, let me know if you have any questions."

The waitress came and both Andy and Leila decided they were in the mood for a beer and chose the local brew called Mack. Andy decided to play it safe with his food order and chose the salmon, while a more-adventurous Leila decided to try the reindeer. Their dinner conversation revolved around the weather and the darkness. They wisely chose not to discuss the case in this public place, and for the first part of the meal they avoided resuming the discussion that had been initiated at the Olive Tree Café. However, aided by the disinhibiting effect of alcohol in the several beers they drank as well as by fatigue, Leila could not muster the mental fortitude to repress her thoughts any longer, so she reopened the discussion begun several evening ago by Andy.

"So, you like me, is that right?" Leila stated matter-of-factly, which resulted in a deer-in-the-headlights look from Andy.

Dammit, why does she always catch me by surprise? he thought. He took a mental deep breath and then replied. "Ah, yes, it is true that I said that, but it was out of line, and I already apologized, and you already made me feel like shit once, so can we let it go, please?"

"I don't want to let it go," replied Leila defiantly.

"I don't get it."

"What don't you get? I asked you a simple question, and I am only looking for a simple answer."

Silence. It was like the silence Andy had expected from this dark and faraway town, but just as this town had already surprised him with its relatively mild weather, so Leila continued to surprise him with her bluntness.

"Well?" Leila demanded.

"Well, what?"

"What are you doing? Are you playing dumb, or are the beers making you stupid. Seriously!"

Silence. Andy got up and walked away, telling Leila that the beers had caught up with his bladder capacity. He went to the bathroom to regroup, as he had the other night. *Did she just call me stupid?* He washed his face and decided he would respond in the most simple and matter-of-fact way to any questions Leila asked—the least likely way to get into further trouble.

When he returned, "Did you just call me stupid before?" Andy asked in a commanding tone.

"Yes, and I'm sorry. That was totally uncalled for. I'm tired and probably a bit drunk—how much alcohol does this beer have in it, anyway?" Leila wondered, purposely changing the subject.

"*Yes*, by the way," Andy said.

"What do you mean, 'yes'? I asked about the alcohol content of the beer—it's not a yes-or-no question."

"That's the answer to your first question," Andy retorted.

"Oh, I'm sorry. I think I am really drunk."

"Then we should end this conversation, pay the check, and go back to the hotel to sleep. We are meeting with Bergeland tomorrow," Andy suggested.

"Good idea."

They were both beyond tired and had been in the darkness for over eight hours at this point, which only served to enhance their fatigue. Humans are evolutionarily trained to sleep at night. A combination of the blackness and the alcohol, along with the fact that they had not slept in beds in over twenty-four hours, brought on a feeling of exhaustion that neither doctor had felt since their residency, when working thirty-six hour shifts had been part of the routine. Upon reaching the hotel, Andy and Leila parted company in the elevator with scarcely another word. Andy reached his room, undressed, and collapsed on the bed. With the last bit of energy left in his being, he rolled over to the nightstand and turned the music of his Sigur Ros "sleep time" playlist on his iPhone. He fell asleep to the haunting piano intro of "Saeglopur" before the vocal part had even begun at the nineteen-second mark of the song.

CHAPTER 14

F elix de Ville awoke to an unusually warm and sunny December day in Basel. He hoped this might be some mystical sign that today some light would be shed on the mysterious death of Mr. Stern. When he reached his drab office at the police station, hoping for some good news, he was encouraged to see a message on his desk requesting that he return a call to Simon Kupfer. However, the only news Kupfer had for his friend was that he would be on his own for at least a few more days due to a demanding Interpol case. He encouraged his now-disconsolate friend to simply wait until the anonymous woman contacted him again. Kupfer felt quite confident this would occur, since the woman seemed to have some valuable information she wanted to impart to him and the investigation and was probably trying to figure out the best way to provide this information while maintaining her privacy. Presciently, he told Felix to be on the lookout for an e-mail, as the woman might choose this less-personal way to make the next contact.

De Ville was at the same time pleased and annoyed that his boyhood friend was once again correct. As he opened his e-mail program and began perusing the thirty-eight e-mails that had made their way silently and unobtrusively to his inbox overnight the way a fresh nighttime snow might stealthily blanket the ground, he found one from double_drapes@gmail.com. He was about to delete it, suspecting it to be spam, but then he decided to open it so as not to chance missing anything. It read:

> *June 27, 1999, Lugano*
> *March 22, 2011, Gstaad*

Felix stared at the screen for several minutes, unsure what to make of the e-mail. Just two dates and two places, apparently associated with each other:

Lugano, the main city of the Italian-speaking section of Switzerland, and Gstaad, the luxurious alpine town where the rich and famous went to ski, shop, and be seen. He wasn't sure where to start, but in 2012, most searches for information began in the same place—Google. He typed the first line of the e-mail, and the first four results were advertisements for touring companies, followed by a mixture of additional touristy-sounding websites and then a list of restaurants and other seemingly useless, yet endless, information. He did the same for Gstaad, only this time he had a bit more luck. On the second page of search results there was a link to something entitled Pharmacology and Pharmacoeconomics 2011. It turned out there had been a conference in Gstaad between March 18 and 23, 2011. *Interesting*, de Ville thought as he pondered his next move. He grabbed his car keys and headed out the door with a new sense of determination.

A loud knock on the door startled Andy, and he leapt out of bed. He looked out the window and gazing southward, noticed the twilight of the sky hovering over the mountains beyond the edge of Tromsø.

"Who is it?" he asked.

"It's Leila. Time to wake up, sleeping beauty. It's almost one o'clock."

"In the *afternoon*?" Andy asked incredulously.

"Yes. I'll meet you in the lobby in thirty minutes."

"Okay."

Andy had slept fourteen hours straight. He felt rested, and while he normally hated waking up in the dark, he couldn't possibly sleep any longer. Besides, it wouldn't get any lighter than the fleeting twilight of this early winter afternoon north of the Arctic Circle. After his shower, he went online to check the weather so he could dress in appropriately warm clothes, but without overdoing it, as he clearly had done the previous night. The screen read, "Periods of light rain and snow. High temperature 1°C and low -2°C." *That would be thirty-four degrees Fahrenheit for the high and twenty-eight for the low*, he thought to himself. *Not too bad. No balaclava.* He headed down to the lobby to meet Leila.

"I'm starving," Andy said.

"Well, the breakfast buffet is long since over. We can have some lunch at the hotel restaurant, if you like."

"Sure, that would be fine. When did you wake up?"

"Ten thirty. I can't sleep more than twelve hours."

"About last night—" Andy began, but he was interrupted.

"Not now. I'm sorry I brought it up. I was way too tired to carry on any reasonable conversation. I don't know what I was thinking," Leila said, putting the notion of any further discussion about their feelings to rest.

"You're right; we have important work to do. Let's review what we know about Bergeland and what we will discuss with him," Andy suggested.

They reviewed the file Alvarez had provided for them on Jan Erik Bergeland. He was forty-two years old and held a PhD. from University of Tromsø, which he'd received at the young age of twenty-three. He'd studied chemical engineering and had worked for Astra Zeneca pharmaceuticals, a Swedish company, in Stockholm, before returning to Tromsø ten years ago to start his own company. He'd received a grant from Statoil, the giant Norwegian oil company, to study an idea that had come to him while watching the news of a major storm that had stranded oil-rig workers on their platform in the North Sea for more than a week. In essence, the idea was to modify existing medications with novel chemical compounds in order to increase the duration of their effect. The oil company was interested in having a wide variety of commonly used medications that would remain in the body for a prolonged period of time, so that a single dose of, for example, an antibiotic would be enough to cure an infection. This would not only save a lot of space in the medical unit of the oil rig, something that was always at a premium on what amounted to an artificial island far from the comforts of a town or city, but would also keep the workers more healthy, as they were notoriously poor at taking prescribed medicines consistently. Using this grant money, Bergeland had devised several compounds, including antibiotics and motion-sickness medications, which Statoil paid his new company handsomely for. Following this early success for products specifically requested by Statoil, he received grants from other pharmaceutical companies and eventually sold his first patent for the formulation that prolonged the duration of action of ciprofloxacin, a commonly used antibiotic, to Astra Zeneca. With this additional money he had been able to start his own company in Tromsø. He called it Sami Innovations in honor of the indigenous people of the Arctic portion of Norway, Sweden, and Finland.

Over the past ten years, his company had developed several novel chemical compounds that could be linked with currently available medications to prolong their effect. His *modus operandi* was to study the structure of the medication, using sophisticated chemical-engineering techniques, and figure out how to best add another compound to the drug to delay its clearance from the circulation, thus providing a longer-lasting effect. His successes had led to the ability to treat pneumonia, for example, with one dose of ciprofloxacin, when normally it would require two pills a day for two weeks to successfully treat most varieties of pneumonia. As a result of these successful innovations, Bergeland had become a very wealthy man, though he lived a modest lifestyle, still maintaining his primary residence in Tromsø. His only indulgence was expensive vacations to the far reaches of the planet in search of adventure, fun, and sun, particularly during the long and dark Norwegian winters.

"So, how do we approach our discussion with Bergeland?" Leila asked. "Remember, he agreed to speak to us because we are doctors. He didn't want to speak to any detectives. The Swiss were planning on coming here to interrogate him, but he refused to speak to them."

"Well then, we should speak to him in his language, pharmaceuticals, and see where that takes us. We can just ask him about how he started his business. Entrepreneurs like talking about themselves and their successes," Leila added. "In fact, I have a good idea. Let's interview him as if we are interviewing a new patient; you know, start with the chief complaint, the reason we are talking to him, like reason for the consult when we do a consultation. We can follow that with the present history, what's happening now, followed by the past, etc. What do you think?"

"Yeah, I like it. We need to be sure to ask open-ended questions and just let him talk—same method as asking patients questions."

"Good, we have a strategy," Leila said.

They went to the lobby, asked the concierge to call for a taxi, and were soon under way to the headquarter offices of Sami Innovations. Their preparation imbued them with a sense of confidence. Bergeland's headquarters consisted of a modest two-story building constructed from giant logs polished to a high gloss and large, square windows; it sat at the top of a small hill in the northern section of Tromsø. It reminded Andy of a high-end ski lodge, complete with a steeply sloped roof. The building was backed by a wooded forest of pine trees, like neat rows of soldiers standing upright at attention with lances by their sides, silhouetted against a dusky sky. It was at once both beautiful and intimidating. Upon arrival, they walked into the lobby, where a security guard greeted them.

"We are here to see Dr. Bergeland," Leila stated. She used the title "Doctor," as they had agreed, even though in Europe PhD holders were more often called "Professor" as a title. They had thought it might demonstrate a higher modicum of respect and equality, which could serve them well in their discussions.

"I'll let him know you are here," the security guard said as he pointed to the chairs in the otherwise empty lobby.

Being asked to sit down surely meant it would be a few minutes, at least. This delay tactic was often used by detectives when interrogating suspects, in the belief that such waits increased the stress of the one being interrogated and led to more mistakes when they are trying to concoct a story, so ultimately lead to more truthful answers. But this time it was Bergeland using it against them, or so it seemed.

Minutes passed, and with the guard watching them, they elected not to speak. Leila notice the automatic pistol holstered at the guard's side, which she found odd in what seemed like a very peaceful place. Leila hated guns—they reminded her of the violence in Iraq during her youth. In fact, her hatred of guns was so profound that she actually felt guilty that she could feel such a strong negative emotion. The gun, the darkness, the pine trees, the waiting—it all felt very intimidating. After they'd waited for thirty minutes, the guard approached them.

"Professor Bergeland will see you now," the guard stated, escorting them to the elevator.

He led them to the corner office on the second floor, where they were greeted by Bergeland. He was five foot ten inches tall, thin, and had a chiseled face with high, protruding cheekbones. His straight blond hair was combed forward with a slight angle toward the right, with a small shelf of hair sticking out over his forehead. He was wearing snug black slacks that tapered narrowly around his lower legs and a black button-down shirt with the top button open. A shiny gray sport coat completed the outfit, and with what appeared to be a very expensive watch, Bergeland's image could have been torn from the cover of GQ magazine. He looked very fit and very European.

The large corner office was tastefully adorned with large floor-to-ceiling windows on two sides and light and well-lacquered wood panels on the other two walls. One of the walls had a large Norwegian flag proudly stretched out from side to side. The room was sparsely furnished, with a large desk and chair facing the window affording a view of the downtown area, the fjord, and the large hill called Storsteinen, just to the east across the fjord, barely visible in the twilight. On the other side of the office there was a setup one might find in a living room, with a sofa, coffee table, and two chairs across the table from the sofa. The sofa and chairs looked expensive and Scandinavian, with lots of tan suede upholstery on top of dark wood, and the coffee table was composed of thick glass squares with beveled edges placed between thin planks of dark wood that matched the base of the sofa. Bergeland motioned to Andy and Leila to sit on the sofa, and he sat opposite them on one of the chairs. The height of the seats on the sofa was substantially lower than that of the chair, offering Bergeland a commanding position. Leila suspected that Bergeland had all of this planned—his office, the wait, and their relative positions in the "living room" area of his office. He wanted—perhaps needed—to feel that he was in charge of the discussion, and not Andy and Leila, though clearly they were here to question him with respect to the two bleeders.

"So, what shall we talk about?" he asked with seemingly sarcastic smile.

"Dr. Bergeland, you know very well why we are here. I believe Detective O'Reilly spoke with you while we were on our way to Norway," Andy began.

"Yes, of course, and please call me Professor Bergeland. I am not a doctor like you."

"Certainly. I am sorry, Professor," Andy replied.

"Not to worry," he answered in impeccable, softly-accented English. "In Europe, we are professors and not considered doctors, though I know in the USA, PhDs often carry the title 'doctor.'"

"Understood." Leila proceeded, "Professor Bergeland, I know that you were made aware that Andreas Stern, the CEO of Terrapharma, was found dead a few weeks ago in his office, having bled to death. We know that you helped Terrapharma develop Provitax and that you felt insulted or slighted by the deal your company made."

"For starters, I don't work directly with the pharmaceutical companies. They come to me with their medication and ask me to find a way to prolong the duration of action. I then work with my team to find a suitable compound that I can link to their medication which, while prolonging the action of the medicine, doesn't interfere with what the drug is supposed to do and does not have any negative effects. It simply makes their medicine last longer. That's it."

"You did work with Terrapharma, correct?" Andy asked.

"Of course, and you know that. Let's cut to the chase, shall we? My company has hired brilliant scientists and less-than-brilliant businesspeople. I made the mistake of underestimating what a conniving thief Andreas Stern is and what idiots I hired to make deals for my company. While I shoulder the blame for hiring imbeciles, it is clear that Mr. Stern's team took advantage of them."

"But isn't a deal a deal, Professor?" Andy replied.

"Yes—if it's fair to both parties. I am telling you that Mr. Stern took advantage of the situation and did not deal fairly. What you probably have seen or heard about are these supposedly threatening e-mails I sent to him in an effort to get him to renegotiate our terms; however those were only sent after I exhausted all other efforts. Finally, the e-mails merely threatened legal action. I never threatened to kill him, and I didn't kill him," Bergeland concluded firmly.

"That's it," Leila said.

"Yes, that's it."

"What if we don't believe you?" Andy asked.

"You can believe what you want, but I am telling you that I didn't kill him, and unless you are going to send the police here to arrest me—and that would need to be the Tromsø police—our meeting is over."

"What are you going to do now with Terrapharma now that Stern is dead?" asked Leila.

"I will wait for a new CEO to be appointed and start over. I will not give up until I have a fair deal with them. That I can assure you."

"Don't you have enough money to last you a lifetime—or several lifetimes already?" Andy followed.

"You don't get it, do you? This is not about money. This is about intellectual property, it's about pride, it's about fairness. You are not business people, are you? Doctors, yes. Scientists, perhaps. Entrepreneurs you are not. By the way, you should come back to Tromsø in the summer—it's quite lovely here then. It never gets dark."

And with that, the security guard was already in the office and ready to escort Leila and Andy back to the entrance, where a taxi he had called was waiting for them.

Back at the hotel lobby, they pondered their next move. They decided to go for a walk and chose to cross the Tromsø bridge to the suburb of Tromsdalen, in order to take the cable car up to summit of Storsteinen. After crossing the bridge, they were met by the beautiful Arctic Cathedral, a white-as-snow triangular structure perfectly lit to stand out in sharp contrast to the dark sky. They walked further to the cable car that would whisk them to the top of the hill for dramatic views of the city, the fjord, and the surrounding mountains. It put into clear perspective how this city was indeed set on an island fully surrounded by water and connected only by two bridges, one from the eastern shore and one from the western shore. As they sat in the cold air, looking southward, the twilight was brighter and they could even see a hint of a sky blue line on the lowest part of the horizon—the nearest sunlight near the latitude marked by the Arctic Circle. They searched their minds for such clarity and light on what they should do next.

"Bergeland is involved, I tell you," Leila stated confidently. "I agree," replied Andy.

"The man played us, intimidated us. I'd like to question him in a more friendly—or shall I say *neutral*—environment. I'm sure he's hiding something," Leila went on.

After he'd received the curious e-mail and learned about the Pharmacology and Pharmacoeconomics conference that had been held in Gstaad in 2011, de Ville left his office. He headed straight for the offices of Terrapharma, walking with a sense of purpose, a sense that perhaps, just perhaps, he would make some headway in this bizarre and puzzling case. He remembered his way around and, after signing in with security at the front desk, went directly to Mr. Stern's office. He found Stern's executive assistant at her desk and asked her where Mr. Stern had been on March 22, 2011.

"Just a moment; let me look back on his calendar. May I ask what this is about?"

"No. I just need to know where he was that day. That's all."

She veered her eyes from de Ville's purposeful eyes and searched through her computer, pressing keys and clicking her mouse. For a moment de Ville wondered if she might be hiding something, but then he realized that it was likely his newly acquired air of confidence that had led her to not reply to his firmly stated no.

"He was at a conference in Gstaad. Why do you ask?"

Before she could even complete her question, de Ville was out the door and heading back to his office. *Interesting indeed*, he said to himself. It was exactly what he'd expected after searching the date and Gstaad. His confidence grew further, and he finally felt he had a lead in the case.

CHAPTER 15

DECEMBER 10–11
TROMSØ,
BASEL

F ollowing the revelation that Mr. Stern had been in Gstaad on March 22 at the Pharmacology and Pharmacoeconomics conference, de Ville wondered whether Mr. Stern might also have been in Lugano on the date in question twelve years earlier. Unfortunately, Mr. Stern's assistant could be of no further help, both because she had not been working for Terrapharma then and because accurate records of Mr. Stern's travels had not been not archived electronically during that time. After exhaustively searching the Internet for other pharmacology and pharmacoeconomic conferences, and even after broadening the search to any conference in Lugano on the date in question, de Ville hit a dead end. Yet, deep down, he felt that Mr. Stern must have been there and that somehow events that had taken place in Gstaad and Lugano were connected to his death. Feeling desperate, he elected to send an e-mail to <u>double_drapes@gmail.com</u>, and to his surprise, he received a response within a minute. His initial excitement at the prompt response was quickly tempered as he read the e-mail.

> *The e-mail account double_drapes@gmail.com does not exist. Please check the e-mail address and try again.*

Despite the fact that he'd replied to the original e-mail, de Ville checked and checked again that the e-mail address was entered correctly, eventually coming to the conclusion that indeed he had typed it accurately. He surmised that whoever was sending these e-mails has gone to great lengths to avoid being identified. It was yet another dead end. He waited until it was morning in New York and made a phone call.

Morning had arrived in Tromsø, though it was quite impossible to tell without glancing at the clock. Andy rolled over in bed, reached for his iPhone, and found that it was already 10:00 a.m. Convinced that sleeping any longer would only make him feel worse, he woke up, peered into the darkness outside, and felt a longing for the warmth and sunshine of Los Angeles. In fact, he'd have been more than happy even for a cloudy, dreary drizzly day, so long as there was some daylight. He thought about calling Leila's room but decided against it for fear of waking her up. He began thinking about how awkward their relationship had become since his confession to Leila in New York, now more than five days ago. He was thoroughly confused. At first, she'd seemed upset that he'd said he liked her. Then she'd asked him to clarify what he'd said, and when he made the effort to do so, she'd suddenly reversed course and decided she would rather not discuss it. On the one hand, his heart was pushing him to engage in this dialog with her, but on the other hand, his mind thought that ignoring the whole discussion would make it go away. Then he could forget about it and begin the process of forgetting about any relationship with her. Andy knew himself well enough to realize that the second option was really not an option—he was never able to suppress his feelings for women—but he also did not how to proceed with the first option. He chose to be patient and let Leila be the one to raise any discussion regarding their relationship. He sensed that at some point she would; perhaps ignoring the subject would, paradoxically, increase the likelihood of it being brought up. He showered and went down to breakfast, which he would just barely be able to make if he was quick.

Upon his arrival at the hotel restaurant, Andy found Leila sitting at a table, sipping coffee and eating a pastry and some fruit.

"Good morning, sunshine," she said, greeting Andy.

"What sunshine? I would love to see some gray skies and drizzle at this point, so long as there was daylight."

"Hey, let's not start the day on such a downer. Besides, we've been here barely two days. I'll agree with one thing Bergeland said. We should come back here in the summer. I bet it's beautiful," Leila said.

"I, for one, hope we are done with this case way before summer rolls around," Andy replied.

"I hope so too. Then we can come back just for the fun of it."

Andy didn't say what he wanted to say, since he had just made a pact with himself not to bring up anything related to his feelings for Leila.

"We'll see," he said. *That was good*, he thought to himself, *'We'll see' is the perfect non-answer answer.*

"What's next?" Leila asked.

Andy couldn't tell whether this was a loaded question or Leila was genuinely wondering what they would do next.

"I don't know. Let's see if I have any e-mails, and if not, we'll call New York."

Andy opened his computer, connected to the Wi-Fi, and began scrolling. "Alvarez sent one saying to call him as soon as we can, no matter the time," Andy said.

"Wow, maybe they've got something," Leila responded. "What time is it in New York, by the way?"

"Almost 5:00 a.m."

"Call him then—he's going to wake up soon anyway," Leila said.

"Uh, maybe that means we should just wait an hour or two, since he'll be awake then?"

"No, he said no matter what time—you said so yourself."

"Okay."

Andy called Detective Alvarez, set the phone to speaker mode, and placed it on the table so they could both hear.

"Yeah," came the scratchy, quiet voice of someone who had clearly been awakened from sleep. "Alvarez here."

"Sorry to wake you, Detective, but you did say to call anytime."

"Who is this?"

Only with that response did Andy realize that, as a detective, Alvarez probably received numerous middle-of-the-night calls throughout the year. "Oh, sorry!" he said. "It's Andy Friedman and Leila Baker, regarding the case of the bleeders."

"Yeah, okay. Give me a minute," he replied. Some twenty seconds passed before he continued. "We have a new lead, and we need you to go to Switzerland to follow up."

"Switzerland," Andy responded, with a note of surprise, frustration, and resignation.

"Yes, I take it you've heard of it," came the sarcastic reply from a now-more-awake Alvarez.

"Detective, we can't. I mean, we really need to get back to LA. Remember, a few days ago in New York I said we'd interview Bergeland and that's it," Andy replied. "And our boss—"

"Do you want to help us solve this thing, or what?"

"I—I do, yes." Andy hesitated, and Leila nudged him. "I mean, *we* do, but our boss is not going to let us. He's already—"

"I'll call your boss," Alvarez interrupted.

"Can't you work with the local police in Switzerland?" Andy kept at it.

"We still need your expertise. The detective in Switzerland doesn't know any hematologists, and he suspects that he'll need that expertise to sort out what happened with the bleeder over there," Alvarez continued.

Andy looked over at Leila. Her big brown eyes grew large, and the Julia Roberts smile decorated her face—the same face he'd seen when the trip to New York had first been mentioned. She stood up and silently made fists of both hands, placing them in front of her hips and symmetrically moving them in a backward motion as if she were skiing.

Andy shook his head and smiled. Her mischievous streak made her only more endearing. Andy relented.

"Okay. Where in Switzerland?"

"Get yourselves to Basel today, and call me when you get there for further instructions."

"I take it we are our own travel agents again?" Andy asked.

"Aren't you both doctors? Figure it out," came the blunt response from Alvarez. "Call me when you get there." And with that came a dial tone. Alvarez had hung up and, no doubt, gone back to sleep.

"Switzerland, yay!" Leila said. "We can't go and not ski—at least one day. Promise me." Leila sounded like a giddy schoolgirl again—just as she had prior to the trip to New York.

"I don't know if we'll have time. Besides, I don't know how far it is from Basel to the nearest ski resort."

"It's Switzerland, Andy. The Alps. And it's not a big country, so it can't be that far. We're going. Trust me, we're going. At least, *I'm* going."

"We'll see." And with that, the conversation about skiing ended. Andy had begun to really like using the 'we'll see' phrase to change the subject.

That same day, de Ville received an e-mail from Alvarez confirming that the doctor detectives would meet him later in the day. Alvarez asked de Ville to prepare a file for them containing all of the detailed evidence that he and Kupfer had collected, as well as the interesting new lead he had uncovered. De Ville then emailed Kupfer with the latest information, though he knew that he was very busy with Interpol-related business. He sent it more for himself than for Kupfer to actually read. He felt proud that he had uncovered what he sensed was an important new lead, and he had to share it with someone.

Andy and Leila booked the tickets for the next leg of their continuing adventure. They boarded the SAS flight from Tromsø back to Oslo, with a second flight to follow to London on British Airways, and from there to Basel. During the flight to Oslo, the sun greeted them for the first time in three days, though it had seemed much longer. Andy had the feeling of reconnecting with a long-lost friend. The blinding rays of the bright sun sitting just above the horizon pierced through the airplanes windows like a laser beam, invigorating both Andy and Leila. Andy, glancing at his watch and noting that it was one o'clock in the afternoon, found the midday sunrise as odd as the midday sunset he had experienced just a few days earlier, but it was much more welcome. After nearly dozing off shortly after takeoff, they were now wide awake and looking forward to the next assignment—and, just maybe, a bit of skiing. There was no further discussion about their relationship, although at one point their eyes had met and locked in on each other's. They were each left to wonder what that might have meant and what the other was thinking, since neither one uttered a word—though neither one seemed intent on breaking the intense eye contact.

After eating lunch at Gardermoen Airport in Oslo, they were off to London. The flight was pleasant and quiet. The sun shone brightly above a blanket of clouds, and each of them sat backed and listened to music. Andy listened to Tears for Fears, though not the morose sounds of the early 1980s but the rather more-uplifting *Everybody Loves a Happy Ending* album from the 1990s. He was not quite sure what had possessed him to make that specific selection at this particular moment. Leila put on Maroon 5's debut album, *Songs about Jane.* While she was enjoying this decidedly different adventure, she missed Los Angeles, and thus she decided to listen to her favorite Los Angeles band to combat her homesickness. Their headphones remained on until the flight attendants motioned to them that they were soon to land and that the headphones had to be removed.

During their short layover at London Heathrow, they wandered the numerous shops in the massive structure known as Terminal 5, bought some Cadbury chocolates—a bit ironic, considering they were on their way to a prolific chocolate-producing nation—booked hotel rooms in Basel, and watched the planes take off. Before long, they were on their third and final leg of the trip to Switzerland. Sitting on the right side of the plane and looking west, they were treated to a beautiful sunset—their first in four days. The rest of the flight was uneventful— no discussion and no eye-locking stares. Andy watched two episodes of his favorite show, the thrilling *24*, with Kiefer Sutherland, while Leila took a nap. By the time they landed, cleared immigration, and reached their hotel, it was past eight o'clock. Andy called Alvarez, as instructed, from the lobby of the Radisson Blu Hotel, and he instructed them to meet Detective de Ville at the Basel Police Station in the morning. Andy and Leila retired to their own rooms and to their own thoughts.

The next morning, de Ville arrived early to the police station. He wanted to be as prepared as he could be for the meeting with the two doctors who had unexpectedly become the key investigators in the case. He reviewed the autopsy report provided by Dr. Costa, the reports from their interviews with the employees of Terrapharma, and—the most recent and mysterious aspect—the anonymous phone call and the e-mail providing just two dates and two cities. After an hour, his desk phone rang.

"Yes, I'm expecting them. Please send them up."

He got up to open his door and waited for a moment as his guests climbed the stairs to his office.

"Good morning. I am Detective Felix de Ville, and you must be Drs. Friedman and Baker."

"Please call me Andy."

"And me Leila."

"Very well, I also prefer to keep things informal, so please call me Felix. I must say you are younger than I expected."

"We'll take that as a compliment, Felix," Leila answered, smiling.

"Well then, shall we discuss the case? Can I get you anything to drink?"

Andy and Leila requested some water, and after a few minutes a cart was rolled into the room with water, coffee, tea, juices, and a variety of freshly baked pastries, which both Andy and Leila eagerly accepted.

De Ville began. "As you of course know, we have two dead men, one in New York and one in Basel, who died the same way on the same day. And I think we all agree that this is far too coincidental to have occurred by chance. I understand that the leads in New York have dried up and that unless this Alexa woman turns up, there may be no new leads there. I also know you have been to Tromsø, and I am curious to hear your thoughts on Mr. Bergeland, especially considering the threatening e-mails he sent and the fact that he has been to Switzerland a number of times in the past year. Finally, we have recently received two anonymous tips that I will discuss with you shortly, as this is where we need your assistance."

"Sounds fine," answered Andy.

"Tell me about your interview with Jan Erik Bergeland, please."

At that, Leila laughed.

"What's funny? It was a straightforward question, or so I thought," de Ville followed.

"I am sorry," Leila said, "but to be honest, it was more like Bergeland was interviewing us—to see what we know," Leila responded.

"How do you mean?"

"Well, first of all, we had to go to Tromsø to meet him; second, we had to go to his office; third, his guard stood by with a pistol on his hip; and well, the whole thing seemed like a setup to intimidate us, to be honest with you. I think Bergeland made us schlep to Tromsø not only for his convenience but also for home-field advantage. I think he even thought that the perpetual darkness would add to the intimidating atmosphere he so well orchestrated, since we're not used to it," Leila stated.

"Go on," de Ville requested.

"He sat us on a sofa that was lower than his chair and spoke to us in a condescending manner. I'm telling you, the only reason he agreed to see us was to find out what we knew—not to help with the investigation."

"That's interesting. Did you find out anything that might help?"

"Frankly, the only thing I took away from it is that Bergeland is involved somehow, some way, though I can't tell you how," Leila answered.

"I agree," continued Andy. "He stated that he did not kill Mr. Stern, but the entire interview left me with the sense that he is either involved or he knows something that he is not telling us."

"Very well then. It seems as if we will need to question Mr. Bergeland again."

"Yes, but not in his office in Tromsø—in fact, not in Tromsø at all. I am sure he owns the police there," Leila added.

"I am sure we can arrange for an interview in a police station—hopefully this one," de Ville said, pointing to the floor. "Let me tell you what I have found out and where we would like you to help us next."

He went on to tell them about the anonymous phone call, and the mysterious e-mail and what he had been able to deduce from it so far.

"Where are Gstaad and Lugano, and can you tell us about each city?" Andy asked.

"Gstaad is a world-famous ski resort city, with very wealthy clientele, high-end hotels, and expensive stores. It hosts conferences, including everything from high-profile political congresses to medical conferences to trade shows."

Leila was smiling from ear to ear. "Is everything okay?" de Ville asked.

"Leila has dreamed of skiing in the Alps."

"Well, you should take advantage while you are here. Ski season is off to a good start as well, but ... you have work to do as well. Shall we focus on that first? Then I can give you some tips on skiing in Switzerland in general."

"Yes, I promise the investigation comes first," Leila replied.

"What about Lugano?" asked Andy.

"Lugano is a lovely city situated in the very south, in the Italian section of Switzerland. It sits in the Southern Alps, just across the border from Italy, and is known for relatively mild winters despite its location. It is rather isolated from the rest of Switzerland, but the people there consider themselves staunchly Swiss and not Italian."

"Does it also host conferences—could Mr. Stern have attended one there in 1999?" Andy asked.

"Good thinking. I looked into that precisely but found none, so I am not sure what the two cities may have in common with respect to this case, I'm afraid," de Ville responded.

"So, I'm a little unclear. What exactly do you want us to do?" Leila asked. "Please understand that for the time being I can't leave Basel, due to other police matters. So, here is what I suggest. The two of you go to Gstaad and Lugano over the next week and investigate events that occurred on or about the dates we were provided by the anonymous e-mail. Hopefully, you will find some connection with Mr. Stern or any other aspect of the case. I, honestly, am not sure it will be fruitful, but this is all we have right now. Does that sound reasonable?"

"Yes, as long as we get some skiing in as well," Leila added with a nod and a smile.

"I can't see why you don't deserve a day off to ski—use your judgment. I will call the police chief in Gstaad to let him know who you are and what you'll be doing there. Please contact him upon your arrival, and he will make sure you get treated well and offer any assistance you might need."

"How do we get there?" Andy asked.

Felix explained that the best way to get around Switzerland was by car and suggested they rent one. Andy and Leila agreed. Felix opened a large map of Switzerland and traced the way to Gstaad and, from there, the way to Lugano. He asked his assistant to find a hotel for them in the two cities.

"Do you need one room or two?" de Ville asked.

Leila laughed, while Andy blushed as they told de Ville they merely worked together.

"Well, you would make a nice couple, I have to say," he added.

This only made Andy blush more, what with all the awkward discussions that de Ville was not privy to. Even Leila couldn't fully hide her embarrassment, though she giggled more rather than blushing.

"Detective, before we head to Gstaad, I have one other thought. Have you tried tracing the e-mail address from where the tip came from?" Andy asked.

"Yes. I asked Detective Kupfer, who's been helping me in the case, to have his IT staff at Interpol attempt to trace the e-mail, but it was not possible, unfortunately."

"So, you don't even know whether this e-mail originated in Switzerland, is that right?" Leila inquired.

"Correct."

"By the way, there is something odd about the e-mail address, which I can't quite put my finger on," Leila continued.

"I agree. Perhaps the drapes are a clue as well. I have looked into that but found no company called Double Drapes or anything like that."

"But why drapes? What are 'double drapes' anyway? Is that a Swiss thing?" Leila continued her inquiry.

"No, we don't have something specifically called that, but do you not think someone in this business could give their company such a name?" de Ville wondered.

"It could, but ..." Leila's voice trailed off while her mind pondered the e-mail address further.

CHAPTER 16

The light morning rain had stopped, leaving scattered white clouds immaculately placed, as if by a designer, backed by a brilliant-blue sky like collections of cotton balls impossibly floating overhead. Andy and Leila were glad to be away from Tromsø. Their common experience in the foreboding atmosphere there had been altogether unpleasant. There had been perpetual darkness, too much drinking, too much sleeping, and too many uncomfortable moments—with each other and, in particular, with the daunting Jan Erik Bergeland. While learning about Mr. Stern's whereabouts in Gstaad in 2011 would be the primary goal of the trip to the ski resort town, they would also investigate whether Bergeland had been there, as well. After all, it wouldn't be surprising for him to attend a pharmacology conference, given his business interests. Andy rented a Škoda sedan, a Czech-made car neither had ever heard of before. The car-rental agent assured them it was in fact an excellent car popular throughout Europe.

Andy took the driver's seat, and after piling their belongings in the trunk, they made their way through the busy streets of Basel, with Leila serving as the navigator using her iPhone and Google maps to guide the way. After about twenty minutes, they made their way to highway E25, which would take them to Gstaad. Driving on the modern highways of Switzerland in the clear, crisp air and gazing at the rolling hills and valleys of northern Switzerland, Andy felt much happier than he had during the (albeit short) stay in Norway. For her part, Leila seemed more relaxed as well. Perhaps it was the more-pleasant environment she now found herself in, or perhaps it was the loss of the tension she had felt for much of the past week after Andy had made his confession regarding his feelings. She sensed this might be a good time to revisit the discussion that Andy had started that day, at the risk of regenerating the tension. They were alone, they had time, they had acclimated to the time zone and were as awake and alert as they had been since leaving Los Angeles, and importantly, there was no alcohol to cloud their judgment.

"Andy, can we—uh—clear the air a bit?" she began.

"About what?" Andy chose to play dumb, but he regretted it as Leila responded.

"Hey, don't play dumb, because I'm not stupid and that shit won't work on me. You and I both know we need to have a talk, and since we have a three-hour drive ahead of us, seems like a good time to do it. Agreed?"

"Yes, sorry. I need to stop underestimating you."

"Yes. That is precisely the problem."

"How do you mean?" Andy asked.

"Do you remember our conversation at Olive Tree?"

"Yes."

"No, really—how well do you remember it?"

"I told you I liked you, and you made me feel like an idiot, and we got drunk on arak to recover any sense of enjoyment for the remainder of that evening."

"That is the truth, but not the whole truth. Think. Why did I get so pissed off? Surely the arak didn't rob your entire memory of that night," Leila continued.

"There was also something about how it was inappropriate of me to say I liked you because I am your mentor or something like that."

"Try *mentor, superior, boss*—and while I was the one who suggested those terms, you agreed."

"Wait a second. You got upset because of that and not because I said I liked you?"

Leila raised her eyebrows, pursed her lips, and tilted her head. The meaning was unmistakable to Andy. She might as well have said, "Duh," as she often liked to.

"Do you get it yet?"

"I think so," Andy said hesitantly.

"I'll tell you what; I will make it crystal clear. You said you liked me and, I … well, I was flattered—really I was. Before I even got a chance to say anything other than 'Really?' you proceeded to insult me and ruin the whole moment."

"Well, you confused me, and I thought that you thought I was being inappropriate. Jesus, I don't think I'll ever figure women out. That's probably why I am still single."

"Fair enough. How do you view our working relationship? And don't think about your answer and don't say what you think I want to hear. Just be honest," Leila said emphatically.

"Yes, okay; I will," Andy replied.

"Oh, and if you haven't figured girls out yet, let me give you some advice. Being honest might not get you the girl, but she will at least respect you. So, let's hear it," Leila demanded.

"Leila, you are an outstanding doctor. You're intelligent, compassionate, caring, and thoughtful. You have all the qualities of an excellent researcher as well. You are curious and inquisitive. Truly, I am absolutely thrilled that you came to CHLA and that we work closely together."

"Thank you. I appreciate that. That's a good start, but I need to hear more," Leila said matter-of-factly.

"Like what?" Andy wondered.

Silence. Andy, still driving, peered over at Leila. She just looked intently, with her eyes meeting his.

Andy continued while he turned his eyes to face the road ahead of him. "Leila, you are my peer—I don't think of myself as your boss or mentor or advisor, though I would be happy to advise and mentor you if you wish. I see you as my equal, like I said: my peer and my colleague at work. We are in the same field of medicine. We not only work in the same place but also are interested in the same diseases. We are a team."

Leila smiled. A small tear held fast to the corner of her eye. She leaned over and kissed Andy on the cheek. He looked at her and smiled. They did not speak any further, instead enjoying the silence, the scenery, and the relief at having finally resolved the confusion surrounding their conversation at the Olive Tree Café. After an hour of driving, they saw the white-capped Alps piercing the blue skies, appearing as if they were moving toward them and slowly filling more and more of the southern horizon. The darkness and stress of Tromsø suddenly seemed so long ago. Time passed quickly, and the wide two-lane highway narrowed to a one-lane country road and began a steady, curving climb through valleys carved ten thousand years ago by the glaciers of the ice age. With the sun beginning to set in the western sky, the brilliant blue color gave way as a line of darker blue took over, moving across the sky from east to west. They reached Gstaad at dusk. It was a beautifully situated and beautifully adorned small city nestled between towering peaks of snow-clad mountains. The lights of the city streets and shops were on, giving the city an almost fairy-tale feel. They found their hotel, parked their car, checked in to their separate rooms, and agreed to meet in the lobby to go to dinner. They both expected the most relaxed dinner together yet.

Andy applied his investigative skills to search for the perfect place to have a romantic, enjoyable, and very Swiss dinner. He settled on Sonnenhof based on its great reviews on TripAdvisor. He and Leila, walked, arm in arm, on a cold and clear night along the quaint streets of this resort village. After twenty minutes, they reached the restaurant and walked in to its elegant yet rustic interior made entirely from wood. It was just what Andy had imagined a Swiss restaurant would look like. The hostess sat them at a table by the window and though the sky had darkened, they were still able to make out the silhouette of the peaks against the black sky. Leila imagined the view during the day would be spectacular. After getting settled and used to their surroundings, their focus turned to each other, and as opposed to the tense evening in the Olive Tree Café, this dinner took on the relaxed atmosphere they both desired and needed. Their conversations were varied but much of it revolved around their distance past. Leila provided Andy details, some horrific, of her upbringing in Iraq, and the difficult transition to life in the United States. Andy was pleased Leila felt comfortable enough with him to discuss such personal details with him. When it came to his turn, Andy was almost embarrassed to begin as his story of a middle-class, suburban childhood was so boring, it would be like comparing a compelling, exciting, action-packed movie to a dull sequel of a movie that should never had been made in the first place. In any case, the conversation—like the wine—flowed easily, and the pair got to know each other in ways they hadn't before.

The next morning, they met with the head of the canton police in Gstaad, who welcomed them warmly to his city. He explained that he had spoken to Detective de Ville the day before and been briefed on the purpose of their visit to Gstaad. He offered them the use of his office. During dinner, Andy and Leila made a list of all the people and places they needed to see in Gstaad, which included the conference center staff, offices of the conference event planners, and the hotel staff at the Gstaad Palace Hotel, where Mr. Stern had stayed. They also decided to work in the mornings and ski in the afternoons. After all, they had not had a day off since the beginning of their part in the investigation, and they felt entitled to work several half days rather than taking a full day off.

As it was yet another beautiful day, they chose to walk to the conference center. They were greeted there by Bulent Afçin, a Turkish immigrant who was the director of operations of the Gstaad Exposition and Conference Center. He gave them a tour of the impressive facilities and then had them sit in a small conference room. Upon his return, he brought in a trolley filled with pastries and coffee, tea, juice, and water. Leila and Andy were continually impressed by the hospitality of the Swiss people.

"So, I am at your disposal," Afçin stated in his thick Turkish accent. "What can I do for you?

"We are interested to know about the Pharmacology and Pharmacoeconomics Conference that took place here in 2011 in March," Leila began.

"Yes, I was told as much, but what specifically are you interested in?"

"Were there any unusual incidents? Security breaches? Reports of misbehavior by any of the attendees?" Leila continued.

"Well, I am not precisely sure what you are looking for, but we can check the security logs, if you wish."

The three of them spent the next several hours combing through the security records and security videos. Through that search, they were able to identify Mr. Stern on a number of video clips; however, they noted no unusual behavior either by him or any of the people whom he associated with or spoke to. Furthermore, they could not find any evidence on the video clips demonstrating the presence of Bergeland. All in all, it was a useful exercise only in that it established the fact that Mr. Stern had indeed been in Gstaad on the date in question. By the time Andy and Leila left, it was time for lunch. They ate quickly and headed for the shops to buy some ski clothes, and then they headed to the slopes.

Upon arrival at the ski center, they were quite shocked at the cost of, well, everything. They didn't feel comfortable using the investigation funds provided by Mrs. Milbank for their leisure activity. Nevertheless, they decided to splurge and pulled out their own credit cards to cover the exorbitant cost for the clothes, rented ski equipment, and lift tickets. Even the half-day pass was in excess of one hundred Swiss francs—nearly a hundred dollars. After forty-five minutes of trying on various boots and skis, they were ready and headed out to the lifts. The glare of the sun was intense, necessitating the expensive sunglasses they'd purchased. They reviewed the trail map and agreed on how to proceed, from the easy green runs to the more challenging blues and eventually the black diamond trails. Neither of them had skied in nearly two years, and they weren't eager to be injured. They got on their first lift without difficulty.

"Andy, did you mean what you said in the car yesterday? You know, that I am your peer and we are a team—at work, that is?"

"Yes."

"Thank you. You have no idea how important it is that you respect me as a professional, as a doctor. I don't want you to consider me as your protégé, mentee—I want you to think of me only as your peer. That is how I see it, and that is how I want you to see it, but only if you really believe it."

"Sure. Okay. And honestly, I do believe it."

"Okay. Let's have a great afternoon skiing. I can't believe that a few weeks ago we were going through our routines at work, and now we are skiing in Gstaad and are investigating a murder case," Leila added.

"An apparent murder case."

"No, Andy, at this point, it is for sure a real bona-fide murder case."

The next day, they met with Anna Frey, the owner of SwissEvents, an event-planning firm based in Gstaad. SwissEvents was in charge of all the logistics for the Pharmacology and Pharmacoeconomics conferences (as well as all other conferences in Gstaad). During their meeting, Leila and Andy were able to confirm a number of important facts. First, they could confirm that Mr. Stern had registered for the meeting and attended all three days of the conference. Registration nametags were barcoded, and attendees had to scan their nametags whenever they entered any of the educational sessions and when they entered the exhibition area, where drug companies touted their approved drugs as well as their pipeline. They were also able to confirm the hotel Mr. Stern had stayed in, as the event-planning company had full control of all the hotel rooms associated with the conference. Furthermore, they were able to ascertain that Mr. Bergeland had not registered at the conference and this, combined with no video surveillance evidence that he was at the conference, more or less proved that he had not been in attendance. Lastly, the event planner was able to inform Leila and

Andy that no complaints had been made regarding Mr. Stern or his behavior during the event. Of course, what might have happened away from the conference center could not be ascertained. With respect to Terrapharma, the event planner could confirm that eight members of the company had attended the meeting, and they provided their names to Leila and Andy, but no names jumped out at them as people of interest. In addition, the event planner could confirm that Terrapharma had purchased a prime location for their booth on the exhibition floor, at a cost of seventy-five thousand Swiss francs. Andy requested a list of the names of all those that had scanned their badges at the Terrapharma booth. Then he had an idea.

"Why do you want to back to the conference center?" Leila asked.

"I don't know. Probably nothing. Just a hunch—like an itch I need to scratch."

"You're not going to tell me?" Leila inquired. "I'll tell you when we get there."

The conference center was a short walk from the SwissEvents office. Andy had called ahead and made a request to Mr. Afçin. Once they arrived, he greeted them and took them to the security office.

"Andy, are you going to tell me what we're looking for?" Leila asked, somewhat annoyed.

"I'm not exactly sure, but I want to look at the video from the exhibition floor, and specifically, the Terrapharma booth."

"I don't understand," Leila responded, now clearly annoyed.

"Okay, let's just watch the video and see if we can spot anything. How fast can you run it?" Andy asked Afçin.

"How fast do you want it?"

"Fast enough so we don't sit here all day, but slow enough that we can spot Mr. Stern, and when we do, let's slow it down."

"Sure; you tell me when to speed it up and when to slow it down."

Andy and Leila watched the video carefully, and whenever they saw Mr. Stern at the booth, they had Afçin slow the tape down to near-normal speed. There appeared to be nothing unusual, and Leila was convinced this exercise was a waste of time.

"Andy, please, this is excruciating, and I'm getting a headache," Leila complained.

"Yeah, me too, but keep looking."

She kept looking. Then suddenly, she yelled out: "Stop!"

"I'm sorry Leila. We can stop and come back tomorrow," Andy said.

"No, no, no! Look!" She turned to Afçin. "Can you rewind to the last time we saw Stern?" she asked.

"What is it, Leila?" Andy asked. "Now, it's your turn to be patient."

She guided Afçin back and forth on the surveillance video. "Hmm, very interesting," she stated almost victoriously. "Care to explain?"

"Mr. Afçin, play the tape," Leila asked, and he obliged. "And stop. Look at Stern here. Do you see who he is talking to?"

"A woman—yes, I see. Go on," Andy replied.

Leila motioned to Afçin to play the tape again and move forward in time until she again asked him to stop.

"Look again," she said.

"He's talking to a woman again," Andy stated matter-of-factly. "Not *a* woman, the *same* woman."

Leila had Afçin repeat the exercise, moving forward in time and stopping whenever Stern could be seen with the woman.

"Don't you see what I am talking about?" Leila implored. "Please explain," Andy replied.

"All right, fine. I will play the sequence again, and I want you to pay attention to her body language."

Leila again had Afçin play the portion of the video she'd requested, and a clear picture of what transpired began to emerge.

"Yes, I see now. Leila, that's brilliant," Andy said.

"It takes a woman to know a woman, and neither of you should take that as an insult."

What Leila had noticed was that in the early part of the conference, when Mr. Stern was at the booth, he had been mostly with other men, but as the conference progressed, this particular woman appeared in his presence more and more. On the first day, she showed up just once. On the second day, she was there several times, and by the third day, she was there every time Stern was there. Even more interesting was the woman's body language, which evolved from professional and distant, to more personal and physically closer, to flirtatious touching of Stern—and he touching her similarly, in a playful, almost affectionate way. In addition, Leila noted that her dress on the third day was more revealing than in the prior two days.

"Leila, what can I say? Great observation. You are amazing," Andy stated glowingly.

Leila wondered if the 'you are amazing' meant anything beyond this singular discovery.

"Afçin, can you zoom in on her name tag?" Leila asked.

"Yes, but I doubt you will be able to read it. This is a surveillance video and not the highest quality, I'm afraid."

He zoomed in during a moment when her badge was fully visible, but there was no way to decipher any of the letters.

"Can you save this image and copy it to a flash drive?" Andy asked. "Sure, no problem."

"With all due respect, we'll send it to an expert team to see if they can get the name off of the badge," Andy said.

"No offense taken," replied the amiable Afçin. "I think I deserve my ski afternoon now, Andy."

"Yes, you do."

He kissed her on the cheek. For a fleeting moment, he was about to regret it, but that feeling was replaced by a sense of pride—the woman he liked, whom he already knew was highly intelligent, had just done something remarkable and potentially critical to their investigation. He was proud of her and proud of himself for liking such an intelligent woman. Unlike in the previous week, he was buoyed by her response to his kiss. She flashed the Julia Roberts smile.

They spent the afternoon skiing. Their skiing technique had improved remarkably over the first two days on the slopes, and they were challenging themselves with more difficult runs, although still being careful. Getting injured while skiing during a work assignment that bore little resemblance to their regular jobs, and which was not part of this specific assignment, would result in numerous upset people. So they took great care to ski safely.

The following day, they went to the next and last of their planned three places to investigate the case. They realized that the previous day's discovery might require further research in Gstaad, but for now, this was going to be their last stop. They were waiting on a reply from de Ville, to whom they had e-mailed the picture of the woman and her name badge in an attempt to identify her. They arrived at the Gstaad Palace Hotel. It was the most expensive place to stay in the city, with a basic room costing 750 Swiss francs per night and suites ranging from SF 1,500 to 7,500 per night. Clearly, this is where the rich and very rich stayed, and this is where Mr. Stern had stayed. They met Sophie Verdier, the hotel manager, in the lobby, and she escorted them to her office. They reviewed the hotel stay of Mr. Stern. He'd checked in on March 17 and checked out March 23. Andy nodded to Leila, and she understood that these dates included the date that had been e-mailed to Detective de Ville—March 22. They reviewed Stern's bill. He had stayed in a one-bedroom suite, which cost SF 2,100 per night. In addition, there had been charges for the mini-bar, laundry, and on March 22, dinner at Le Grill, the highly acclaimed restaurant situated in the hotel. The restaurant bill itself was SF 1,874.43.

"Do you have the actual bill?" Andy asked Sophie. "Not here, but I can request it from the restaurant."

"I am wondering if this was a dinner for two with the woman in question or a corporate dinner for him and his Terrapharma colleagues."

"Let me go and find it," Sophie said and stepped out of her office, leaving Andy and Leila to speak privately.

"What are you thinking, Andy?" Leila asked.

"While you said it takes a woman to know a woman, I can equally say it takes a man to know a man. If Mr. Stern had dinner with the mystery woman and shelled out nearly two thousand francs—which is what, about two thousand dollars?—he, uh ... how shall I put this ... would expect an enjoyable dessert, and I don't mean crème brûlée."

"I see," Leila replied.

"Leila, men of means and power expect to be rewarded for showing a woman a good time."

"What about you, then?" she said, smiling.

"I have neither the power nor the means, and regardless, I am just not like that."

"I know. I was joking, silly."

Sophie Verdier returned with the restaurant bill.

"Here is the bill, but I also have another piece of information you may be interested in from the restaurant staff," Sophie said.

"Well?" Leila wondered.

"Let's put it this way: there is no doubt, based on the order, that it was dinner for two, which included a couple of cocktails and a SF 850 bottle of wine. Not only that, what's not on the bill is a SF 325 bottle of champagne that Mr. Stern purchased from the bartender, using cash."

"When did he buy the champagne?" Andy asked. "At the end of the meal, as they got up to leave."

Leila was skeptical. "That was well over a year ago. How could the bartender remember that?" Leila asked.

"I asked the same thing, and the bartender replied that he always remembers getting a seventy-five-franc tip—Mr. Stern just gave him four hundred francs and told him to keep the change."

"Do you happen to have surveillance video that goes that far back?" Leila asked.

"I knew you were going to ask that," said Andy.

"Yes, I believe it is archived that far back. I'll need to check with security, though."

"Please do," Leila requested. Sophie Verdier stepped out again.

"What are you thinking?" Leila asked.

"I think he got to know this woman here at the conference, lied about his marriage, had a fling with her, and then dumped her when he got back home."

"Or even before he left here," Leila added.

"I am sure this is what the anonymous caller is tipping us to, and maybe in some way this woman became bitter and did something to Stern," Andy stated.

"I don't know. I don't think it is that simple. I'm not sure what is going on, but I agree that we found out what the anonymous tipper was leading us to."

"The date and place, March 22, Gstaad—this is where the mystery woman had dinner with Stern. So we need to find out exactly what happened," Andy said.

Sophie returned and escorted the two of them to the security office, where the head of hotel security had already spooled the video to the night in question. Elevator cameras showed Mr. Stern with the woman at 10:37 p.m., exiting on the floor at 10:38. They were flirting and laughing—seemingly having a great time.

"Do you see the woman leaving at some point? Leila asked.

"No, she never gets back into the elevator," the security chief replies. "What about Stern?" Leila asked as a follow-up.

"He is seen entering the elevator at 8:49 the following morning, but no woman."

Andy and Leila gazed at the moving black-and-white image on the screen, with Mr. Stern walking down the hallway from the front and then from the back, followed by an image of him in the elevator.

"He looks fine, but what happened to the woman? Are there cameras in all the elevators?" Leila wondered.

"There are cameras in all the elevators, and our cameras cover the lobby, parts of the hallways, the registration desk, and the front door."

"Is there another way out?" Andy asked.

"The stairs, of course," replied the security chief. "No cameras there?" asked Leila.

"No, I'm afraid not."

"But she would have had to go through the lobby, no? And she would have been caught by cameras there, right?" Leila said.

"Well, not necessarily," replied the security chief. "The stairs are also the fire escape, and at the bottom of the stairwell, there is the option to go straight outside in case of a fire."

"But why would she do that?" Andy asked.

"Embarrassment," Leila said. "It takes a woman to know a woman, as I said before. Sophie, what do you think?"

"I suppose, but why would she be embarrassed?" Sophie said.

"One-night stand. Maybe she's married and didn't want anyone to see her leaving. I'm sure there could be other reasons," Leila replied.

"We have to assume that is how she left, but we don't know why. Can you give us a print of her face from the lobby or the elevator?" Andy requested.

"No problem."

Andy and Leila were left to ponder the identity of the woman and to wonder what had transpired that night that was somehow related to the case. They returned to the slopes one last time, realizing that it would soon be time to move on to Lugano. While coming down the last run of the day, Leila came to a sudden stop. Andy stopped right behind her.

"Tired?" Andy asked as he loudly exhaled a cloud of vapor.

"No. I just had an epiphany. I think I know what happened to the woman."

Chapter 17

Andy and Leila had agreed to meet in the lobby at 8:00 a.m. the next day, eat a quick breakfast, and head back out with the Škoda sedan, for the drive to Lugano. The trip promised to offer spectacular scenery, as the route would cut through the heart of the Alps to take them to the Italian portion of Switzerland. Although Andy had repeatedly asked Leila what her "epiphany" was, she'd asked for his patience and told him she would reveal her thoughts some time later, after they began their investigation in Lugano. They had agreed to discuss their strategy for the investigation there during the three-to four-hour drive, and both realized that his part of the investigation would be more difficult. For one thing, there was no specific event, such as the pharmacology conference, that would serve as the launching point for gathering information. In addition, the date that had been referenced in the e-mail for Lugano was much further in the past than was the date for Gstaad—nearly twelve years, in fact. More than likely, such a time gap would have eroded people's memories and erased any evidence that might have been present previously. Since the Gstaad investigation pointed toward something nefarious involving Mr. Stern—specifically, the one-night stand with the mystery woman, they agreed that their focus should be on Mr. Stern in Lugano as well. The drive was pleasant, with few cars on the narrow mountain roads, and the scenery was as spectacular as promised. They passed various small towns that sat in U-shaped valleys between staggeringly high mountains. Each town had a river running through its central district and several bridges connecting the opposite sides. Leila was in the mood for another conversation.

"Andy, how come you never got married?" Leila asked. "Why are you asking me this now?" Andy asked back.

"Just making conversation. We have a ways to go on this drive."

"Okay, how come *you're* not married? Don't women marry young in your culture?" Andy retorted.

"First of all, I asked you first. Second, are you making fun of *my* culture? "I'm not making fun at all. Don't Muslims marry young?"

"Wow, you have a lot to learn, my friend."

"Okay, educate me." Andy requested.

"Fine. First of all, saying Muslim is like saying Christian, or perhaps I should use Jew, since you'd be more familiar with that. Islam is a religion, and like all religions, there are varying sects, and varying levels of adherence even within each sect," Leila said before pausing briefly, trying to gauge Andy's response.

"Go on."

"So, for example, some Muslim women wear the *niqab*, a black garment covering everything but their eyes and would never wear anything else in public. Others wear bikinis and thongs on the beaches of Greece and even Los Angeles. Some are very adherent and never eat pork and fast every night of Ramadan, while others have bacon for breakfast and don't even know when Ramadan is. You just stereotyped what you called my culture, which I assume you meant my religion, and you know that it is wrong to do that."

"Indeed. I apologize. That wasn't the right thing to say."

"How about Jews? Where is your yarmulke, or skullcap, whatever you prefer to call it?" Leila asked, not hiding her sarcasm.

"Not all Jews wear one—as you well know."

"Exactly. Some Jews wear them, some don't. Some Jews are ultra-orthodox, like those who have beards and wear their black garb, and others wear regular clothes. I believe I have seen you eating shellfish, haven't I?" Leila continued.

"Okay, you've made your point." Andy replied in a conciliatory tone. "So, would you like to ask your question again? Your first one."

"Yes. Leila, how come you aren't married yet?"

"Ah, much better," Leila responded playfully. "But, I still asked you first."

"Okay. Fine. I just haven't met the right person, I guess."

"Does the person you marry have to be Jewish?"

"Well, I had always planned it to be that way, but at my age, I don't think I can be that picky anymore."

"Well, of course you can be picky. No one is holding a gun to your head to get married," Leila continued.

"My mom doesn't own a gun, but if she did, she would do just that," Andy replied.

"Your *mom!* How old are you? You've got to be kidding me? You're—I think you can make your own life decisions."

"Well, that is part of my culture—the overinvolved mother."

"You don't like your mother?"

"No. I love my mom. She has been a hugely inspirational figure in my life, and I have a great relationship with her, but she does tend to still treat me like I'm a teenager sometimes," Andy replied.

"So, does the woman you marry have to be Jewish?"

"No. She just has to be perfect," Andy said, smiling. "Does being perfect mean she can't be Muslim?"

"I didn't say that."

"Agreed, but a Jew and a Muslim. Sounds like a volatile mix."

"Maybe, but for the right woman, that wouldn't stop me," Andy added.

Silence. *Where is she going with this?* Andy wondered. Leila, now realizing where the conversation had gone, decided to retreat from the personal nature to which it had meandered. Her intent was not to insinuate anything regarding their relationship—the conversation had just naturally flowed into that uncomfortable direction. She decided to ease the awkwardness that had resulted.

"Look, Andy, I was not talking about us when I asked if you would marry a Muslim. God knows, my family would have a fit if I told them I was even dating a Jew."

Andy suddenly felt a lump in this throat. *What the fuck happened on the drive from Basel to Gstaad, then?* he wondered. *And what was the kiss for? Is she leading me on, just flirting?* Andy felt a surge of anger and embarrassment boil within him. He made every effort to contain his feelings, like a pressure cooker straining to keep its contents in the pot, so that Leila wouldn't notice, but he also felt the urge to say something. The pressure had to be released, for fear of an explosion of emotion.

"Really. Your family would never approve of you marrying anyone other than a Muslim?" Andy asked.

"Not just Muslim. A Kurdish Muslim. With respect to my culture, you need to understand that Kurds have been persecuted for hundreds, if not thousands, of years and nearly always by other Muslims. We have no homeland, and neither Iraqis nor Turks nor any other nations trust us. We are the ultimate outsiders."

"I didn't realize that, but I have to say that while I don't know Kurdish history, it would take a lot to top Jews as the ultimate outsiders," Andy responded.

"So, both our cultures have been persecuted, hated, killed by the establishment. Our ancestors have a lot in common, then," Leila continued.

Andy decided to take a chance. He had been thinking about what to say next, and while he had made several gaffes in the past two weeks, he felt what he was about to say would help him fathom his standing with Leila, which he was desperate to do.

"What if I called your dad and told him you kissed me?" Andy stated affirmatively.

"Kissed on the cheek, you mean."

"Leila, please don't be so aloof. You know what I mean."

"Look, Andy, I like you, and I am enjoying spending time with you, but don't get ahead of yourself. Let's not get into such a discussion now," Leila responded.

"You started this conversation," Andy protested. "I was trying to get to know you better, that's all."

"Fine!" Andy said, exasperated. "Let's change the subject."

Just as it seemed their relationship was blossoming, Andy realized, there was a big roadblock. *A Jew and a Muslim*, he repeated to himself several times and finished the thought with, *Never gonna happen*.

The rest of the drive was uneventful. They discussed where they would stay and their schedule of events, which of course included skiing. Midway through the drive to Lugano, they stopped for lunch, following which Leila took over the driving duties.

"Hi Simon, any word on the pictures of the woman from the pharmacology conference?" de Ville asked loudly into his mobile phone.

"Yes, we have identified her. We were able to get her name off the badge and matched it to her photo with her driver's license and passport. Her name is Karina Hummels. She works for Novo Nordisk, a pharmaceutical company, based in Copenhagen but with a major office in Zurich. She is a Swiss national and currently lives in Zurich."

"Thank you so much, Simon."

Felix wondered whether she was the anonymous caller. He was still puzzled by the fact that she'd masked her voice. After all, who at the police station would know her? He e-mailed Andy with the all the information he had on her.

By the time, Andy and Leila arrived in Lugano, it was too late to meet anyone. They decided to go for a walk through the town.

"It's, like, almost warm here," Leila stated. "Yeah, weird."

Neither of them realized that Lugano was part of an Alpine microclimate that resulted in relatively warm temperatures, even in winter, as a result of the prevailing winds coming off the high peaks, with the air being compressed and thus heated. Regardless, they were pleased to not have to wear heavy coats and gloves for a change. Lugano, like many Swiss cities, rested on the shores of a lake. The architectural style was decidedly different than that of Gstaad, with a clear Italian influence. In addition, the common language heard on the streets was Italian, though they could also hear German, French, and English being spoken. They checked into the Hotel Walter au Lac near downtown. It was conveniently located and much less expensive than the trendy boutique hotels that abounded. They met for dinner in the hotel lobby and headed to Ristorante Cyrano, as recommended by the concierge.

"So, are you going to tell me your slope-side epiphany now that we are in Lugano, Leila?"

"Not yet. I'm sorry, but please be patient. I promise I will soon."

"Felix e-mailed me," Andy said lifting his eyebrows.

"Oh, and?"

"His friend at Interpol was able to confirm the identity of the woman from Gstaad. Her name is Karina Hummels, and she works for a drug company in Zurich and lives there."

"That's great. I guess that will be our next stop on the tour of Switzerland," Leila suggested.

"Probably, but you know, we've been gone almost two weeks. We need to go home at some point, even if it means we have to come back."

"I suppose."

"Don't forget we're doctors; we have patients to see," Andy reminded Leila. "Of course," Leila responded, not hiding her disappointment. "But we have to try to meet the woman in Zurich before we return."

"We'll see. Let's focus on our work here first, though we now have two names to look into here in Lugano—hers and Stern's."

They decided their first stop would be to meet with the canton's chief of police, and they would follow that with a trip to the local newspaper office to research events that had occurred on the date in question.

Chief Roberto Conti greeted Andy and Leila in his office with a broad smile and pulled up chairs for them across from his desk. He was a genial and friendly man; however, his English was rather poor, and coupled with his heavy accent, he was nearly impossible to understand. To his credit, he knew this and had brought along Detective Angelo

Grilli, who had spent a good deal of time training with detectives in the United States and spoke fluent and clear English.

"We were briefed by Felix de Ville about your investigation and have searched our files for events around the date in question. While we had a number of arrests, they were mostly for public drunkenness, bar fights, and one burglary. We didn't find any connections to Mr. Stern or Ms. Hummels. We don't even know whether they were in Lugano then, so I am not sure we can help you very much," Grilli explained.

"That's okay," Leila said. "Do you know if there were any medical or pharmaceutical company conferences in Lugano in June 1999?"

"No, we don't keep that information here; however, you can check with the conference center. Fortunately, there is only one here in Lugano."

"Thanks. It's on our list of places to go," Andy stated. And with that, the two doctors got up and left the police station. They headed directly for the conference center, where they met with the manager, only to hit another dead end. There had been, in fact, no events at the center spanning the week before to the week after the date in question.

Their next stop was the local newspaper office, where they searched the archived files for the names Andreas Stern, Karina Hummels, Terrapharma, and other search terms but found no matches. Clearly frustrated at what appeared to be a wasted trip, they got up to leave and headed back to the hotel.

"I'm not up for skiing today, Andy," Leila said. "I am sore as hell."

"What do you want to do, then?" Andy asked.

"Beautiful lake. Not too cold. How about we rent a boat and go for a ride?" Leila suggested.

"Sure."

They walked to the marina and were able to rent a small motorboat for two hundred francs for the rest of the afternoon. They bought some food for lunch and headed out on to the deep-blue water of Lake Lugano. They found an isolated area on the far side from the town, where they turned off the engine and let the boat and their minds drift with the current as they unpacked their sandwiches and chips. They sat on the cushioned chairs of the boat, facing each other.

"Andy, something must have happened here with Mr. Stern. I just know it. The first location and date gave us some important leads, and I am sure there is something here, too," Leila said.

"Agreed. Let's brainstorm, then. You know, just throw out some words and let's see if it leads us to any ideas."

"Stern," Leila said. "Money, women, hotel."

"Medication, pharmaceutical company, marketing," Andy continued the brainstorming.

"Cheater, abuser, asshole," added Leila. Andy laughed.

"Education, knowledge ..." Andy continued with his train of thought regarding the pharmaceutical company and the conference.

"Lecture ..." Leila said, shifting her thought pattern.

"University. Yes, university. Stern was a doctor and a specialist in pharmacology, right? And before he went to Terrapharma, he worked at the University of Zurich."

"You think that's his connection to the woman? But it appeared he just met her at that conference," Leila said, and she wondered.

"No, that's not what I'm thinking. Maybe he was here in Lugano to give a lecture—you know, like a visiting professor. That wouldn't make the police rolls or the newspaper," Andy said.

"Okay. I like that idea, and we've got nothing else, anyway. Let's go to the local university and see if we can find some connection with Stern and June 1999."

"But not now. It's getting late, and this is so relaxing. Plus, I think we should keep brainstorming for a while—maybe we'll come up with some other ideas," Andy said.

They spent the rest of the afternoon on the lake. As the winter solstice was approaching, the sun began its descent early. By three thirty, it was behind a mountain to the southwest. Leila restarted the engine and headed back to the marina. Once back at the hotel, they went online and learned about Lugano's University, known locally as the Universita della Svizzera Italiana (USI). It was the only one in the

Italian area of Switzerland. They called and spoke to the secretary for the director of education, who advised them to come by the next day at 11:00 a.m.

The campus of the University of Lugano sat not far from downtown. The campus had a number of small, modern buildings built of steel and glass and one older one made of large logs that looked like the stereotypical Swiss chalet. It was in this building that they were to meet with Professor Massimo D'Antoni, the director of education. They requested that Detective de Ville call ahead and explain the nature of their visit, figuring D'Antoni would be more forthcoming with information than he otherwise would have been. After all, to him, they were just a couple of American tourists. Professor D'Antoni hadn't been at the university in 1999, but he assured Andy and Leila that the university kept meticulous records of visiting lecturers—it was a source of pride, he said.

"Fortunately, we have recently computerized and archived all of the lectures from the past fifteen years, so if Mr. Stern gave a lecture here, we will find it," D'Antoni assured them. He had them sit next to him in front of a large computer screen in the conference room and entered the date in question, June 27, 1999, but there was no mention of Stern. Andy asked him to look at the days before and after.

"Aha!" D'Antoni shouted out. "June 26, 1999, Professor Andreas Stern gave two lectures to our students—one on general pharmacology and one on pharmacokinetics."

Andy and Leila looked at each other, and each gave a slight smile of satisfaction.

"Do you have a list of the students that attended those lectures?" Leila asked. "Well, we're not that meticulous, but I can give you a list of the students who were enrolled at the university at the time the lecture was given."

"Thanks, that would be great. Uh, about how many students did you have in 1999?" Leila asked.

"Well, the university was quite new then—I think only about four hundred or so."

"Thank you," Leila added. "This has been most helpful."

D'Antoni gave them the list his secretary had prepared while he and the American doctors spoke about the different university systems in each of their countries. Before leaving, they asked if he could e-mail them the list so they would have an electronic version, to which he obliged. They thanked the professor for his hospitality and help.

"Let me know if you need any more help," he said as he stood up to escort them out.

Andy and Leila walked back to their hotel and found a quiet spot in the lobby to sit down. Leila pulled the list out of her pocket and began perusing the alphabetized record, looking first for Karina Hummels. Neither of them expected to find her name there; they were quite convinced that the meeting between her and Stern in Gstaad had indeed been their first meeting. They perused the list of names, mostly Italian-sounding, though there were some German and French as well. However, they didn't recognize any of them. Once again, a feeling of frustration came over them.

"Let's e-mail the list to de Ville and see if he can come up with any suggestions," Andy suggested.

Andy went up to his room in order to retrieve his computer, while Leila went to the bar and ordered some lunch. Within a few minutes, Andy was online and had e-mailed the list to de Ville.

An hour later, Andy's phone rang. "Dr. Friedman, regarding the list of students you e-mailed me, can you tell me where you got this list?" de Ville asked, launching straight into the conversation.

Andy explained how they had had the idea of going to the university to see if Stern had happened to give a lecture corresponding roughly to the date in the e-mail.

"Are you 100 percent sure about this?" de Ville asked in an excited tone, making no attempt to hide his concern.

"Yes, what is it?"

"Something very strange. I'll explain it to you when you are back in Basel."

"We were actually planning on going to Zurich to look for Ms. Hummels,"

Andy stated.

"No, I need you to come to Basel, immediately. This is, uh … very disturbing." And with that de Ville hung up.

"Well, what is it?" Leila asked.

"Seems like de Ville just had an epiphany."

"What is it? What did he say?"

"He didn't say. Now we have two epiphanies. We're going to Basel. Now." Andy said firmly.

"Do you want to hear my epiphany?" Leila asked. "Actually, no. I'd like to hear them together."

They gathered their belongings, checked out, and began the long drive back to Basel.

CHAPTER 18

By the time they reached Basel, Andy and Leila were exhausted from their travels and retired to their rooms. They were going to meet de Ville at the Basel Police Station the next morning. The drive was quiet. Leila slept. Andy thought. He thought about the case, about the yet-to-be-revealed epiphany Leila had had, and about the disconcerting degree of anxiety de Ville had expressed when he'd inquired how they had obtained the list of students from the University of Lugano. Andy also thought about the need to return to Los Angeles to see patients, and as he grew more tired, his mind wandered to the mental minefield of his relationship with Leila. The fatigue drowned any sense of rational thought, causing his anxieties to surface like a submerged buoy. Did he really like Leila that much? With her latest statement that her family would never approve of any man other than a Kurdish Muslim, was there any chance they could ever have a meaningful relationship? *How could I even consider a relationship with a Muslim? What was I thinking? But wait, I was taught not to judge people by their color, ethnicity, religion, or anything else, for that matter. What am I supposed to do?* Though he exerted what mental energy he had left to migrate his thoughts elsewhere, they nevertheless returned to Leila and then to Leila and him. He couldn't help it, and he knew what that meant.

"Well, good morning, doctors. I hope you got some time to enjoy the beauty of our country. You have gone from the east to the far south, and now you are back in the north. I should think you have seen more of Switzerland in the last few days than most of the natives have in their lifetime. We Swiss prefer to spend our vacations abroad."

"We did get to ski in Gstaad and take a boat ride on Lake Lugano," Leila offered.

"Great, fantastic. How was the skiing … and Gstaad?"

"Lovely town and really nice skiing," Andy said.

"I should go there some time—perhaps one weekend this winter," said de Ville.

"You've *never* been to Gstaad?" asked a surprised Leila.

"No, and not Lugano, either. Well, shall we discuss what you found and what our next steps should be?"

"Yes, of course. That's why we're here. By the way, any word on the investigation in New York?" Andy asked.

"Nothing. They are stuck, and they fear that they will never see this Alexa woman again. The fate of the investigation, for now at least, rests with us, but I believe you have made some … well, interesting progress, it seems."

"Are you going to tell us about the list and what you find so disturbing about it?" Andy asked.

"Yes, but I would like to review the Gstaad piece first."

"Leila, why don't you give de Ville an overview," Andy suggested. "Sure."

Leila explained the steps they had taken in Gstaad and de Ville was clearly impressed at their methodological approach. She told him about Mr. Stern and the woman he'd met, whom they now knew was Karina Hummels, and about the fact that they'd seemingly become fast friends during the conference and how it appeared they had gone to Mr. Stern's hotel room after a lavish dinner.

"After the presumed tryst at the hotel, the woman, Hummels, disappeared." Andy stated. "Leila, I think it's time for you to reveal your so-called epiphany, which I have been painstakingly and patiently waiting to hear."

"You had an epiphany?" asked de Ville.

"Well, as I have mentioned to Andy, you need to be a woman to think like a woman, and Andy assured me the same was true in the reverse."

"Go on," de Ville implored.

"The woman was seen entering the elevator with Stern in the lobby and exiting the elevator with Stern on the seventh floor, which is where Stern's room was located. Of course, there are no cameras in the rooms, but we assume they ended up there together. Then, strangely we never see the woman again."

"How did she leave, then?" de Ville asked.

"There are the stairs, of course, in case of a fire, and we assume the woman went down the stairs. She was not caught on any of the lobby or exit area cameras," Leila continued.

"So, how did she exit the hotel, then?" de Ville asked.

"The security guard suggested that she probably left via the fire exit door on the first floor and then into town. There are no cameras in the stairwell nor outside the fire door."

"I see, though I would add that it is a rather peculiar thing to do, don't you think?"

"Indeed," Leila continued. "So I asked myself as a woman, why would she do that?"

"And?" de Ville coaxed her to continue.

"The answer is either she didn't want to be seen leaving or she was embarrassed to be seen leaving or perhaps a combination of both. Since we know Stern left unharmed, I doubt she was escaping from anything that she may have done to him."

"Leila, please get to the point and your epiphany. I'm dying here," Andy chimed in.

"Okay. I know I have no proof and there was no report made, but …" Leila paused briefly, looking both Andy and de Ville in the eyes before proceeding. "I think she was raped."

"Raped!" shouted a shocked de Ville. "*Raped?* Are you sure?" Andy asked.

"Well, of course I'm not sure—there is no proof or even evidence of rape, but my gut is telling me that is what happened. You said it yourself, Andy, that a man that shows a woman a great and expensive evening is expecting, you know—sex."

"Sex, yes. Rape, no. Rape is not sex. Rape is about power and control, isn't it, Felix?"

"Indeed it is. You are correct."

"I agree—well, mostly—but it is also about sex. Not consensual sex, obviously, but you can't take the sex out of rape. It is about power and control *and* sex," Leila responded firmly.

Felix was stroking his chin, mulling over this quite audacious, though plausible, suggestion. He knew as a detective that most rapes went unreported, and it would be no surprise if Ms. Hummels chose to leave the hotel stealthily, not reporting the rape, and attempted to just go on with her life as if nothing had happened.

"Leila, I think you may be on to something. I actually think your suggestion is rather plausible. We don't know for sure, but we suspect the vast majority of rapes in Switzerland are not reported," de Ville stated.

"All right, now it's your turn, Detective, to reveal your surprise," Andy requested. "You seemed really upset about the list we sent you."

"Very well, but you must promise to keep this to yourselves. It is critical to the investigation that you don't reveal this to anyone, not the New York detectives nor anyone else. Is that clear?"

"Felix, I, uh, don't understand," Leila stated.

"You will. Please affirm that you will keep it to yourselves for now."

"Yes," Andy and Leila said simultaneously.

"I will discuss this with the detectives from New York, rest assured, but I don't want you to do it."

"Okay. Go on," Andy insisted.

"I recognized one name on the list."

"Oh, who?" Leila asked.

"Angelina Costa."

"That name sounds familiar, but I'm afraid I don't recognize it," Andy said. "She's a pathologist. In fact, she's the coroner who did the autopsy on Mr. Stern."

"What! You're kidding. It must be a coincidence. There's probably another Angelina Costa," Leila suggested.

"I, uh, don't think so. She is from Lugano and did go to the University of Lugano, and I reviewed her history, and she was there in 1999 before going to medical school here in Basel."

"Still, it could be a coincidence," Andy stated with a hint of skepticism.

"It could be, and I thought it probably was—but then I remembered the anonymous phone call," de Ville said glumly.

"Wait, you think Dr. Costa made the call?" Leila asked.

"I do. Remember the caller disguised her voice? Why would a supposedly anonymous caller have to do that? I mean that the caller went through a fair bit of trouble and cost to obtain a device that disguises the voice, not to mention that she called from a pay phone at the airport. Who uses pay phones, anymore—unless they are trying to stay anonymous. That's when I thought Angelina must be the caller."

"Remind us what she said, please," Leila asked.

"She talked about meeting a woman who'd had an encounter with Mr. Stern. She would not elaborate on the encounter but said the woman began to cry when discussing the incident."

"Wait, I'm confused. An anonymous caller that you think is Dr. Costa reported an incident between a woman she met and Mr. Stern. That's quite a bit of hearsay, don't you think?" Leila asked.

"Well, I suppose it is, but why would someone call the police to report this if it didn't happen? I mean, what's the point?" replied de Ville.

"Well, fine, let's assume that what the anonymous caller, possibly Angelina Costa, reported is true. Then, you are also assuming that the woman whom she met is Karina Hummels, and that is based on my assumption that Mr. Stern raped Karina," Leila continued.

"Yes, and that is why the woman, Hummels, was crying about the incident," replied de Ville.

"I don't know, Detective, that's a lot of assumptions," Andy questioned.

"Do you have an alternative explanation?" de Ville challenged Andy. "No, I don't, but that doesn't mean what you are theorizing is correct."

"Let's review the Lugano piece of this," Leila said. "Mr. Stern was in Lugano to give a lecture the day before the date in the e-mail you received, which we now know was meant to be an anonymous tip."

"Yes. And now we know that Angelina Costa was also in Lugano on that date and presumably the next day—the date in the e-mail—as she was a student there," de Ville continued.

"Do you think something happened between Stern and Costa," wondered Andy.

"Perhaps," said de Ville. "Why don't we continue this line of assumptions and thinking? Is it possible that Stern and Costa met, as did Stern and Hummels, and is it possible that Stern ... er, forced himself upon Angelina?"

"You mean *raped* Angelina!" Leila exclaimed, clearly annoyed at the euphuism de Ville had used.

"Yes, sorry, raped her. God, I hate to think that. Angelina is just such an angel—like her name, a little angel. That would be just so awful."

"So, who sent the e-mail about the dates?" Andy asked.

"I assumed it was the same person who made the call—so that would be Angelina, if we are right," replied de Ville.

"Oh my God! The e-mail. The e-mail! Felix, open it, please—now!" Leila demanded vehemently.

"What. What is it?" de Ville demanded.

Leila's heart began beating fast, and sweat formed on her forehead and lips.

She looked almost panicked. De Ville couldn't open the e-mail fast enough. "Come on, come on!" Leila urged.

Felix opened the e-mail.

June 27, 1999, Lugano
March 22, 2011, Gstaad

As she gazed at the monitor of de Ville's computer with the e-mail displayed in the window, her eyes opened wide and her jaw dropped. It was as if she had just seen a ghost.

"Leila, are you okay? What is it?" Andy demanded in concern. "Don't you see? Don't you see!" cried out Leila.

"No, what," de Ville stated exasperated. "June, 27—"

Leila interrupted. "No, not the content of the e-mail, the e-mail address!" They all looked at it: <u>double_drapes@gmail.com</u>.

"Sorry, just tell us, will you?" Andy yelled.

"Move the *d* of drapes back to the word *double,* and what do you get?"

"Doubled rapes," Andy said quietly, increasing his pitch as he said the word *rapes*, as if he were asking a question.

The three of them sat silently staring at the screen, and it all began to make sense. The assumptions they had made were seemingly correct. In June, 1999, Mr. Stern was in Lugano, and so was Angelina Costa. After he gave a lecture, they must have met, and during his visit he'd raped her. Due to the shame and embarrassment, and perhaps concern for a future career in medicine, not to mention not knowing whether anyone would believe her, Dr. Costa had not reported the rape. She'd lived with this awful event for years without saying a word. She might have been able to mentally move past it, but then she'd met a woman, seemingly coincidentally, and through that encounter had learned that Andreas Stern had raped that woman as well. Perhaps she'd wondered how many other women he'd raped in between. The detective, Andy, and Leila came to the conclusion that Angelina was confident that Stern was a serial rapist. She had no longer been able to contain her awful secret, and after Mr. Stern had died, she'd placed an anonymous call to Detective de Ville. Since they were acquainted, she'd had to disguise her voice. She'd followed up the call with an e-mail giving the detective an additional and vital lead that had led to the discovery that Mr. Stern was a serial rapist—or, at the very least, that he had raped two women.

"Even if we assume for the moment that this is all correct, I still have a couple of questions," Andy said. "Why didn't Angelina simply tell you, Detective, about this after Mr. Stern died? Why is she being so secretive about it all—anonymous calls, e-mails that can't be traced?"

"Because, perhaps she is involved in Mr. Stern's murder, and she figured anonymous calls and e-mails would prevent us from suspecting her or at least prevent us from having additional evidence against her," de Ville offered.

"Do you think she killed Mr. Stern?" Leila asked incredulously.

"I, uh … can't imagine she could do such a thing, but I also can't even begin to know what it's like to be raped," de Ville answered.

"Yeah, well, I can't really help you there since that's thankfully never happened to me, but I can believe a woman who has been the victim of a rape could have that much rage—especially considering she found out about at least one other rape," Leila said.

"I think we have our second suspect in Mr. Stern's murder," Andy said. "Bergeland is such an asshole—I can see him being a killer," Leila added.

"Felix, could Angelina be a murderer in your view?"

"One thing I learned early in my career is that you cannot discount anyone. Angelina had a motive and she was in Basel the day of the murder. Bergeland had a motive; however, while he had been to Basel several times, his passport record indicates that he was in Norway on the day of the murder."

"Now what?" Andy asked.

"I, uh, have to talk to Angelina, but I know her, and police procedure is such that I really shouldn't be the one to interview her."

"What are you suggesting?" Andy asked.

"Leila, I think you should talk to her. You are a woman, and you have great intuition. I think that you might be able to get some information from her without her suspecting that she's, well, a suspect," de Ville said.

"Hmm, I doubt she won't suspect anything. She's a doctor, and I am sure she is very smart."

"She is indeed very smart, but still I don't think she will think anything of it. She doesn't even know that you and Dr. Friedman are investigating the case. I think you may be able to gather some valuable information. At least, it's worth a try."

"So, I basically, play dumb—is that what you're saying?"

"Well, yes. I don't see how it can hurt."

"But under what premise do I talk to her—she's the coroner and she's done her part in the investigation," Leila countered.

"Good point. I am open to suggestions," de Ville said.

"How about this. Leila meets with Angelina, doctor to doctor, to review the autopsy report, as she has been asked to assist in the investigation. Then, Leila, you bring up the anonymous phone call and the e-mail and see how she reacts and what she says," Andy suggested.

"I like that idea," responded de Ville. "Okay, I am up for it," Leila said.

"Great. I'll set it up," de Ville said. "In the meantime, Andy and I will try to track down the whereabouts of Ms. Hummels. Perhaps we can get them to come forward about the rapes."

They took a break then for lunch. Andy and Leila decided to take a walk through Basel.

"Leila, we really need to get back to LA. We need to catch up on seeing patients and to meet with the team to go over all the patients that they have seen the past couple of weeks. We also need to show our face to the boss. After you meet with Angelina, we're going to go back home."

"I understand, but I have to admit that this sleuthing has really got me excited—I want to stay involved until we figure out this mystery."

"I'm certain we will stay involved somehow, and I am sure we can keep in touch with de Ville, and O'Reilly and Alvarez, too," Andy continued.

"Mr. Stern is turning out to be quite the asshole. Seriously, if he really did rape two women, I bet there are more—perhaps many more," Leila said.

"So, you think he deserved to die, then."

"You mean to be killed. I don't know. That's a tough one. On the one hand, as a physician, I am trained to preserve life, and I certainly don't believe in the death penalty, but on the other hand, if he was a serial rapist and no one was doing anything to stop him, then perhaps he did deserve it," Leila responded.

"Let me throw out a hypothetical—though one that may come to reality. Let's say Dr. Costa did kill Mr. Stern. What should happen to her?" Andy asked.

"She should be prosecuted. I don't believe in vigilantism," Leila replied confidently.

"Really. And what about the rapes? Obviously, they can't be prosecuted anymore—I doubt the Swiss justice system will prosecute a dead man."

"The rapes can be in a sense prosecuted during Dr. Costa's trial—she can bring that up as a defense, don't you think?" Leila suggested.

"I am no law expert, but that kind of evidence probably couldn't be brought to trial. So, do you think she should be prosecuted, assuming she is charged with his murder? Do you think she should be found guilty?" Andy replied.

Leila didn't answer.

"When you meet with Angelina, you probably shouldn't think that far ahead anyway," Andy stated.

"I won't. I will be very matter-of-fact, I promise."

They sat down for lunch at a café. The sunny skies of the previous days had disappeared and the more typical gray skies of winter returned. It was colder than it had been, and the chill of the air penetrated Leila's clothes to her skin. After sitting down inside the café, she kept her coat on and placed her hands between her knees, bent her neck, and hunched her shoulders. Though it was warm inside, the chill took time to shake off. Her mind wandered. She pretended she was Karina in the hotel room with Mr. Stern. What would she have done? Could she have been strong enough to fight him, or would she have succumbed to his violent, despicable act? She pretended she was Angelina in Lugano. Angelina must have been in her early twenties in 1999, perhaps younger. She wondered what the scene might have been like when an older man —a doctor, a lecturer, someone she would respect—had forced himself upon her. Leila again wondered how she might have reacted. In Iraq, women were constantly being raped by men, except it wasn't always seen that way. Men had all the power there. Women's rights were nonexistent. Then she thought of the United States—the nation that had accepted her family as refugees from a horrible war and a horrible dictator hell bent on committing genocide against the Kurds. Yet, even in the United States, she could recall several cases of rape or at least sexual assault where men who were clearly guilty had been acquitted—famous men, too. Even in a country whose principles were based upon equal protection under the law, it seemed that men were more protected than women. According to de Ville, it seemed much the same in Switzerland. How could it be that in such a civil society as existed in Switzerland, the quintessential neutral country, men could get away with such horrific acts? Maybe Stern did deserve to be killed, even if Angelina had done it.

"What are you thinking about, Leila?" Andy asked, looking up from his menu.

She did not reply.

"*Hello!*" Andy waved his hands in front of her face.

"Yes," Leila replied, seemingly oblivious to the fact that she wasn't paying any attention to what Andy was saying.

"You are quite deep in thought, aren't you?"

"Oh, sorry. I'm ... just tired and hungry."

"Perhaps, but you were thinking about something. I know you much better now that we have spent the past two weeks together."

"What are you going to order?" Leila asked, clearly intent on changing the subject.

Andy took the cue and decided not to persevere.

"I think I'll have the Niçoise salad. How about you?"

"The same," Leila replied.

"Did you even *look* at the menu?"

Leila smiled. "I'm sorry. I was thinking about what Karina and Angelina might have gone through, and, well … it's horrifying. Most men get acquitted of rape and sexual assault, don't they?"

"I don't know, honestly."

"They do. I am quite sure of that."

They spent the rest of their lunch talking about their plans to go back to LA and to see the patients that they had more or less neglected over the past two weeks. Of course they trusted their nurse, Andrea, and the other physicians who were helping her, but they missed their team and the clinic and the patients as well. They missed the warmth of Los Angeles, too. They planned to go back to LA shortly after Leila spoke to Angelina, regardless of any new developments. They wondered whether they would be coming back to Switzerland, or Norway, for that matter. They both still felt bad about how they had been so manipulated by Bergeland, and they still considered him a suspect, despite the fact that he had been in Norway the day Stern died.

CHAPTER 19

The next morning, they met de Ville at the police station again. He discussed the conversation he'd had with Angelina the previous day and stated that she would be more than happy to meet with the American doctor to review the autopsy. She apparently had no inkling that she was actually going to be interrogated—in a manner of speaking—about the case and her potential involvement. De Ville drove Leila to Angelina's office, and Andy stayed behind. Upon reaching Angelina's office, de Ville introduced Leila and explained how she had become involved in the case as a consultant trying to unravel the mystery of the bleeders. He left shortly after the introduction. Angelina escorted Leila to her office, offered her coffee, juice, and pastries, and they sat down at a table in the office facing each other. They recognized that they were more or less the same age and that they had some other things in common with respect to their families.

"Italian families are very close too, you know," Angelina said. "But you're Swiss, aren't you?"

"Yes, staunchly Swiss, but my heritage is Italian, and our family values are very much in line with that. We believe in maintaining close family ties even as we get older."

"My mom is still asking me about my personal life, virtually on every phone call," Leila said, laughing.

"Yeah, mine, too. She says 'Angelina, your sisters and your friends are all married; what about you?'"

"Oh, *please*. In my culture, people think something must be wrong with me that I am not married at my age—you know, like I have a mental illness or something like that," Leila responded.

"So, are there no men in your life that are possibilities?" Angelina asked.

The two seemed to hit it off like old friends. Both were doctors, both were in their thirties, and both were surrounded by men in their professional lives but were without men in their personal lives.

"Well, there is one. He is a doctor like me, and he is a really nice guy, but I don't know. It seems like a bad idea on several levels," Leila replied.

"Like what?" Angelina asked.

"Well, for one thing, we work together—in the same practice."

"So what! Where are you supposed to meet professional men of your level and type—not in bars, that's for sure," Angelina said, laughing.

"The other problem is that he is Jewish and I am Muslim."

"Well, if you were living in the Middle East, maybe that could be a problem, but you live in America. Don't people with different religions and races marry each other all the time in America?" Angelina asked, questioning Leila's concerns.

"Yes, I suppose, but you don't understand. Imagine a devout Italian Catholic wanting to marry a Jew or a Muslim—how would that go over with your close-knit family?"

"Not well. But are you devout? I mean, I would have never guessed you were Muslim."

"No, my family is definitely not that religious—"

"Is his?" Angelina interrupted, continuing along that line of questioning. "I don't know, honestly, but I don't think so."

"So, I don't see the problem. If you like him, and he likes you ..."

"You know Angelina, I haven't had a conversation like this with my friends, let alone someone I just met, but it's comfortable talking to you," Leila said.

"Me, too. I think had we met earlier in our lives, we would be good friends."

"I agree," Leila said. "This has been a nice discussion, but really we should talk about the case. Felix will be expecting me to come back with some helpful information. You see, he is quite baffled by the events of Mr. Stern's murder."

"You are sure it is murder?" Angelina questioned.

"Yes, at this point we are quite sure," Leila said trying not to give away that they were, in fact, absolutely sure they were dealing with two murders. "You know, given the two nearly simultaneous deaths—you are aware of the other death in New York, aren't you?" Leila replied.

"Yes, I know of it."

"So, doesn't the manner of death seem so odd, particularly that they died on the same day?" Leila continued.

"But people die of diseases, drug overdoses, or infections simultaneously all the time. Why are these two cases so suggestive of murder?"

"Really, you think these two cases are just a coincidence?"

"I don't know, but to conclude that these are both murders is a bit premature, in my view," Angelina replied.

"Fair enough, but Mr. Stern definitely bled to death, right?" Leila continued with her questions.

"More or less. He bled in his brain, and that is what caused his death."

"But he bled in multiple organs, didn't he?"

"Yes, he did," Angelina responded.

"And he was still bleeding after he'd died?"

"That is what the police said. By the time he got to me, he was no longer bleeding."

"What do you supposed could cause that? I mean, I can tell you as a hematologist that this is very odd," Leila said.

"Indeed, it sounds odd," Angelina responded, keeping her replies short.

"And the man in New York also died in the same manner and was bleeding after he died too," Leila went on.

"Where are you going with this, Leila? I feel as if I am being interrogated," Angelina said.

"I'm sorry. I didn't mean to make it sound that way but, well, you know why we were brought onto the case, and I am just trying to make some headway."

"That's okay. I understand. How long have you been in Switzerland?" Angelina attempted to change the subject.

"About ten days now," Leila replied innocently, not realizing at that moment that this would open up the opportunity to discuss the anonymous phone call and e-mail and perhaps even what she, Andy, and de Ville had theorized happened.

"Ten days!" Angelina said, surprised. "Really, what have you been doing all this time? I hope you got some sightseeing in."

Leila now sensed her opportunity. "Yes, we got to visit Gstaad and Lugano, would you believe."

Leila was now carefully watching Angelina for those ever-so-subtle body-language clues that might give something away.

"Gstaad and Lugano, what odd choices. I mean, don't get me wrong, beautiful cities and, as you probably know, I am from Lugano, so I have nothing but good things to say about it—it's my home, after all." Angelina paused.

Leila remained purposefully silent, allowing Angelina to continue her thoughts.

"Still, strange choices," Angelina continued, still not suspecting anything. "Why not Zermatt and Geneva?"

Leila decided to keep probing. "To be honest with you, we went to those cities because of the case. Detective de Ville received an e-mail for which the only content was dates and cities. Specifically, a date in Gstaad in 2011 and a date in Lugano in 1999. Isn't that odd?"

"Indeed it is."

Leila perceived the slightest bit of discomfort, a nearly imperceptible quivering in Angelina's voice in her last response.

Leila chose to remain quiet and watch Angelina's next response.

"So, you went to Gstaad and Lugano to find out what happened on those dates?" Angelina asked. Now it seemed she was questioning Leila, who took note of that and played along as long as she could.

"Well, we did some investigating and found out some interesting things."

"Oh, really. Something to help the case of the supposedly murdered Mr. Stern?" Angelina kept probing.

"I can't really talk about it, of course. De Ville told me that we can't reveal what we found to anyone at this point."

"I understand, of course," Angelina said.

Leila sensed that Angelina was becoming more and more uncomfortable. Each question she posed was asked more rapidly, with more intensity, and with a hint of increasing anxiety in her voice. As much as Leila wished Angelina had not played a role in Mr. Stern's murder, she couldn't help but feel that she might have had a part in it.

Their conversation continued, shifting to discussing the minute medical details of the autopsy and what plausible scientific explanations could be made for the massive bleeding and even the post-mortem bleeding. They did not resume any discussion regarding the visits to Gstaad or Lugano. Leila thought it odd that the subject of Lugano, Angelina's hometown, wasn't further discussed. People usually loved to talk about their hometown with strangers and especially foreigners. Leila felt that Angelina was purposely avoiding the subject. After they had discussed for over an hour the potential medical aspects of the case, mixed in with some small talk, de Ville returned, knocking on the door to Dr. Costa's office. Upon being invited in, he was reunited with the two women he had left a couple of hours prior. They exchanged pleasantries, and Leila said her good-byes to Angelina and left with de Ville.

As soon as they got in the car, de Ville could barely contain himself. "So, what did you find out?" he said excitedly.

"I hate to say this, but my instinct tells me she is involved in Stern's murder."

"Really! How so? And how awful if you are right."

Leila reviewed the discussion with de Ville, and he interrupted numerous times with his own questions. She became quite exasperated at his excitement and his many interruptions and questions and told him they could discuss the rest with Andy upon returning to his office. She did leave him with one final thought, though.

"There is definitely one thing that weighs the most in my mind regarding Angelina's demeanor and responses, but you will need to wait until we are with Andy to discuss it."

Leila and de Ville picked up some takeout Turkish food and brought it back to the police station, and the three of them ate lunch while they reviewed everything they knew about the case up to this point, to ensure they were all on the same page. Once they were all caught up to the point of Leila's meeting with Angelina and Andy and de Ville's investigation of Ms. Hummels, they then discussed these last two important pieces of the investigation.

"So, Leila, what can you tell us about your conversation with Angelina?" Andy asked.

"Let's see. First, her demeanor. She did seem, well, rather defensive at times, I have to say, as if she sensed that we knew more than she had hoped. Second, what she *did* say. She was very surprised, it seems, that Andy and I went to Gstaad and Lugano, though I am not sure why, since we think she is the source of the e-mail. Perhaps, that was a ploy to make me believe she didn't send it—or maybe she, in fact, didn't send it."

"What do your instincts tell you, Leila?" de Ville chimed in.

"Like I said, she was very defensive the whole time, and I felt as if she *knew* that I knew something," Leila replied. "Anything else?" Andy asked.

"Yes, as a matter of fact. What was most telling to me was what she *didn't* say."

"I'm sorry; I don't follow," said de Ville.

"Well, I discussed that we went to Lugano, her home town, yet she didn't ask me a thing about the trip nor anything about what I thought of Lugano. I thought that was odd. If someone ever asked me about Kirkuk, where I was born, I would be thrilled to tell them all about—the good and the bad. However, she didn't ask a single question nor make a single comment about Lugano."

"So, you think she purposely avoided discussing Lugano for fear that the conversation would lead to the alleged rape. Is that what you are thinking?" de Ville asked.

"Yes, exactly. Because she didn't want to discuss or reveal even the possibility of an encounter, much less being raped by Mr. Stern. For one thing, she may still feel the shame, but more relevant perhaps, is that we could then say that she had a motive to kill him."

"Okay, you may have a point there," Andy said.

"But the strangest thing I noted, again about what she *didn't* say, relates to the discussion about the e-mail that Felix received," Leila continued.

"What did you find strange about it?" de Ville asked.

"You see, I purposely did not mention anything about who'd sent the e-mail. I just said that Felix *received* an e-mail. I went out of my way to make sure I didn't say that it was anonymous or really anything about the sender," Leila said and then paused for effect and smiled the type of proud smile one would have when they'd solved a riddle.

"Well—are you going to tell us or keep us in suspense?" Andy said, nodding and staring directly at Leila.

"She never asked *who* sent the e-mail," Leila replied.

"So?" Andy said, implying he didn't believe this meant anything.

"Really, Andy. Think about it for a minute," Leila said, clearly annoyed at Andy's doubts.

"I don't see where you are going with this, I am—" Andy replied but Leila interrupted.

"Andy, I tell her about a critical lead that we received that sent us to Gstaad and Lugano, which she was surprised we visited in the first place, and she doesn't even bother to ask who sent the e-mail. Come on. Felix, what do you think? After all, you are *actually* a detective," Leila said clearly implying that Andy's opinion was not as valuable as de Ville's.

"Andy," Felix responded, "I've got to side with Leila on this one. That would be my first thought: Who sent the cryptic, yet important, e-mail?"

"So, what are the two of you saying—that this means Angelina sent the e-mail?" Andy asked.

"Yes," Leila answered, with a quiet yet confident tone of voice, signaling an end to this part of the discussion. "Felix?" Andy persisted.

"Yes. She must have sent it, and she must have been the anonymous caller."

The three of them sat silently, finally getting to take a few bites of their doner kebabs and *boreks*, the famous Turkish filled pastry.

"So, did you find Ms. Hummels?" Leila asked. "In a manner of speaking," Andy replied.

"She does live in Zurich; however, we couldn't get in touch with her," de Ville added. "I will set up a meeting with her so we can gather more evidence regarding what remain a list of assumptions, albeit sound ones, regarding the alleged rape." And with that, their discussions regarding the case ended. They agreed to have one final meal together later that evening, a nice dinner at Cheval Blanc, the famous Basel bistro. They agreed further that there would be no discussion of the case during the meal.

Andy worked on the travel arrangements back to Los Angeles. He booked the two of them on Swiss International Airlines flight 41 from Zurich to Los Angeles, as it was nonstop. It was the fastest and easiest way to get back, and the airport in Zurich was just one hour by train from Basel.

Chapter 20

December 21
Basel, Zurich,
Los Angeles

A s the winter solstice hit northern Switzerland, Andy awoke to a start with his iPhone alarm ringing its marimba tone. It was 8:00 a.m., yet dawn was just breaking. He rolled over in bed and suddenly sensed a quite pounding headache. *How much wine did I drink last night?* he asked himself. His recollection was not complete, yet he did remember de Ville, Leila, and himself sitting together and drinking several bottles of red wine. *God, I hope I didn't say anything stupid,* he thought. As much as he tried to remember, he could not recall any specifics of their discussions nor how the night had ended. He reached over, grabbed the phone, and rang Leila's room to be sure she was awake, but there was no answer. He figured she was either still sleeping or perhaps in the shower getting ready. He hung the phone up, and within a few seconds it rang.

"Did you call me?" It was Leila.

"Yes, just wanted to be sure you were awake."

"Oh, really. I think I should have been the one checking on you, mister."

"Uh, why is that?" Andy asked, unsure of what to expect for an answer. "Well, you had quite a bit to drink last night and, as they used to say on *Seinfeld*, 'the vault was opened,'" Leila said, implying that Andy had said things he might have preferred to keep to himself.

Andy, now wide awake, his pulse bounding and on the verge of panic, yelled out, "Oh God, what did I say?"

"I am sure you know the expression '*in vino veritas*,' yes?"

"I do—are you going to tell me what I said or what?" Andy replied, his anxiety changing to annoyance as quickly as a chameleon changes colors.

"Well, we will have lots to talk about on the train and the plane today, I think," Leila replied coyly.

"Oh no!"

"Look, it's not that bad, but you did say some things that we need to talk about. And don't worry; I know you were under the influence."

"Fine," Andy replied, calming down slowly. "But you have to tell me one thing now. We … er, um, you know …"

"No. What!"

"We, uh, slept in our own rooms, right?"

"Yes, silly. I'm not that easy," Leila said with a laugh. "I'll meet you in the lobby at 9:00." And with that she hung up.

Andy lumbered out of bed, dizzy, dry-mouthed, and with an unrelenting pounding behind his forehead. He found some ibuprofen, took four tablets in his hand, and swallowed them all with a handful of water. He stepped into the shower and dialed the warm water over to cold. He started feeling better, not sure whether the cold simply numbed his head or just startled him back to reality. He dried off, packed his bags, and headed down to the lobby. Leila met him with some Pedialyte, a balanced electrolyte drink made for dehydrated babies, now favored by hung-over college students. He smiled as she handed it to him and drank the twelve ounces in less than a minute. Leila smiled and pulled another one out of a shopping bag. They both laughed. Within a few minutes, de Ville showed up to take them to the train station. He looked fine, as did Leila, which led Andy to wonder whether he was the only one feeling hung over. They arrived at the train station in a few minutes. Leila gave Detective de Ville a warm hug, which caught him somewhat off guard.

"In my culture, we hug to say good-bye," she said when she sensed his discomfort.

Andy looked at Felix and held out his hand to shake. He told him that he was a hugger too but that he would spare the detective any further embarrassment.

"I, the Canton Police of Basel, and the people of Switzerland thank you and applaud you for your efforts. You have both done a wonderful job," de Ville stated.

"Well, we haven't solved anything yet, so don't you think the accolades are a bit premature?" Leila replied.

"Yes, but nevertheless I think you have accomplished much, and I am sure all that work will lead to the answers we seek." And with that they parted company.

Andy and Leila found their way to the express train to the Zurich airport and started the long journey home. With their luggage stowed, they found their way to the cabin with the fewest people and sat in the large and comfortable seats. These were more comfortable than anything they had experienced on trains in the United States. They each pulled out a book that they'd purchased at one of the airports they'd sauntered through on this long journey, though neither could recall which one. Andy pulled out the latest offering from Jo Nesbø, the Norwegian crime novelist, entitled *Phantom*. He had been a fan of his novels long before this investigation had taken them to Norway. Leila had purchased *The Tipping Point*, the best-selling social science exploration by the award-winning writer Malcolm Gladwell. As if to avoid discussing what he might have said the night before, Andy quickly buried his head in his book, desperately trying not to look up. When he did, though, his eyes met Leila's as if she had been staring at him the whole time or at least had the intuition to look up at just the right time (or, in Andy's mind, the wrong time). She unleashed a warm, closed-mouth smile, her eyes narrowing slightly, attempting to insinuate that all was well, she was happy, and Andy could and should relax. With her high degree of emotional intelligence, she sensed that Andy was not ready to discuss their relationship again, so she only held her smile long enough for Andy to get the message she intended before looking down into the pages of her book. Taking the cue, Andy reached for his iPhone and headphones and scrolled through his playlists. He chose Pink Floyd's *Wish You Were Here*, preferring to listen to atmospheric-sounding music with limited vocal portions while he read. Leila did the same but chose Hothouse Flowers' *Songs From the Rain*. She had never heard of this outstanding and underrated Irish band until she'd heard it in Andy's office. Leila liked Hothouse Flowers' songs, as they were on the more upbeat side of Andy's eclectic, yet occasionally brooding, music library. They shared not a word during the hour-long journey.

Upon arrival at Zurich International Airport, they found their way to the check-in area, received their boarding passes, and within minutes reached the satellite terminal from which their flight was to depart. As they knew they would receive a reasonable lunch in business class, they held off on eating and instead continued their self-imposed silence and read their books. After another hour passed, they boarded the large Airbus A340 jet and found themselves in a small forward cabin with few other passengers. Andy sat by the window, with Leila sitting next to him by the aisle. Andy was looking out the window at the other planes parked at their gates, twiddling his fingers and fidgeting restlessly. Leila took note, and feeling the time was right, she tapped him on the shoulder, gave him the same comforting smile as she had on the train, and ended the silence.

"So, Andy, I believe this is a twelve-hour flight. What are you planning on doing?" she asked matter-of-factly.

"Not sure, but probably have some lunch, watch a movie, and do some work."

"So, in other words, you are planning to treat me as if I am not sitting here or as if you don't know me. Really?"

"Well, we can talk, if you like, Andy replied sheepishly. "Don't do me any favors," Leila responded sarcastically.

"Okay, fine. I want to know what I said last night ... and, uh, please remember that I was under the influence," he said, making a drinking motion with his hand to his mouth.

"I took that into account, but if you don't recall what you said, maybe you shouldn't get so defensive," Leila said.

"I'm sure I said some stupid things, and let me apologize now for anything that might have offended you."

Leila pursed her lips and stared at Andy for a moment while shaking her head.

"I don't get you. At work, you are Mr. Confident, even arrogant at times, and with me, you are such a wimp. Can you explain that?"

"It's because I am confident in my professional life, but when it comes to women, I ... I, well, I have made many bad decisions, and I can't ever seem to make a good decision. I guess that's why I'm still single."

"Andy, women like confident men. I can imagine that there have been many women who have come in contact with you in your professional life who were attracted to you and wanted you to approach them, but either you never did talk to them or perhaps you did, but with your Clark Kent persona, and they were turned off."

"I suppose you are right. Now, are you going to tell me about last night or what?"

"That's better! Threaten me. That shows confidence," Leila replied, laughing. "Very funny."

"Where shall I start? Leila wondered.

"How about at the beginning," Andy suggested.

"How long is this flight again?" Leila asked, toying with Andy. "I'm not sure twelve hours will be enough to cover the entire evening." She laughed. Andy loved her laugh, even if it was at his expense. So he said nothing.

"Okay, I'm sorry. I'm just teasing you," Leila said.

Then her tone of voice changed suddenly, like a teenager who, after being caught tormenting other students and confronted by the principal, adopts a repentant tone. And as if her facial expressions had a switch, her appearance changed from that of a giggling child to that of a serious and even-emotioned adult. Her eyes suddenly went from playful to rueful and her mouth from smiling and laughing to solemn. Her eyes became glassy with the hint of a tear ready to emerge from the corner. Andy became alarmed at the rapid change in demeanor, but he chose to remain quiet and let Leila begin this part of the conversation.

"Andy, do you remember anything you said at all?"

"I remember the small talk in the early part of our dinner, but if you mean do I remember what I said about you, then no."

"It's too bad, you know."

"Why?"

"I'll tell you in a minute. Have you blacked out before?" Leila continued.

"Yes, but not very often. Where are you going with this?" Andy was confused.

"I'm trying to find out if you meant what you said last night—if that was the real Andy or the under-the-influence Andy."

"I don't remember what I said, but I've been told that I am a blatantly if not brutally honest when drunk. Apparently, alcohol simply exaggerates my normal bluntness. By the way, you're killing me here."

"I know. I'm sorry, and I'll get to what was said soon. I am just trying to find out before I tell you whether what you said was what you really think."

Andy sat motionless for a moment, looked out the window, and gathered his thoughts. While he was distressed that he didn't know what he might have said, he looked back over at Leila, staring into her eyes, and replied, "Look, I don't remember what I said, but I am sure I meant every word of it, for better or for worse, okay?"

"I believe you," Leila said. Her eyes now filled with tears, like a cup so full of water that merely breathing on it would cause the water to spill over the brim.

"Are you okay?" Andy asked, with concern in his tone. Leila shook her head up and down in the affirmative.

"Yes, yes," she said. "Andy, you said things about me that no one has ever said—not my teachers, not my friends, and not even my family."

Andy's face lit up, with his eyebrows arching and eyes open wide; he could only muster, "Oh!"

"After Felix had left and we were alone, you said, 'Don't you think it is unfair that you are so intelligent *and* so beautiful'—and by the way, I wrote it down, so I wouldn't forget."

"What did you say?"

"I just smiled and I was speechless, but you weren't speechless, that's for sure."

"What else did I say?" Andy asked.

"You said that I was not just intelligent and beautiful—that was your expression of the evening—'You're not just intelligent and beautiful' and then you added that I had a great sense of humor, that I was nice to everyone all the time, and that you are the luckiest person on earth that I somehow came into your life."

"Really—I said all that. I don't mean to say that I don't feel that way—I do, but I can't believe I just let all of my feelings for you come out like that."

"*In vino veritas*, I guess." Leila was now visibly shaking, and tears were streaming down her face. The flight attendant, who had been about to ask for our drink order, said she would be back in a few minutes when she noted the intensity of the conversation.

"I'm obviously sober now, and I am glad I said those things, Leila. I really do think that highly of you," Andy stated; he had now gained the confidence to speak forthrightly.

Leila, still sniffling through her tears, said, "That's not all you said, either."

"There's more?" Andy said; he was surprised yet no longer fearful.

"Yes, one more thing, actually," Leila said, pausing to wipe the tears. She looked Andy straight in the eye. Andy waited patiently. Time stood still for the moment. "You said that you love me."

Andy, without any hesitation and speaking as confidently as he had to any woman in his life, said, "I do love you, Leila. In the past two weeks I have gone from liking you as a colleague, to admiring you as an investigator, to caring for you as a friend, to loving you as a woman."

A tear appeared at the corner of Andy's eye, while the tears on Leila's face streamed down her cheeks and over her lips. Andy leaned over and kissed her on the lips, tasting the salt of her tears. Their lips stayed in contact for a few seconds before parting.

"I must look like an idiot right now," Leila said.

"No, not at all. You look beautiful. You always look beautiful."

"I love you too, Andy, and I am sorry I gave you such a hard time during this trip when we discussed our relationship a few times, but I needed to know how you really felt about me," Leila said, gathering her composure and wiping away the last vestiges of tears.

"It's okay. I understand why you did it."

"Well, not really. You see in Muslim and Kurdish culture women are not generally seen as the equals of men. I am proud to be a Muslim and to be Kurdish, but I can't stand that aspect of my religion and nationality."

"I am not sure where you are going with this," Andy wondered.

"Look Andy, I don't know anything about Jewish culture. I never even saw a Jewish person until I moved to the United States ..."

"Let me ..." Andy interrupted.

"Please, Andy. Let me finish my thoughts, and then you can have your say, OK?"

"Sure, go on."

"What I mean is that even though you seem very liberal about your views on women, both at work and in society at large, I just really need to be sure. And so, I also need to know that when you say things like 'we are equals' and 'we are a team' that you really mean it and are not just saying it because you think it is what I want to hear. Do you understand?" Leila said passionately.

"Yes, I understand. We have lots of time to talk about Jewish culture, and in some ways and with some groups, it is still quite traditional, as you described your culture to be, but in modern Jewish culture, women are held in high regard and equal to men. At least, that's my take on it. For example, women can be rabbis and cantors and hold other important leadership roles in religious and social groups. And I was indoctrinated by my mom that women are equal to men so this has been my view ever since I can remember."

"Okay. Thanks Andy. I believe you, and I am sorry to be carrying on about this, but it is just so different in my culture. You know when I talk to my family and friends back in Iraq or other Arab countries, I am proud to tell them that more women than men attend university in the US and that women can and have achieved very high leadership positions in corporate America," Leila said.

"We still have a ways to go here to, Leila. If you look at the CEOs of corporate America, it's still mostly old, white men," Andy replied.

"I know, but it's changing. Slowly but surely, it is changing, and I believe medicine is leading that change. I mean look at our hospital. Lots of women are in major leadership roles."

"True," Andy replied succinctly.

"Look at our team. It's mostly women—and you hired almost all of them. And not only that, we have a mix of Caucasians, Asians, Latinos, African Americans—almost everything."

"Yes, well, I don't discriminate on any basis—gender, race, ethnicity, sexual orientation, whatever—I just want the best people to work with. It just so happens that we've had lots of great candidates who are women," Andy stated.

"Yeah, well not everyone is like you, believe me."

Leila was clearly impressed, though not surprised, with Andy's views. He closed by saying that living half your life in New York and the other half in Los Angeles, it was impractical to be intolerant, not to mention obviously wrong. Leila finished the conversation by reminding Andy that intolerance should not be accepted anywhere, to which he, of course, agreed.

The flight attendant returned and served them drinks and lunch. After the intensity of the previous hour's conversation, Leila and Andy agreed that they should allow their minds some time to escape and decided to watch movies while eating. Andy decided that he needed a really escapist movie and chose to watch *The Bourne Identity*, with Matt Damon, while Leila, still feeling the warmth of love in her heart, chose a romantic comedy, *The Wedding Singer*, with Drew Barrymore and Adam Sandler. Andy enjoyed the relative isolation of long-haul flights. International flights mostly did not have Internet capabilities, and while a phone was available, it was prohibitively expensive to make calls and was probably used only for emergencies. He could be in his own little world for many hours and could catch up on movies he'd missed and books he had wanted to read but never got to, or he could work on grant applications or papers that were due or overdue. Often he would spend parts of the flight partaking in all three activities.

Only, this time he was not alone. While the movie had provided two hours of respite regarding his thoughts about Leila, his mind then returned to her and their prior discussion. He recognized that neither he nor Leila were young college students, and he started to ponder how quickly their relationship could become very serious. Ironically, despite their discussion regarding freedom of religion and not discriminating based on religion, Andy's thoughts turned back to the many thoughts he had had over the past several weeks—a Jew and a Muslim. Could such a relationship really work? If they had children, what would their religion be? What about his parents? What about her parents? The warmth that had surrounded his heart when Leila had said she loved him was quickly replaced by nervous fluttering when his thoughts turned to the practicalities of the situation. Regardless of their liberal views, such a relationship wouldn't be easy—at least not at first. He decided that this should be a topic of discussion before they landed in Los Angeles. He would have a difficult time sleeping without the subject at least being broached. He looked over at Leila—she was sleeping. He scrolled through the movie choices and decided he needed a comedy. Thankfully, *The Hangover* was one of the options. He needed to laugh a bit.

"Leila, wake up," Andy gently prodded her. "They're serving a light lunch—a Los Angeles-time lunch. You are probably hungry."

Leila rolled over on the chair that had reclined to a flat bed and stretched her arms.

"Are we there yet?" she asked, like a child on a long, unwanted road trip. "A couple more hours," Andy replied.

Leila got up, went to the lavatory—*Why do airplanes call them lavatories?*

Andy wondered—and returned, having washed her face and brushed her hair. "I must have looked hideous," she said.

"That's not possible," Andy replied. Leila smiled.

The flight attendant served them a light lunch consisting of a small salad and bread, which they eagerly devoured. Andy saw an opportunity.

"Leila, before we land, I would like to know what your family would say if they knew you told a Jewish man you loved him."

"Do we need to go there right now? Can't we just enjoy the moment?" Leila countered.

Andy, having shed his insecurities earlier, decided he needed to be adamant about this point.

"I am enjoying the moment, but I don't want it to only last a moment. I mean, if a long-term relationship with you is not possible or not a good idea, I'd like to know that now."

"The truth?" Leila stated, though it was more in the form of a question. "I take it you want the truth."

"Yes—should I get you some wine?" Andy said jokingly.

Leila laughed and shook her head no. "Okay," she said. "My dad will be pissed off. He will tell me I am crazy. He will probably say some things he will regret about Jewish people, because he is not a bigot, I promise you. My mom," Leila paused and chuckled, "she just so badly wants me to get married that I don't think she'll care. I mean, she will care, but more about who you are as a person than your religion. I told you that in my culture a thirty-something woman is either a lesbian or mentally ill. Well, I'm being a bit extreme, but it's not that far off."

"Will your dad stand in the way of what you want, or will you not go against the wishes of your father?" Andy asked in a deathly serious tone.

Leila thought about her reply for a few seconds. "Will he stand in my way? Maybe. I don't know. Will I go against his wishes? No, I won't. I can't. He's a good father, a good man. He took us out of Iraq not for his own best interest but for his family. If it were just him, he never would have left. I can't defy that."

"So, despite everything we discussed earlier, we may have no future together," Andy said ruefully.

"We may not. I am sorry, Andy. I asked if you wanted the truth— well, that is the truth."

"Thanks for being honest."

"Like I said before, let's enjoy the moment and see what happens. I'm afraid that you and I will have to live with that uncertainty for a while." She went on to say, "There is always uncertainty with budding relationships. Perhaps the nearly three weeks of being together nonstop in far-off countries, and working so closely on an intense investigation, is what is bringing about these feelings we have for each other."

"I will agree with you regarding the uncertainty, but please don't question my feelings for you. I know that I love you," Andy stated firmly.

Leila smiled her Julia Roberts smile.

The plane landed on time at LAX. Andy turned on his iPhone and took it off flight mode. After a couple of minutes, the text-message tone sounded. Andy tapped the button and read the message from Felix de Ville:

I know you are in transit, but you must call me right away.

Almost simultaneously, Leila's iPhone registered a text message. It was from Detective Alvarez:

I have spoken with Detective de Ville. Great work. You won't believe what we have uncovered here in New York. We need you and Andy to come back. Please call.

They passed the phones to each other, and after a brief pause, looked at each other, shook their heads, rolled their eyes, and laughed.

CHAPTER 21

After arriving home the previous evening at 6:00 p.m., Andy had been so exhausted he'd fallen asleep on the couch in front of his television. He wasn't sure what time that had been. His alarm woke him up at 7:00 a.m., and he got up feeling refreshed. *I must have slept twelve hours,* he thought. He hopped in the shower and got ready for what would be a busy day of seeing patients and attending to meetings that he had neglected the past few weeks. It was Thursday, and Andrea had scheduled many patients over the next two days, taking into consideration that they would be short on staff the following week, with many people opting to take off the week between Christmas and New Year's Day.

On his drive to work, which frequently took an hour on the congested freeways and roads of Los Angeles, his thoughts turned to Leila and their multinational, multiple-stop journey. He sensed that they had, in just a few weeks, gotten to know each other in ways they never could have in their routine daily lives at home. He felt a great sense of accomplishment considering how close he and Leila had become, yet he fretted about whether or not it would mean anything in the end. Though he felt that they could get past their religious and cultural differences, he felt much less confident that their parents, and particularly Leila's parents, would feel the same way. This notion caused his stomach to churn and his mind to race. *Why am I feeling this way?* he asked himself. Then he came to the realization that that this was the result of the warmth and joy one feels when newly in love, combined with a sense of dread that this love might lead to a painful outcome. He loved Leila, and she said she loved him, but in spite of that, their relationship might never blossom. Like an early-budding daffodil embracing the warmth of spring, it could be killed by a cold, unexpected frost. *A Jew and Muslim.* With a measure of relief, he was happy when he reached the hospital, where his wandering mind could instead focus on the task of taking care of patients in lieu of thinking about Leila and the what-ifs.

After a brief stop in his office, he found his way down to the clinic, where he was warmly greeted by Andrea and the rest of the team, including the social workers, physical therapists, and receptionists.

"Welcome back, Andy. We missed you. How was it?" Andrea asked.

"How much time do you have—it was quite a whirlwind, exhilarating, exciting, and exhausting, too," Andy replied.

Prior to his departure, he had explained to his team the reasons he and Leila would be leaving. Andy now went on to tell them that he couldn't really discuss the investigation and that, in reality, with the number of patients scheduled, there was no time to get into a lengthy explanation either. He didn't say a word about what had transpired between him and Leila, of course.

"Hi, everyone," came the cheerful voice of Leila.

She came into the conference room in the clinic and hugged each and every one of the staff. She was in a great mood and was clearly happy to be back home and back at work. When she caught Andy's eye, she winked. He winked back, ensuring that no one else would take notice. Together they reviewed files for the patients who were scheduled for visits that day. It was a mixture of patients with hemophilia and other bleeding disorders as well as some patients who had had blood clots.

Through their meeting, they decided who would see which patients and then immediately got to work.

Andy saw that Diana Vasquez was scheduled and told the team that he would see her and her family. Diana was one of Andy's favorite patients, and he'd had a strong bond with this family ever since the untimely and tragic death of the older sister. In fact, he was quite concerned about Diana, since her sister had died from a blood clot while on the blood thinner Coumadin, and Diana was seemingly following in her path, with the same history and now taking Coumadin. The only difference thus far was that the older sister, Vanessa, had developed a second blood clot while on Coumadin, while Diana, fortunately, had not. Although Andy had tried to switch her to Lyzanda, the new blood thinner, her insurance company had refused to pay for it. He was hoping they would not have to review the same conversation that he had had with the family over and over again regarding Vanessa's death and their enormous sense of guilt.

When he entered the exam room, Vanessa and her parents greeted him with warm embraces, as was the norm. Indeed, despite Diana's death, the Vasquez family remained steadfastly grateful to Andy for all that he had tried to do for her.

"Hi, Diana! How are you?" Andy asked.

"I'm doing great, Dr. Friedman. How about you?"

"I'm doing great also," he replied. "Any bleeding symptoms?"

"No, same as always. A few bruises, but no bleeding," Diana replied.

They continued discussing her medical situation for several minutes, after which Dr. Friedman examined her and advised her and her parents that she needed to continue to take her Coumadin. He once again reviewed with Diana and her mother the symptoms of a blood clot and a pulmonary embolism. They had heard this many times before, but they never once interrupted Dr. Friedman; they were like young children who want to have the same book read to them over and over again to provide a sense of familiarity and safety. Paradoxically, the grave discussion offered Diana and her family some comfort. There was an understanding between Dr. Friedman and the Vasquez family that these visits had to cover the same ground. After completing his examination and discussion, Dr. Friedman then chose to change the subject.

"How is your brother, Diana?"

"Bryan is great. Thanks for asking. He's still working with ExxonMobil. He has such a cool job. He gets to travel all over the world, you know, looking for oil."

"Really? That's fantastic. You sound jealous."

"Yeah, I am."

"What countries has he been to?" Andy asked.

"In just the last year, he's been back and forth to Nigeria, Brazil, Qatar, and Norway several times," Vanessa replied.

"Wow, he's hit four continents with those trips. Does he have a favorite?"

"He told me Norway is his favorite. He keeps telling me how beautiful it is and that one day he'll take me there."

"Well, I hope you get to go sometime," Andy replied.

"I had no idea there was a lot of oil off the coast of Norway. Anyway, that's his main project now—trying to convince his managers that they should invest a lot of money there and to get some good deals for Exxon. Have you ever been to Norway, Doctor?"

Andy hesitated momentarily. On the one hand, he didn't want to lie to Diana, but on the other hand he felt an obligation to keep the investigation secret.

"I have been there, and I hope you get to go one day. How long has Bryan been away?" Andy replied, purposefully moving the discussion back to Bryan's travels rather than his own.

"Oh, he's back now for Christmas, but he was gone for most of November and the beginning of December. I'm so proud of him," Diana said, while her mom looked on, beaming, clearly very proud of her son.

"Well, Merry Christmas to you and your family, and I'll schedule your next visit for a month from now," Andy said as he concluded the visit.

"Thanks and Happy Hanukkah to you," Diana said. She knew that Dr. Friedman was Jewish.

With that, the visit ended, and Andy moved on to the next patient that Andrea had seen. It was a young family with two boys who had hemophilia. They were doing well with their prescribed treatment, and Andrea had taken care of everything, making his visit more of a social than a medical visit. He then returned to the conference room.

"Andy," Leila called, but she got no answer.

"Hey, Andy," she said a bit louder, but again there was no reply. She walked up to his side and shouted a staccato *Hey* in his ear.

"Oh, hi; what's up?" he asked.

"*What's up?*" Leila said sarcastically. "What planet were you just on?"

"I'm sorry. Between the jet lag and—" Andy began.

"And what," Leila said with a frustrated tone.

"I can't talk about it now. I'll tell you over lunch," he said.

Leila stood closer to Andy and whispered, "Uh, we are not supposed to talk about you-know-what here."

"Huh?" Andy replied, confused, but then he realized what Leila was referring to and quickly corrected her. "No, no—it's not what you're thinking. It's about the Vasquez family. I'll tell you at lunch. Please be patient."

The conference room was where the doctors, nurses, and the rest of the team worked in between seeing patients: checking laboratory results, calling other doctors, and working with the staff to schedule the follow-up visits. It was a crowded room, with lots of people coming and going, and clearly not the place to discuss what was on his mind; that would require a modicum of secrecy. It was nearly noon anyway, and he and Leila planned to have lunch together off-site at a local restaurant, where he would be able to share his thoughts with her.

The last patient of the morning was Steven Findley, the sixteen-year-old high school student who was forbidden from playing football since he was still taking Coumadin to treat his blood clot. Thankfully, his mother had convinced her son to sit out this season, despite his pleadings. At least football season was over now, and Andy wouldn't need to get into the same discussion he'd had with him previously. He and his father, though, remained quite bitter about the whole experience, fearing that missing the entire football season would jeopardize Steven's chances of landing a college scholarship. His father continued to express a lot of resentment regarding the whole experience, though it was not aimed directly at the health-care team.

"Steven, how are you?" Dr. Friedman said as he walked in.

"Can I finally stop this medicine?" Steven asked expectantly, not hiding the mixture of hope and frustration in his voice.

"Probably soon. I just need to review your ultrasound to be sure the clot is fully resolved."

"You know, my dad says I might not be able to get a scholarship anymore."

"I understand, but your health had to come first, Steven, and we've discussed this many times before," Andy replied tersely.

"He did some research about the medicine you suggested, what was it called, Lyz ... something."

"Lyzanda," Andy filled in.

"Yeah, that's it. He found out why I couldn't get it, you know."

"Well, it's really expensive, and your insurance—"

"Wouldn't pay for it," Steven completed Andy's sentence. "Let me tell you, when he found out that they wouldn't pay for it, he called one of his friends from college who's a lawyer to find out if he could sue them."

"And?"

"His friend looked into it but found out that Empire Health has fought off hundreds of lawsuits like this and that we had no chance. My dad was so angry he said he could kill someone—of course, he was joking."

"Did you say Empire Health?" Andy asked. "Yeah, why?

"No reason. Just curious," Andy replied.

Andy went to the conference room to see if the ultrasound results were in the computer yet and sat in front of the monitor, but he hesitated for a moment. *Empire Health,* he said to himself. *It must be a coincidence.* He pulled up the results of Steven's ultrasound and returned to the exam room.

"Great news. Your clot is completely gone which means … you can stop the Coumadin."

"Really, doc? That's great news!" Steven said, elated.

"Dr. Friedman, is that true? Really?" Mrs. Findley followed.

"Yes. And that means you can go back to playing football. You have plenty of time to get in shape for next season, and if you are as good as I hear you are, you should still have a great chance at a scholarship."

"Thanks so much, doc," Steven replied happily; there was an ear-to-ear smile on his relieved face. With just a few more instructions and plans for a follow-up appointment, the visit ended. Andy had yet one more thing to discuss with Leila.

The morning clinic was complete. All in all, Andy, Leila, and Andrea had seen fifteen patients, had another twelve scheduled for the afternoon, and would see another twenty-five tomorrow. It was going to be a busy two days, but with all their time away, Andy and Leila knew they had to catch up. Andrea left them and headed out to lunch with several other nurses, which gave Andy and Leila the opportunity to take the short walk to Bianca's, a small Greek deli-style restaurant just across the street from the hospital. As they were walking, Leila's patience ran out.

"So, what's up, Andy? You're acting all weird. Remember, we're not supposed to talk about *that* at work."

Andy knew what *that* meant and added, "No, it's not anything about *that*, I promise. It's … well, more coincidences."

"Do tell, then," Leila requested.

They reached Bianca's, ordered their Greek salads, and took a seat outside in the warm winter sunshine of Los Angeles. Thankfully, there were only a few people at Bianca's that day, probably because this was the day the hospital was offering its free Christmas lunch to all the staff.

"Out with it, now! I'm tired of waiting," Leila demanded. "You remember Diana Vasquez, right?"

"Sure, of course. What a horribly sad story what happened with her sister."

"Indeed, but this is about her brother."

"Does he have a clot too?" Leila asked.

"No, nothing like that." Andy hesitated for a moment and then continued. "You have to understand that the family was—well, *is*—still very bitter about what happened to their beloved sister and daughter. They still feel guilty that they didn't pay for the Lyzanda and can't understand how or why a medicine could cost so much money."

"I'm not following," Leila said.

"When I say angry, I mean, very bitter and angry—not at us or the hospital but rather with Empire Health, because they wouldn't pay for the medicine, and with the drug company for charging so much for it," Andy continued.

"O-o-k-a-a-y ..." Leila said slowly. "And?"

"It turns out Bryan, Diana's brother, works for ExxonMobil as an oil exploration engineer, and ... he's doing a lot of travelling."

"Go on."

"So, he was in Norway, for pretty much the whole month of November. Isn't that interesting?"

"Come on, Andy, you don't think he has anything to do with the murders, do you?" Leila added, surprised at Andy's accusatory tone.

"Well, he would have a motive, and he was in Norway, and—"

"Andy, Norway has a big oil industry. I'm sure he was just there for work."

"You're probably right, but I'm going to have de Ville look into it a bit, just in case," Andy said matter-of-factly. "And that's not all. I have another weird coincidence for you, would you believe?"

"Oh, there's more?" Leila said, raising her eyebrows. "Remember Steven Findley, the football player with the clot?"

"Yes," Leila answered. "You're not going to tell me he's been to Switzerland, are you?"

Andy laughed and said, "No, but his dad is pretty upset that he couldn't get Lyzanda either, thinking that if he had, he could have played football this past season."

"You wouldn't have let him play, regardless, though."

"Well, I wouldn't have recommended it, but I might have looked the other way a bit since the risk for bleeding with Lyzanda seems to be so much less than with Coumadin," Andy answered.

"So, who is his dad so angry with?"

"His insurance company—*Empire Health*," Andy stated with the emphasis on Empire Health for dramatic effect.

"Are you kidding me?"

"No, I'm not. His son even said that his dad was so angry he could have killed someone. He said his dad was joking, of course, but … who knows?"

Andy stated.

"So, exactly how many suspects do we have now?" Leila said, not hiding her sarcasm.

They returned to clinic after lunch and spent the afternoon seeing patients with all manner of bleeding and clotting problems. Thankfully, no more suspects emerged among the remainder of the patients. Andrea sensed something was bothering Andy, but he shrugged her concerns off by simply stating that he was tired and jet-lagged, and she accepted his explanation, though deep down, having known Andy for the past ten years, she sensed that this was not the real reason. Leila was able to maintain her usual demeanor better than Andy and didn't elicit any similar concerns among the team. By the time they'd finished clinic, it was nearly 6:00 p.m. Both Andy and Leila were exhausted and dared not think that it was now 3:00 a.m. in Switzerland and Norway. They parted company and each headed home for an early night of sleep.

The next day was much the same as the previous one—lots of patients and lots of paperwork to catch up on. There was one difference, however, which was the meeting with the boss. He needed an explanation for their extended time away. Andy arranged for the meeting.

"Hi, Candice, I'm here—just wanted to let you know I'm ready," Andy said, knowing full well he would be waiting in the corridor for some time.

"I'll let you know when he's ready for you. Would you like to wait here, or should I call your office?"

"I'll wait here, if that's okay," Andy said clutching the newspapers he'd brought with him under his arms. He flipped one of them open to read last week's news. After five minutes, he pulled his iPhone from his pocket and flipped through his recent e-mails. Another five minutes passed. Then Candice appeared in the hallway and called him in.

"So, Andy, you and Leila have been away quite a bit. Can you tell me what you've been doing?" the boss said matter-of-factly.

"Well, I, uh, can't get into the investigation, other than to say we are making progress in finding out how the two men died," Andy replied.

"I think you and Leila have been gone enough, don't you think?

"We've been away a lot, I know, but we've become an integral part of the investigation, and they really need us—the detectives, that is," Andy said.

"Well, we need you here, too. I don't see how it is helping your program and our center for you to be away so much," the boss said sternly.

Andy pulled out the newspapers he had been holding on his lap. Of course he'd selected the ones he figured would help his cause the most. He handed the most sensational one to the boss, Its headline read,

LA Blood Docs Chasing the Bleeders Killer

"Interesting," the boss said, suddenly more interested. "What does it say inside?"

"I took the liberty of highlighting the relevant portions for you," Andy added as he helped the boss flip to page three of the newspaper.

> *Drs. Andy Friedman and Leila Baker, of Children's Hospital Los Angeles and Children's Center for Cancer and Blood Disorders, are foremost experts in conditions that cause bleeding problems. They have been called in by the NYPD to help with the mysterious death of Creighton Millbank.*

"They are both brilliant and are really helping us with getting to the bottom of this. Children's Hospital Los Angeles is lucky to have them," says NYPD Commissioner Garrett Williams.

Andy had the boss review several other newspapers with similar comments and quotes and watched his boss flash a rare smile of approval. He knew right then and there that they were headed back to New York.

By the end of the meeting, the workday was nearly over. Since Christmas was approaching and many of the staff were going to be off the following week, Andrea had arranged a holiday dinner for the team at Cha Cha Cha, a local Caribbean restaurant. Andy had already delivered his Christmas gifts to each of his staff members, carefully concealed in an envelope and stealthily delivered to their offices. It was his way of offering his sincere thanks and rewarding his staff with a personalized note and a gift card to their favorite store. The dinner was an enjoyable and carefree evening—just what Andy and Leila needed, although as the evening drew to a close, Leila couldn't help but think of the text messages they had each received upon landing in Los Angeles two days ago. As Andy and Leila walked to their cars, she felt an urge to discuss them.

"Andy, I hate to bring it up now, but what about the text messages from de Ville and Alvarez? I totally forgot to reply to them," Leila said.

"Don't worry. I didn't forget. I called each of them, and … uh …," Andy said with a sheepish smile, "told Alvarez we would see him next week."

"You did what? What about some time off? It's Christmas," Leila said, annoyed.

"First of all, you are Muslim, so you don't celebrate Christmas, and second of all, I know you want to go back to New York," Andy replied, smiling.

"Fine, and right on both counts, but I need a few days off first. I have to catch up on my sleep and rest, okay?"

"And you shall have them. It's not like Alvarez wants to work on Christmas either. We'll go two days after. Oh, and by the way, New Year's Eve in New York is a blast," Andy said.

"So, I've heard," Leila said, flashing her Julia Roberts smile. "What did de Ville want?"

"Let's just enjoy a few days off, and we can talk about it on the way to New York," Andy responded.

"Normally I wouldn't let you get away with that, but since I am in no mood to think about the case right now, that sounds just fine."

"So, I'll make the arrangements, and I'll call you. I guess I won't see you until at least Monday, then," Andy said.

"Actually, I'll see you Sunday."

"Oh, really? Where?"

"At my house, my dear. You're coming to meet my parents."

"Uh, I am?" Andy replied, clearly caught completely off guard.

"Well, if you really do love me, you'll be there," Leila said, raising her eye brows and tilting her head to the side with the hint of a mischievous smile on her face.

"Just tell me what time and your parents' address."

CHAPTER 22

Following a few well-deserved days off, Andy and Leila were back at the airport. Andy had contacted Detective Alvarez, who suggested coming to New York on December 27, after he'd had a few days off for Christmas with his family. Although Detective O'Reilly was anxious for the two doctors to return as soon as possible, Alvarez convinced him to take an additional day off after Christmas—this despite the fact that they still had not found Alexa. Ordinarily, O'Reilly would have been completely opposed, but he relented, since that gave him the opportunity to spend a social day with Julie Millbank, whom he had grown to like despite his best instincts telling him not to get involved with a rich widow. O'Reilly spent Christmas Eve and Christmas Day with his sisters and their families, and though he was surrounded by family members, he nevertheless felt lonely. He was amazed how lonely someone could feel even amongst family.

Given the additional day off by Alvarez, who was determined to spend three full days with his large family, O'Reilly sought the cure for his loneliness with the equally lonely Julie Millbank. When he called her to ask her to spend the day with him on a date, she was so shocked she could barely utter the word *yes*. O'Reilly figured that so long as they were not discussing the case, it was reasonable for him to spend some social time with her, but he wasn't completely sure.

As a result of Alvarez's request, Andy and Leila had three consecutive days off—something Andy had not had since a vacation nearly a year ago. The three-day weekend afforded Andy the opportunity to catch up with friends, spend time with his family—at least via Skype—and, of course, to meet Leila's parents and siblings. Leila's parents lived in a modest house in El Segundo, just south of LAX, and the roar of planes taking off every few minutes a few miles away was unmistakable. Andy wondered how the din of the airport wasn't disruptive to the daily lives of the people who lived there. Leila assured him that after living there for a few months, your mind tuned it out and you didn't even notice it anymore. Now the two of them were actually at the airport, awaiting their flight. Terminal 4 was the American Airlines terminal at LAX, and it bustled with business people and tourists from before 5:00 a.m. to just past midnight every day. The only time of day when activity was at a lull was in the late afternoon, after the rush of the morning and early afternoon and before the red-eye flights and international flights taking off between 7:00 p.m. and midnight. Leila and Andy's flight, American Airlines flight 2, was due to depart at 9:30 a.m. and arrive at New York's JFK airport at 6:10 p.m. They'd agreed to meet near the gate and had no trouble finding each other.

"Good morning, Andy," Leila greeted him with a big smile.

As Andy approached, his mind was in a state of confusion. *Do I hug her? Kiss her? Just say hi?* he was asking himself. While meeting Leila's family had been a wonderful experience, and he genuinely liked her parents, he wasn't quite sure what it meant for their relationship. Certainly, her father hadn't left him with the impression that he'd accepted Leila being involved with a non-Muslim, let alone a Jew. He decided to play it safe and just say hello, with no physical contact of any kind. That was a mistake.

"Hi, Leila—how was your trip in?" Andy asked.

"What the hell is wrong with you?" came Leila's terse, if not rude, reply. "Uh … sorry, did I say something wrong?"

"No, you didn't *say* anything wrong," Leila replied sarcastically. "Okay … then what?" said a confused Andy.

"Listen, you need some, shall we say, relationship lessons."

"Oh," Andy replied, not exactly sure where Leila was taking this discussion. "How many times have you kissed me?"

"Uh, several."

"Yeah, several—whatever that means. And now you greet me like I'm some long-lost male friend from college. Although, who knows, you might even give that person a hug."

"I'm sorry, Leila. I am confused. First, I think we are going to be a couple, and then I meet your parents, and well, it seems so unlikely that we could ever have a relationship—what with your dad's feelings about, you know, our differences," Andy tried to explain his aloofness.

"Listen, Andy. You don't need to worry about my parents. That's my problem. If you love me, if you want me to be your girlfriend, then you better start acting that way, or you're right, we won't ever have a relationship," Leila replied clearly, challenging Andy, if not threatening him.

"Okay, but it's not easy, not after meeting your dad. Perhaps we should have waited longer before I met your family."

"No, I disagree. It's always good to meet the family early—especially in my culture. It is what it is, and if our relationship will become that serious, my dad will probably come around."

"Probably?"

"Well, I don't know for sure," Leila replied. "So, as I said to you a few days ago, let's just take things one day at a time. I know that's a stupid cliché, but I think it actually makes sense for us."

"Fine," Andy replied.

"Uh, so where is my hug and kiss?" Leila said, smiling. Andy obliged.

They boarded the 767 and found their way to their seats, thankful that this plane's 2-3-2 seating configuration afforded them some semblance of privacy, as they had a window and aisle seat. Andy and

Leila were once again airborne. They both realized that they had been spending a lot of time on airplanes lately, but neither seemed to mind. Each flight brought them to a new adventure and seemed to bring them closer, as the hours of idle time together allowed them to learn more and more about each other. For now, however, Leila, was more anxious to discuss the case and felt she had waited long enough to find out what de Ville's text message was about.

"So, why was de Ville so anxious to talk to you?" Leila asked.

"He met Karina Hummels—remember her?" Andy replied.

"Sure, sure. She's the one who I said was probably raped by Dr. Stern in Gstaad. So, what did he find out?" Leila responded excitedly.

In an attempt to elicit some emotional response, Andy purposely delayed his answer, sensing Leila's excitement.

"Well, are you going to tell me?" Leila said. She had raised her voice over the sound of the white noise of the airplane, thinking Andy hadn't heard her.

Andy simply raised his eyebrows and turned his head in a playful manner, teasing Leila while Leila responded by pursing her lips and squinting her eyes. Andy kept the suspense going just a bit longer, like a parent holding back a great surprise he is about to spring on his child.

"Ms. Hummels denied everything at first, but de Ville sensed the tension in her voice when he mentioned Mr. Stern. He pressed her gently but she still resisted, but he found a way to crack the safe."

"Oh, how?"

"It's all thanks to you, actually. He showed her the still images from the video at the pharmaceutical conference in Gstaad. I still think that was really brilliant how you figured that out," Andy answered.

"So, what did she say?"

"It's not so much what she said—more what she did."

"Go on," Leila implored.

"She apparently broke down crying and couldn't utter a word for the rest of the meal."

"That's it."

"No, she agreed to meet de Ville another time if he left her alone for the rest of the day, and he agreed," Andy said.

Andy relayed the rest of what had transpired when de Ville had met Ms. Hummels the following day, and she, in fact, had had a lot to say. After unleashing a flood of emotions during their first meeting, she unloaded a flood of information at the subsequent meeting. She had kept this dark secret for the last couple of years, and Ms. Hummels seemed almost relieved to be able to remove the albatross and share the horror of what had happened to her with someone. De Ville said that she had been especially relieved to finally tell a law enforcement officer that she had been raped. She apparently had been so ashamed of having been duped on the one hand and then raped that she'd refused to tell anyone—not her family, not her friends, and certainly not any law-enforcement personnel, for fear that no one would believe her and that the case would become public knowledge. De Ville went on to say that Ms. Hummels had thought she would be able to suppress her emotions; however, she'd also confessed to crying herself to sleep every night and to no longer being able to carry on a relationship with any man. The rape had essentially destroyed her life. The only thing she could do was her job, which turned out to be the only vestige of sanity that remained in her life.

"That is just horrible, Andy. I could never imagine how that must feel—nor do I ever want to. Did she mention Angelina Costa at all?" Leila asked.

"Yes, she did. She told de Ville that she had met Angelina last summer on a hiking trip in the Alps and that they had hit it off really well and spent the whole trip together talking and becoming fast friends. And as they got closer, they talked about men and their love lives ... and eventually she told Angelina that she had been raped."

"Holy shit!" Leila exclaimed.

Several heads turned from the seats next to them. Leila apologized—she hadn't realized how loud her voice was nor her level of excitement upon receiving confirmation of her assumptions.

"That's not all," Andy added.

"Yeah, go on, and don't pull that keeping-me-in-suspense crap again," Leila demanded.

"Karina also told de Ville that Angelina had told her that she had been raped too."

"Oh my God," Leila said in a decidedly quieter tone. "This is incredible, Andy. I can't believe you were able to keep this from me the whole weekend. Anything else?"

"Yes, one last thing, but it should be obvious to you by now," Andy said.

"Uh, no, it can't be that obvious, because I have no idea what's going to come next."

"Karina also told de Ville that she and Angelina had come to the realization that they had been raped by the same man, albeit ten years apart."

"No way! Are you serious? What a crazy coincidence—though this case seems to be one coincidence after another."

"Indeed," Andy replied.

"It makes you wonder how many women Stern raped, doesn't it?" Leila pondered.

"What do you mean?" Andy wondered.

"Well, do you think we just happened to come across the two women that Stern raped over that twelve-year span?" Leila responded.

"I don't know," Andy replied.

"I know. Believe me, there is no way he only raped two women over that span of time. I am sure there are more, perhaps many more. I am sure he is a serial rapist."

"Should we ask de Ville to look into it?" Andy asked.

"Well, it might take him away from other aspects of the investigation, but it might uncover some other potential suspects, and ..." Leila replied and then paused.

"And what?"

"And shed some light into what a terrible man Stern was—though it doesn't mean he should have been killed."

"It could provide mitigating evidence if Karina or Angelina are somehow involved in his murder," Andy stated.

Andy told Leila he would ask de Ville to look into other unsolved or, if possible, unreported rapes, though he wasn't sure how he would be able to uncover unreported rapes. Perhaps Karina Hummels, now that she had finally come forward, could act as a spokesperson for the presumed other women and ask them to report the rapes—if they'd occurred. Leila then requested that Andy brief her on the new information that Alvarez had uncovered. Although Alvarez had texted Leila, she'd asked Andy to contact him, figuring it made sense for the same person to contact de Ville and Alvarez following their return to the United States, in case some of the information from one of the discussions would trigger questions for the other discussion.

"So, what are we going to be doing in New York, besides celebrating New Year's? What made Alvarez so anxious that he needed us to come back to New York so soon?" Leila asked.

"Let me start by saying that it is amazing what you can do with computers, phones, and the Internet these days. I mean, these tech advances have become indispensable, but ..." Andy paused.

"But what?"

"But everything you do leaves a permanent footprint. It's really quite frightening, if you stop to think about it. I am sure you know that tapping Delete and emptying your recycle bin or trash doesn't forever eliminate that e-mail or text message you sent that you wish you hadn't sent," Andy began.

"What does this have to do with the case?"

"The New York Police Department now has a forensic-information technology team that apparently can in little time find that e-mail you sent to a friend ten years ago."

"Oh, really," Leila said with a doubtful tone.

"Yes, and they can also go into Mr. Millbank's computer and Empire Health's servers and find every e-mail he ever sent and received, regardless of whether he deleted it or not," Andy continued, hinting at what was to come.

"And what did they find, do tell?" Leila pleaded, intrigued.

Andy explained that the forensic tech experts had searched all of Mr. Millbank's files, e-mails, etc., looking for anything possibly related to the case, like a disgruntled employee, an upset patient, or anything salacious like sexual innuendo or the like. At Leila's request, he explained to the extent that he understood it how the tech experts could conduct multiple searches using complicated algorithms to find the proverbial needle in the haystack among tens of thousands of e-mails and thousands of files.

"They found one e-mail exchange where Mr. Millbank used a personal e-mail account that had the name Alexa in it," Andy stated, and he opened a file on his computer.

"Here is the exchange," Andy added, pointing toward the screen of his iPhone.

July 23, 10:35 a.m.
craynyc@gmail.com

Hi Alexa, last night was incredible. I can't wait to see you again. J

July 23, 11:07 a.m.
axela@hotmail.com

Creighton, please don't ever mention my name in an e-mail or text—only in person. I have a reputation to uphold, and I need to be 100 percent discreet. So do you, by the way.

July 23, 11:23 a.m.
craynyc@gmail.com

Sorry. I'll call you later.

"Interesting," Leila said, "but doesn't seem very helpful. We already knew they were seeing each other. This just confirms that it goes back at least four months before Millbank died."

"Well, that's not the interesting part, actually," Andy replied. "Then I don't get how this helps."

"It's not so much the exchange, other than it confirms who the two parties were," Andy stated. "Craynyc is Creighton Millbank, and—"

"Axela is Alexa spelled backward—not all that discreet, if you ask me," Leila said, smiling. "But I still don't see how this helps."

"The forensic tech experts were able to determine the IP address of the computer from which Alexa sent her message and, well, you're not going to believe this, but ..." Andy took a breath. "It was sent from a computer in New York Hospital."

"Get out! Really!" Leila responded, her voice rising again.

Andy put his hand up and moved it palm down toward the ground indicating to Leila to keep her voice down. Despite his gesture, though, he thoroughly enjoyed seeing Leila get so excited.

"Yes, and that's not all. They were able to trace it to a computer in the department of pathology," Andy continued.

Leila stared wide-eyed at Andy, her eyebrows rising in anticipation. But she was let down somewhat when Andy told her that the computer they'd traced it to was a public computer used in the conference room and that while mostly the pathologists and their fellows and residents would use it, it could have been used by anyone from the chief of pathology, to a medical student, to the cleaning staff.

"How about fingerprints?" Leila asked. Andy laughed.

"That was my first thought, but Alvarez said such a public computer would have so many users that it would not be possible to even lift a clean print off."

"Can the tech experts look for digital fingerprints?" Leila inquired.

"Great minds think alike—I asked the same question. They said that they could try to see who had been logged in at the time the message was sent, but that may not be possible, and even if they could find out, people leave their log-ins open on such computers all the time, which could result in falsely accusing someone who is only guilty of not logging off a publicly utilized computer. Alvarez thought that since the subject was so sensitive—cheating, sex—that he wanted to avoid any chance of that happening."

"Makes sense. So, with all of this new and fascinating information, I am not quite sure what we are going to be doing in New York to further the investigation," Leila replied.

Andy explained that Alvarez had suggested the two of them spend some time in the hospital, inconspicuously looking around and trying to determine who Alexa might be. Alvarez explained that while it was true that numerous people had access to this specific computer, it was likely that the user was familiar with the conference room and the computer and wasn't just someone who'd wandered into a room that was often locked. Alvarez stated that his own investigation at the hospital, and the tech team's intuition, was that there were hundreds of other computers in the hospital that were far more anonymous than the one in the pathology conference room and which a random individual could have used. Andy told Leila that they would be granted access to the pathology area under the guise of a research project they were working on with Lisa Goldberg, their hematology colleague and the bleeding-disorders expert at New York Hospital. He had already secured their ID tags, which would grant them access to all public places in the pathology department.

"Andy, what are we going to be looking for, exactly?"

"Alexa. She, or whoever she really is, could hold the key to uncovering the circumstances of Millbank's murder—even give us the murderer."

"I don't get it. Alvarez knows what she looks like, right, and he hasn't found her, so how are we going to find her?" Leila asked, with a hint of desperation in her voice.

"I'm not sure, but I have a hunch we will." Andy smiled. "Just use the same brilliant intuition you used to identify Karina Hummels on that video from the Gstaad conference."

They spent the rest of the flight in silence, each of them listening to music and reading. Andy chose a recent offering from Yes, the famous progressive rock band who had had their heyday decades ago. The title of the album he chose was *Fly from Here*; it featured for the first time a vocalist other than the high-pitched, airy Jon Anderson. With songs titled "We Can Fly from Here,"

"The Man You Always Wanted Me to Be," and "Into the Storm," it felt somehow to be an appropriate selection.

Following landing, Andy and Leila switched on their iPhones, almost expecting another enticing text message, and they were not disappointed. Following the electronic triple tone on Andy's iPhone, they glanced at the message together while still seated on the plane.

Andy, call me. I have some information on Bryan Vasquez

Andy and Leila looked at each other, smiled, and shook their heads.

CHAPTER 23

"Good morning." Sean O'Reilly welcomed Andy and Leila into the same familiar conference room they had been seated in just weeks earlier prior to heading to Norway. "Good morning," Andy and Leila replied simultaneously.

In front of them lay a tray with some large and fresh-looking bagels and small containers of cream cheese, along with juices, coffee, and water. They each happily placed a bagel on a plate and began eating. After all, bagels were Andy's favorite New York treat, and Los Angeles had failed him miserably in being able to replicate the texture and taste of a New York bagel.

"Good morning," Detective Alvarez greeted them as he walked into the conference room looking a good deal more refreshed than the last time they'd seen him. In fact, they also noted that Detective O'Reilly was in a far different mood than when they had last seen him. Neither Andy nor Leila could quite put their finger on it, short of sensing that O'Reilly seemed to be happier.

Alvarez continued, "I want to thank you both so much for coming back to New York so soon after getting back to Los Angeles following your long trip to Europe. You are both doing a great job, and the

248

investigation, which seemed stalled just a few weeks ago, is now moving forward at an excellent pace."

"I want to add my two cents," O'Reilly began. "We were getting frustrated, taking a lot of shit from our superiors. I was beginning to think we would never find out what happened, but I am sure now, with you on board, that we will solve this damned case. You know that the papers are calling it 'the mystery of the Bleeders,' so we decided that is what we'll call it, too."

"I am glad you have such confidence in us, but I have to admit it is a bit intimidating. I mean, we may not figure this out. There are still so many holes and I—I don't know, Detective," Andy said hesitantly.

"We'll figure it out," Leila boldly stated. "I am confident we will figure it out—of course, with your help and the help of Detective de Ville."

"That's the spirit!" Alvarez responded. "Andy, you need to work on your self-confidence."

Leila laughed, looked at Andy, and said, "You can say that again."

She stared into Andy's eyes and gave a quick wink and slight smile as if to say "just teasing."

"Let's review what we'd like you to do," Alvarez replied in a matter-of-fact tone, clearly moving the team past the small talk. "It's another situation where having doctors on the case has become a necessity."

He explained that they had good reason to believe that Mr. Millbank's alleged mistress, Alexa, worked at New York Hospital, possibly in the pathology department. He reminded them of two important facts. First, that Alexa had been on her way to see Mr. Millbank at the Plaza Hotel on the day he'd died, and second, that Mrs. Millbank, while trying to find out who Alexa was, had followed her several times from a meeting with her husband, and the trail had ended at the front entrance to the hospital. Based on this information and the e-mail traced to the pathology computer, they were virtually certain that Alexa worked in the hospital. Alvarez provided a grainy photograph of Alexa, taken that day in the Plaza Hotel with a surveillance video. He then handed them their New York Hospital ID tags, which he explained were coded with a magnetic strip that security had programmed to allow them access to all of the rooms in the pathology department, with the exception of the doctors' and other staff's private offices. He reviewed the pretext under which they were working in the pathology department and gave them a flash drive with the fictitious research study's files. He instructed them to study those files well, as doubtless they would be asked what they were doing in the pathology department. Finally, he told them that their first meeting was to be with Lisa Goldberg, to "review" the study. She would then escort them to the pathology department and introduce them to the staff.

"Any questions?" Alvarez asked.

"I have one," Leila said. "Since you have this picture of Alexa, and since all the hospital employees have a picture ID, can't you cross-reference this picture with the hospital database?"

"Brilliant, as usual, and I hate to disappoint you, Leila, but we are pretty smart detectives, and we indeed thought of that. Unfortunately, the picture of Alexa from the surveillance video is pretty grainy, and her face is not fully visible—it is not a straight-on shot like the ID photos—so the facial recognition software has not been able to make a match. We are trying to find other pictures from the other places we know Alexa has been, but we haven't been able to find a better picture," Alvarez replied.

"What about hospital surveillance cameras?" Andy asked.

"Another good idea, and I am glad you brought that up. We thought of that too, and have been through literally thousands of images and had our computer programs scour them, but still no match," O'Reilly replied.

"Isn't that odd," Leila said, "and doesn't that shoot a hole in the theory that Alexa is a hospital employee?"

"Not really. We are very confident that she works in the hospital. One possibility is that she disguised herself, but that is just a guess," Alvarez replied.

"Disguised herself as Alexa or as the hospital employee?" Leila asked. "Either/or, but I think it would be easier to disguise herself as Alexa,"

answered O'Reilly. "Good questions. Anything else?"

"When do we get started?" Leila asked.

"Right now. We set up a meeting with Dr. Goldberg at 10:30, so let's get going," Alvarez said and got up from his seat at the conference-room table.

Andy and Leila got up as well, but not before Andy had grabbed another bagel. Leila looked at him, and Andy let out a sheepish smile and took a bite.

They arrived at Lisa's office after a short ride along Manhattan's east side.

Lisa hugged them both warmly.

"Andy, you have poppy seeds in your teeth," she said, and a chorus of laughs erupted from the detectives and Leila.

"Serves you right, you bagel hog," Leila said, still laughing as Andy's face turned bright red and he excused himself to find the bathroom.

"Sean and I have some other cases we need to follow up on, so we're going to move along," Alvarez said. "Tell Andy we'll save him some bagels tomorrow morning when we regroup."

"Better make them egg bagels or plain ones—I don't think Andy is going to eat one with seeds on it for a while, if I know him," Leila said.

Andy returned, and the tone of conversation turned more serious. Lisa explained that she had been mostly kept in the dark about what Andy and Leila were supposed to be doing at the hospital. All she had been asked to do was come up with the skeleton of a research project that could serve as a pretext to allow them to spend time in the pathology department. She was curious, however.

"So, I assume this is about the murder of the bleeding dead guy, but can you tell me why they want you in the pathology department?" Lisa asked.

Andy puffed his cheeks. "Lisa, I'm sorry, but we were told we can't tell anyone anything about the case—they are worried about leaks and compromising the investigation."

"Fair enough, but does this mean they suspect someone in the pathology department of being involved?"

Andy just shook his head, insinuating that he couldn't answer her question, but he thanked her for playing her part in helping them and assured her that he would tell her as soon as he was allowed to, though he had no idea how long that might take.

They left Lisa's office on the sixth floor and headed to the pathology department, which was in the basement of the main building. On the way, Lisa told them that she'd met with the chief of pathology, Caroline Simmons (who happened to be the only African American department head in the whole hospital) and had explained that Andy and Leila were friends and colleagues and were helping her with a research study on children with frequent nosebleeds. She'd told Dr. Simmons that Andy and Leila needed access to all the records of patients who had blood testing done that looked for platelet-function defects, a common cause of nosebleeds. When Leila asked if Dr. Simmons had asked any questions or seemed suspicious of anything, Lisa reassured her she was quite sure that she hadn't sensed anything out of the ordinary. Doctors and medical students from many different hospitals had made similar inquiries and spent time in the pathology area.

After a few long walks through hospital corridors, and two elevator rides, they arrived in the pathology department, where they were warmly greeted by Dr. Simmons. She gave them her office and pager number and told them to call her if they had any questions. Dr. Simmons was a very impressive woman: tall and articulate with a blazing smile. Leila said she reminded her of Michelle Obama, only with a white lab coat. Andy concurred. She led them to the pathology conference room—the very same one from where Alexa had sent her e-mail—and provided them with two computers. Andy told her they had been granted log-in usernames and passwords, and they would be able to access the information they needed without further help. Dr. Simmons left just as a young woman walked in, wearing a short lab coat that cut just below the waist.

"Hi, I'm Taylor Davis. I'm a medical student from Cornell. Are you Dr. Simmons?" she asked Leila.

"Uh, no, no. We are visitors too. We're just here doing research. My name is Leila Baker, and this is Andy Friedman; we're pediatric hematologists from Los Angeles."

"Oh, cool. I'd like to go to LA one of these days. Is it as awesome as it seems on TV?"

Andy and Leila both laughed. It was not the first time they had heard such a comment about their city. Hollywood had done well to cultivate an image of "coolness" for Los Angeles, and it remained a big draw for the young and ambitious who dreamed of the kind of life neatly glorified in movies and television shows.

"It's not that cool," Leila replied.

"Still, I'd like to go there one day—at least for a visit. I have rarely ever left Manhattan, if you can believe that," Ms. Davis responded.

"What year are you in?" Andy asked.

"I'm a third year doing a rotation in pathology now. It's kind of boring, though."

"Maybe next year you can come to LA and spend a month with us as an elective," Leila offered.

"Really? That would be awesome!"

Leila gave Taylor one of her business cards and suggested she e-mail her next summer when she was planning her fourth-year electives. Taylor was elated.

"Don't get too excited about LA—you just might be disappointed. It's just another big city," Andy said.

"I doubt that. No one says New York is just another big city," Taylor replied. "So, where is Dr. Simmons—I am supposed to report to her?" They pointed her to the reception desk to get the help she needed. Andy and Leila felt confident that they'd passed their first test of explaining who they were and why they were there. Fortunately it had been an innocent and equally lost medical student.

They sat down at the computers and began working on their "research." The usernames and passwords that they'd been granted allowed them to access the hospital intranet, which gave them access to the pathology web page—which included the names and biographies of all the pathologists in the department. Leila opened her laptop and opened a Word file, which she used to distill the information from the pathology web page. There were forty-five pathologists altogether, of which twenty were women. Pathology was a popular field with women, in part due to the fairly predictable hours, which at least some women preferred. Leila typed the names of the twenty female pathologists, each on a new page of her document. Andy then opened the page for each of the women. The profile for each doctor included a photo and information regarding where she went to medical school, and where she did her residency and fellowship. It also stated each one's specific area of interest in pathology, such as surgical pathology or hematopathology, followed by a list of any papers that she'd authored in medical journals. Leila furiously typed the salient information that Andy was reading. Every few moments, Andy would look up at the open door at the front of the conference room to be sure no one was about to walk in and discover the true nature of their research. Leila and Andy agreed to keep the door open, sensing it would arouse fewer suspicions if someone walked in. After they had collected what they felt was the most important information on each of the female pathologists, Leila suggested they look at the picture they had of Alexa, however grainy it was, and see if they could match it to one of the web-page photos of the pathologists. Despite going back and forth from the grainy photo to each of the headshots on the web pages, they couldn't make a match. Andy told Leila that the case wouldn't be that easy.

"Did you really think we could find a match when Alvarez and the computer guys couldn't?" Andy asked.

"Sometimes women's intuition is more valuable than all the men and computers in the world, so it was worth a shot, but I agree I don't see a match."

"Remember, anyone could have sent an e-mail from here. You just saw how easy it was for a medical student to walk in," Andy said. "She could have chosen to sit at the computer in question, access her e-mail account, send an e-mail, and be off—it's that simple. While focusing on the pathologists is reasonable to start with, we need to find out what other groups might come in and use this conference room."

They decided that the front-desk receptionist would be a good target to question, since she sat like a sentry guarding the gates of some secret vault buried in a huge castle. They again used the pretext of their research to deflect suspicion.

"Hi, Shirley," Andy began, eyeing the nameplate on her desk. "We are from LA and are doing some research here. Since we plan on using the conference room quite a bit, I wonder if you could tell me who tends to use the room and when, so we can plan our schedule. We don't want to interfere with anyone else's activities."

"Oh, well, there are several conferences each week with the pathologists," she said, and she listed four weekly meetings involving several other departments: oncology, gastroenterology, surgery, and nephrology.

Leila cajoled the list of the usual participants from Shirley, though Shirley informed them that there were often guests, including medical students and residents, as well as others. They thanked her and returned to the computer, looking at the web pages for each of these departments. Fortunately for the sake of their investigation, the number of women in these departments was relatively small, and Leila noted each one of them in her new file. They decided to break for lunch and called Lisa, who was happy to meet them in the main cafeteria.

They sat together eating in silence. Leila sensed the tension and decided to break the ice.

"What, Andy, no bagel for lunch?" Leila said and laughed.

"Very funny. Do I have something in my teeth again?" Andy asked sarcastically.

"You're such a Jew," Lisa said with brio; she felt that the oft-stated excuse of being Jewish herself provided her with immunity from what would otherwise be construed as an anti-Semitic slur.

Leila pounced on the opportunity and added, "Imagine if I said that as a Muslim—I could probably go to jail."

"I didn't know you were Muslim," Lisa stated matter-of-factly. "Yup," Leila responded proudly, "and Kurdish."

"Really. I think you might be the first Kurd I ever met," Lisa said.

"I doubt that—we are everywhere, but since we don't have a homeland, we are often mistaken as Turkish or Iraqi."

"Which one is your family from? Lisa asked.

"Those aren't the only countries Kurds are from. You can add Iran, Syria, and Armenia, at the very least, to that list, but I was born in Iraq, and my family moved to the US after the first Gulf War."

"Wow. I would have thought you were born in the USA—you seem, how shall I put this ... uh, very American."

"Well, I am, right down to my American passport. Aren't most Americans from somewhere else?"

"Sure, I suppose it is just a matter of generations," Lisa added, and then she went on. "Can I ask you something personal?"

"You can ask me whatever you like, but I reserve the right to refuse to answer," Leila stated bluntly.

"Are you expected to marry a Muslim? And I am only asking because if I am dating someone who isn't Jewish, my parents freak out."

"I am definitely supposed to marry a Muslim, but I don't know that I will," Leila responded, as Andy stirred uncomfortably in his seat, decidedly unhappy with the direction the conversation had turned.

"Will your parents accept someone who is Christian?" Lisa asked.

"Why just Christian? What about Jews, Hindus, or others?" Leila replied. "Jews!" Lisa exclaimed wild-eyed. "I don't think there is any chance of that happening."

Andy fidgeted nervously, not sure if or how he should join the conversation or, better yet, turn it toward a completely different direction.

"Why can't I marry a Jew?" Leila asked, clearly getting annoyed.

"Well, it's like oil and water—they don't mix well together. Don't you agree?"

"Not at all. The problem is the perception that people like you have. We are all just people, aren't we? Maybe I can figure out a way to arrange a date for you with a handsome, intelligent, successful, and Muslim man, only I'll figure out a way to ensure that you have no idea he's Muslim until after you meet."

"I'm sorry. I know that sounded bigoted, and it is not that I have a negative views of Muslims. It's just that I think a Jew and Muslim together—well, it would be difficult."

"Only in your close-minded view!" Leila exclaimed and got up and walked away.

"Sorry, Andy, I, uh, didn't mean to …" Lisa began as Andy got up and chased after Leila.

Leila walked swiftly toward the far end of the cafeteria, where the restrooms were; Andy picked up the pace to catch her and reached her just as she was about to enter the bathroom. He gently grabbed her and turned her face slowly toward his, only to discover a stream of tears flowing from her eyes down her face like condensed water dripping down the outside of an ice-cold glass of water. She looked at Andy's face, held his eyes for a moment, and then pushed him away and barged through the bathroom door, leaving Andy helplessly watching as the door closed behind her. Lisa caught up to him and tapped him on the shoulder.

"Is everything okay?"

Andy turned to Lisa and gritted his teeth; he was ready to explode. But he gathered his composure and let out a deep sigh.

"No. It's not okay. You see …" Andy began, but then he stopped. "What? What is it?" Lisa asked.

"Do me a favor, and just leave me alone … please," Andy pleaded. "I'm sorry. I—"

"It's okay. I just need to be alone now."

Lisa turned and walked slowly away, unsure of how she'd provoked such a sudden turn of emotions.

Andy waited and waited, pacing back and forth like a family member standing outside of an emergency room anxiously expecting someone to emerge and report the condition of a family member. And like a worried family member, he felt his stomach turning in knots; the pangs increasing with each passing minute. At last Leila emerged; her face was cleaned up and she appeared to be back to normal. Andy embraced her warmly, and the knots in his stomach calmed, only to return in an even more violent and sharply painful twist than before, as he comprehended Leila's whispered proclamation.

"It's over. I'm sorry."

CHAPTER 24

A ndy woke up in his hotel room to the ring of his iPhone. By the time he reached it, he had missed the call. In the fog of his half-awakened state, he couldn't recall if yesterday's nightmarish conversation with Lisa at lunch had been a nightmare or been real. As the fog cleared and his mind sharpened, he sat up on the edge of the bed, looked out the window at the gray winter dawn, and came to the sad realization that the romantic part of his relationship with Leila had come to a sudden, crushing end. Moreover, he was increasingly concerned that his friendship and working relationship with her might be on the brink as well. These thoughts left him unsettled. He set out to clear his mind with a walk in the cold, gloomy New York morning. After showering and dressing, he grabbed his phone, almost forgetting the call that had awakened him nearly an hour ago. He'd figured it might be Lisa, or worse yet, Leila, and chosen to ignore it. However, when he glanced at it, he noted the number was international. Fortunately, the author of the call had left a voice mail.

Andy, is everything okay? I texted you two days ago and haven't heard back. Please call.

It was Felix's unmistakable voice and accent. Andy felt bad that he hadn't called back; however, he elected to take his walk first and call back later. As he exited the hotel wearing just a sweatshirt and jeans, the concierge informed him that it was twenty degrees outside and that he would be cold, but Andy proceeded as if on a time-sensitive mission. As he exited the hotel, the frigid air punched his face and pierced his throat; it felt as if he were inhaling small shards of ice. After stopping momentarily, he began to walk briskly across Central Park West, entering Central Park not far from where Mr. Millbank had been killed. Although the cold penetrated his body to the core, Andy kept moving, at first a brisk walk, then practically speed-walking, and finally breaking into a jog. It was all he could do to keep warm. As his heart pumped harder and harder, more and more blood reached his brain, and more and more clarity came to his mind. He felt better. He kept running. No human was in sight. The more he ran, the better he felt. Running in the freezing cold, with his body now warm, he felt exhilarated—even euphoric. *This must be what athletes feel when they reach that endorphin high*, he thought. He finally reached the east side of the park and the limits of his endurance, and he stopped. He was sweating, but the small, warm beads quickly cooled. The freezing air became slowly more noticeable once again. Andy thought about starting to jog again, but he was too tired. He stopped on Fifth Avenue, glanced around, and spotted a Starbucks. He headed there for a break and a drink.

He got a bottle of water and a vanilla latte, a curious combination, but he needed to rehydrate and recaffeinate. As he drank his water, he remembered the call from Felix, pulled out his phone, and dialed.

"Felix, Andy here. I am so sorry I forgot to call back. I was on board a plane when you called a couple of days ago, and after I landed I forgot to call, and then yesterday—well, anyway, sorry."

"No problem. I just want to relay some interesting information to you," Felix replied.

"You always do, my friend. Go on."

"Do you even remember what you asked me to look into?"

"Sorry, no. It's been such a whirlwind," Andy replied, embarrassed. "Does the name Bryan Vasquez ring a bell?"

"Yes, of course. He's the brother of one of my—oh, yeah, now I remember. God, I hope you didn't find out anything I don't want to hear," Andy stated, suddenly recalling that Bryan's sister had said he had been to Norway.

"Well, this Bryan has been doing some serious travelling recently," Felix replied.

"He works for an oil company, as an engineer, so I'm sure—"

Felix cut him off. "Andy, he has been to Norway, as you know, and yes, to Stavanger, the major oil-industry city, but he's also been to Tromsø—and Andy, there's no oil up there."

"Oh my God. Perhaps he was just sightseeing. It is possible that it's just an innocent trip."

"Not in November. No one goes on holiday to Tromsø in November. Trust me. It's dark, cold, rainy, and snowy. No festivals. No Aurora. And that's not all, Andy."

"Oh no. What else?" Andy asked with a resigned, despondent tone.

"After this revelation, I decided to look a bit more into his travels than you had asked." Felix paused momentarily and then continued, "Andy, he went from Tromsø to Oslo for a few days, and then he flew to Switzerland on November 10—less than two weeks before the murder of Mr. Stern."

"Say it ain't so, Felix," Andy responded.

"Indeed he did—I have proof from immigration that he entered Switzerland at the Zurich airport."

"It could just be a coincidence, don't you think?" Andy said in a hopeful tone.

"It's not," Felix replied confidently. "I have investigated enough murders to know that this is no coincidence. Nevertheless, there is one thing that is difficult to explain."

"What's that?" Andy wondered, his voice filled with optimism that his patient's brother would be exculpated by this additional information.

"He left on November 15—seven days before Mr. Stern was murdered."

Andy was thrilled and relieved, stating that it meant Bryan could not have been the killer.

"Perhaps, but we don't know the manner of death, and I wouldn't rule him out based solely on that," Felix said.

"Come on, Felix. He couldn't have killed him if he wasn't in Switzerland the day of the murder—especially if he left more than ten days before the murder," Andy protested.

"Andy, there is one more fact that adds to my suspicions of Mr. Vasquez."

"You're kidding me. What else could there be?"

"He flew from Zurich to New York the day he left. That would place him in New York shortly before Mr. Millbank was murdered."

"So? He might have had a meeting there, or he was going to spend Thanksgiving there, or he might not have been able to get on the flight to LA."

"No, Andy, you are wrong, and you need to rid yourself of this bias and think objectively if you are to continue to be part of this investigation. I looked into your alternatives and can tell you that there were plenty of seats on the Zurich to LA flight that day. He wasn't simply transiting through JFK, because he didn't leave New York until November 23—the day after the murder."

"Okay. You're right, Felix. I'm sorry. My emotions momentarily got the best of me. Trust me, I want to get to the bottom of this as much as you do."

"Fair enough."

"Do O'Reilly and Alvarez know about this?" Andy asked. "No, I wanted to tell you first."

"Thanks."

"I think we need to tell them now, though—do you want to do that, or would you rather I do it?" Felix queried.

"You do it. We are meeting with them later today. If you can inform them soon, we'll review this as a group and decide where to go next."

"Very well, then. Say hi to Leila for me." And with that, the phone call ended.

Andy's mind was swirling with so many thoughts and so many emotions going to and fro, from Bryan Vasquez, to Leila, and back again. It was like being seated courtside at a tennis match, head and mind going from one side of the court to the other and back again. He finished his water and coffee and grabbed a taxi back to the hotel. The concierge was right—it was too cold to be walking outside.

Leila hadn't left her room in nearly twenty-four hours. She'd slept for twelve hours and was contemplating her next move. She yo-yoed back and forth between only leaving the investigation all the way to extricating herself from everything related to Andy—the investigation, her job at CHLA, and her friendship and relationship with Andy. She felt sick to her stomach and hadn't had anything to eat or drink in all the time she'd been in her room. She felt she needed to get out and get some fresh air, not to mention something in her stomach. As she stood from the bed, she felt a sharp pain in her lower back. *That's what you get for being in bed for twenty-four hours*, she thought. She walked over to the window, put both hands to her head, and then lifted a bunch of her thick black hair in a stretching motion. She stared at the gray skies and bare, brown trees of Central Park far below. She then bent at the waist, keeping her legs straight, beckoning the sore muscles of her legs and back to loosen. Arching her lithe upper body from side to side, she continued to coax her muscles to stretch out the effects of excessive sleep. After several minutes, she walked back to the window. She couldn't help but wonder where Andy was, though she wasn't sure that she cared. She checked her phone and was simultaneously relieved and annoyed that Andy hadn't tried to communicate with her. She decided not to call or send him a text message. She needed to shower. With her muscles more limber, a steaming hot shower was in order.

Leila was quite sure her forty-five-minute shower had used up all the hot water the hotel tanks had. She felt better. She got dressed and headed out. She decided to head to the Metropolitan Museum of Art on Fifth Avenue. She'd never been there and decided this would be the best, and perhaps only, opportunity she'd have. She also hoped that focusing on the art and the tranquil nature of the museum would calm her frayed nerves.

Andy's taxi pulled up to the hotel moments after Leila left. He thought about calling Leila, but he was in no mood to get into *that* conversation again. The cold air, his run through the park, and de Ville's phone call had rallied his spirits and focused his mind squarely back on the investigation, and he had no intention of letting the good vibe be gutted by talking to Leila. He got back to the room, showered, and was preparing for his meeting with O'Reilly and Alvarez at the police station, scheduled for 2:00 p.m. *But what about Leila?* he thought then. They were supposed to go there together, of course. He decided an impersonal text message was the best approach.

> *Hey there, are you planning on coming to the police station with me?*

Andy waited. No reply. It was almost noon, and he needed some lunch. He got dressed and, rather than brave the cold again, headed down to the hotel restaurant. At 12:20 there was still no reply from Leila. He was sure she'd gotten the message but completely unsure as to her whereabouts or whether she would respond. He ordered lunch.

Leila sat at a nearby vegetarian restaurant and ordered a salad with mixed greens and sliced ahi tuna and a glass of water. She looked at her phone, glanced at Andy's message for the third time, and shook her head. *What am I going to do? I need some advice,* she thought to herself. She decided to call her mom, who had always been a great source of wisdom. She had comforted Leila on the trip from Iraq and upon their arrival in Michigan and then California, and Leila needed her levelheaded and sage advice now more than ever.

"Mom."

"Leila, such a pleasure to hear from you, darling. How are you?" came her mother's comforting accented voice.

"I'm okay."

"No, your voice tells me you're not okay," her mom replied with a mother's intuition. "What's the matter, dear?"

"I need some advice."

"Yes, dear. Tell me what's bothering you."

"Andy and I are no longer a couple—I guess you can say we broke up, but that sounds silly, considering we were in a relationship for less than a month." Leila let out an awkward laugh.

"It's true it was short, but you had spent so much time together that it was a more mature relationship than is usual for one that is so short," her mother responded.

"Yeah, that's so true. I have one friend who has been seeing someone for four months or so, and I know Andy and I have spent way more time together."

"So, why suddenly there is a problem?" asked her mom, who still occasionally lapsed into grammatically incorrect English.

Leila explained to her mother what had transpired the day before and how that had made her feel that her dad had been right about her not getting involved with a Jewish man. She told her mom that she was more determined than ever to meet a Muslim man, and preferably a Kurd.

"You may be waiting a long time then, you know."

"Yes, I know, but that is what I feel I should do. Am I making a mistake?"

"Darling, you have always had great instincts, and you are very emotionally intelligent. You should decide what you want based not on Father's feelings or mine, but on yours and only yours," her mother said.

"Thanks, Mom. You always know how to make me feel better," Leila responded. There was renewed confidence in her voice.

"Just follow your instincts, and if they are telling you to find a Muslim man, then this is what you should do."

"I will, Mom. Thank you so much—as always."

"I love you, Leila."

"I love you too, Mom."

The conversation elevated Leila's mood. She knew now what she had to do.

Andy, sorry, I was talking to my mom. I'll meet you at the hotel lobby at 1:30.

Andy waited a few minutes on purpose, in part not to sound too eager and in part in an attempt to annoy Leila. Then he typed his two-letter response.

OK

Andy was relieved that Leila had texted him back. While he had no illusions about the status of their relationship, he had hoped she would continue to work on the investigation with him. They had formed a formidable partnership and had made more headway than any of the experienced detectives had thought possible. He couldn't walk away now, despite the emotional anguish he was feeling, and now he sensed Leila couldn't either. After finishing his lunch, he sat in the lobby and waited for Leila to arrive. He spent the next twenty minutes contemplating how to greet her. He still felt the sting of Leila's sharp comments to him when they'd met at LAX just two days ago, but their relationship had taken on a decidedly different tone now. The one positive was that he didn't care now if Leila didn't like how he greeted her. Then he saw her walk in. He got up and walked over to her.

"Hi, Leila. Are ..." he hesitated momentarily and then proceeded. "Are you okay?"

"Yes, I'm fine. Thanks. I had a good talk with my mom, and I feel a lot better. How about you?"

"I'm fine too," he replied.

"Look—" Leila started, but Andy interrupted.

"I don't want to talk about it. You said we were over, and I will come to accept that. I understand why, and it's okay."

Andy responded with the most confident voice he had ever shown Leila when discussing their relationship. Leila was rather stunned, the way Lois Lane was when she heard Clark Kent speak in Superman's voice for the first time.

"Fair enough," Leila said.

"Let's focus on the case," Andy said. "Agreed."

They arrived at the police station right on time and were whisked into the now-familiar conference room. No bagels this time, though. In fact, there was no food. O'Reilly and Alvarez were seated at the table, with files stuffed with paper in front of them and stern-looking faces.

O'Reilly opened the discussion. "Hi, Andy. Hi, Leila. Let's get started. We've got a lot to do."

"Sure thing," Andy answered.

"I understand you spoke to de Ville this morning, right?" Alvarez asked. "Yes, I did, and—" Andy was interrupted.

"Is Leila up to speed?" Alvarez continued.

"No, uh, sorry, we didn't get a chance to talk after—" Andy was again interrupted. He noted that the detectives were in an altogether different frame of mind today. Determined—more so than he had noted previously.

"No problem. I think it's a good time to review everything anyway," O'Reilly interjected. "Jose, go ahead."

Detective Alvarez stepped to a white board, where he had summarized the case thus far. There were three columns with the headings: New York, Norway, and Switzerland. Under each were listed the names of individuals. Under New York, the list included Creighton Millbank—deceased, Julie Millbank, Alexa, Lisa Goldberg, Jennifer Carmichael, Vinh Tran, and Mr. Ridgewell.

"Why do you have those names—are they all suspects?" Leila asked curiously.

"No, not at all. These are just the names of the key people we have interviewed in the case. It is not a suspect list, for sure. We don't suspect Mr. Ridgewell, for example," Alvarez answered.

"Why not? He was at the scene of the crime, after all," Leila replied with renewed focus. Andy wondered if she had erased her memory since yesterday's breakdown.

"That's a fair question, Jose," O'Reilly chimed in.

Alvarez continued. "You're right. We have not ruled anyone out, but I am stressing that while this might look like a list of suspects, it is not intended to be that. Let me move on to Norway. Here we have just two names: Jan Erik Bergeland and Bryan Vasquez."

"What the hell! Why is Bryan listed there? Andy, what is this?" Leila was clearly shocked to see his name on the board.

"Go ahead, Andy, I think you need to explain that one," Alvarez said. "Remember I told you that Bryan's sister told me he had been going to Norway—" Andy began, but Leila interrupted.

"That was for work, Andy. He's in the oil industry."

"I know, but I had de Ville look into his travels. It turns out he didn't just go there for his work with ExxonMobil."

"How do you know that? Come on, Andy; there is no way that he's involved in this."

"Because he went to Tromsø, Leila."

"So, he might have had a meeting up there for work."

"No, Leila, he didn't—we checked with his boss," Alvarez added.

"So, he could have gone up there for some vacation time," Leila continued her defense of Bryan Vasquez.

"No one goes to Tromsø for vacation in November. Remember, we were there just after he had been there and … well, you saw it for yourself," Andy said.

"Well, that's pretty thin if you ask me."

"Okay, fair enough, but what if I told you he went from Tromsø to Switzerland?" Alvarez moved the conversation forward.

"He did that?" Leila responded, surprised. Her tone was much less defiant as she scanned the faces of the three men in the room, and she came to the same realization they had hours earlier.

"Do you know if he was in Basel?" she asked.

"No. Not yet, anyway. We are checking with rental-car companies in Zurich, where he flew into, and running his credit-card statement to see if he purchased a train ticket, but we have little doubt that he did," Alvarez responded.

"Leila, two other facts regarding Bryan. First, he left Switzerland seven days before the murder, and then …" Andy paused for a moment, "he came to New York. He left New York the day after Mr. Millbank was found dead."

"You're kidding me! What—what does all this mean?" Leila said. She was stunned.

"That is why we're meeting here today—to brainstorm ideas. Let me finish first, though, with the last column." Alvarez continued working the white board.

Under the last column, headed by Switzerland, were the following names: Andreas Stern—deceased, Mrs. Stern, Philippe Boudreaux, Reto Ingler, Angelina Costa, Karina Hummels, Bryan Vasquez.

"So, anyone care to start—just say whatever comes to mind," O'Reilly stated. "Bryan Vasquez is the only one on all three lists," Leila noted.

"There are only two names under Norway," added Andy.

"Good, so let's start there. We are alleging that Bryan Vasquez had a meeting with Jan Erik Bergeland in Norway. But why?" Alvarez said.

They all stared at the board but said nothing. Then Leila broke the silence. "We know Bergeland threatened Mr. Stern, from the e-mails Reto uncovered and from Boudreaux's interview—but wait a minute! Andy, oh my God! No, I don't even want to say it."

"Say it!" O'Reilly demanded.

"That's what they have in common! They both had a problem with Mr. Stern. You see, Bryan's older sister died last year from a pulmonary embolism—er, a blood clot in the lungs. She had not responded to any of the treatments we had, and we tried to get her on Lyzanda, but her insurance denied it due to the cost. The family couldn't afford the astronomical price—something like twenty-dollars per day—so they kept her on Coumadin, which we knew wasn't working that well for her. I suppose he might be blaming Stern, the CEO, for charging an unaffordable price for a medication that could have saved his sister's life."

"You're brilliant, Leila. That's it! That has to be the connection between Bergeland and Bryan Vasquez!" Alvarez exclaimed.

"Fine, I agree with that, but what could they accomplish in Tromsø? Something is still missing," Andy added.

"Indeed, and we need to figure out what the missing piece is," O'Reilly stated. "Let's move on to New York, then. Any thoughts?"

The group seemed at a loss as they tried to weave connections between the main players, save for the obvious ones, such as the fact that Lisa Goldberg and Jennifer Carmichael knew each other through work. Leila suggested they start with Bryan again; however, there was no clear connection between Bryan and anyone else on the list. For once, Leila didn't seem to spark the investigation. Alvarez suggested they move on to the Switzerland list. They again acknowledged the already-established connection between Angelina Costa and Karina Hummels, but they couldn't make any other connections, least of all with Bryan Vasquez. Then, as if shot from a cannon, Leila jumped up, ran to the white board, and drew a line—not between two people from the same column but between two people from different columns.

"I don't get it," O'Reilly said.

"Me neither," Alvarez followed.

"What kind of memory do you guys have—do you guys drink too much?" Leila said, tongue in cheek, raising the eyebrows of her expressive face.

O'Reilly fidgeted in his seat, uncomfortable with the reference to drinking too much.

"Andy, come on—think!" Leila urged.

"Yes, yes, I remember! Leila, tell them," Andy responded.

Leila's smile spread across her cheeks. Andy gazed at her glowing face and for a fleeting moment felt sorrow but just as quickly suppressed the feeling.

"How did you find out there were two dead guys, the bleeders, as you call them?" Leila challenged the detectives.

"Yes, the Great Coincidence—I see where you are going with this," Alvarez replied, himself now standing up and walking toward the white board. "Go on, Leila."

"Detective O'Reilly, we found out about the second case when Jennifer Carmichael e-mailed Angelina Costa to get some advice. They know each other. That's the connection."

"Yes, I remember that now, but I am not sure what you are trying to say," O'Reilly said.

"Well, I'm not sure either, but let me think aloud for a moment," Leila continued. "Angelina Costa clearly has a motive to kill Mr. Stern—he raped her and she found out he was at least a double rapist, right? Angelina knows Dr. Carmichael, as they are both pathologists and they trained together here in New York."

Leila hesitated momentarily, looking at her three colleagues and hoping one of them would draw some inspiration from her suggestion. And just then it hit her like a thunderbolt.

"Oh my God! I got it!" Leila exclaimed. "Pathologists. Department of Pathology. The computer. The e-mail sent from the computer in the pathology conference room."

"Yes, yes, I see where you are going with this now," Alvarez added, now in sync with Leila's thoughts.

Yet Andy and detective O'Reilly, who were still lost, just held their hands up. Just then, a young police officer stepped into the room and motioned Alvarez and O'Reilly to come with him without saying a word. He quietly said something to the two detectives out of earshot of Andy and Leila, and then Alvarez returned.

"We have to go. Unrelated case," Alvarez explained. "Well, who knows at this point if it's unrelated? Why don't the two of you take the rest of the day off? Leila, I think you know what we need to do next— I'll take care of the paperwork we will need. Stay in touch." And with that, O'Reilly and Alvarez were gone, leaving Andy and Leila together in the suddenly quiet conference room. It was awkward. Andy couldn't stand the awkward silence.

"Are you going to tell me what the hell is going on? Obviously I am missing something."

"I'll tell you tomorrow," Leila replied tersely. "And what paperwork was Alvarez talking about?"

"I'll tell you tomorrow," Leila politely repeated her prior answer.

"Fine, I don't want to argue with you." Andy resigned himself to being kept in suspense until the next day. "Now what?"

"What do you mean?"

"Leila, what are we going to do between now and tomorrow—that's what I mean," Andy asked, getting annoyed because he sensed Leila was being purposefully aloof.

"Look, Andy. When I said it was over, I meant that it will be too difficult for us to have a meaningful relationship, but we can still be friends."

How many times had Andy heard that one? He couldn't quite recall. He had even gone so far as to use that euphemistic soft landing himself several times when breaking up with girls. Of course, they never stayed friends. Men never stayed friends with women they had been romantically involved with. At least Andy never did. He knew that *We can still be friends* was the first step toward the end of any contact. It was the ultimate relationship oxymoron. Nevertheless, he needed to respond and find some way to make it until tomorrow when they could get back to being sleuths. No need to be friends then.

"Sure, we can still be friends. So, do you want to have dinner together later?"

"Yes, of course. I don't want to eat in my room by myself."

"You did yesterday," Andy replied sarcastically.

"No, yesterday …" Leila began and paused for a fleeting moment before completing her thought, "yesterday, I didn't eat. Now stop being an asshole, or you *will* be eating by yourself."

CHAPTER 25

DECEMBER 30

NEW YORK

ndy and Leila met promptly at 9:00 in the lobby. They'd had an uneventful dinner the night before, with the conversation consisting of office gossip, thus avoiding any discussion about their own strained relationship. They hopped into a taxi on yet another frigid winter morning. Leila directed the taxi driver to take them to the police station.

"Why are we going to the police station, Leila?"

"To pick up the papers, remember?"

"No, what papers?"

Leila told Andy she would tell him what the papers were for after she'd picked them up. Andy looked at Leila and rolled his eyes. His feelings regarding her great intuition in the case had changed from being the proud boyfriend to the jealous sibling. While she was *his* girl, he'd been proud of her and honored to be her significant other, despite the short duration of their romantic relationship, but now that she was no longer his girl, the pride had drained out of his body like the blood lost from a deep laceration. In fact, he'd started thinking she just made him look bad. During the drive, an icy coating of condensation lined their windows, obstructing any view of the city. The rest of the taxi ride was carried out in silence—the frost was not limited to the windows. They arrived at the police station and were taken by a uniformed officer to the conference room, where Alvarez greeted them.

"Let's go," he said.

"Oh, you're coming with us?" Andy said, surprised.

"Yes, sorry, but only a police officer can serve a search warrant. I thought I could get the judge to agree to let you serve it, since you were functioning like police officers, but she wasn't buying that, so I'll be joining you, if that's okay."

"Sure, no problem, but what search warrant are you talking about?" Andy asked.

"Leila didn't tell you?" Alvarez responded, surprised.

"No, she likes keeping me in suspense," Andy said, not hiding his annoyance. Leila smirked, the double meaning of Andy's statement clearly evident to her.

"We are going to search Jennifer Carmichael's office, and we have been approved to seize her computer and any laptops, flash drives, or other memory devices she has in there."

"Dr. Carmichael—not the nicest person in the world, but how did you swing a search warrant?"

"Andy, I think she's Alexa. Remember, Mrs. Millbank followed Alexa to the hospital, and Alexa has access to the pathology computer from which the e-mail was sent to Mr. Millbank," Leila explained.

"Seems pretty thin to search a doctor's office, but, well it's not for me to judge, I guess," Andy said.

They hopped into Detective Alvarez's car and in no time reached the hospital. The detective told Andy and Leila that Dr. Carmichael was on vacation this week, so they would not need to confront her when they served the warrant. In response to Andy's question, Alvarez explained that the warrant would be served to the hospital's chief operating officer, who was responsible for all the hospital space, and that Dr. Carmichael need not be present. Her office was hospital property; however, since she had an expectation of privacy in her office, a search warrant was still required. After serving the warrant, the COO escorted them to her office.

"I don't get something, though, and this is why I can't honestly be suspicious of Dr. Carmichael," Andy said. "Isn't she the one who initiated the contact with Angelina Costa with regard to the autopsy? I mean, why would she do that if she killed Mr. Millbank?"

"That's a good point, Andy," Alvarez said, and he continued, "and I am not convinced that she is Alexa—not as much as Leila is, in any case, but when a forensic pathologist can't solve a case, they routinely seek help. Remember that, as the coroner, she is also an employee of the City of New York and has a duty to provide answers in cases of suspicious deaths."

"I would add that if she didn't provide a robust report—a believable report—she might have thought that would cast suspicion on her," Leila said, "and that by being forthcoming and seeking help not only from Dr. Costa but Dr. Goldberg as well, she might have thought this would deflect attention away from her as a suspect. In any case, we'll find out soon."

"You seem really confident, Leila," Andy suggested. "We might not find anything, you know."

"Yes, I know."

They arrived in the pathology department. The COO asked them to wait outside in the hallway for a moment so he could explain to Dr. Simmons the purpose of this visit; he furthermore requested that she not discuss the warrant or the search with anyone else—discretion was paramount. He then stepped into the hallway and motioned to Alvarez that they could enter the pathology suite. He also put a finger to his lips to indicate he wanted no discussion until they were in Dr. Carmichael's office.

The suite was largely devoid of people, as many had taken this holiday week off for vacation. They stood outside the door to Dr. Carmichael's office, and with the key Dr. Simmons had provided, the COO opened it. He stepped aside, and Alvarez, Andy, and Leila slowly walked in. Alvarez had brought a box with him in order to carry her computer and any other items they deemed necessary to take back to the station. The office was fairly small, with a large, darkly stained, wooden L-shaped desk in the middle of the room. On one side of the desk was a microscope with a camera mounted at the top, while on the other was a computer monitor resting atop the computer itself. Alvarez unplugged the computer from all its accouterments and placed it in the box. Besides the desk, there was a matching bookcase sitting on top of a cabinet with long drawers. The bookcase was adorned with a variety of medical textbooks and some medical journals. The drawers in the cabinet they found to be locked. The three of them searched for the keys but could not find them. Alvarez stepped out and returned after a discussion with Dr. Simmons, who informed him that she didn't have keys to the drawers. Alvarez asked the COO to call the hospital locksmith.

"Why would she keep these locked?" Alvarez asked aloud.

"I don't know—maybe to keep her purse in. Unfortunately, office thefts are not uncommon in hospitals," Leila replied.

"Do all the doctors have locked cabinets in their offices?" Andy wondered. "I'm not sure—they each order their own office furniture, I believe," the COO responded. "I can tell you that I have a locked cabinet similar to this one, but I rarely lock it."

"I bet there's something in there," Leila said.

They searched the drawers of the desk, which were not locked, but didn't find anything of note. Leila was getting frustrated—her intuition told her there was something important in this place. She went to the bookshelf and pulled all the books out, almost believing that pulling one of them would lead to some secret passage behind the wall, as in a scene from some fantastical movie. Finally the locksmith entered the room. He examined the lock and expertly pulled a small key from his circular key chain that contained at least a hundred keys. The key fit perfectly, and he unlocked the cabinet. Leila was naturally the first to the drawers—there were three, one on top of the other—and began rummaging through the bottom one. It was filled with medical articles ripped from journals or simply printouts, but nothing else. The second drawer had a small coffee maker, filters, and a bag of Starbucks' coffee. Leila, unable to contain herself, emptied it out and moved on to the top drawer. That drawer had a box for a Bose sound system and numerous compact discs.

"Nothing! Damn it!" Leila exclaimed in clear frustration.

"Did you check the box—maybe the CD player isn't inside and she's hiding something in there," Alvarez suggested.

"Of course," said Leila, excited. How could she have overlooked such a detail? She pulled the box out, but inside was the player encased in its Styrofoam as if it had just come out of the store. They all took one more look around, but they were resigned that there was nothing obviously incriminating in Dr. Carmichael's office.

Alvarez thanked the COO and the locksmith as they replaced everything precisely as it had been, with the exception of the computer and some CD-ROMs. The COO told them that to be fair he would inform Dr. Carmichael of the search, and Detective Alvarez told him they would return the computer and the CD-ROMs before Dr. Carmichael returned. As they were about to leave the office, Andy stopped.

"Just a second. I want to check one more place, if that's okay?"

"Go for it," Alvarez responded.

Andy stepped back into the office and sat down at the desk. He looked around carefully and systematically. He imagined himself sitting at his desk—he had an L-shaped desk as well. First, he looked around the microscope, then around the computer monitor—nothing. Then he looked down, and as if lured by a scent, he got off the chair and kneeled underneath the desk, and that's when he saw it. At first, the large FedEx envelope seemed innocuous, but its position was strange— it was almost as if it were hanging in midair, eluding gravity. On more careful examination, he noticed that it was taped to the inside panel of the desk to ensure it wouldn't fall. *That's odd*, he thought.

"What are you doing? Come on, Andy. Let's go," he heard Leila call. "Just a moment."

He pulled the envelope toward him, ripping the tape from its adhesive contacts, and noted that it was stapled shut.

"What are you doing?" he heard Leila say as she came back into the office. "Where are you?"

"Down here."

Leila walked around the side of the desk and saw Andy on his knees, head fully under the desk.

"Did you find something?" she asked.

"Just a big FedEx envelope, but it's weird—it was taped to the inside panel of the desk, and it's stapled shut," Andy said as he emerged from under the desk squeezing the envelope with his hands.

"Open it!" Leila demanded.

By this time, Alvarez had also returned to the office and stood next to Leila. Andy sat at the desk. He asked for a staple remover, and Alvarez obliged him.

Before removing the staples, he palpated the contents from the outside, using his keen physician's skills to try to discern what might be underneath the skin of the envelope. What he felt was soft and amorphous, and as he maneuvered his hands around the package, a gentle scratching sound emanated, like that of a drummer playing with brushes instead of drumsticks. He looked up at Detective Alvarez and Leila and shrugged. Alvarez nodded his head, indicating he should open the envelope. With a surgeon's touch, he carefully unclasped the staples so as not to disrupt what might be inside. He gently, and with great anticipation, pried open the envelope and then flipped it over, dumping the contents onto the desk. Leila's jaw dropped, her big dark eyes grew wide, and her mouth was agape. Detective Alvarez calmly leaned over closely to examine the object, squinting his eyes just a bit. Andy sat at the desk with a closed-mouth smile on his face, staring at the object as if he had just solved the Sudoku puzzle no one else had been able to.

"Well, I'll be darned," Andy said in a faux Southern accent, "it seems as if Andy's intuition finally kicked in."

Detective Alvarez put on latex gloves, picked up the wig, and placed it back in the FedEx envelope. This he put into a large, clear plastic bag, which he marked with the date, time, and location.

"It's the same auburn color I remember when I first ran into Alexa five weeks ago. I would never have guessed it was Dr. Carmichael," Alvarez stated.

"You know, Jose," Leila said, using his first name for the first time, "it's not the hair or the clothes. It's the attitude—she probably fooled you by carrying on a completely different personality when you met her as Alexa."

"Yeah, she had attitude, I can assure you of that."

They left the office and returned to the police station to give the wig to the forensics experts. Alvarez thanked Andy and Leila again for all their great work and said he would be in touch after New Year's. He called O'Reilly, told him what they had found, and instructed him to get a search warrant for Jennifer Carmichael's apartment. He suggested to Leila and Andy that they stay in the city for New Year's Eve and enjoy the greatest party on earth, and with that he shook Andy's hand and gave Leila a warm hug.

Andy and Leila returned to the hotel and sat down in the restaurant to have some lunch. "Andy, that was truly awesome. What made you go under the desk?"

"I keep all kinds of shit under my desk. When you have a big desk, it's a great place to store things you don't use often."

"Or things you don't want others to find," Leila added. "I suppose."

"Well, I have to thank you," Leila said. "For what?"

"Remember, I was the one who thought Carmichael could be Alexa, but I was ready to leave her office empty-handed. Your amazing find confirmed my suspicions."

Andy remained silent.

"Andy, we make a great team, you know—and not just on this case," Leila said proudly and gleefully.

Andy's heart began to beat hard in his chest with excitement, but this turned to disappointment when Leila continued, "We are also a great team at work. Thanks for hiring me."

For hiring you, Andy repeated in his mind. *I wish I never had.* He had to summon up the will to acknowledge Leila's comment. "Yes, it's a pleasure working with you," he said blandly.

"So, what are we going to do for New Year's Eve?" Leila asked.

"You know, Leila, with all that's transpired and the emotional rollercoaster I have been on with this case and, well, with you, also, for the past six weeks, I need a break."

"A break from the work or a break from me?" Leila asked with a hint of concern in her voice.

"Both."

"Oh," Leila said flatly.

"I'm going to fly home tomorrow and spend the weekend catching up on neglected work and just resting my mind—my detective mind, my doctor mind, and my ... well, you know what I mean."

"Okay. I, uh ... understand. Well, I'm going to finally do some shopping."

"Enjoy. I'm going to begin my rest in my room and then fly home early tomorrow," Andy said. "Are you going to stay here all weekend?"

"I don't know. Call me when you're ready to, okay?" Leila said. "I will."

With that they parted company, each to their own thoughts. Andy felt strangely at peace. He had started the process of grieving over the relationship that had been as intense as it had been short. *A Muslim and a Jew—it's just not meant to be.*

CHAPTER 26

L eila woke up at eleven o'clock, aware that Andy would soon be on his way back to Los Angeles. She suddenly found herself alone in a city of millions who were about to celebrate the coming New Year. She felt like an uninvited guest at the biggest party of the year. She had never felt so alone in her life—lonelier even than when she'd left all her friends in Iraq and arrived in the United States. Lonelier still than her first day of school in Michigan as a sixth grader. And even more lonely than her first day in California. Sadness suffused her being. *What have I done?* she thought. She picked up her phone, only to realize Andy had just boarded his flight to Los Angeles. She decided to shower and go for a walk.

Andy was nearly an hour into his flight. He was seated toward the back of the 767 at a window seat. He had been happily surprised to see the seat next to him unoccupied. *New York has a much better New Year's Eve party than Los Angeles,* he said to himself, figuring that might be the reason for the good fortune of the extra space. Gazing out the window at the snow-covered hilly landscape, he figured he was somewhere over the northern Appalachian mountains of Pennsylvania or West Virginia.

He felt relieved and sad at the same time; it reminded him of the time his grandmother, suffering from Alzheimer's disease and barely able to recognize anyone, let alone care for herself, had died. While he'd honestly thought that he and Leila could have a future together, there was some sense of relief—*A Muslim and a Jew*, he said to himself several times. He chuckled for a moment, thinking what his religious grandmother would have thought. She would not have been pleased. He was pretty sure of that. With several more hours in the air ahead of him, he buried himself in his music. In this moment of sadness and vulnerability, he retreated to his favorite musical artist of all time, The Waterboys, and the whimsical, mystical, and philosophical music and words of what Andy felt was surely the most underrated musician in history, Mike Scott, the founder and leader of the group. He chose to listen to *Room to Roam,* with its Irish folk influence layered over Mike Scott's rock 'n' roll roots.

The skies over New York were slate gray and the air cold as Leila set out on a long walk through Central Park. She wasn't sure where she was going, but she was sure she needed to think. For better or worse, she couldn't stop thinking about Andy. Yet her thoughts yo-yoed back and forth. First, she felt a strong conviction that she was doing the right thing by breaking the relationship off now at its infancy. But then, as her heart began to beat harder and an unsettling feeling churned her stomach, tears formed in her eyes as she realized that she was in love with Andy. She tried to ignore her body's urgings and built arguments in her mind one brick at a time as if erecting a wall between her and Andy—or was the wall between the two halves of her own mind? She thought of her family, and with that, her thoughts returned to Kirkuk, where as a brave, yet naïve, girl, she had fought with her dad about leaving the only home she knew. *But what about our family, and what about our friends?* she had shouted and cried. Then her dad's voice had filled her ear: *My dear Leila, I am doing what is best for you. Trust me. I know.* Her father had been right then, and she knew it now. Was he also right this time? Should she trust him now with what she felt was the second-biggest decision he was making on her behalf?

Andy's eyes were closed, though he was most definitely awake. He was subsumed by the music. The Waterboys had provided him comfort many times before, but now tears began to well in his eyes as the song "A Man Is in Love" came on. He'd always known it was a beautiful love song, and he'd sworn he would never link the song with anyone, especially a woman he cared for. He'd never wanted to risk associating this favorite song of his with a girl for fear that it would be forever tainted if the relationship didn't flourish. But he couldn't help himself thinking of Leila as the object of the adoring singer as he sang the last verse:

> *A man is in love.*
> *How did I guess?*
> *I figured it out*
> *While he was watching you dress;*
> *He'd give you his all if you'd but agree;*
> *A man is in love … and he's me.*

It was painful. He was about to switch it off, but at the end he chose not to. *Leila is worthy of this song*, he thought.

After an hour of walking and thinking and thinking some more, Leila felt her thoughts come into sharp focus. To her, it was reminiscent of the sudden reappearance of a clear-blue sky after a sandstorm had blown through Kirkuk. She circled back to the hotel with a newfound confidence, walking tall and purposefully. It was just passed noon on this New Year's Eve in New York City, and she knew now how she would spend her New Year's Eve.

CHAPTER 27

A ndy awoke to the sound of his cell phone. It was only 6:30 a.m. *Who the hell is calling me now?* he wondered.

"Andy, it's Jose," bellowed Alvarez's voice as he heard Andy's raspy voice. "Oh, sorry, I forgot about the time change. Did I wake you?"

"Uh, no, no. I had just woken up," Andy lied. He didn't want Alvarez to feel bad. "What's going on?"

"Well, I hope you had a nice New Year's, but we need to get back to the bleeder case. The chief of police has made this case our number-one priority until it's solved. I think the mayor has been putting a lot of pressure on him."

"Why would he do that—is this case that important?" Andy asked.

"I think it's the tabloids and newspapers. The story keeps showing up on the front pages—people in the city are fascinated by it, and well, the tabloids keep suggesting that it might be some kind of bioterrorism. I don't need to tell you how sensitive New Yorkers have become when it comes to terrorism," Alvarez replied.

"Okay, so what do you want me to do?"

"I would like to have a conference call with you and Leila later today, if possible, so we can decide what our next step will be."

"Have you called Leila yet?" Andy wondered whether he was the only one to get an early-morning wake-up call.

"No. I thought you could talk to her."

Andy didn't want to tell Alvarez that he had not seen nor spoken to Leila since New Year's Eve. He was convinced that would only lead to questions he would rather avoid answering, not that he even had answers for them.

Nevertheless, he agreed to get hold of Leila and arrange a conference call with the detectives later that day—despite the fact that he had not spoken to her in four days and he wasn't sure what kind of response he would receive upon contacting her again. Hoping that Leila's obvious enthusiasm for the case hadn't waned over the long weekend, Andy mustered up a bit of courage and resolved to call her.

Although Andy might have ordinarily gone back to sleep at this point, the thoughts of calling Leila and determining what exactly he would say to her kept him awake. As he mulled over a number of options, he resorted to practicing each one aloud in an attempt to minimize the awkwardness he knew would invariably surface. He also foreshadowed a variety of reactions Leila might have and rehearsed his own responses to those various scenarios. Recalling the many words he had said to her just before returning to Los Angeles—most of which he now regretted—he was determined to be as prepared as possible for whichever direction the conversation turned. Although it had been just four days since they'd last spoken, it seemed like an eternity, considering that they had spent so many hours together nearly every day in the preceding two months. At least the respite had provided him sufficient time to ponder his relationship with Leila and allowed him to become convinced that it was indeed the right decision to not pursue a serious relationship further. As a self-soothing measure, he pacified some of his pain by reminding himself that he'd initially thought it was not even appropriate, given their roles at work, and that if it hadn't been for Leila's response—her rather heated response, at that—he would not have let their relationship blossom as it had. While his mind was more and more persuaded by this decision, his heart still ached. He got out of bed, showered, and rehearsed one last time what he would say to Leila when he called her.

"Andy, it's great to hear from you," came Leila's voice in what Andy thought was an overly cheerful tone.

Is this the same girl? he wondered. He'd fully expected either a very businesslike response or a more somber tone to her voice. He wasn't sure what to make of this.

"How are you?" she continued. "I missed you, but ... I didn't want to call.

Well, you pretty much told me not to, remember?"

While Andy had rehearsed the entire discussion he was prepared to have, it just didn't seem appropriate given Leila's seeming joy at hearing his voice. He shelved his rehearsed speech.

"I'm doing well, thanks. It was nice to have a few days off. I feel refreshed and, well, just content," Andy said.

Leila wondered what *content* meant, but she chose not to ask. "So, what did you call about?" she asked matter-of-factly.

"Detective Alvarez called this morning. Apparently, the mayor of New York has been putting a lot of pressure on him and O'Reilly to solve the case. There is rampant speculation in the New York media that the bleeder case is somehow linked to bioterrorism, and while we all know this is a criminal case, the papers and news shows are playing up this angle—probably to enhance their ratings and sales. So Alvarez wants to have a conference call to regroup and decide on our next step."

"Great. I can't wait to get back into it. You know, I missed working on the case, and it has been playing in my mind. I had trouble sleeping a couple of nights, thinking about the possibilities. I have some ideas, in fact."

That's what you were losing sleep over? Andy thought. He was losing sleep as well, but his mind was not on the case.

"Shall I tell Alvarez we can talk later this afternoon?" he asked. "Sure. How about 1:00 p.m. in your office, then?"

Andy agreed. He contacted Alvarez and confirmed the time. He decided he should spend some time thinking about the case, too—Leila has been one step ahead of him throughout much of the investigation. There was no doubt her intuition was sharp and keen, but Andy felt that he needed to demonstrate to Alvarez and Leila that he was just as capable of elucidating important facts about the case. He spent the rest of the morning in his house thinking over and over again about the numerous details of the case and trying to piece the puzzle together. There were many people and many places. And there were still many gaps. Could Bryan Vasquez really be involved? If not, why had he been in Norway and Switzerland and New York? *It couldn't be just a coincidence*, Andy thought. But he hadn't been in Basel when Mr. Stern was killed—that was a fact. Andy ruminated over the minutiae for a few hours. The more he thought, though, the hazier the picture got. What was missing? What one fact could be the first domino to fall? He didn't know.

Andy sat in his warm, sun-drenched office. During the winter, with the sun's much-shallower arc and relatively low position in the sky, the south-facing window acted like a magnifying glass, concentrating the sun's rays into warm drafts of air like a space heater. Unlike most of his colleagues with offices on the same side of the hallway, he refused to close the shades, for the warmth and glow of the January sun in California energized him as if he were a solar-energy panel. His office, filled with the upbeat Los Angeles pop sound of Maroon 5, had Andy in a profoundly positive mood. He was ready to resume working on the case. He was ready for Leila—ready to return to the collegial friendship they'd had before the first trip together to New York. The knock on the door came a few minutes into the jazz-rock beats of *Sunday Morning* with the soulful voice of Adam Levine filling the room.

"Hi, Leila," Andy greeted her gleefully.

"Well, you're in a bright mood today, aren't you?" she replied. "Bright office, new year, good music—why not?"

"I'm happy to see the old Andy back," Leila replied.

"I'll dial Alvarez and O'Reilly," Andy said, continuing while dialing, "and I'm feeling like I'm about to figure out something important about this case. I don't know why or what it is—it's just a hunch."

"Awesome! We really seem to be stuck again, so we need some more brilliance from you."

"What do you mean, *more* brilliance? You're the one that has figured out most of the key findings," Andy said

"Uh, who found the wig, Einstein?" Leila replied sarcastically.

Just then Alvarez picked up the phone. "Andy, Leila, thanks for calling in on such short notice."

"No problem," Leila replied. "Is it still freezing cold over there?"

"Yes. Well, it is January, and it is New York. How about you guys— how's your weather?"

"Oh, just the usual. Sunny and 75," Leila said with a laugh.

"Well, we might need you back here soon, so don't make too much fun of our winter," Alvarez replied.

"You asked us to call you, so can we assume you have some updates for us?" Andy asked.

"Well, yes and no. We searched Alexa—er, Dr. Carmichael's— apartment, but we found nothing of value. We reviewed Bryan Vasquez's credit-card transactions; he was in the city over at least the six days before Mr. Millbank was killed and left the day he was killed. I am sorry to have to say this, Andy, but he is becoming our number-one suspect," Alvarez explained.

"God, I can't believe he would have anything to do with this, but I see where you are coming from, and I promise to be objective," Andy replied.

"We also know he was in Switzerland, and tracing his credit card again, we know he was in Basel. The problem is that he couldn't have killed Mr. Stern, because he left Basel seven days before Mr. Stern was killed. So, that's the bad news—we have strong reason to suspect he killed Mr. Millbank but just as strong a reason to say he couldn't have killed Mr. Stern," Detective O'Reilly stated.

"Andy, can you review what you had said before about Bryan possibly having a motive to kill both men?" Alvarez requested.

"Sure. Bryan's sister died from a pulmonary embolism—a blood clot in her lungs. I had recommended that she be treated with a new blood thinner called Lyzanda because she was not responding to warfarin, the usual blood thinner that we use. Unfortunately, she couldn't get the Lyzanda, because her insurance company wouldn't pay for it and the medication was too expensive for the family to pay it themselves," Andy replied.

Leila put in, "And let me add that Bryan's family's insurance plan was with Empire Health, and Lyzanda is manufactured by Terrapharma, so I can see how Bryan would feel as if these companies were somehow culpable for his sister's death."

"So you think Bryan could hold the CEO of each company personally responsible?" O'Reilly concluded.

"I suppose so," Andy added in a sullen, almost defeated, tone.

"But again, he was not in Basel when Mr. Stern died, and what the hell was he doing in Norway? Why do we think he went to Tromsø? To meet with Bergeland?" Alvarez asked, exasperated.

Silence. At least ten seconds passed before Leila broke the pause.

"And what about Carmichael and Angelina Costa—is there a common thread that links them and the bleeders?"

"We've looked for those connections, but all we know is that Jennifer Carmichael and Angelina Costa knew each other years ago during their pathology training and that they each conducted the autopsies of the bleeders. However, there doesn't seem to be a connection between Angelina and Millbank or Carmichael and Stern. We also tried to find a connection between Bryan and Carmichael and Bryan and Angelina, but nothing came up," O'Reilly stated.

"So, what's the next step?" Leila asked.

"We need to question Bryan Vasquez? He needs to explain why he was in Tromsø and Basel and New York in the weeks leading up to the murders. Andy, do you want to talk to him?" Alvarez asked.

"No, that doesn't seem right. I mean, I am his sister's doctor, and I've known this family for a few years—I need to keep their trust."

"Perhaps, you boys need some winter LA sunshine?" Leila suggested playfully. Andy's cell phone rang. It was from within the hospital.

"Hello, it's Dr. Friedman," Andy began. The voice on the phone was frantic.

"What? Oh my God! We'll be right down." The urgency in Andy's voice was unmistakable.

"Detectives, medical emergency; we need to go. We think you should come out to LA. Let us know what you decide. We have to go now. We'll call you back. Bye."

Andy got up swiftly, pointed Leila to the door of his office, and began to run down the hallway, with Leila chasing after him, pleading him to tell her what was happening. Breathless and wide-eyed, Andy got in the elevator, with Leila, barely able to keep up with him, sticking her foot in the elevator door just as it was about to close.

"Andy, what the hell is going on?"

He stared straight into Leila's eyes. "Diana Vasquez, Bryan's sister, is in the emergency room—she's bleeding to death!"

CHAPTER 28

"How is she doing?" Andy asked Leila as he entered Diana Vasquez's room at Children's Hospital Los Angeles.

"Better. She's going to be okay, thank God," Leila replied, displaying the hint of a smile.

Andy and Leila hadn't left the hospital until past midnight the previous night. Diana had needed numerous blood transfusions to keep up with all the blood she was losing. Thankfully, none of the bleeding had occurred in her vital organs, sparing her body from any serious damage. After rushing to the emergency room following the call, Andy and Leila had found Diana on a gurney, bleeding from her mouth and nose and covered in large bruises. Leila immediately assumed that she had too much warfarin in her blood and prescribed her both the antidote to warfarin, vitamin K, as well as a medication to immediately stop the bleeding, called a prothrombin complex concentrate, or PCC. Although this did stop the bleeding eventually, it took far more of the PCC than it would normally take to reverse warfarin. This was one of the reasons Leila was suspicious that something unusual had occurred. The other reason, as it turned out, was that the laboratory tests did not indicate that Diana had had too much warfarin in her blood. While

Diana was still upset over her sister's death, her mother was sure she would never try to kill herself.

Leila's suspicions drew her to interview Diana's mother, not in the manner a detective might but in the nonconfrontational fashion doctors are trained to use. Leila explained that it was critical to know every last detail of information that might explain what had occurred, in order to save Diana. The persistent questioning eventually led to a rather unexpected piece of information, which Leila wasn't sure quite how to interpret. Mrs. Vasquez told Leila that Diana had recently started taking Lyzanda. When Leila inquired how she'd gotten it, since neither she nor Andy had prescribed it, due to the lack of insurance authorization, Mrs. Vasquez told her that Bryan had been able to buy it relatively inexpensively on his last trip to Europe. Further questioning informed Leila that Diana had just taken the first dose two days earlier, the day before she'd started bleeding, and that her mother was quite sure Diana had taken just one pill. Leila was perplexed.

"What can I tell you, Andy? That's what Diana's mom told me."

"Something is not right," Andy responded.

"I agree. Let's review the lab results again."

Andy and Leila sat at the computer in Leila's office and accessed Diana's medical records. The lab results suggested that the level of warfarin in her blood was a bit lower than they'd expected, which was consistent with the fact that she had stopped taking the warfarin. A variety of other blood tests, including those assessing the function of her blood-clotting system and determining the degree of blood loss, were very abnormal, which was consistent with the fact that she'd nearly bled to death and that her blood was not clotting normally. Numerous other tests were done as well; however, none of those were informative. Andy had an idea.

"Do you think we can ask the lab to measure the amount of Lyzanda in her blood directly?"

"I'm not sure. We would need to ask the lab director," Leila replied.

"I'm sure there is a way. Let's have them save all the blood samples they have left and find someone who can do it. Maybe she just overdosed or got the wrong dose," Andy contemplated.

"Why don't you look into that? I'm going to see if we can find a connection between Bryan and Carmichael and Bryan and Angelina Costa. That part of the case is driving me nuts. Why was Bryan in Basel and then New York around the times of the murders? There must be a connection," Leila stated affirmatively.

They agreed to regroup later in the day and to alternate checking on Diana, who was improving but still recovering from the shock to her body.

"Hello, I'm looking for Felix de Ville. Please tell him it's Leila Baker from the United States and that it is important that I speak to him."

After being on hold for several minutes, finally Leila heard the voice and accent of Felix de Ville floating out of her speakerphone.

"Yes, Leila, it's good to talk to you. What can I do for you?" Felix asked politely.

"I'm not sure if Detective Alvarez or O'Reilly has spoken to you recently—"

"Yes, earlier today," Felix interrupted.

"Great. That'll save us some time. I am calling because I am very troubled by the presence of Bryan Vasquez in Basel just a couple of days before the murder of Mr. Stern. I can't understand why he would go there if it wasn't to kill Mr. Stern, yet he was gone well before the day of the murder. I want to elicit your help in trying to figure this out."

"Yes, of course. I have, in fact, been wondering about this myself. I think we need to try to connect him with Karina Hummels or, dare I say, my friend Angelina Costa," de Ville responded.

"Indeed. The problem is that all three have a motive—two rape victims and Bryan, who may hold Mr. Stern responsible for his sister's death."

"So, you are thinking one of them is the perpetrator?" de Ville asked. "No, I'm thinking that perhaps they worked together!"

"Really!" de Ville exclaimed.

"I think it is possible—perhaps likely."

"But we don't know how Mr. Stern died. In fact, if it wasn't for the simultaneous deaths of the bleeders, we would have concluded that Mr. Stern died from natural causes."

"True, but we know he didn't die naturally. Something caused him to bleed... to ... death." Leila completed her sentence in halting fashion, as if she were speaking about one thing while thinking about something else.

Silence.

"Leila, are you still there?" Silence.

"Leila?"

"Oh my God! Uh, I need to go. I, uh, just thought of something."

"What? What is it?" de Ville asked.

"I'll tell you later. Listen, do me a favor and see if you can somehow place Bryan and either Karina or Angelina, or all three of them, in the same place. Please let me know immediately if you find out anything, okay?"

"Sure, no ... prob ... lem," de Ville responded, realizing he was completing the sentence to himself only as he heard the electronic beep of Leila's phone disconnecting.

Leila barged into Andy's office. He was on the phone and motioned to her to have a seat. Leila was too excited to sit—she paced back and forth in Andy's small office like an excitable yet bored hamster moving to and fro in its small cage. Andy turned to her, still holding the phone to his ear and spreading his arms out in bewilderment.

"That's great," Andy spoke into the phone. "I'll have someone courier the samples to you this afternoon ... that's great ... tomorrow afternoon ... perfect. Just call my office as soon as you have something ... thanks," Andy spoke his phone number into the phone and hung up.

"Leila, sit down! You are making me crazy walking back and forth like that.

What is it?"

"You first. What was that call about?"

Andy, at first flustered by Leila's sudden intrusion, grew annoyed that her first instinct was to ask him what he had found out, while she clearly had discovered something important.

"Me first. You look like you just discovered the cure for cancer," he replied in a frustrated tone.

"Well?" Leila demanded, flashing an impish smile. Andy knew he wasn't going to win this game of chicken, so he relented.

"I just got off the phone with a gentleman from the LA County drug lab, and he told me they could test her blood. He needed some information about Lyzanda, which I gave him, and he told me he could get something back to me by tomorrow."

"That's great, and perfect timing, because I have an idea," Leila said, still with a broad self-satisfied smile on her face.

Andy momentarily just stared at her face. While he mentally began to put his feelings for Leila behind him, the Julia Roberts smile and the accompanying glow on her face caused his love for her to surge back up like the incoming wave of a new high tide surging further up the sand than the previous waves. He suppressed the thoughts he had the best he could.

"Well, are you going to sit there and smile, or are you going to tell me your latest morsel of brilliance?" Andy said.

"Andy, how did we not think of it the moment we heard about Diana?" Leila wondered aloud. "Don't you see the similarities?"

"Go on," Andy said with a nod. He sensed where this conversation was heading.

"Diana showed up in our emergency room looking the way the two bleeders did when their bodies were discovered—bleeding from everywhere, right?"

"Yes, yes, I see where you are heading," Andy replied. "And once again, Bryan is in the picture. I think you're onto something."

"The Lyzanda. He brought her back Lyzanda from Europe, right, and she took it, according to her mom? Perhaps she took too much, and—"

"No, that's not it. There's no way she took too much—but what if—? Nah, that's not possible. Never mind," Andy said, not completing his thought.

"Andy, what is it? Just say what you're thinking," Leila encouraged him. "Okay, but it's pretty out there," Andy started and then proceeded. "What if Mr. Stern and Mr. Millbank were poisoned with a blood thinner, the way rats used to be killed with powerful, warfarin-like poisons."

"Keep going—I like the train of thought," Leila coaxed Andy like a teacher trying to extract her student's knowledge.

"All right, I'm going to tell you what I'm thinking, but you have to promise me you won't laugh."

"Of course not, Andy. We're talking about life and death—I won't, I promise."

"Let's say Bryan got hold of some super-strong blood thinner, let's say a souped-up version of Lyzanda, and he somehow was able to get Stern and Millbank to swallow it—I don't know, perhaps slipping it into a drink or food. They could bleed to death, don't you think?"

"Yes, could be; that could be," Leila replied thoughtfully.

"Let's say that's true and that Bryan still had some of this super-Lyzanda with him when he returned from Europe. Perhaps he gave that to Diana or, well, why would he do that?"

"How about this?" Leila picked up the theory. "He comes home from Europe with some real Lyzanda and some of the super-Lyzanda, and he accidentally mixes them up so that Diana mistakenly takes the same thing that the bleeders ingested."

"I don't know. You'd think he would be extremely careful about that. You know he loves his sister to death," Andy opined, failing to notice the morbid pun he had just uttered.

"Andy, he was on a whirlwind tour, probably exhausted, jet-lagged, and he very well could have made an innocent, albeit nearly fatal, mistake. I think it's possible."

"Why would he bring home such incriminating evidence, though?"

"Maybe he's not done killing people," Leila stated bluntly.

"Okay, let's assume all of the assumptions we have made so far are correct," Andy added. "Where would he get what I called the super—"

Andy and Leila looked at each other, the jaw-dropped look of one was like a mirror image of the other. Then they suddenly, simultaneously and softly, uttered one word: "Bergeland!"

"Andy, that's it!" Leila said, bursting from her seat like a jack-in-the-box. She grabbed Andy out of his seat and hugged him. In that moment of embrace, Andy didn't know what to do, but as if the weekend in New York had never happened, Leila kissed him warmly on the lips. Andy was thoroughly confused, but rather than attempt to address his confusion at this time, he merely elected to enjoy the moment.

"Let's review our theory, shall we?" Andy began. "Vanessa Vasquez, Bryan's sister, dies of a pulmonary embolism. We had tried to get her Lyzanda since she was not responding well to warfarin or the other blood thinners we tried, but it gets denied by her insurer, Empire Health, and the family can't afford to pay for this expensive new drug, which is made by Terrapharma."

"Right," Leila confirmed.

"Bryan at some point decides to exact revenge by killing the CEO of Empire Health, Mr. Millbank, and the CEO of Terrapharma, Mr. Stern," Andy continued. "Either for practical reasons, or perhaps to make a point, he decides that poisoning them with some super-strong version of Lyzanda is the way to kill them."

"So," Leila picked up the story line, "while on a trip to Norway for work, he learns about Bergeland's company and their ability to make enhanced versions of various medications, like the ones used on the Exxon oil rigs in the North Sea. He finds out that the company that makes these drugs is Sami Innovations, and while in Norway, he tracks down Erik Bergeland in Tromsø."

"And Bergeland is more than happy to oblige, because he isn't exactly thrilled with Mr. Stern," Andy adds.

"Bergeland supplies him with the super-Lyzanda, and Bryan heads to Switzerland ... Oh my God, Andy! It fits in with everything we know about Bryan's whereabouts. This has to be true," Leila stated. There was an ever-increasing tone of resignation in her voice at realizing that Bryan, their patient's brother, could easily be the murderer.

"I agree, but here is where we have a problem, Leila."

"Yes, of course. You're right. He wasn't in Switzerland when Stern was killed.

That is a problem," she said with a nod.

They realized that while their theory had seemed logical up to that point, some major holes existed as they moved forward in time. First, Bryan had left Switzerland a full seven days before Mr. Stern had died. Given the rapid onset of bleeding Diana had experienced after allegedly taking the super-Lyzanda, it was not possible Bryan could have poisoned him. Furthermore, how would Bryan have gotten close enough to Mr. Stern to slip him one or more of the pills without him knowing about it? Regarding Mr. Millbank's murder, while they did know that Bryan had left Switzerland and was in New York at the time of his murder, it was hard to believe that he could have had close enough access to a man who was especially secretive and suspicious of others. Something was still missing. They called Alvarez and O'Reilly to discuss their theory.

"That's interesting, but seems like quite a stretch, don't you think?" O'Reilly stated. "Regardless, while you may have convinced us that he had the motive and perhaps the weapon, the poison, if that's indeed what was used to kill the bleeders, it doesn't look like he had the opportunity. No opportunity, and he can't be the murderer."

"And while I am thrilled you have both thought this through and come up with this theory, I have to say that it relies on a lot, and I mean *a lot*, of assumptions," added Alvarez.

"Let me play devil's advocate for a second," O'Reilly stated. "Bryan goes to Norway for work, but he never goes to an oil rig out on the North Sea. Right, we have no evidence he went to an offshore platform. While in Norway, he is asked to go to Tromsø to speak to Bergeland about Sami Innovation's products, in order to see if they can help the oil workers with the various ailments that occur on an oil rig. They have a purely business discussion, during which Bergeland states that his company doesn't actually make the medications—they only develop the enhancements. He suggests to Bryan that he meet with Mr. Stern, with whom Bergeland's company has worked, to see if Terrapharma would agree to manufacture the medications that Sami Innovations develops."

Andy and Leila look at each other disconsolately. They realized that in their zeal they could have gotten carried away in developing their theory and that O'Reilly's story was just as plausible. Then Andy realized there was one other fact that O'Reilly had neglected.

"What about Bryan's trip to New York—there are nonstop flights from Zurich to Los Angeles. Why would Bryan go to New York instead of going home?"

"That's a good point, and I don't have an answer for that," O'Reilly responded.

"Maybe that is the key to unlocking the mystery, then," Leila said. "If we can connect Bryan to Mr. Millbank, whom he would have no reason to meet—or to Carmichael, or even Costa—then we may yet be correct."

"Yes," replied Alvarez and O'Reilly in unison.

"So, can you do us a favor and contact Bryan's supervisor and find out if he had any reason to be in New York—or in Tromsø, for that matter?" Leila requested. "Also, why don't you see if you can find a connection between Bryan and Mr. Millbank, Jennifer Carmichael, or Mrs. Millbank. We'll work on seeing if there's a connection with Costa, and we may have some information on the super-Lyzanda tomorrow."

"I think we are forgetting something," Alvarez said. "What's that?" Andy asked.

"Bryan. Where is he? I think we need to bring him in for some questioning.

Do either of you know where he is? Has he visited his sister in the hospital?"

"Uh, no, not that we know of," Leila answered.

"Isn't that odd, considering how sick she was and how much he loves her?"

"It is odd. Very odd, in fact," Andy answered, disappointed that he hadn't thought about that.

They ended the call. Andy and Leila looked at one another, perplexed at the notion that Bryan, one of the most devoted older brothers they had ever met, had not, to their knowledge, come to see his critically ill sister. Andy told Leila he would go talk to Bryan's mom to see if she knew whether he had visited or where he might be. Leila decided to call de Ville to see if he had made any progress.

Upon arriving in Diana's room on the fourth floor of the newly opened building at Children's Hospital Los Angeles, Andy found Mrs. Vasquez holding her daughter's hand tightly in hers, while Diana lay in her bed looking intently at her mom. Andy entered slowly, not wanting to startle either one of them; they seemed to be lost in thought and in the gaze of each other's eyes. Diana sensed his presence and turned her head to face him.

"Well, young lady," Andy began, "you've made a remarkable recovery."

"Thanks to you and Dr. Baker—as usual. You are saints, the both of you."

"Thanks for the kind words. We were just doing our jobs, Diana," Andy responded.

"You always say that, but your job saves people's lives and helps people get healthy. It is not like painting a house or fixing a car," Diana said.

"Still, thanks. I actually came to ask you a few questions so we can try to figure out what happened and make sure it doesn't happen again. Is that okay?" Andy asked.

Diana looked at her mom and nodded, and Mrs. Vasquez motioned to Andy to have a seat, as she sensed there would be more than just a few questions. Upon prompting by Andy, Diana explained that her brother had recently returned from Europe on one of his business trips and brought back a bottle of Lyzanda that he had been able to purchase. Mrs. Vasquez explained that Bryan hadn't explained how he had gotten it, only that it was much less expensive there and that he would be able to keep up the supply of medication so that Diana could remain on it. Diana told Andy she had just taken the one pill and later that day had started bleeding. When pressed for specifics, she intimated that her bleeding had started about twelve hours or so after taking the pill and that she had stopped taking the warfarin three days before, in anticipation of starting the Lyzanda. She had correctly learned from Andy and Leila that it took about that long for warfarin's effect to dissipate. Andy's face went from inquisitive to disappointed, like a father on learning that his daughter had deceived him.

"I am so sorry, Dr. Friedman," Diana said, choking back tears, "I promise I will never do something like that again. I promise I will always follow your advice and … I don't know what got into me. Bryan was so excited to give me that first dose—he even brought it me on a shiny plate, like it was some delicacy worthy of a beautiful presentation."

"Bryan didn't just give you the bottle?" Andy asked.

"No, he presented the pill like a gift, and I took it. He gave me the bottle afterward."

"Do you have the bottle with you?" Andy asked.

"No, it's at home," Mrs. Vasquez answered. "Do you want me to get it?"

"Yes, but you don't need to do it right now."

Andy continued his questioning. "Did Bryan say anything else about where he got the medication—like from whom or in what country?"

"No, just that it was somewhere in Europe, and I don't know his crazy travel schedule. He is a grown man now. He doesn't have to tell his mother where he is going," Mrs. Vasquez said with a hint of pride in her voice.

"Does it matter, Dr. Friedman?" Diana asked. "Does what matter?" Andy replied.

"Why are you asking where he got it from—do you think there was something wrong with the Lyzanda?" Diana asked.

Andy was caught off guard by Diana's excellent intuition. After all, an altered version of Lyzanda was the cornerstone to their current theory regarding the murders of Mr. Stern and Mr. Millbank. He decided for the sake of the investigation that he needed to play dumb for the moment.

"Uh, I don't know. Do *you* think there was something wrong with it?"

"No. Well, I don't know. I guess I am wondering if you know why I nearly bled to death. Maybe I just had a bad reaction to the Lyzanda, or maybe it was the wrong dose—are there different doses for teenagers?"

"Those are great questions. First, there is only one size pill for Lyzanda. Second, although you are a teenager, I assume your dose would be the same as that of an adult, since you are adult-sized."

"So, Doctor, why did I nearly die?" Diana asked pointedly.

"I don't know yet, but we do have a blood test that will tell us how much Lyzanda was in your blood. I know you told me you took just one pill, but I need you to tell me for 100 percent certainty that you didn't take more."

"Dr. Friedman, I swear to you, I just took the one that Bryan brought to me on a plate. That's it!" Diana stated emphatically.

"Okay, I believe you. Can I ask you a personal question about you and Bryan?" Andy asked, though as soon as he'd finished the sentence he wished he could suck the words out of the air and back into his mouth.

He had been going to ask Diana if Bryan would have any reason to try to hurt her, thinking he might have slipped her the same alleged super-Lyzanda that had killed the bleeders. But he realized that any query about Bryan's intentions would raise suspicions, and although he couldn't recall the question the way he could recall an unread e-mail, he chose to ask a completely unrelated question.

"Sure, Dr. Friedman, what is it?"

"It has been more than a year since Vanessa died, and with this close encounter for you, I was just wondering if you and Bryan are doing okay?"

"Yes and no, I guess, is the best answer. I mean, we have to go on with our lives, and so I am doing my best in school, and Bryan is ... well, we are so proud of him, doing great working for Exxon. He keeps getting new projects and is in line for a big promotion soon," Diana answered, glancing at her mother, who began crying.

"You said yes and no," Andy prompted.

Diana hesitated; tears welled up in her eyes and a slow trickle started moving down her cheek, like a raindrop on a window that has exceeded its allotted weight and begins its gravity-induced journey to the ground. She couldn't bear to look at her mom, who had gotten up and walked into the bathroom, the sound of faint whimpers emerging from beyond the slightly ajar door.

"We still cry every day. We miss her terribly. Is that normal?"

"Are you still all getting counseling?" Andy asked, working hard to contain his own emotions, which was like trying to prevent a sneeze from emerging during a moment of silence.

"No, not really. It helped for a while, but not anymore. Look, we are managing. Mom and Dad have resumed going out and socializing with their friends, and I am doing well in school and have plenty of friends, and Bryan … well, Bryan seems to have made a complete recovery. I haven't seen him cry in a while."

Andy felt bad that he'd had to redirect his line of questioning back toward Vanessa and the family's grieving. He felt as if he had just picked off a nearly healed scab and now it had resumed bleeding. It was the only question that had come to his mind once he'd realized he shouldn't say anything to Diana regarding their suspicions of her brother. He was curious, though, to note that Diana mentioned that Bryan had made "a complete recovery," and that he no longer cried about the loss of Vanessa. It wasn't just the words she'd said; it was more the way she'd said them—she seemed partly perplexed but partly annoyed that he suddenly could move on while she still cried every day.

Mrs. Vasquez emerged from the bathroom, no longer crying, and with a smile on her face as she gazed at her only remaining daughter.

"Diana, Mrs. Vasquez, do you know where Bryan is?" Andy asked in the most innocent tone he could bring forth.

"I assume he's at work—I mean, it's early afternoon, so that's where he would normally be," Diana said matter-of-factly.

"Has he come to visit you since you were admitted?" Andy asked.

"No," Mrs. Vasquez answered succinctly.

"How come—I mean, I would have thought he would be here with your parents during this crisis."

"Doctor," Mrs. Vasquez answered, "it all happened so fast. We've only been here for a day, and Bryan is very busy, you know."

"Yes, I understand. It's just that he has always been so involved," Andy said, but he decided not to press the issue. He figured it would be best to try to hunt Bryan down himself. "Do you have his office number?" he asked.

Mrs. Vasquez fumbled in her purse and pulled out Bryan's card. She carried them in a silver case, protecting them as if they were, in fact, a part of Bryan himself. She handed them out to anyone who asked and even those who didn't ask. It was as if one's pride could be distilled to a business card and handed to others like pictures of one's children. Andy thanked them for answering his questions and informed them that, if all went well, Diana would be discharged the next day and resume her warfarin at home.

Andy looked at Bryan's card on his way to his office. It read:

Bryan J. Vasquez 310-555-5451
Exploration Engineer +1 310 555 1789
ExxonMobil (mobile)
190th Street, Torrance, CA

Impressive and useful, Andy thought. It has his cell phone number clearly written out for Europeans with the +1 for the United States country code and the word *mobile* underneath rather than the American-preferred *cell phone*. Andy dialed his office first and was surprised to hear a woman pick up the call. He was expecting either a menu option or Bryan's voice mail.

"ExxonMobil USA, can I help you?" the voice of what Andy assumed to be his secretary rang through his iPhone.

Andy hesitated for a moment and was about to hang up, but then he had an idea.

"Yes, may I speak to Bryan Vasquez, please?"

"He's not in today. Who may I say is calling?" the voice asked.

"Do you know if he's in town?" Andy asked, hoping to avoid having to lie. "I'm sorry, I need to know who is inquiring," the operator insisted.

"Okay, I am hoping you can keep this discreet," Andy said with a rehearsed tone of resignation. "I am an executive recruiter calling on behalf of my client, British Petroleum, and I wanted to speak to him about an opportunity."

Andy waited. He assumed Bryan was somewhere in the Los Angeles area at a meeting. Then the reply came.

"Uh, are you sure?" Andy said, practically giving away his alias. "Yes, I made the arrangements. I'm sorry, I didn't get your name." Andy hung up, perplexed.

CHAPTER 29

A ndy and Leila had spent the morning busy with patient-care duties. Andy had conducted rounds on all the hospitalized patients, including Diana, while Leila was seeing numerous patients in the clinic. Between their time away and the holidays, a backlog of patients requiring visits had been building, and they had decided to spend several busy days ensuring their patients were seen in a timely manner. After all, this *was* their job, they had said to each other, and thus their primary responsibility, and while the case intrigued them to no end and offered a break from their routine, they felt they were at least to some extent neglecting their patients. Andy had visited Diana, who had made a rapid, if not spectacular, recovery and was ready to be discharged. He elected not to divulge to them what he had learned about Bryan's whereabouts, which only made his suspicions regarding Bryan grow. He felt excited on the one hand that they were getting closer to solving the bizarre mystery of the bleeders, yet on the other hand he was horrified that the perpetrator could be a family member of one of his patients. Despite his warm feelings for the Vasquez family, he was committed to solving the mystery and helping bring the perpetrator to justice, regardless of who it was or what the outcome would be.

Detectives Alvarez and O'Reilly had been put on notice that their sole mission for the time being was to solve the mystery of Mr. Millbank's death. The mayor had communicated this in no uncertain terms to the commissioner of police, who chose to meet directly with the detectives rather than go through intermediaries, to signify the importance. The New York Post's lead story nearly each day involved the bleeders, and raucous headlines such as "Millbank Bleeds, NYPD in the Weeds" suggested that the NYPD and the detectives named in the article had no clue regarding the case and were not making any progress. The media reports were filled with rumor and innuendo suggesting everything from involvement of the mafia to experiments with Ebola virus, all of which raised the tension of New Yorkers. This hysteria, of course, is precisely what the newspapers wanted to help them increase circulation at a time when fewer New Yorkers were buying print media. O'Reilly was quite sure that the media would be perfectly happy if the mystery remained unsolved, so long as they could keep stoking the buzz with each fresh rumor, like a new log on an ever-growing fire. The commissioner admonished the detectives to make some progress and to do it quickly. While Detectives O'Reilly and Alvarez informed him of the progress that was being made regarding Bryan Vasquez and the other leads they were following in Switzerland and Norway, he stated emphatically that he needed to see some local progress. He reminded the detectives that Mr. Millbank had been found dead in one of the city's most prestigious hotels, in the middle of a major tourist area, in the middle of a busy tourist season. Neither O'Reilly nor Alvarez had a good answer for that.

They decided that they should divide and conquer, following up on the leads they had. Detective O'Reilly would visit with Mrs. Millbank, with whom he had developed a good rapport—perhaps too good for his liking—in order to see if she had any knowledge regarding Bryan Vasquez. Detective Alvarez would follow up with Jennifer Carmichael, a.k.a. Alexa, now that she had returned from her vacation, and with the security office at New York Hospital. He also planned to go back and visit with the staff of Empire Health. His goal was to find a connection between Bryan Vasquez and Mr. Millbank. If Andy and Leila's theory was correct, he or someone he worked with in New York must have slipped the super-Lyzanda into Mr. Millbank's body. Alvarez reminded O'Reilly that Mrs. Millbank must still be considered a potential suspect or collaborator—clearly she had the easiest access to Mr. Millbank, and certainly she had a motive, despite her previous statements to the contrary.

After parting company with the others, Detective Alvarez returned to his desk. He had one other task to follow up on before heading over to the offices of Empire Health and New York Hospital. After spending the morning tracking down Bryan Vasquez's manager, Stanley Allen, at ExxonMobil, he had arranged to speak with him at 12:00 Eastern Time/9:00 Pacific Time, when Mr. Allen arrived at his Torrance, California office. Detective Alvarez didn't want to get into a detailed discussion, lest he raise even more suspicion than he already would with his questions about Bryan's travel schedule. He decided he would limit it to two key questions. In particular, he was not going to inquire about Bryan's current whereabouts, since Andy was already working on that.

"Good morning, this is Detective Alvarez. I have a call scheduled with Mr. Allen."

"Yes, he is expecting your call—just one moment," came the voice on the other end of the phone, which was presumably Mr. Allen's secretary.

Alvarez waited for about a minute, and then a confident-sounding deep baritone voice emerged from his receiver.

"Detective Alvarez, Stanley Allen here. What can I do for you?"

"Thanks for giving me a few minutes of your time—I promise I'll be brief."

"Go on," Mr. Allen responded.

"I have two questions about one of your engineers, Bryan Vasquez. First, I understand he went to Norway in November—is that correct?"

"Well, I can't recall the dates—his assistant can help you with that, but we do have operations in Norway, and he is leading some of our efforts there, so it would be reasonable that he would have been there in November."

"Okay, then. Can I ask you if you have business activities in Tromsø?" Alvarez asked.

"Well, probably not, because I have not heard of it, but you will need to tell me where Tromsø is, because I am not an expert on the geography of Norway."

"Tromsø is a city in northern Norway, north of the Arctic Circle. I did some rudimentary research and did not find that there were any oil company offices or operations there—not for ExxonMobil nor for any other oil companies, for that matter."

"Well, then, it looks like you answered that question for yourself," Allen replied.

"Okay. Second question. We know that Mr. Vasquez was in Tromsø, after which he went to Basel, Switzerland, and from there to New York, before returning to Los Angeles. Are you aware of any reason why? You know, like any assignments he might have been on, in Basel or New York?" Alvarez continued with his brief interrogation.

"Well, no I am not, and I didn't send him to those cities, but you have to understand that we trust our employees, particularly our engineers, to come up with solutions to problems or new ideas on their own, and it is not unusual for someone like Bryan to have such a travel schedule. Can I ask you a question?" Mr. Allen requested politely.

"Sure."

"Why aren't you asking Bryan these questions? Is he in some kind of trouble?"

Alvarez had anticipated such a question and had an answer prepared. "No, he is not in any trouble," Alvarez lied. "It's just part of a routine investigation we are conducting."

"What kind of investigation?" Mr. Allen pressed.

"It's nothing out of the ordinary, and you're right; I will simply ask Mr. Vasquez to answer those questions," Alvarez replied, hoping that vague answer would satisfy Mr. Allen. He did not want to delve into any more details on the one hand or raise any more suspicion on the other hand.

"Thanks so much for your time, and I do need to run. Good-bye Mr. Allen," Alvarez said and waited for what he hoped would be a farewell wish. He didn't want to simply hang up.

"No problem. Let me know if I can be of any further assistance," responded Mr. Allen.

"I appreciate it. Take care." And with that, Detective Alvarez hung up.

Detective O'Reilly had arranged to meet Mrs. Millbank at a café on Fifth Avenue, not far from the Metropolitan Museum of Art. She had planned to spend the afternoon there and thought it would be a convenient place to meet. It turned out that Café Andre was not the type of café O'Reilly had expected. It was, in fact, a small bistro. O'Reilly had to remind himself that this meeting was to be all about the investigation and that he needed to remain professional and objective. He'd enjoyed their two dates, especially the one in Queens, near his apartment in Astoria, where they'd had an inexpensive and relaxed dinner at the Aegean Café, a Greek restaurant. But he in no way wanted to take advantage of their relationship in order to further the cause of the investigation. He quickly spotted Mrs. Millbank at the café, already seated at a table and sipping a red-colored drink.

"Sean," she called out to him and waved her hand over her head, while displaying a warm smile that was at once both welcome and dreaded. He was pleased that she was happy to see him, because the truth was he really liked her. Yet at the moment he felt conflicted that he was about to question her as a potential suspect in the case he was investigating.

"Hi, Mrs. Millbank," he responded.

"Mrs. Millbank," she replied sarcastically, raising her eyebrows and pursing her lips. "Haven't we been down this road before, Sean?"

"Yes, I'm sorry, but since I'm here to ask you questions about the case … and since, well … you know, you are still a suspect, I wanted to greet you professionally."

"Well, forget that, Sean—oh, and I'm going to call you Sean regardless of what you say. Listen, I understand you need to do your job, and I will help you however I can. I have nothing to hide, I assure you," she replied.

"Still, it's just … you know—" O'Reilly muttered before Julie interrupted. "Please, stop being so nervous. You can continue to consider me a suspect, and you can ask me whatever you like. As I said to you many times, I have nothing to hide."

"Okay. And you're sure you don't want to have a lawyer present for this discussion?"

"Sean, how many times do I have to say it? I … have … nothing … to … hide!" she stated emphatically, enunciating each word in the sentence as if Detective O'Reilly were hearing impaired. "By the way, I don't collect the insurance money until this is all resolved, so if anything, I have a motive to help you figure out what happened."

That unexpected, yet sensible, answer finally convinced the detective to relax. O'Reilly proceeded to order a drink. He decided to get the raspberry iced tea that Mrs. Millbank was drinking. As at their last lunch at a French restaurant in the city, she ordered their food, since O'Reilly could barely read, much less pronounce, the items on the menu.

"So, how can I help?" Mrs. Millbank asked once their order had been taken. "As usual, I can't tell you much of what we know or think we know, but let me simply start with a name—Bryan Vasquez. Does that ring a bell?"

"No. Should it?"

"I don't know. You tell me," O'Reilly continued.

"Never heard of him—is he one of Creighton's colleagues or friends?"

"Like I said, I can't tell you much, and with apologies, I think this will work better if I ask questions and you just answer them if you can, okay?"

"Sure, no problem," Mrs. Millbank responded with a smile.

"What I can tell you is that this man, Bryan Vasquez, was in the city on the day your husband died. In fact, he had arrived a couple of days earlier. We think he might be involved in the case, but we are having a hard time linking him in any way to your husband."

"Okay, but I'm not sure I can help. I've never heard of him, don't know what he looks like, and didn't keep up with Creighton's business world, you know."

O'Reilly thought for a moment and then realized that Mrs. Millbank had given him an idea.

"If I show you a picture of him, perhaps you'll recognize him. After all, he might have been using an alias, so maybe you did meet him and don't know it."

O'Reilly removed his cell phone from his pocket and opened the file that contained the pictures of all the players in the case. He scrolled through them and, after finding the one he was looking for, turned his screen toward Mrs. Millbank. She looked at it intently, put her lips together, and shook her head. O'Reilly then asked her whether it was possible that Bryan had come into contact with Mr. Millbank in their home, and she again shook her head, saying that Creighton had never brought business home with him. O'Reilly was at a loss as to where to go next in his inquiry. Meanwhile their food arrived, and he thought it made sense to take a break from the interrogation. While they were eating, they purposely avoided any discussion about the case and chose instead to discuss current events. After they'd completed their meal, Mrs. Millbank asked O'Reilly if she could ask him just one question regarding the case, and he motioned for her to go ahead.

"Is it possible that Mr. Vasquez might have met Alexa? Maybe that's the link between him and Creighton. Maybe he's a boyfriend, or family member, or who knows what?"

"Interesting. I hadn't thought about that. Detective Alvarez is going to question—uh, never mind." O'Reilly realized that he had been about to divulge that they had identified Alexa, and he didn't want Mrs. Millbank to know—at least not at this sensitive point in the case.

"Excuse me!" she replied. "Question *Alexa*? Is that what you were going to say?"

O'Reilly decided he shouldn't deceive Julie—not about this issue, for sure.

"I am not supposed to tell you about this—not now, I mean. I was going to tell you at some point, but—"

"Well, I think I have a right to know if you found Alexa," Mrs. Millbank replied, sitting back in her chair and folding her arms.

"Yes, you do, but you must promise me that you will in no way interfere with the case—no contacting her, nothing. Please. If you do, you can get me in big trouble—really big trouble." O'Reilly pleaded.

"I won't, I promise. Who is she?"

"She's a doctor at New York Hospital."

"Huh. So that's why she would go there and then disappear and never come out again. What's her name?" Mrs. Millbank demanded.

"I, uh, I shouldn't tell you. Besides, you don't know her, so what's the difference?"

"The difference? She was the woman my husband cheated on me with. I just want to know her name."

"Can I tell you later?" O'Reilly begged. "No. I want to know now, Sean."

He relented. "Her name is Jennifer Carmichael, and she's a pathologist at New York Hospital. Satisfied?"

"Yes, and I promise I won't say or do anything—at least until the case is solved," she said, flashing a Cheshire grin.

They sat there looking at each other. O'Reilly felt that he had now betrayed both Mrs. Millbank and the police department, the first by questioning her as a suspect and the second by cluing her in to more details about the case than he had wanted to. She broke the silence.

"So, do you think this Bryan Vasquez person might have known Alexa?"

"Like I said, I don't know, and I hadn't thought about that."

"Hey, I have an idea," Mrs. Millbank offered. "Are you open to suggestions, or are you going to be the typical New York stubborn, know-it-all cop?"

"Uh, where did you get the idea that New York cops are like that—because you're wrong."

"TV. Aren't you all like Detective Briscoe from *Law & Order*, or you know, that guy from *NYPD Blue*—I don't remember his name."

O'Reilly laughed. "TV cops are all overdramatized, Julie. I can't believe you really think we're like that."

"Thanks—for calling me Julie. It makes me feel like you actually believe me."

"So, what's this idea you have?" O'Reilly inquired. "I'll take anything reasonable at this point. We need to connect Bryan to your deceased husband, or else our leading theory goes to hell in a handbasket."

"So, how much do you know about my efforts to check up on Creighton?" Mrs. Millbank asked enticingly.

"Nothing, other than what you told us about tailing Alexa to New York Hospital that one time. Did you do more than follow her here and there?"

"A lot more. For one thing, I hired a private detective to follow Creighton after work and when he left the house for a so-called business meeting," Mrs. Millbank replied. She continued, "He's the one that discovered the affair Creighton was having with Alexa, or whatever her name is—"

"Dr. Carmichael, or Jennifer," O'Reilly interrupted, briefly intrigued by what he was hearing.

"Well, whatever. You even said it shouldn't matter to me. Anyway, once my private eye discovered the affair with—I'll just call her Alexa, I asked him to follow her around, and I got so curious I followed her occasionally too."

"Do you think your private detective might recognize Bryan?"

"I don't know, but I don't think so," Mrs. Millbank replied confidently. "Sorry, I am not following—how might this help us?"

"I have pictures. Thousands of pictures," Mrs. Millbank added, wide-eyed and smiling.

"Pictures of what exactly?"

"Geez, do I have to spell it out for you?"

"Please do," O'Reilly replied, confused.

"Sean, I have thousands of pictures of Creighton with Alexa, without Alexa, and of Alexa with other men all over the city. Maybe you can match one of the men in the picture to Bryan Vasquez, making the link you say you need."

O'Reilly sat staring at Julie, processing what she had just told him, and slowly his facial expression changed. The corners of his mouth symmetrically rose, while his eyes appeared to grow in size as they brightened till he looked like a cartoon character.

"That's a great idea, Julie—a great idea! How many pictures do you have, exactly?" O'Reilly stated, his excitement growing.

"I don't know, Sean, but thousands. They're all on my laptop. I take it you want them?"

"Yes, yes. Of course. This could be the breakthrough we need," O'Reilly responded gleefully.

"No problem. When do you want them?"

"Uh—now!" O'Reilly stated emphatically.

Mrs. Millbank indicated the door to Sean, who got up from his chair, and they headed out of the café. As it was a reasonably pleasant afternoon—at least for January—with temperatures in the high forties, they decided to walk to her apartment. On the way, they discussed where they could go together after the case was solved. O'Reilly already was developing feelings for Mrs. Millbank, and any talk of going away together at once filled his heart with warmth and his stomach with nausea. It had been many, many years since he'd spent more than a few hours straight with any woman. When they arrived at her apartment, Mrs. Millbank went to her bedroom and returned with her computer. After turning it on, she opened the folder where she stored the pictures and indicated to Detective O'Reilly the number of items in the folder—3,894. Detective O'Reilly sat back in his chair, realizing that with that number of images it would be no small task to find Bryan Vasquez—assuming that he actually *was* in any of them. Mrs. Millbank put a flash drive in the computer and began copying them over. The indicator on the computer stated it would take forty minutes to make the transfer. They decided to talk about where they might go once the case was solved. They were both happy.

Alvarez arrived at New York Hospital unannounced and having no planned meeting with Dr. Carmichael. He figured she would simply do her best to avoid him, so his strategy was to try to surprise her. Perhaps catching her off guard might lead her to make a mistake, he thought. He showed his badge at the front desk and received a pass to give him free access in the hospital. He decided to head down to the pathology conference room first. He figured that if she wasn't there, someone might know where she was. Upon his arrival, he saw the medical student that he had met previously, though he didn't recall her name.

"Hello, I'm—"

"Detective Alvarez, I remember," she replied.

"Oh, good memory. I apologize that my memory isn't as good as yours."

"I'm Taylor Davis."

"Hi, Taylor. Do you know where Dr. Carmichael is?"

"She stepped out to get something to drink—she should be right back. We were just reviewing a patient's case."

Clearly she has no idea that Dr. Carmichael is under suspicion for committing a horrible crime, Alvarez thought. He told Taylor that he needed to speak to Dr. Carmichael briefly and he would sit and wait for her. No sooner did he sit down than Dr. Carmichael walked into the conference room with a bottle of iced tea. "What the fuck are you doing here?" she asked bluntly, clearly upset at the sight of the detective who'd searched her office and her apartment. Taylor, terribly uncomfortable witnessing what to her was Dr. Carmichael's unprovoked attack on a police officer, walked out of the conference room.

"I need to ask you some questions, Dr. Carmichael," Alvarez stated in a calm, professional tone, in contrast to the doctor's obvious anger.

"Who the fuck let you in here, anyway—and I have nothing to say to you," came her terse reply.

"I understand that you are upset with—"

"Damn straight. Now get the fuck out of here. I'm going to call security, and unless you have a warrant of some kind, I don't think you can stay here—you're not invited."

"You know, your anger only makes me more suspicious that you did something wrong. If you could just answer a few questions, perhaps we won't need to bother you again—and more importantly, not suspect that you're involved in Mr. Millbank's murder," Alvarez said calmly, taking notice that the medical student who had left the room briefly had now returned and was standing in the doorway observing the unusual scene in front of her.

"Of course I did something wrong. I committed adultery, and I feel horrible about it. I don't need you reinforcing my guilty feelings. Now, if you have an arrest warrant, go ahead and arrest me, and if you don't, then please leave. I don't need to talk to you."

Alvarez stood silently, stealing a glance at Taylor Davis, who simply looked back at him and then over at Dr. Carmichael.

"So, what's the deal? Do you have one or not?" Dr. Carmichael insisted.

"No. I have no reason to arrest you. I just had a few questions, and then I'll be on my way."

Alvarez remained calm, as if he were the eye of the hurricane that was Dr. Carmichael moving to and fro, clearly agitated.

"Are you deaf?" she said, suddenly more calm. She took two steps and leaned her head toward Alvarez, suggesting he hadn't been able to hear her.

"No, I'm not. Last chance to—" Alvarez tried one last time to engage her, while remaining as calm as he had been when he'd walked into the room.

"Are you threatening me?" Dr. Carmichael interrupted. "Look, I don't know what you are looking for, but besides cheating, I didn't do anything wrong. I don't feel the need to, nor do I want to, answer your questions. I'm still pissed off that you searched my office and my apartment. Now, please leave."

Alvarez accepted that he was, for the moment anyway, defeated. He apologized to Taylor for placing her in this uncomfortable situation. As he left, he heard Dr. Carmichael apologize to her as well, and while he had half a notion to stand in the hallway for a moment or two to see what else she might say, he decided that was not a good idea and left.

Andy glanced at the clock in his office. It was 5:00 p.m., and he figured Leila should be done seeing patients by now. He called her cell phone. She picked up, said she was on another call, and asked him to come to her office. When he arrived at Leila's office, she was sitting in her chair, reclined, with her head back, raven-black hair following gravity's line toward the ground behind her chair. He could tell she was tired.

"Hey, there," he said. "Hey, how are you?"

"Tired," Andy replied. "Me too."

"I can tell," he said. "How many patients did you see today?"

"I don't know," she said softly. "More than I have seen in one day in a long time."

"Why didn't you call me for help?" Andy wondered.

"Because you were busy with Diana and the other inpatients."

"Next time, please call me to help out," Andy replied. "Hey, listen, I have some news."

Leila sat straight up and turned her chair to face Andy. No matter how tired she was, she could always muster up energy for the case. Andy reviewed his discussion with Diana and her mom regarding the Lyzanda, explaining that she had just taken the one pill and describing the manner in which Bryan had presented it to her, like a gift.

"That's odd," Leila said.

"Indeed it is. Clearly he gave her the one pill she took that almost killed her," Andy added.

"But you don't think he would try to kill her, do you?"

"No, not at all, but your idea that he might have brought home both the regular Lyzanda and the super-Lyzanda and that he mixed them up and accidentally gave his sister the wrong one is definitely possible," Andy said.

"That reminds me. Aren't we supposed to have the lab results back to see how much Lyzanda was in her blood?" Leila asked.

"Yes, let's call the lab now. By the way, that's not all I found out, but let's call the lab first," Andy said.

"Do you get some kind of thrill keeping me in suspense like that?" Leila said with a hint of annoyance.

"Probably the same rise you get when you do it to me," Andy replied, smiling.

They dialed the lab's number.

"Dr. Friedman, did you say?" came the voice over the speakerphone. Andy replied affirmatively.

"I'm glad you called. Is your phone working?"

"Yes, why?"

"Well, we've tried calling a few times and just get your secretary's voice mail."

"Oh, sorry. She's out on vacation and maybe her backup called in sick.

Anyway, what's this about?"

"Dr. Raj wants to speak to you—let me see if he's still here."

Leila put her hands up in the air, motioning that she was confused. Andy explained that Dr. Raj was the lab director at the LA County drug lab.

"Hello, Dr. Andy," came a heavily accented voice over the speakerphone.

"Just Andy is fine."

"Okay, Dr. Andy." Andy looked at Leila and rolled his eyes, and they laughed silently. Doctors from India tended to call other doctors by their first name but always with the salutation, Dr., first.

"Do you have some information for us?" Andy asked.

"Yes. Very interesting. Very interesting," the Indian voice continued. "First, we ran the actual drug dissolved in a diluent. Do you know much about high-performance liquid chromatography, Dr. Andy?"

"A bit, but not much."

"Well, what we do is run the known sample, that is the drug in the diluent, and then find the peak on the chromatograph where the molecule is found. We also look for contaminants—other smaller peaks. Basically, if the sample is pure, the readout shows a single spike, kind of like the spike you would see on a Richter scale if there was an earthquake. The only difference is that we would see just one spike, not many, over a period of time. Depending on the location on the graph and how high the spike is, we can tell you what chemical is in the blood and how much."

"Got it; go on."

"When we run your sample from the patient, we look for the peak in the same location so we know it is the same drug, and then we can measure the height of the peak, which tells us how much of the drug is in the blood."

"So, what did you find?" Andy asked.

"Very strange, very strange," Dr. Raj stated quizzically.

"Yes," Andy stated impatiently. "Please tell us what you found."

"Your patient has a very high spike at the location of the Lyzanda, but it has a double peak. Very strange."

"Dr. Raj, please get to the point," Andy demanded, finally losing his patience.

"Yes, sorry. I tend to—never mind. This means that what was in the patient's blood is Lyzanda, but it has been altered in some way. The spike is so high that it would be like taking at least twenty Lyzanda pills, but if that were the case, it wouldn't have the double peak. Do you know how many pills she took?"

"She swears she took just one," Andy replied.

"Good. That makes sense, actually. So, this pill she took is Lyzanda, but it's like a highly potent version of it. Does that help you?"

"Dr. Raj, you have no idea how much. Thank you so much for running the test so fast and explaining it all—I am sorry if I lost my patience a bit," Andy said, his face brimming with excitement.

"Oh, don't worry. It drives my wife crazy, too, how I have to explain everything."

"Thank you again. We'll call you if we have questions. Oh, one more thing—can you please store the blood sample you have? This might be a criminal case."

"Sure thing—we store such samples here all the time."

With that, Andy hung up. Leila sat silently staring at Andy, eyes practically popping out of their sockets and mouth wide open. She looked as if she'd seen a ghost as she came to the realization that their theory about Bryan was irrefutable now. Andy looked at her with a much more sober face as he came to the same realization, that the acclaimed and successful brother of two of their patients was the perpetrator of two murders. Or so they thought.

"Andy, if Bryan is the killer, I still don't see how he could have killed Mr. Stern if he was not in Switzerland at the time of his death. From Diana's near-death experience, we know that the super-Lyzanda works within about twelve hours. So I don't get that."

"Me neither. Unless he had help," Andy suggested. "You mean from Carmichael and Costa or Hummels."

"Yes."

"But he didn't know any of them … and I don't know how he could have pulled it off. I mean, why would they even agree to work with him?" Leila wondered.

"Well, we still have some work to do to figure that out," Andy responded. "You said you were going to tell me one more thing. What is it? Though I confess I am not sure I am ready for another big surprise," Leila told Andy.

"Oh, yeah. Well, I have no idea how this fits in, but well, I called Vasquez's office and spoke to his assistant, and well, it's weird …"

"Yes?"

"She booked him on what she said was a business-related trip to Aberdeen, Scotland."

"*Aberdeen?*"

"That's what I said."

CHAPTER 30

A ndy couldn't believe he was back at the airport yet again. This time he hadn't even met with the boss. He had e-mailed him to arrange another meeting and had been told to take whatever time he and Leila needed to solve the case. He'd responded to Andy's rather stunned e-mail reply by saying he had taken an interest in the case and was following the developments in the New York media.

After Andy's discussion with Detectives O'Reilly and Alvarez on Friday, he'd agreed to return to New York. Leila had agreed to go but only after a weekend of rest. He didn't remember ever flying so much in such a short time, and while he loved going to New York, he preferred his visits to be more spread apart and preferably in the spring or fall, not in the middle of winter. On another level, he wasn't sure how to greet Leila this time. Last time they'd met at the airport, she'd nearly torn his head off when he didn't hug her and kiss her. Since that trip, they had decided not to pursue their relationship any further, which elicited a great sense of *what if?* He knew he loved Leila; however he was beginning to accept that he would never have a meaningful relationship with her. But then she'd kissed him just a day or two ago—and not just a friendly peck on the cheek but a full-on-the-lips kiss backed by what he sensed was warmth and passion. He had no doubt about that. He was very confused. He had no doubt about that, either.

Leila had spent the weekend at home, hardly leaving her apartment. She was physically and emotionally exhausted from the investigation, a busy week at work, and the numerous conversations with her parents that she'd initiated over New Year's weekend when she'd left New York. She'd needed two full days to recharge—she was the iPhone and her bed the charger. She didn't want to get up until fully recharged, especially knowing that she was headed back to New York.

She entered Terminal 4 at LAX yet again, cleared security, and stopped at the first Starbucks she saw. While she indeed felt reenergized, a vanilla latte was the way most of her days began—a morning ritual not to be skipped under any circumstance. She headed to the gate and saw Andy. He saw her out of the corner of his eye but purposely did not look her way, instead staring intently at the screen of his iPhone, pretending to be distracted to ensure that Leila would be forced to make the first move—and so she did.

"Hey," she said, tapping Andy on the shoulder and embracing him warmly. There was no kiss. He hugged her tightly—the type of hug reserved for a significant other—and she squeezed his back. While still in their embrace, they pulled back just enough so that their faces were within inches of one another. Andy waited. He didn't know what to do. Leila looked at him intently and then let go. He did the same. He wasn't sure what to think. At least he hadn't incurred any ire this time. He considered that a small victory. They talked about their weekend, with Leila explaining that she hadn't called simply because she'd needed a break. Andy told her how he had spent his weekend catching up on writing papers he had neglected and exercising his body, which he had also been neglecting the past few months. He told her how he'd gone on a hike in the Hollywood Hills and a jog on the beach in Santa Monica.

After they'd boarded the flight and taken their seats, Andy caught Leila up on his earlier conversation with O'Reilly and Alvarez. He explained that, while there was as of yet no link between Bryan and Mr.

Millbank or Alexa, they were more hopeful now than they had been previously. Andy explained O'Reilly's discovery that Mrs. Millbank had thousands of pictures taken by a private investigator who had followed Mr. Millbank and Alexa, a.k.a. Jennifer Carmichael. Both he and Alvarez hoped that the analysis of this trove of photographs would provide the key pieces of information they still needed to solve the mystery. He went on to describe Alvarez's attempt at interviewing Carmichael and how she had unfortunately been far less than accommodating—though it made Andy wonder whether or not she was involved. After all, why would she act in such a hostile manner if she really were Mr. Millbank's killer? That would only increase everyone's suspicions and intensify the scrutiny already brought on by her actions and secrecy.

Andy and Leila agreed, as on past flights, to keep to themselves. Andy wanted to do some writing, while Leila had downloaded the second season of *Royal Pains*, a medical drama she'd gotten hooked on after she'd found out there was a character with hemophilia on the show—something she had never heard of before. As soon as Andy heard the sound of the familiar ping indicated it was okay to use electronic devices, he reached first for his iPhone and noise-cancelling headphones and then his computer. As his computer was waking up, he dialed through his iPhone to decide what music he was in the mood to listen to. *Definitely nothing romantic or sexual*, he thought, which ruled out Maroon 5 and some of the Waterboys' music he so loved; thus he settled on Black 47 with their Irish rock sound and politically charged songs. He set the iPhone to shuffle through Black 47's selections, and in a moment his ears were filled with a haunting female voice singing in Celtic as the intro to the song, "The Big Fellah," began filling his ears. This was quickly followed by rhythmic electric guitar and pounding drums, before the horns and the Uilleann pipes, sounding like a victorious anthem, heralded the lyrics that were to come. The sound was rich and full, orchestral, despite the relatively small number of instruments. No love songs, for sure, but music intense in its sound and the stories it told.

Leila was sitting cross-legged, iPad nestled comfortably on her knees, watching the opening segment to *Royal Pains*. She and Andy were both content. Andy would find the right opportunity later to figure out what was happening with Leila. As "The Big Fellah" finished, the song "Blood Wedding" came on, and Andy laughed. *Why do the songs with the word* blood *keep popping up on these trips? There aren't that many, after all.*

In preparation for Andy and Leila's arrival, Detectives Alvarez and O'Reilly began perusing through the thousands of pictures Mrs. Millbank's private detective had taken. O'Reilly, complaining the whole time, harkened back to the days prior to digital photography, when each photo taken had had a fixed cost for both the film and developing process, so that people were far more careful about how many pictures they took. At least they didn't have to rifle through thousands of printed pictures, which surely would have made the task that much more tedious. Instead, they sorted the digital images into separate folders based on where they thought they were taken: Mr. Millbank's office, a restaurant, hotel, coffee shop, etc. Neither of them was convinced that this would help them find anything useful, but they did it nonetheless. They had also had the audio-visual team set up the conference room so that the images would display on a large LCD monitor, and they alerted their digital photo expert to be available at 10:00 a.m. sharp the next day. The detectives were hoping the key to solving Mr. Millbank's death was somehow digitally painted across one or more of the pictures. While the evidence against Bryan Vasquez was mounting, they were still perplexed as to how he could have gotten close enough to Mr. Millbank to deliver the super-Lyzanda into his body. He had the motive and the means but hadn't had the opportunity. This was the final piece they needed before they could proceed to arrest him.

The flight was uneventful, boring even, and Andy and Leila's plane touched down at JFK International Airport just as dusk turned to night. They quickly gathered their things—they'd brought far more than they'd thought they might need; they didn't want to be stranded in New York without enough clothes. For this trip, Detective Alvarez had requested that they purchase open-ended tickets. He'd told them that he didn't want them to keep flying back and forth across the country, but Leila sensed that he simply didn't want them to leave until they'd solved the mystery. He related to them how much pressure was being applied, not just by the police commissioner but also by the mayor, to solve the case. They were all getting tired of the around-the-clock media coverage this case was receiving. The *New York Post* headlines were bad enough, but having "The Bleeders" be the lead story on Anderson Cooper 360 every evening on CNN, raising all kinds of questions about the competency of NYPD detectives, was quite unbearable. No one in the NYPD team was quite sure why Anderson Cooper was so fascinated by this case, until one of them suggested that it was probably due to the fact that he was a native New Yorker.

Andy and Leila checked into the Westin Times Square Hotel and agreed to meet in the lobby and head back over to Little Italy for dinner. Though Andy had suggested they go to Chinatown, as he'd wanted Leila to experience as many of New York City's neighborhoods as she could while they had the opportunity, she'd insisted on returning to Little Italy. As they walked outside from the lobby, Andy remarked that it was not as cold as their last visit, to which Leila rolled her eyes, exhaled strongly and pointing to the fog of condensed air emerging from her mouth, reminding Andy that you never saw that in LA.

After dinner at Sal's on Broome Street, they headed to Greenwich Village to catch some live music at the Bitter End before returning to the hotel. There was no relationship discussion, kissing, or hugging this evening. Whatever might have been going through their minds, it seemed their focus was solely on solving the mystery of the bleeders. Andy placed his iPhone in the docking station, put on the most recent release by Bon Iver, and drifted off to sleep with the soothing guitar and soft falsetto of Justin Vernon's voice as the song "Holocene" seemed to float out of the speakers toward the ceiling, and his eyes closed.

"Good morning, Leila. Good morning, Andy. Please have a seat," Alvarez said. "How about some breakfast?"

He pointed to a pile of bagels surrounded by several containers of different flavors of cream cheese. He suggested they eat and then get comfortable, as they were likely to be in this conference room all day. He explained that their mission for the day was to sort through the thousands of pictures taken by Mrs. Millbank's detective. He reiterated to them the pressure they were under to solve the case and said that he was hoping—in fact, praying—that they would be able to link Bryan to Mr. Millbank or Jennifer Carmichael with one or more of the pictures.

"Good morning," Detective O'Reilly greeted them as he walked into the conference room. With him was a young man wearing horn-rimmed glasses, with wild curly hair so long it looked like a wig for a Halloween costume. In fact, he looked as if he'd been ripped from the pages of a circa 1976 teen magazine. "This is Evan Belkin; he is going to be our computer whiz for the day."

Andy and Leila stood up, shook his hand, and introduced themselves. Evan didn't look much older than a high-school student; however, O'Reilly had assured them that Evan was the brightest IT expert their division had and that he was very adept with the best imaging software available, which would help them sort through the 3,894 photographs Mrs. Millbank had provided them.

"I'm sorry, but did you say 3,894 pictures?" Leila inquired, clearly surprised by the volume.

"Yup," O'Reilly answered. "Digital photography—gotta love it. No cost to take as many fucking pictures as you want, so why not?"

"What exactly are we looking for?" Andy asked.

"Well, we're not exactly sure, to be honest, but I suppose for starters just looking for Bryan in any picture would be a small victory, so how about that for now?" Alvarez replied.

"Can't your software do that?" Leila asked. "I mean, iPhoto on my Mac can do it."

"Well, yes and no," Evan responded and proceeded as if he were teaching a sixth-grade computer class. "You see, the software is great if there is a clear picture of someone's face, and they have not altered their appearance, and the lighting is good and, well, a few other things. If the picture is dark, if the face is partially hidden. I could go on—"

"Leila, on your Mac you have pictures of yourself, your family, friends—mostly candid pictures," Alvarez interrupted, "but the nature of these pictures, which are mostly shot through a telephoto lens from significant distance, at odd angles … basically, Bryan was not staring into the camera and saying cheese, so the software can't detect his face that well."

Evan continued, "Yesterday, we did sort through many of the pictures and asked the computer to match pictures to the one we have of Bryan from his work ID—"

"And?" Andy interrupted.

"Well, the way we had the settings, it didn't pick up any matches. So we altered the settings, but then it flagged hundreds of pictures," Evan completed his thought.

"We looked at those pictures and after the first fifty that weren't Bryan, we decided to stop; we came to the realization we were going to have to do this one by one, with our own eyes," Alvarez stated.

"I have to say this actually makes me feel good," Leila said. "I am glad to know that computers and software still can't fully replace the human eye and brain. Let's get started, shall we?"

"Great. We did sort the pictures by location—Mr. Millbank's office, restaurants, hotels—as best we could, anyway. Any preferences as to where we start?" O'Reilly asked.

"How about his office?" Andy said. "I think if Bryan were going to meet him directly, he would need to start there."

"Okay. Evan, please." Alvarez motioned to the young computer whiz.

Evan opened a folder with 389 pictures. The thumbnails revealed a sequence of pictures beginning with ones taken of the entrance to the large office building that housed Empire Health on Thirty-Fourth Street and continued with pictures taken in the lobby.

"With all the security, I am surprised the private detective was able to get a camera in there—especially one with a telephoto lens," Andy wondered aloud.

"The ones in the lobby were taken using a hidden camera, apparently," O'Reilly explained.

"Could Bryan have been wearing a disguise?" Leila asked. "After all, if he was going to kill Mr. Millbank, you'd think he would try to hide his identity."

"Maybe, but on the other hand, it couldn't be something too obvious. After all, if he was going to meet him, it would be in the context of a business meeting, don't you think?" O'Reilly replied.

"Who knows?" Leila replied. "Let's just look through them slowly and see if we find any with Bryan."

Evan selected the first image and displayed it in the full-screen view, moving slowly through the pictures one by one as the two detectives and two doctors viewed them on the large LCD monitor at the front of the conference room. The pictures were displayed in time order, as agreed upon by the group, and Evan used the date and time stamp for each file to sort them in that sequence. The earliest pictures were from March— eight months before the murder. Andy, Leila, and the detectives looked at each one intently, pointing out the people they recognized in the picture like a toddler pointing to the familiar characters in a book being read to him by his parents. By taking the time to go through them meticulously, they were confident they wouldn't miss Bryan if he were, in fact, to be found in any of them. Since only Leila and Andy had seen Bryan in person, the detectives were relying on them to identify him. Mr. Millbank was visible in nearly all the pictures, occasionally by himself; however, he was usually with a variety of other people, many of whom were employees of Empire Health. The pictures from the lobby showed Mr. Millbank with his assistant, Mr. Vinh Tran, the Vietnamese doctor they had interviewed, and several other employees the detectives recognized. Unfortunately, none of the people in the pictures bore any resemblance to Bryan. Detective Alvarez also pointed out that in none of the pictures was there even the suggestion of anything particularly suspicious. Lastly, Detective O'Reilly stated that he had been paying particular attention to the women in the images but he could not spot any picture that suggested the presence of Alexa, a.k.a. Jennifer Carmichael.

After nearly three hours of gazing at hundreds of images, they took a brief break, but they all then agreed to proceed, clearly intent on making the breakthrough they so desperately wanted and needed. Next, they elected to view all the pictures that were presumably taken in hotels—in the lobbies and in the bars, with Mr. Millbank inside as well as entering and leaving. This set yielded a lot more interesting information. Again moving forward chronologically, at first they saw Mr. Millbank only with men and occasionally older-appearing women in tailored suits. The assumption was that these people were business associates or friends that he was having lunch with or enjoying happy hour with. Then, beginning in May, they spotted Jennifer Carmichael in one of the pictures. She was seated at the far end of a bar near the edge of that particular frame without her wig and dressed in an elegant, yet very sexy, outfit. She had a tight halter-top cocktail dress accentuating her ample breasts and revealing fit and toned shoulders, arms, and legs. It was clear she exercised, and it was clear she was hoping to get noticed.

"Jennifer Carmichael—and no wig," Andy pointed out to the group.

"Yeah, well, she didn't need a disguise if she's out to meet men, right?" Alvarez followed.

"Right!" Leila said, smilingly indicating that as the only woman in the room she probably should have answered Andy's query.

As they looked through the sequence of photos from that day in May, they got to their first picture with Mr. Millbank and Jennifer Carmichael next to each other. He was standing next to her holding a clear drink, while she was holding a bright-red drink. It was clear they had struck up a conversation. As they continued to look at the hotel folder of pictures sequentially, it played like an old movie shot in still frames and then patched together. Then suddenly, in September, they spotted a picture of what appeared to be the two of them again in a hotel lobby, only this time the woman's hair was quite different. Leila pointed out that it was indeed still Jennifer Carmichael, only in the latest picture she had donned the now infamous wig.

"I wonder why she started wearing the wig?" O'Reilly asked. "I have an idea," Leila said in a wondering tone.

"Yeah, what?" Andy asked.

"Well, perhaps Mr. Millbank was spotted with Jennifer, either by an employee or a friend, or ..." Leila hesitated.

"Or what?" O'Reilly urged her to continue.

"Or Mrs. Millbank found out—perhaps from the pictures—confronted her husband, and instead of ending the relationship, he asked Jennifer to be more discrete."

"Makes sense, I guess," said Alvarez.

"I can find out about that—at least the second part," O'Reilly replied, indicating he could ask Mrs. Millbank if and when she'd confronted her husband about the affair. He said he would call her when they took another break from viewing the pictures.

"Let's keep going," Alvarez suggested. "We already know that Dr. Carmichael, Alexa, was Mr. Millbank's mistress. What we really need is to find Bryan in one of these pictures if we're going to link him to the murder."

At Alvarez's request, they continued to look at the pictures from the hotel file, but there was no sign of Bryan or any other persons of interest. The information that emerged from the remainder of the pictures was that Mr. Millbank and Dr. Carmichael were seeing each other more and more often. As they moved from late October and into November, they met nearly daily. Furthermore, in some of the picture series, the last photo of the day demonstrated Mr. Millbank and Dr. Carmichael entering one of the hotel elevators, presumably heading to a room for a late afternoon or early-evening tryst. Several of those alleged trysts took place at the Plaza Hotel where Mr. Millbank was found dead later in November.

"Well, that's the last of the hotel file," Evan announced. "Which one do you want me to open next?"

"I've got a headache. Can we please take a break?" Andy requested. "We've been going at this for more than five hours. Damn, this is going to take a long time. How many pictures have we actually gone through Evan?"

"Let me see. There were 389 in the office file and 226 in the hotel file, so that's 615. That's about sixteen percent," Evan declared, showing quick math skills and no hint of emotion.

"That's okay. I think we've made good progress for one morning—er, morning and early afternoon. We just need to keep plugging away. This is our only lead right now," Alvarez said. And with that, the group took a short break.

Upon returning to the conference room twenty minutes later, they found that a tray of fruit and granola bars as well as drinks had been placed on the table. Andy, Leila, and Evan each grabbed a drink and a snack, while O'Reilly and Alvarez hadn't yet returned from their offices. A few minutes, later, they did return.

"Mrs. Millbank agreed to meet me for an 'afternoon tea'—her expression, I swear," O'Reilly stated, not that any of them would have expected him to utter that term. "I'll see what I can find out." Thus they all parted company, agreeing to meet again at 6:00 p.m, that same day.

Andy and Leila were in the mood for pizza, and there was no better place for pizza in Andy's mind than New York City. They headed out of the police station and melted into the crowd of humanity walking down Lafayette Street toward Greenwich Village. Detective O'Reilly, meanwhile, headed over to Mrs. Millbank's apartment.

"Sean, so good to see you again," Julie Millbank said as she welcomed Detective O'Reilly to her enormous apartment in Park Avenue. "To what do I owe this nice surprise?"

"Julie, I am just here for information today, and I have to get back to the office. I'm sorry, but if we can just get to the point of my visit quickly, that would be great."

"Well, do have some tea, and I have some fresh sandwiches and scones. You will allow me to feed you, yes?" she replied.

"Sure. Thank you. Look, we have been looking through all the pictures you so kindly provided, and we found lots of pictures of your husband with Dr. Jennifer Carmichael. Up until September, she did not disguise herself when she was with your husband, but after that, in all the remaining pictures right up until your husband's death, she's wearing a wig. Any idea why?"

A broad smile came across Mrs. Millbank's face. "But of course I know why, Sean," she said.

"Well, are you willing to share that information?"

"What kind of detective are you, Sean? Surely you've figured that out," Mrs. Millbank added playfully.

"Julie, please, we've been working for eight hours straight. I am not in the mood for a guessing game."

"Okay. I'm sorry. After my private detective showed me the many pictures of Creighton with Dr. Carmichael, I confronted him. He told me he was sorry and that he would stop seeing her."

"Did you tell him you had someone following him and taking pictures?"

"No. I, uh, didn't want to give that away. I told a white lie, making him believe that I had followed him and saw him with a young woman," Julie continued.

"So, you think he wanted to continue seeing her and asked her to wear a disguise when they were together in public?" O'Reilly asked suggestively.

"I am quite sure that is what happened," Julie replied confidently.

"Okay, thanks so much again—you've been a very helpful witness, Julie.

And, er—um, well, I—" O'Reilly uttered haltingly.

"I understand, Sean. I like you, too," Julie replied, seemingly understanding where O'Reilly was taking the conversation. "Let's wait until this is over and go from there."

"That would be great," O'Reilly replied, regaining his composure.

"How was the pizza?" Alvarez asked as he walked back into the conference room and noticed the empty cardboard box with dried cheese and crumbs on the bottom.

"Really good," Leila replied. "It's going to be hard to eat pizza in California again after that. What makes it taste so good?"

"Lots of cheese, a perfectly cooked crust, and oregano in the tomato sauce," Andy replied as if he were the pizza maker. "Is Detective O'Reilly back?"

"Not yet, but he called and is on his way. We'll get started in about twenty minutes. He should be back by then," Alvarez responded.

It was approaching 6:00 in the evening, but Andy and Leila felt energized—perhaps it was the pizza, perhaps the excitement of the now fast-moving investigation, or perhaps because it was only 3:00 p.m. in Los Angeles and their brains were still very much in work mode. Alvarez returned with Evan Belkin and a cart with coffee and more energy bars and fruit, insinuating that they were all in for a long evening. There would be no dinner in another New York City neighborhood this evening. Andy and Leila made small talk with Evan, finding out that he was twenty-nine years old and a graduate of Rensselaer Polytechnic Institute, a well-known and highly touted engineering school in upstate New York, not far from the capital of Albany. He had moved to New York City for the simple fact that life in Rensselaer—or Utica, also in upstate New York, where he had grown up—was, in his view, dull. He had always dreamed of living in New York City and, master's degree in hand, he'd headed down to "the city" and found a job in the police department. For all his nerdy appearance, he was very conversational and seemed quite self-confident. Leila asked him about the hair, to which he blushed and nodded his head, stating that he knew it was time for a more modern haircut and promised her he would get to work on that soon. Andy and Leila liked Evan—they found him to be very genuine. Andy suggested that there was one major difference between New Yorkers and Angelinos (as those from Los Angeles are called). While Angelinos liked to pretend to be something they were not, altering their appearance and not infrequently their persona, New

Yorkers were comfortable in their own skins and their own personalities. Despite Andy's convincing argument, Leila was not so sure; she'd noted that there were plenty of plastic-surgery offices lining the streets of the city.

With O'Reilly back in the room, Detective Alvarez, cup of coffee in hand, got up from the table and asked if the team were ready to proceed, to which affirmative nods were cast all around the table. They decided to open the folder wit the cafés next. Evan announced that it had 158 pictures in it. O'Reilly, relieved that it was a relatively small folder, suggested this would be the last set of pictures to be viewed for the day. Again there were affirmative nods all around.

Evan began the same procedure he had now perfected—arranging the images sequentially per the time-and-date stamp and displaying them one by one in full-screen view. The first thing they noticed was that the private detective had used a different technique with this set, whereby he first took a picture of the outside of the building prior to entering it to shoot the pictures of his intended target. This helped the investigators by identifying the precise location of the interior pictures that followed. Each group of five to fifteen pictures was thus preceded by the storefront and, in the case of this folder, name of the café. The first few sets had Mr. Millbank alone at various Starbucks around the city, all of which seemed pretty innocuous. Others had Mr. Millbank with what looked like co-workers, at Midtown Coffee House, not far from Empire Health's headquarters. Again, nothing of interest appeared, but as they proceeded through time, the ever-more familiar face of Dr. Carmichael reappeared, first with no wig and later with the wig. In response to Andy's question, Evan stated that the wig had appeared around the same time in this set of pictures as it had in the hotel set. At that point O'Reilly reviewed his discussion with Mrs. Millbank, confirming Leila's theory about the wig. At this, Leila smiled proudly, ensuring that each of the team members saw the smile before she put it back in storage, ready to be revealed when she next felt she needed to remind the team of men of her keen woman's intuition.

The next set of pictures was from Café de Bon Salud which, not surprisingly, based on its name, was located on the campus of the New York Hospital. It was clearly a major hangout for hospital employees, as the first pictures of the storefront were dotted with men and women in lab coats and hospital scrubs.

"Does anyone else think it's odd that there is a set of pictures from this café so close to the hospital?" Alvarez asked.

"What do you mean?" O'Reilly replied with his own question.

"Well, first, this is pretty far from Mr. Millbank's office, and you'd think he wouldn't meet Dr. Carmichael so close to her place of work," he replied.

Leila added, "I wouldn't think Dr. Carmichael would even want to meet him here—too many people she knows would see her with him, and I doubt she would want that."

"Well, let's see what we find," Andy added.

After the first few pictures of the outside of the café, the scene of the pictures shifted to the inside. It was a fairly large space with small round tables in the center and square tables adjacent to the surrounding walls. The first interior picture showed a line of people ordering coffee and pastries, although they recognized no one, but as they proceeded, a familiar face emerged.

"There's Dr. Carmichael—no wig," Andy stated. "Well, that's odd," Evan said.

"Why?" Alvarez questioned.

"Well, this picture is dated after Dr. Carmichael started going incognito," Evan answered.

"Leila, time for some woman's intuition." Alvarez looked over at Leila as she flashed a smile.

"I would say the only reason is that she's not expecting to meet Mr. Millbank here. And, you know, that makes perfect sense. I very much doubt she would want to see him anywhere near the hospital."

"That makes me wonder why we have a set of pictures from this location," Andy said, looking at Detective O'Reilly. "Did Mrs. Millbank tell you anything about having the detective follow Dr. Carmichael."

"Yes, in fact, she told me that on some days the private detective followed Dr.

Carmichael around."

"Well, this should be interesting," Leila said quizzically. "Explain, please," Andy demanded.

"Well, I'm curious to see if she will ever be seen with the wig at this work hangout."

"What do you think?" Andy asked.

"I predict we won't see any pictures of her with the wig in the Café de Bon Salud nor any pictures of Mr. Millbank there either," Leila replied.

Evan began to scroll through this set of pictures, and indeed, most of them were shots of Jennifer Carmichael, sometimes alone, but often with other people from the hospital. Andy recognized Dr. Simmons, the chief of pathology, in a few of the pictures, seated at a table with Dr. Carmichael, having coffee. Certainly nothing out of the ordinary. At O'Reilly's request, Evan began moving through the pictures more quickly, as it appeared that there would be no sighting of Mr. Millbank at the café, as Leila had predicted. In addition, there was no indication that Bryan, who remained the most important person they were hoping to find in the pictures, would actually make an appearance. Then, suddenly, Andy leapt out of his chair as if he had just spilled a hot drink on his lap.

"Stop!" he yelled. "Evan, go back one picture!" Evan did so.

"That's weird!" Andy said loudly as he walked closer to the monitor and gazed intently at the image on display. "Yeah, that's definitely her. Weird."

"Oh, I see. Yeah, that *is* weird," Leila confirmed Andy's finding. "Can you clue us in, please?" O'Reilly demanded in an irritated tone. "Don't you see who Dr. Carmichael is sitting with?" Andy added.

Alvarez now noticed. "Yeah—yeah, I remember her."

"For fuck's sake, will someone tell me who the hell the girl is?" O'Reilly burst out in frustration.

"Well, that's Taylor Davis," Andy said slowly, his head tilted slightly to one side as if he were looking at a piece of art he couldn't quite figure out.

"And who the hell is Taylor Davis?" O'Reilly asked, still annoyed.

"She's just a medical student we met briefly in the pathology department before we searched Dr. Carmichael's office," Leila added, with the same sense of wondering in her voice Andy had had upon making the discovery. She was both somewhat bewildered and somewhat disturbed by this finding.

"So what?" O'Reilly said.

"I'm sorry, Detective, we're not trying to make you guess, but I think we're just not quite sure what to make of this," Andy said.

Leila picked up the line of thought. "You see, in the doctor world, medical students usually hang out with other medical students or residents, and well, mostly they stay in the hospital. It's a bit odd that Dr. Carmichael is having coffee off-site with a medical student she barely knows, that's all."

"Well, doctors, in the detective world, this doesn't mean shit. After all, they are both medical professionals working in the same hospital— they're allowed to have coffee together. So, I still don't see the big deal," O'Reilly stated firmly.

"I see your point. I, uh … just didn't expect to see her, that's all," Andy stated.

"Call it a woman's intuition if you men like, but I still find it odd. Andy, when was the last time you had coffee with a medical student outside the hospital?"

"I don't recall ever doing that, to be honest."

"Yeah, me neither," Leila added.

"Well, what now?" Alvarez asked.

"We just keep looking at the pictures; only now, let's keep our eyes out for Ms. Davis as well as Dr. Carmichael," Leila replied.

"Isn't it Dr. Davis?" Alvarez asked.

"Not until she graduates," Leila said with a cheeky smile.

Evan moved forward through the sequence of pictures. Several more of Taylor Davis and Dr. Carmichael from the same day in the café showed up and then a few more of Dr. Carmichael by herself or with other hospital employees. There were none with Mr. Millbank, and no sign of Bryan Vasquez, either. Another dozen or so later, they spotted another one of Dr. Carmichael with Taylor Davis; this was now on a different day.

"I still say that's weird. What's the date on this one, Evan?" Leila asked. "November 17."

"Wow, that's less than one week before the murder."

Evan put up the next picture, and Detective Alvarez spotted something. "Look at Carmichael's face. Do you see what I'm seeing?" Alvarez said as heads nodded around the conference room.

Dr. Carmichael's face had contorted from a rather blank, uninterested stare to one of surprise; it was like a sped-up video showing the transformation of a new pumpkin to the animated face of a jack-o'-lantern. Her eyebrows rose high up her forehead, and her wide-open eyes seemed to be bulging out of her skull. Her mouth was agape and cheeks tense. It was a look of disbelief—there was no doubt about that. Cleary the private detective had taken note, as the next picture was just a second or two after the previous one. Dr. Carmichael's expression this time was one of growing astonishment. In this picture, the eyebrows had come down and the eyes moved back into their sockets; she was squinting as her expression morphed from recognition to ire. Then in the next picture, the cheeks were sucked in, the squint was tighter, and the recognition had changed to anger. Her eyes were fixed on her object with such ferocity it was as if she were trying to destroy it with her stare. Then the mouth closed, the lips pursed tightly, and the anger now clearly turned to rage. Viewing the pictures one at a time was like watching a movie in super-slow motion.

In the same sequence of pictures, Taylor had at first been looking at Jennifer Carmichael, her back to the photographer, but then, when she'd noticed the dramatic change in Jennifer's facial expression, she had slowly turned around. As she now faced the photographer, the next several frames demonstrated an even more dramatic facial transformation on Taylor's face than the one on Dr. Carmichael's face, if that were possible. Her expression morphed from curiosity, to shock, and finally to undeniable horror.

"What the *fuck* is going on?" O'Reilly broke the silence, clearly unsure what to make of all this.

"I don't know, but Leila, I think you're going to prove yourself right again.

Something odd is going on, that's for sure!" Alvarez stated.

Evan flashed the next picture. The first thing that was immediately noticeable was that the photographer had changed his point of view. Registering the direction in which the two women with their stunned faces had now focused their gaze, he had apparently motioned his hidden camera toward that very direction and began taking picture after picture in rapid sequence. At first it was hard to see what the women were looking at, as the photographer had not yet framed the subject of their attention, but as Evan moved through the sequence, it became eminently apparent. Initially, all they saw were legs moving between tables; then a briefcase with a gloved hand came into view, then the torso of a man in a business suit and overcoat, and finally, the face came into full view. The detectives, Andy, and Leila stared in stunned silence. No one said a word. They just kept staring. Their eyes fixed on the large monitor in the front of the room as the unmistakable face of Creighton Millbank became apparent. His shoulders and head were held high, and his eyes were keen on his target, which no doubt was Dr. Carmichael's table. In the next three pictures, Mr. Millbank got closer to the photographer until he passed him, unaware of picture after picture being taken, until he finally reached the table where Dr. Carmichael and Taylor Davis were sitting. Evan stopped moving the pictures forward at O'Reilly's request.

"Well, Leila, I think you are actually wrong for the first time. You said you didn't expect to see Mr. Millbank in the café," O'Reilly stated aloud.

"You're sort of right," she replied.

340

"*Sort of right*? What are you talking about?"

"Well, you're correct; I didn't expect to see Mr. Millbank in this café, but it is clear that neither did Jennifer."

Andy interrupted as O'Reilly was about to retort.

"I don't get something about this. We didn't agree about whether Ms. Davis and Dr. Carmichael having lunch was odd, and that's fair, and we can come back to that later. But, while I understand why Dr. Carmichael was surprised to see Mr. Millbank in the café, I don't get Ms. Davis facial expression at all."

"She looks absolutely terrified," Alvarez said.

"I agree," Leila added. "She has a look of horror as if someone is about to hurt her or even kill her."

"Uh, correct me if I'm wrong, but she's not even supposed to know who Mr. Millbank is," Alvarez said.

"No, she's not," Leila agreed, "but clearly—very clearly—she does. And she's definitely not pleased to see him."

"You know, going through these pictures was supposed to give us some answers, but now I have a thousand more questions racing through my head," Andy stated, exasperated.

It was nearly nine o'clock. They were all beyond tired. They must have looked at nearly eight hundred pictures in one day. Evan looked at Alvarez, who motioned his hand across his throat in the "cut" sign. Evan turned the monitor off.

"Let's all get some sleep and reconvene in the morning."

No one moved—not right away, anyway. They were all lost in their own thoughts, wondering how many more surprises this case was going to conjure up for them.

CHAPTER 31

JANUARY 11
NEW YORK

"Tall vanilla latte, two pumps, no foam, please," Leila requested.

"Grande peppermint hot chocolate," came Andy's request.

"The holidays are over, Andy," Leila said.

"They must still have peppermint syrup, don't you think?"

The clerk rang up their drinks while the barista shouted out their orders. Indeed, there was still peppermint syrup. And with that, Leila and Andy left Starbucks in the lobby of their hotel and headed back to police headquarters. They passed on breakfast, knowing Detective Alvarez was sure to wheel in a cart full of food. They didn't discuss the case at all, preferring to reserve their thoughts for the full team. Andy told Leila he had been on the phone with Andrea back in LA to discuss some patient matters, and she had assured him that the coverage they were getting from the other doctors was excellent and there was no need to rush back. Andrea told Andy it was good that they had spent many hours the previous week seeing the most complicated patients and that nothing terribly complicated or difficult had cropped up.

Since, it was a rather pleasant morning, considering it was January, with the temperature up to forty degrees, Andy and Leila had skipped the hotel gym workout and instead gone for a long jog in Central Park—how different it was from just two weeks ago when Andy had tempted the New York winter to give him frostbite by going for a walk inadequately dressed. With the sun shining, the park took on an early spring-like feel, though it would be nearly three months before the trees would start budding and the flowers would start blooming. The vigorous jog had sent a surge of blood to their brains, not to mention their legs, preparing them for what they expected to be a mentally grueling day. Now, with their morning elixirs in hand, they hopped into one of the ubiquitous New York City yellow taxis for the ride downtown to police headquarters. After they'd entered and gone through security, a young officer asked them if they needed help finding their way.

"Young man, I can give you a tour of this place," Leila said, chuckling. "Yes, ma'am," the polite officer replied.

"Wow, you're a ma'am now. Congratulations!" Andy said teasingly. "What does that make you?"

"I'm not that much older than you," Andy responded. "Nevertheless!"

They reached the now-all-too-familiar room and found a young man sitting at the table eating a bagel and cream cheese. At first they didn't recognize him, but as Andy was about to introduce himself, he noticed it was Evan.

"Uh, you look ... different," Andy said, at somewhat of a loss for words. "Hi, Evan; don't listen to Andy. You look awesome," Leila said.

Evan had had a drastic makeover. His hair was much shorter, cropped close on the side, with small, tight curls on top, and he wasn't wearing glasses. He winked at Leila, and she winked back.

"As we were leaving yesterday, I gave Evan a little fashion and appearance advice," Leila said.

"And you definitely took it to heart," Andy added. "May I ask what she said?"

"She said, 'You're not in upstate New York anymore' and then made some reference to Justin Timberlake. I didn't even know who that was, to be honest, so I looked him up, understood the message, and went to a salon."

"At 10:00 at night?" Andy asked, astounded.

"Hey, it really is the city that never sleeps—you can do almost anything in the city at that hour," Evan replied.

Like the screech of a subway car pulling into its next stop, the sounds of a metal cart with familiar squeaky wheels heralded Detective Alvarez's arrival. It was the usual spread of coffee, bagels, cream cheese, and fruit. Andy, bagel lover that he was, didn't mind. Leila was more than ready for a different choice, but she realized that a homemade Kurdish-style meal was at this point in time only a dream.

"Good morning, everyone. Hope you had a good night's sleep. Excuse me," Alvarez began as he looked at Evan. "Holy shit, what the hell happened to you!"

"I, uh, might have said something," Leila said coyly.

"Well, whatever you said, he certainly didn't waste any time—do you have this influence on all men, Leila?" Alvarez asked.

"Funny—I wish!" she said and glanced over at Andy, who merely looked back at her without altering his bland expression.

"Detective O'Reilly is on his way. Evan, let's get ready to pick up where we left off, but don't put any images up on the monitor just yet."

"Good morning," came the familiar Queens accent of Detective O'Reilly. He looked at Evan quizzically. "Did you get cut from *That '70s Show*? And you can suddenly see okay, or what?"

"Contacts. Justin Timberlake," Leila responded on his behalf.

"Justin Timberlake. You're going to have to do more than that, Evan," O'Reilly said, laughing out loud.

"Hey, I think he looks a bit like Justin Timberlake—and unless you're gay, I think only my opinion counts," Leila replied, defending the nice young man they all genuinely liked and appreciated.

"Well, I'm glad we're all in a good mood this morning. I was a bit worried we overdid it yesterday, "Alvarez said. "I'd like to briefly review yesterday's unexpected discovery before we move on with the pictures. Honestly, I can't wait to see what's next. If I hadn't been so tired, I don't know that I could have slept last night. Still, let's first go over yesterday."

They reviewed first the set of pictures from Empire Health's offices and surroundings. They all agreed that there were no sightings of Bryan and nothing else of note from all those pictures. Next they discussed the pictures from the hotels and came away with a number of important facts. First, Mr. Millbank had met Jennifer Carmichael in March—eight months before the murder. Second, they had clearly started to have an affair, with frequent meetings beginning in May and overnight trysts at various hotels beginning in July. Third, Mrs. Millbank had confronted her husband about the affair sometime in July, after which Dr. Carmichael had donned a wig for all of the subsequent meetings with Mr. Millbank. Then, they'd uncovered the strange events at Café de Bon Salud.

Alvarez began summarizing. "Okay, so at the café we see Jennifer Carmichael and Taylor Davis having coffee and chatting. Andy and Leila both found that to be a bit odd, given that medical students and attending physicians don't often socialize, and this appears not to be a work-related get-together."

"Well, I might let one such coffee get-together slide, but not two," Andy said.

"You know, I'm going to change my mind on this one," Leila said. "Dr. Carmichael is not that old—what is she, about thirty-seven or so, and Taylor is probably at least twenty-five. Maybe they both realized they liked the coffee at this café and decided to go together. I'm less convinced it is unusual than I was yesterday."

"Fair enough; let's move on to the sequence of pictures involving Mr. Millbank. So, Dr. Carmichael who, of course, knows him, seems to be caught off guard that he shows up at the café, right?" Alvarez continued.

"Caught off guard and pissed off as all hell," O'Reilly added. "Thoughts?" Alvarez asks.

"Well, obviously Jennifer doesn't expect him there, and perhaps she had warned him not to come to or near the hospital, you know, to maintain some discretion," Leila replied.

"And she is at first surprised to see him and then upset that he's there. That makes sense based on what the pictures show," Andy added.

"Fine, but then we have Taylor Davis also clearly reacting to the presence of Mr. Millbank, and we agree she's not even supposed to know who he is. Any ideas before we proceed with the pictures to see how this encounter unfolds?" Alvarez asked, trying to encourage some discussion and perhaps some theories before they revealed the next set of pictures.

He was met with silence. Each of the team shifted his or her gaze from one to the other as if waiting for someone else to take the risk of embarrassment by espousing a theory.

"Anyone? Leila?" Alvarez pleaded, pointedly asking the only woman in the room and the leader among the quartet in important revelations.

Leila, sensing that a response was required, began. "I don't have a clue, to be honest, but I do have a question. Is the fact that Jennifer is with Taylor at the café when Millbank shows up merely a coincidence, or was it somehow planned for her to be there at that time? In other words, is this some kind of setup or trap, or is it purely coincidental?"

"I think it's a coincidence, given Jennifer's reaction," Andy said. "It seems pretty obvious that she was not happy to see him, so there is no reason to think she set up the meeting, and since Taylor was equally surprised, I can't see how she could have set up a meeting."

"Sure, unless one of them is feigning her reaction—acting," Leila responded. "Interesting thought. Anything else before we move on?" asked Alvarez. "Let's move on," O'Reilly replied impatiently.

Alvarez motioned to Evan, and his fingers began tapping on the keys of his computer. Alvarez asked him to quickly flash the sequence beginning with Carmichael's reaction, to paint the scene for the upcoming set of pictures, and Evan ran through them, allowing about fifteen seconds for each one. They all gazed intently at the monitor. When they reached the last picture they'd viewed yesterday, the one showing the look of terror on Taylor Davis's face, Evan looked at Alvarez, who motioned to him to go to the next picture. With one tap of a key, he brought up the next picture. It showed Mr. Millbank, with his back to the photographer and facing Dr. Carmichael. She had stood up, her mouth was wide open, and it was apparent that she was yelling at Mr. Millbank. Andy pointed out that people at the other tables in the café had begun turning their heads and were looking at Dr. Carmichael and Mr. Millbank, suggesting that they were causing a commotion. In this frame, Taylor was still seated, but now her back was to the photographer. It appeared that her hands were covering her face, as if she were feeling ill, crying, or both. Alvarez motioned to move to the next picture. Now Dr. Carmichael had her finger pointed at Mr. Millbank, with her face animated and mouth open, in all likelihood in a heated exchange with her married lover. Now all the faces of the people in the tables behind her were fixed on the apparent argument going on between her and Mr. Millbank. Taylor had one leg turned out from underneath the table; her hands were now off her face, with one hand on the table and the other by her side. It wasn't clear what she was doing at this point, though her face peered downward and away from the argument. Evan moved to the next picture; each one was just a second or two in time after the previous, playing out like a stop-motion animation sequence being viewed frame by frame.

The private detective clearly felt he was capturing an important event. The next picture now had Mr. Millbank leaning forward, one hand on the table, his face closer to Dr. Carmichael, while she had placed both hands on the table and was also leaning forward. Again, the crowd behind them appeared mesmerized. Taylor, it was now clear, was getting up out of her chair, ostensibly making an effort to avoid eye contact with either Dr. Carmichael or Mr. Millbank. She, in fact, was the only one in the café who seemed disinterested in their discussion. As the sequence of shots proceeded, the following became clear. Dr. Carmichael and Mr. Millbank were in a heated argument, and now both were standing. Dr. Carmichael's face was the only one visible, and she was yelling and gesticulating animatedly. Meanwhile, Mr. Millbank was noted to be gesticulating, and though his face could not be seen, it was likely not a one-way argument. As this was going on, Taylor Davis swiftly got up, and a second run through the pictures, advanced in a much quicker fashion, showed her obviously running for the exit. The photographer took a series of pictures of Taylor as she hurriedly escaped the scene at the café, momentarily diverting his attention from Dr. Carmichael and Mr. Millbank. Upon returning to the argument, the series of photos showed Dr. Carmichael turning around and walking deeper into the café, while at first Mr. Millbank stood waiting. As the time passed, first seconds and then, with the photographer now shooting pictures at a slower pace, minutes, Mr. Millbank continued to wait, but eventually he ran out of patience and left. For a few minutes, no pictures were taken, until Dr. Carmichael emerged from deep in the back of the café. She stopped at the cash register, appeared to be asking a question, and then walked out the same front door as Taylor and Mr. Millbank had some minutes earlier.

"So, does someone want to take a shot at piecing this together? Sean, how about you start—you're the most seasoned investigator in the room," Alvarez suggested.

"Yeah, I'll tell you exactly what happened—I think it's pretty obvious. First, we see Carmichael and Davis having coffee. Mr. Millbank walks in. Neither one expects him to be there. He and Carmichael have a major argument. Not sure exactly why, but people who cheat get into arguments and fights all the time. Don't you agree, Jose?"

"Well, I wouldn't really know, Sean," Alvarez answered briefly.

"Carmichael is pissed off, you know, because he showed up in her territory—so close to the hospital and around many people who probably know her. While they're arguing, Taylor Davis leaves, and eventually Carmichael manages to ditch Millbank somehow. Then he leaves after losing his patience waiting for her, and then she eventually leaves, probably after asking the cashier when Millbank left."

"Thanks, Sean. That's a good start," Alvarez said, serving as the de facto moderator of their discussion. "Leila or Andy, care to interpret what you think happened?"

"Sure, I'll start," Leila replied, eager as always to demonstrate her intuition. "I'm going to stick with what I said before, that the coffee date between Jennifer and Taylor is innocent and totally coincidental to the subsequent events—just my gut feeling. I agree with Detective O'Reilly's assertions about what transpired as the facts."

"Thanks, Leila. I think that's the first time you've ever agreed with me," O'Reilly said jokingly.

Leila chuckled and then continued. "For some reason, Mr. Millbank feels the urge to find Jennifer. Perhaps she'd been avoiding him or dumped him. Maybe she got busy with work or, who knows, started seeing someone else, either instead of or in addition to her relationship with Millbank. I wouldn't expect single women in such affairs to be monogamous. Regardless, Mr. Millbank probably has tried to contact her by other means, phone or text messages, which have been ignored."

"That's something we can check on," Alvarez said writing something down on a notepad.

"In any case, he shows up uninvited and confronts Jennifer. They have an argument, presumably over some aspect of their relationship. Then she's had enough and leaves the argument. I'm going to suggest she goes to the one place in the café that he can't—the lady's room, and hangs out there for a while until she senses he would have left. Only then does she return."

"Hey, that sounds really logical. I like that train of thought," Andy stated. "Excellent. I think I agree as well, so that makes four of us on that aspect of the events," Alvarez concluded. "Now, what about Taylor Davis. Who's got an idea?"

The room now turned silent. It was apparent that this facet of the events was much less obvious. Again, everyone's eyes shifted to one another, but this time they all eventually fixated on Leila, who noticed almost immediately.

"Well, Ms. Intuition," Andy cajoled Leila. "Fine. I'll take a crack at it," Leila replied.

She hesitated, looked up at the ceiling, and then asked Evan to bring up the picture of Taylor's facial metamorphosis after Mr. Millbank had walked in. She asked him to move slowly forward, and then back, and forward again. The detectives and Andy looked at her expectantly, with bated breath, fully anticipating that she would provide the most logical explanation; they were like schoolchildren about to hear the final chapter of a mystery story. Leila continued to gaze at the monitor with the picture of Taylor's frozen, frightened face. Then, at first slowly, she got up out of her chair and walked to the front of the conference room to get a closer look, turned her head slightly askew, and finally turned back to the four men in the room. Her look was somewhere between curiosity and understanding, but she remained silent for a moment.

"Well, it seems you've figured something out—are you going to tell us?" O'Reilly asked.

"I'm not sure what is going on, honestly, but I do have one question about this set of pictures; I am not sure what to make of it. Anyway, here goes. If you look carefully, it's obvious that Taylor recognizes *him*, but interestingly, Mr. Millbank doesn't recognize *her*. Either he is fixated on Dr. Carmichael and is simply not paying attention, or he simply doesn't really recognize her."

"Good point. Let's think about that for a second. Under what circumstances is there a lack of mutual recognition? In other words, when does someone recognize a person while that person does not recognize them back?" Alvarez asked.

"A celebrity," Andy said.

"Yes," acknowledged Alvarez. "When else?"

"When one person is in a more senior position—like a superior," O'Reilly added. "I can tell you that all the NYPD officers would recognize the commissioner, but he wouldn't recognize any of them back."

"Okay, so perhaps Taylor recognized Mr. Millbank from such a position. Maybe she worked for him at Empire Health or something like that?" Andy responded.

"But I doubt she worked there. I mean, she's a medical student and looks young enough that she has probably never worked—not a real job anyway. College then medical school. No job," Leila said.

"Keep going. How else might there be non-mutual recognition?" Alvarez pressed.

No other ideas came forward.

"Fine, let's keep this recognition issue in our heads and move on to Ms. Davis's response to seeing Mr. Millbank. Who'd like to start? How about you, Andy?"

"I think she looks scared. Terrified, actually. And, almost as soon as Mr. Millbank arrives at their table, she hurries out."

"Runs out," Sean added, "but she covers her face first. Is she crying, or just shocked, or what?"

"Maybe she covers it because she doesn't want Mr. Millbank to recognize her," Leila said.

"But we already said he doesn't recognize her, so why does she feel the need to cover her face, Leila?" Andy asked.

"I'm just guessing now, but maybe she's afraid he will recognize her when he gets closer."

"Interesting," Alvarez states. "But why?"

Again silence hit the room, only this time Leila interrupted, requesting that they take a quick break. Alvarez agreed. They all got up and walked out of the conference room. Leila and Andy both made calls on their cell phones, while O'Reilly and Alvarez returned to their desks to check e-mail, as if hoping a break in the case would simply show up in their inboxes. There had still been no sighting of Bryan Vasquez, and for all the fascinating findings of Mrs. Millbank's detective's pictures, it had brought them no closer to solving the case. After fifteen minutes they returned to the conference room.

"I hope that break helped. Leila, you have that smile on your face again—the one that seems to come before you make some dramatic revelation. Care to share?" Alvarez pleaded.

"I *do* have an idea, but it—it's weird; it actually came from a call I literally just made to my mom. You see, we have some relatives visiting from Detroit that we hadn't seen in years, and she was wondering when I might be coming back to LA," Leila said quickly and then stopped.

"And?" O'Reilly prodded her to keep going.

"Well, she said something that made me think about the scene at the café. She said 'I hardly recognized your cousin, Kalan, he's grown so much,' and it got me thinking."

"Go on," Alvarez said.

"Well, another situation in which there isn't mutual recognition is just as my mom described—when you have not seen someone that you know for a really long time, particularly if that person is a child. Kalan, I'm sure, recognized my mom—she's an adult and likely looks more or less the same despite the five or so years that have passed since he has seen her, but she didn't recognize him because he had grown and matured so much."

"Where are you going with this, Leila?" Andy asked inquisitively.

"Okay, don't laugh if you think this is ridiculous, but what if … what if Taylor Davis is Mr. Millbank's relative—maybe even his daughter, and—"

"You can stop right there," Detective O'Reilly interjected. "Mr. and Mrs. Millbank don't have any children. That I know for sure."

"May I ask how you came about that information? I know that you have interviewed Mrs. Millbank, but I'm curious exactly what you asked her," Leila said.

"*Duh*, I asked her if she had any children," came O'Reilly's terse response. "Right, you asked *her* if *she* had any children, but did you ask her if *he* had any children—from a previous marriage, for example?"

"Hmm," O'Reilly replied more cordially.

"Well, I, uh, I don't think I did."

"Continue, Leila," said Alvarez.

"I know it's a bit far-fetched, but let's assume for the moment that Taylor is Mr. Millbank's estranged daughter—"

"Now she's his estranged daughter," O'Reilly huffed, clearly still not buying into this hypothesis.

"Well, of course she's estranged, because remember, he doesn't recognize her. So she's the child who has now grown up. Perhaps he left her when she was much younger, which could explain how she recognizes him but he doesn't recognize her. As he gets closer, she covers her face in case he might identify her; she obviously doesn't want him to."

"Let's say you're correct. Why is she so frightened, then?" Andy wondered. "I'm not sure—but, well, if you'll indulge me?" Leila hesitated.

"Keep going. We need something, anything, at this point," Alvarez encouraged her.

"Perhaps Mr. Millbank did something bad, maybe something horrible, god-awful, to Taylor or her mom when she was young. Then he left them or was forced to leave and never saw her again until this chance encounter in the café. I know it sounds crazy, but it would be a plausible explanation for her reaction. Don't you think?" Leila suggested.

Detectives Alvarez and O'Reilly looked at each other, while Andy and Leila looked at them as if they were children seeking the approval of their parents. The two detectives excused themselves and stepped out of the conference room, stating that they would be back shortly. Andy and Leila remained in the room, along with Evan, who told Leila he thought her theory made a lot of sense; he was the third sibling offering support while the parents chatted outside of earshot. Detective Alvarez returned a few minutes later, explaining that they would take an early lunch break and that O'Reilly had set up a meeting with Mrs. Millbank to see if she could shed light on whether Mr. Millbank had a daughter. He'd also requested the retrieval of Mr. Millbank's mobile-phone records for the days leading up to the encounter at the café. He asked them all to return in two hours. Andy and Leila nodded in agreement.

They walked out of the police station and headed to yet another New York landmark, The Original Soup Man, formerly the Soup Kitchen International, made famous on the *Seinfeld* television show in the 1990s, when the chef was not so amicably referred to as the "soup Nazi." As they had two hours and it was a nice day, they chose to walk there, though it was a fair distance from police headquarters. Along the way, Andy described the "Soup Nazi" episode to Leila, which helped pass the time. There were a number of other *Seinfeld* references Andy mentioned along the way, telling Leila that while the show had been an international hit, only New Yorkers could truly appreciate every nuance.

Detective O'Reilly made his way back to Mrs. Millbank's apartment. He had called her in advance and requested that Alvarez give him two hours, since his last visit with her had been so brief. He felt that she would be more cooperative if he offered her more time. Alvarez reminded his partner to keep their discussion solely to the case and to stay away from any social talk until the case was over. O'Reilly assured him any other discussion would be small talk only. He arrived and was escorted to the elevator by the doorman, who by now recognized him from his previous visits.

"Hi, Sean," Mrs. Millbank greeted him with a smile. "Don't worry, I know the rules by now," she added, indicating that he didn't need to remind her about avoiding any discussion of their relationship.

"Thanks, Julie," he replied.

They sat in her large, ornate dining room, while her maid brought them lunch. Shrimp cocktail, served with lemon and cocktail sauce, was the appetizer. They made some small talk while eating. After the appetizer, the maid brought a cold steak salad with avocado, corn, and black beans. O'Reilly, hungry, happily dug in.

"So, how's the case going? You know I'm anxious for you to finish it," she said.

O'Reilly, somewhat arrogantly, surmised it was more so they could move their relationship forward than because she was curious to know who'd killed her husband.

"Well, first of all, your pictures have been—how can I say this?—really helpful, but they have raised a bunch of new questions."

"Such as?"

"Well, for starters, your husband showed up at the Café de Bon Salud near New York Hospital just a week before he was killed, apparently to confront Dr. Carmichael—"

"That's not surprising. She probably was ignoring him, and Creighton was never good at dealing with women who didn't treat him like he was God's gift to them," Mrs. Millbank interrupted.

"I see, and you think she was the one who broke contact?"

"Why else would he confront her?"

"Good point. But there was something else that occurred. Can I ask you first whether you've looked at all the pictures?"

"All of them! God no! There are thousands. My detective was quite good, wouldn't you say?"

"Perhaps. I'm asking because, in that café, there is a young woman who was having coffee with Dr. Carmichael, and this young woman also recognized your husband," O'Reilly said.

"Who is she?"

"That's what we need to find out, and that's why I'm here today."

"Why would I know her?" Mrs. Millbank asked.

"I didn't say you do. Anyway, I'll spare you the details, but one of the doctors thinks that young woman might be related to your husband. Is that possible?"

"How old is she?"

"She's probably in her midtwenties."

"What does she look like?" Mrs. Millbank asked with an expectant tone. "Attractive. Long brown hair, fair skin. About five foot five, tall, thin."

"Oh God," Mrs. Millbank said, her face becoming dreadfully serious. Out of nowhere, a few tears formed in her eyes.

O'Reilly, suddenly alarmed, wondered what had led to Mrs. Millbank's sudden change in demeanor as she dabbed the tears with her napkin.

"Is she a medical student?" Mrs. Millbank asked, and O'Reilly's mouth opened with astonishment.

"Uh, yes," said he said incredulously. "Julie, how did you know that?"

Mrs. Millbank gathered herself, paused as she gazed at Detective O'Reilly, and said: "That's Creighton's daughter."

O'Reilly, realizing that Leila's theory was correct, sat motionless for a moment. Mrs. Millbank, noticing that she had caught the detective by surprise, reached across the table and put her hand on top of his in a comforting gesture. She then explained that sometime in November, she couldn't recall exactly when, a young woman had called and asked to meet with her. Mrs. Millbank explained that she had been reluctant at first but ultimately had agreed, and they'd met for lunch at the same French restaurant in which she and O'Reilly had first had lunch. The young woman had told her that her name was Taylor Davis, but that she had changed her name; her birth name was Cassandra—Cassandra Millbank—and she was Creighton Millbank's daughter. Mrs. Millbank went on to say that Taylor had told her she was estranged from her father and had not seen him in many years. Mrs. Millbank told O'Reilly that she had not known that Creighton had a daughter, and when she confronted him later, he'd told her that it had been long ago, and his daughter was not part of his life anymore.

"When I asked her why she wasn't in contact with her father, she burst into tears. I don't mean a couple of tears. She was bawling—uncontrollably," Mrs. Millbank continued.

"I assume you asked her why?"

"Naturally, but she wouldn't say. She said it was too painful."

"Did you ask your husband about it?" O'Reilly continued.

"Of course. He said it was because he left her and her mother just as she was becoming a teenager, and it was painful for both of them," Mrs. Millbank replied.

"When did you meet Creighton in relation to that?"

"I'm not sure. I met Creighton ten years ago."

"So, if Taylor is twenty-five, and let's say he left when she was ten or twelve, that would be thirteen years ago, meaning that you met him about three to five years or so after he left them," O'Reilly surmised.

"I hope I don't have anything to do with this poor girl's painful memories."

"I doubt it. It seems you came in years after he left her," O'Reilly said.

"Still, I wonder why Creighton didn't maintain a relationship with her. Sure he was an adulterous asshole, but he had a good heart in general, and I'm surprised he would treat flesh and blood like discarded trash," Mrs. Millbank opined.

O'Reilly asked Mrs. Millbank if she could remember the exact date Taylor had come to her. She didn't recall, but at O'Reilly's insistence, she called her accountant to get the dates her credit card had been used at Chez Boulant. O'Reilly asked how she could be sure of the date, since she frequented that particular bistro, and she replied with a wry smile, saying she didn't go there *that* often. She held the phone while her accountant looked it up.

"Must be nice to have someone deal with all your bills," O'Reilly said to break the awkward pause.

"Yes, it is." Mrs. Millbank said, and as O'Reilly was about to say something else she motioned with a finger to her lips, asking him not to speak. "Thanks, Clark," she said into the phone. Then she told O'Reilly, "It was November 19. Does that help?"

"Every bit of information helps."

They finished their lunch with chocolate mousse and more small talk, and then O'Reilly headed back to the police station.

The investigative team gathered once more in the conference room. Detective Alvarez began by telling the team that the mobile phone records of Mr. Millbank indicated multiple daily calls and text messages to Dr. Carmichael, which were at their most intense from July to October. Then, after October 31, there had been several changes. The calls became much shorter—most of them only a minute. In addition, the calls, which had been both incoming and outgoing throughout the spring and summer, were now only outgoing; Dr. Carmichael had stopped calling him altogether. The text messages were numerous. At first they were flirtatious, and then they turned to highly sexually charged ones, including some with explicit pictures. But after October 31 the tone changed, and the ones from Millbank to Carmichael ranged from pleading to angry and then back to pleading. Alvarez asked Evan to display the most telling exchange on the monitor. It was dated November 6 and read

> *Millbank: I'm sorry I got angry. I just want to talk. Can we meet?*
>
> *Carmichael: To talk. You never just want to talk.*
>
> *Millbank: I'm serious this time. I love you, Jennifer.*
>
> *Carmichael: Then you know what you have to do.*

Millbank: If we can just meet and talk, I can explain.

Carmichael: I am not meeting with you until you do what I asked.

Millbank: Jennifer, please. Carmichael: No.

"I figure they hadn't seen each other in a week at this point, after having met nearly daily in the preceding few months," Alvarez said. "It seemed as if Dr. Carmichael had given Millbank an ultimatum regarding their relationship, and he was hesitant as to what he would do, so he asked for a meeting."

"Right, and Jennifer simply chose to ignore him until he did what she asked, which I think had to be that he ended or was going to end his marriage," Leila added.

"That explains the confrontation at the café," Andy said.

"Sean, please brief the team on your conversation with Mrs. Millbank," Alvarez requested. Detective O'Reilly had already discussed it with him.

As Detective O'Reilly described his conversation, Andy and Leila were both stunned. Leila was amazed that her intuition once again had proven correct, as was Andy, though he thought to himself that he shouldn't be surprised anymore by Leila's uncanny sixth sense.

"Leila, congratulations again," Alvarez said. "Now, while we know that Taylor Davis is Mr. Millbank's daughter, and we know her father left the family around the time she was twelve or thirteen years old, there are still lots of questions, like Why did Mr. Millbank leave her and her mother? Why did she seem to be terrified of him? And why did she break down crying at her meeting with Mrs. Millbank?"

"I would also add another oddity, which is this: Why did she out of the blue choose to visit Mrs. Millbank?" Andy wondered.

"Yes, of course, Andy. And not only that, it happened to be just two days after the encounter at the café," O'Reilly added.

"And four days before the murder," Alvarez put in, which further added to the intrigue.

"So, is she a suspect now?" asked Leila.

"Yes, she could be or should be," O'Reilly said. "But what would her motive be?"

"Obviously, we need to talk to her—she's the only one who can answer all these questions we now suddenly have about her," Alvarez stated.

"So, where does this leave Bryan?" Andy asked. "I'm getting more and more confused," Leila said.

The four of them reviewed these surprising new details for the next hour. They now had three suspects for Mr. Millbank's murder: Bryan Vasquez, Jennifer Carmichael, and now Taylor Davis—that is, assuming Mrs. Millbank could be definitively ruled out. While her involvement was becoming less and less plausible, there was nevertheless still the possibility that she was involved. They briefly turned their attention to Mr. Stern's murder, and they discussed the fact that while Bryan had definitely been in Basel, he hadn't been there the day of the murder. As for Jennifer Carmichael, she indeed had a connection with Basel in her friendship with Angelina Costa, but records showed that she had never been to Switzerland. They didn't know yet whether or not Taylor Davis had been to Switzerland. After that discussion, and considering the fascinating new information regarding the identity of Taylor Davis, Andy requested to review all the pictures from the café one more time.

"Oh Andy, are you for real?" Leila said, rolling her eyes. "I'm going to go blind looking at that monitor."

"Well, Leila, there are a bunch more pictures we have yet to see. Why don't we go through the café pictures one more time, and for now, we can hold off on the next set. I agree with Andy that our eyes may see things they missed before now that we know more about the status of Millbank and Carmichael's affair and about Taylor Davis," Alvarez said. "We can deal with the other pictures tomorrow."

"Jose, I think tomorrow we need to track down Taylor Davis, her mom, and anyone else who may know something about Mr. Millbank's previous marriage," O'Reilly said.

"Good idea. We need a break from the pictures anyway," Alvarez replied. "Thank God," Leila said.

Evan turned the monitor back on and had the folders with the pictures at the ready, and the group began the tedious task of going through the pictures one by one again. Andy repeatedly asked to go back and forth through the same pictures like a squirrel sniffing the ground back and forth over the same patch of grass until he finds the precious acorn. Leila focused on Taylor's face and reaction, looking for the faintest hint to clues about her previous life with her father. The detectives gazed intently, hoping for the clue that would be the key to solving this crime. They had repeatedly reminded Andy and Leila how much pressure they were under, and Andy and Leila reminded them that they were keenly aware of this fact, thanks to the many previous times the detectives had mentioned just that. It was perhaps the only reason Leila had reluctantly agreed to look at the café pictures again. One by one by one the pictures came up, but no immediate revelations were made. They were now looking at the ones of Taylor getting up to leave and then running out of the café. Still nothing—until Andy leapt from his seat again and ran to the front of the room to look at the monitor from just inches away. He then moved back and then forward and back again. He asked Evan to zoom in to the background—to a specific table in the background.

"Holy shit! I couldn't believe it at first. It was just too improbable. But, yes, I have no doubt about it now."

"What! What!" Leila yelled out. "Look, don't you see!"

Leila stared intently at the monitor. Then her eyes grew large, and she saw what Andy had discovered.

"Yes, yes, I do. Oh my God," Leila cried out.

"Detectives, do you see this person sitting alone at the table, looking toward his right, toward the argument?"

"Yes," the detectives said in unison. "That's Bryan Vasquez!" Andy yelled out.

CHAPTER 32

Andy woke up before his iPhone alarm went off. After falling asleep exhausted, he had been tossing and turning in his hotel room bed for the past few hours. He couldn't stop thinking about Bryan. He resigned himself to the realization that Bryan, a person he admired for his strong bond with his sisters, was repeatedly turning up at critical moments in the case. First, he'd happened to end up in Tromsø—home of Erik Bergeland, who had been the original suspect in Mr. Stern's murder—for no apparent reason, though it was possible, Andy thought, to explain that coincidence away. Then he'd traveled to Basel, the city where Mr. Stern had been murdered, again for no clear reason. His presence there was even harder to explain. Following his trip to Switzerland, he'd ended up in New York, scene of the other murder, but not only had he been in New York in the days leading up to the murder, he'd just happened to show up in a picture at a café where Mr. Millbank and one of the other suspects, Jennifer Carmichael, had had an argument. Andy now had little doubt that Bryan is involved in both murders, and it saddened him greatly. He even harbored feelings of guilt himself, noting that it had been the death of his sister Vanessa that had undoubtedly led him to take such drastic and horrible action.

While all of this would have been enough to distract Andy from the sleep he so desperately needed, at this moment what was being knocked back and forth in his head like a Ping-Pong ball was the idea that Bryan had taken a trip to Aberdeen, Scotland. This specific location hadn't come up in this puzzling case before. What on earth was Bryan doing in Aberdeen, Scotland?

Leila had slept soundly. All of the excitement at the discoveries the team had made the day before had exhausted her mind to the point that all it could do was shut down for the night. She was sleeping so soundly that she didn't even hear the beeping sound of her phone signaling that a text message had come through. Finally, at 8:30, she rolled over to the side of the bed, glanced at the bedside clock, and reached for her phone. She noted that she had received a message from Andy nearly an hour ago, merely asking if she were awake. She figured that her lack of response had provided Andy the answer. She texted back to tell Andy she had just woken up and that she would meet him in the lobby in a half hour.

"So, you were able to sleep well, I take it?" Andy asked. "Yeah, my brain was fried. How about you?"

"So-so. I've been tossing and turning since about five o'clock."

"What were you thinking about?" Leila asked, anticipating that it had something to do with their relationship. At least she hoped so.

"After seeing Bryan in that picture at Café de Bon Salud, I couldn't stop thinking about him. Anyway, I remembered that his assistant said he flew to Aberdeen, Scotland, and I was trying to figure out why he went there."

"Oh," Leila said with a twinge of disappointment in her voice, though Andy took no notice. Leila realized that Andy had missed her clue.

"Aberdeen—what the hell is in Aberdeen?" Andy wondered aloud. "Maybe another victim?" Leila suggested.

"No, I doubt that. First, I think the killings are over—it's been nearly two months since the double murder. Second, Bryan is not stupid, and he must realize that there's an investigation going on and that he might be considered a suspect," Andy replied.

"How about oil—any possibility it is related to his work?" Leila continued to offer ideas.

"I don't know."

"Where is Aberdeen, anyway?" Leila asked.

"I told you—it's in Scotland," Andy responded.

"*Duh*, I know that. I mean *where* in Scotland?" Leila replied, irritated.

Andy picked up his iPad, opened his web browser, and pulled up a map of Scotland. Leila pointed to Aberdeen on Scotland's east coast. Neither one noted anything peculiar about its location. Leila suggested they zoom out to take in a broader view of Scotland's surroundings. Then she noted something interesting. "Andy, in this wider view, take a look at the country that lies to the east of Aberdeen."

"Hmm. Norway."

"And look what city in Norway is closest to Aberdeen."

"Stavanger," Andy said.

"And the North Sea, with all its oil platforms in between. Maybe Bryan was getting suspicious that someone would be looking into his travel," Leila said.

"Are you suggesting he flew to Aberdeen in order to, well, sneak into Norway aboard one of his company's ships?" Andy asked.

"Perhaps."

"But why is he going back to Norway, and if it is work-related, why doesn't he just go the conventional route—you know, fly into Oslo or Stavanger?"

"I don't know—I'm just thinking out loud," Leila replied. "I hate when you do that." Andy stated.

"Why?"

"Because you're usually right, and I don't like the idea of our patient's brother acting in this very incriminating way."

Following a quick stop at Starbucks for the usual morning beverages, they headed back to police headquarters yet again. Andy suggested they should ask Alvarez for NYPD badges, given all the time they had spent on the case. Leila laughed while they walked and glanced at

Andy, holding her gaze until he glanced back. She smiled. He smiled back, though it was an uncomfortable smile because he couldn't quite understand why they were smiling at each other. For her part, Leila kept her eyes fixed on Andy's until he turned to face forward. She had so much she wanted to tell him, but she needed to find the right time and place. For now, she just kept smiling each time their eyes met.

When Leila and Andy arrived at police headquarters, security personnel now greeted them by their first names. No longer were they offered directions to the conference room.

"Good morning, Detective O'Reilly," Leila said as she walked into the room. "Please call me Sean," O'Reilly replied.

"Really!" Leila exclaimed in surprise.

"Well, you've been calling Alvarez Jose for a while now, and I've been waiting for you to start calling me Sean."

"Oh, I'm sorry. I didn't know it was okay," Leila continued. "Why? Because I'm old, er ... older?"

"I suppose ... Sean," Leila said, flashing her Julia Roberts smile.

Detective Alvarez joined Andy, Leila, and O'Reilly in the conference room. "Where's Evan?" Andy asked, noting his absence along with the absence of the computer he had been using to project the pictures.

"We're not going to be looking at more pictures for now," Alvarez replied. "Basically, we have to move more quickly in sorting this crazy case out, and even more important, we obviously have some new leads we need to track down.

"Here is what we suggest," O'Reilly continued. "We want the two of you to go back to the hospital and find Dr. Carmichael and Taylor Davis. Leila, we want you to meet with Taylor and have a, well, friendly chat with her and try to find out as much as you can about her. Remember, she doesn't know that *we* know who she is and why we're interested in her."

"You don't want me to be there, I take it?" Andy asked.

"No, we think it will be more productive if it's just Leila—woman to woman."

"What do you want me to do?"

"Well, we haven't had time to officially question Dr. Carmichael. She knows we found the wig, and she knows that she's a suspect and that we are going to have to bring her into the station for interrogation," O'Reilly added.

"So, shouldn't you be doing that—the questioning, that is? Why do you want me to talk to her?" Andy asked.

"To be honest, we don't think she'll talk to us without us arresting her. I tried talking to her one time in the hospital, and I got nowhere. She completely blew me off. We think if you talk to her, maybe you can get some much-needed answers," Alvarez replied.

O'Reilly put in, "Jose and I talked about it, and we think we should let Carmichael know about the pictures from the café. If you offer that information to her, and she really had nothing to do with it, she may talk to you," he continued. "It's a long shot but worth a try."

"If she does agree to talk to you, Andy, we'd like you to find out about just two things. First, her relationship with Taylor Davis—why were they at the café together? Second, we want you to ask her what the confrontation with Mr. Millbank was about, to confirm if we're on the right track," Alvarez said.

"Uh, why would she agree to discuss any of this with me?" Andy asked.

"She might not, but I think *that* would be telling in and of itself," Alvarez replied. "Anything she tells you couldn't be admissible as evidence, since it would be hearsay, and it would be absolutely fine for you to tell her that. Even if she doesn't ask, you can volunteer it."

"Doesn't she know that already?" Andy asked.

"Probably. I mean, after all, she is the coroner and has testified in many trials, so she's familiar with the rules."

"I get it," Leila chimed in. "Get what?" Andy asked.

"May I?" Leila asked, looking at Alvarez. "Please."

"Andy, you and I are doctors, not detectives, so we're not, how shall I put this, threatening or intimidating—you know, not like the detectives would be. So, for both Jennifer and Taylor, they are more likely to be open with us—we're all doctors, after all."

"And if they're not, then they're probably hiding something," Andy finished the thought.

"So it's a win-win, as we see it," O'Reilly said. "They either give you some useful fuckin' information, or they clam up. We will learn something either way. If we, you know, Jose and I, question them, the dynamics and rules are completely different."

"Okay. So, do we just show up and find them or set up an appointment?"

"We'd like it to be spontaneous, if possible," Alvarez replied. "We have cleared you with hospital security again—you'll get temporary ID badges—and then we also told Dr. Simmons that you will be heading over to Pathology. You remember her, right?"

"Yes, the head of pathology," Leila answered.

"Right," Alvarez continued. "She informed us that Dr. Carmichael is working today and that Taylor Davis is still on her pathology rotation and has been hanging out either with one of the pathologists or in the pathology conference room. So, you should have no problem finding them. The rest is up to you."

"You have a lot of confidence in us, Jose," Andy said.

"Why shouldn't I? Without you two, we wouldn't be as close as I think we are getting to figuring this out."

Having been assigned their mission, Andy and Leila headed back out to the concrete jungle that is New York City and hopped into a taxi to New York Hospital. Leila purposefully glanced over at Andy several times during the drive uptown, smiling widely each time he returned her gaze. After the fifteen-minute taxi ride, they arrived at the hospital and quickly refamiliarized themselves with the way to the pathology department. They discussed several options for splitting up and initiating contact with their targets, but they realized it all depended on what and whom they would find upon reaching the pathology conference room. As luck would have it, they found Taylor alone in the conference room. Leila glanced at Andy, and taking the hint, he greeted Taylor briefly before turning around and heading back down the hall he had just come from. Fortunately, they had discussed just such a scenario, as this was how they had found Taylor when they'd met previously, and they'd made a plan. Andy assumed Leila would follow through with that plan, so he ducked into the men's room and hid there for ten minutes. Upon emerging, he noted that the hallway was empty, and so he headed back down to the pathology conference room. He stood outside for a minute or two, gathering his thoughts and rehearsing what he was going to say. He was like a predator hiding in the grass, stalking its prey and waiting for the right moment to pounce.

Meanwhile, Leila had convinced Taylor to show her to the cafeteria, following through on the plan she had made with Andy. She was even prepared to drink the dilute, tasteless, brown liquid the cafeteria referred to as coffee in order to open a dialog with Taylor. At first, Taylor didn't want to leave; she was concerned that she would be labeled as "uninterested"—almost the worst comment a medical student could receive on her report card. Leila, however, astutely asked Dr. Simmons to excuse Taylor for a short time, which alleviated those concerns. Leila noted Taylor to be a very pleasant young woman. She was confident that Taylor had absolutely no suspicion that she was about to be probed for information. Although Leila felt somewhat guilty for being deceptive, her determined will to solve the case took precedent. After getting their drinks, they sat at an isolated table toward one corner.

"So, are you actually interested in pathology, or is this rotation a requirement?" Leila began with an innocent question.

"The truth?" Taylor began her reply, looking across at Leila with a slight smirk on her face. "Well, the truth is that I heard this was a really easy rotation, and I'd had three brutal months in a row, with lots of overnights in the hospital, so I needed a break."

"That's funny," Leila said. "I did the same thing, only I chose dermatology for my 'break.'"

They both laughed. Leila sensed she could get what she was after, but she knew she had to be patient.

"So, *has* it been easy?" Leila went on.

"Oh God. So easy that I'm bored." Taylor said with a laugh. "How have you dealt with that?"

"Just like this—having coffee or lunch with people. That breaks up the monotony of doing nothing."

"So, you meet other students—or do you wait for strangers like me to come and steal you away to the cafeteria?" Leila asked, smiling.

"No students. My friends are either at another hospital or are busy with actually taking care of patients. Mostly I've hung out with Dr. Carmichael," Taylor replied.

"I actually met her once," Leila said, though not sure it was the right decision.

On the one hand, she didn't want to let on how she knew Jennifer, but on the other hand, she didn't know if in their conversations her name had ever come up. She'd decided to play it safe and be honest.

"In what context?" Taylor asked.

Shit, Leila thought to herself as she was thinking of a good response. "It was about a case. You remember I'm a hematologist, right?"

"No. I knew you were a doctor and that you're from LA, but I didn't know that you were a hematologist—not sure we ever discussed that. You were here for some research or something like that."

"Yes, you have a good memory," Leila replied and noted that Taylor indeed had a good memory and was clearly very bright. She would need to tread carefully.

Andy sat at the conference room table, pretending to read a medical paper that was lying on the table while periodically gazing around, hoping Dr. Carmichael would show up. After thirty minutes, and following the comings and goings of several pathologists, Carmichael emerged from her office. Andy, still in predatory mode, leapt from the table and greeted her.

"Hi, Dr. Carmichael—do you remember me?" Andy asked.

"Yes, of course," she said tersely. "What are you doing here? By the way, there are no more wigs or other paraphernalia for you to look for, if that's why you're here."

Andy, stunned that she somehow knew that he'd found the wig, took a few seconds to gather his composure and then chuckled. "I'm not looking for anything this time," he said.

"So, why *are* you here then?" she asked in an annoyed tone.

"The truth is I'm here because I want to talk to you—about the case, of course," he responded.

She was still standing in the doorway to her office. She quickly glanced around the conference room and saw no one. She motioned for Andy to come into her office. The predator had its prey—or was it the other way around, Andy wondered. At first it seemed that perhaps Andy was going to be interrogated, as Dr. Carmichael opened the questioning. "What's the deal with the NYPD? How come they can't find the killer?" she asked.

Andy was surprised she'd delved right into the hunt for the killer. Was this a deft way for Dr. Carmichael to deflect attention away from herself? Andy knew she was extremely intelligent, so anything was possible.

"I don't know, but it's not for lack of trying, I can assure you," Andy said. "You know we, Leila and I, are working with them, of course."

"Yes, that's how we met the first time—I reviewed the autopsy with you, remember?"

"Yes, of course. So, since you are aware that I am working with them, you know, to help with the medical aspects," Andy lied, "they asked me to come and speak with you."

"Go on," Carmichael responded, seemingly interested.

"Okay. Well, we happened to get our hands on some pictures that were taken at the Café de Bon Salud, and one set showed you in what appeared to be a confrontation with Mr. Millbank a few days before he was killed. Do you remember that?"

"Pictures! Where the hell did you get those?"

"It's a long story—let's just say we have them," Andy answered, attempting to avoid that topic.

"Dr. Friedman, if you want any answers, I need to be able to trust you, and so I need honest answers to my questions. Where did you get the pictures?"

"Fair enough, I'll tell you. Mrs. Millbank hired a private detective to follow her husband and, well … you around, and he took lots of pictures—with him and also a lot with you."

"Oh my God! Are you kidding me?"

"No."

"Uh, are any of them ... you know, uh, sexual? Have you seen my naked body?" Dr. Carmichael asked, trying to hide a degree of panic that had set in.

"Oh no, not at all. I swear. They were all in bars, hotel lobbies, the café—none of them are those kind of voyeuristic pictures," Andy replied.

"Thank God. I have a reputation to uphold, you know."

"So, do you recall the confrontation with Mr. Millbank at the café?"

"Of course; what about it?" Carmichael answered matter-of-factly. "Uh, do I need to spell it out for you?"

"Yes, please do."

"O-o-k-a-a-y," Andy began. "You were in what appeared to be heated argument with a man you were having an affair with less than a week before he was found dead."

"Yes, that's true," Carmichael responded calmly.

"And let me remind you that you also just happened to turn up looking for him the day he died. It seems pretty suspicious don't you think?" Andy stated, pressing Carmichael.

"Yes, it's very suspicious," Carmichael replied, disarming the argument momentarily. "I completely agree with you, but I had nothing to do with Creighton's death, I can assure you."

"Can you tell me then what the argument was about?"

"Sure. Happy to. I had been avoiding him, and he got pissed off, so he somehow hunted me down at the café, which I was not happy about."

"Why were you avoiding him?" Andy cajoled her to offer up more information.

"You see, I gave him an ultimatum—I told him he needed to choose his wife or me, and I refused to keep seeing him unless he agreed. We had talked about that issue a bunch of times in person, and he kept promising he would tell his wife their relationship was over, but then he wouldn't do it. So I told him I wouldn't see him anymore."

"That's it."

"Well, he started calling me over and over again and began texting me incessantly, and ... well ... I didn't respond. You have to understand that he is a man who is used to getting his way—even if it means getting his cake and eating it, too, if you know what I mean."

"And so he tracked you down—" Andy said.

"Yup—tracked me down as if I belonged to him," Carmichael interrupted. "Well, that doesn't sound so unreasonable if you look at it from his point of view."

"Perhaps, but the main reason we got into a heated debate at the café was because I told him one condition of our relationship was that he never come anywhere near my place of work, and when he unexpectedly showed up, I was pissed as hell," Carmichael replied.

"Makes sense. One more question, if I may. How come you came to the hotel the day he died if you had cut off all communication with him?" Andy asked.

"Well, I know it's going to sound crazy, but he texted me and told me he was going to get a divorce," Carmichael responded. "So I agreed to meet him. He wanted to celebrate in the hotel room. It freaks me out to think I could have been in there when he died. Look, I'm not stupid. I know that you all consider me a suspect now. Just imagine how bad it would have looked if I'd been in the room with him when he died—that's what scared the shit out of me!"

"Are you sure he told his wife he wanted a divorce?"

"I don't know if he actually did or not. I mean, he could have lied, sure, but I was willing to meet him because I think he was telling me the truth," Carmichael responded.

Andy couldn't help but think that this all made sense. Furthermore, she relayed the information in such a cool and matter-of-fact manner that Andy was convinced she was either telling the truth or she was a pathological liar. It was clear that Dr. Carmichael knew her activities were suspicious, yet she went to no lengths to defend them or minimize their meaning. *Wouldn't the murderer act more defensively?* Andy thought.

Leila and Taylor had spent the past half hour getting to know each other, mostly regarding their interest in medicine and what it was like being a woman in what was still often an old white man's world. Leila sensed that Taylor was warming to her. She felt that rather than asking point-blank questions, the best way to learn about Taylor's past would be to first discuss her own upbringing in the turmoil of Iraq and the move to the United States.

"Not only is it hard to be a woman in medicine sometimes, but to be an immigrant with a funny name is even harder," Leila began.

"You're an immigrant?" Taylor asked, surprised. "You don't have an accent, and your name isn't funny."

"Well, some people think my name is funny. Anyway, I grew up in Iraq."

"Iraq!"

"Yes, but it's worse, actually. I'm Kurdish. Have you heard of the Kurds?"

"A little, but honestly, I don't know much about Kurds," Taylor answered.

"Maybe we can have a chat about that another time. Let me tell you how I ended up in the United States. The Kurds are a persecuted people, always have been. We don't really have a home, you see. We are scattered around in Iraq, Turkey, Syria, and Iran, but none of those nations really want us there. They're afraid we will want our own country one day and they will lose some of their territory. Anyway, after a couple of wars and Saddam Hussein's massacre by gas of so many of our people, my parents decided to leave to make a better life for me and my family."

"That's awful—about the gas and all the hatred. I hate that about the world. Bad people seem to get away with behaving badly all the time. Where's the accountability?" Taylor wondered aloud.

"Agreed. So, when I was twelve, we moved and ended up in Dearborn, Michigan, for a few years. Lots of Iraqi refugees ended up there. Then we moved to LA and have been there ever since."

"Amazing. I would love to hear more," Taylor requested, but Leila sensed it was a good time to shift the discussion.

"What about you? Are you a lifelong New Yorker, or should I say *Noo Yawka*?" Leila said, attempting her best New York accent.

Taylor laughed. "Born and raised," she said.

"Yet not much of an accent, I must say." Leila decided to begin her subtle inquisition. "Are your parents doctors?"

"No," Taylor said. Her demeanor clearly changed when Leila asked about her parents. She became suddenly quiet. Leila decided to carefully press forward.

"Your parents must be *so* proud of you. It's hard to get into medical school these days, with the economy the way it is, when lots of smart young people head for the security of a career in medicine. What does your dad do?"

"Uh, my dad. Well …" Taylor began and drew a deep breath. "He … he's not part of my life. He left me and my mom when I was young."

"Oh, I'm sorry. I didn't know. I don't want to open up any old wounds," Leila said with false sincerity.

"Old wounds," Taylor said in a contemplative tone. "Old wounds. There are definitely lots of those."

"Look, we don't need to talk about this. I'm sorry."

"Fuck it," Taylor said suddenly. "Let's get out of here. Sorry, are you busy?"

"Not really. What do you have in mind?" Leila was a bit bewildered by the sudden change of tone.

"Let's go to the museum. Have you been to the Met?" Taylor asked, referring to the Metropolitan Museum of Art on Fifth Avenue.

"No, I haven't."

"I like you, Leila. Let's go have some fun instead of sitting in this sterile cafeteria."

"Okay, but what about Dr. Simmons and—you were so worried about leaving the pathology area in the first place. I mean, I don't want you to get into any trouble."

"They don't give a shit. They won't even notice. I'm like a fly they try to brush off but keeps coming back. Once I'm gone, they won't care. Teaching me pathology is the least of their concerns. So, what do you say—do you want to go?" Taylor asked.

"Sure, but I need to use the restroom first. Two cups of coffee already today," Leila said, acting out her best wry smile.

Leila excused herself and retreated to the restroom. She texted Andy and told him she would meet him at the hotel later in the afternoon. He acknowledged but offered nothing further, as he was seated in front of Dr. Carmichael.

Dr. Carmichael continued to be forthcoming with information. She revealed to Andy how she'd met Mr. Millbank and about the details of their affair, save for the intimate aspects. Andy carefully pieced her story with the pictures of her and Mr. Millbank at various hotels and restaurants that he had seen in the preceding days. He grew more and more confident that she was telling the truth and less and less confident that she was involved in the murder. *Why would a killer be so open and so honest?* he wondered. Was Dr. Carmichael so cunning as to be able to be this apparently truthful and yet not give up some morsel of information tying her to the murder? When discussing the murder, she mentioned how awful it had been for her to conduct the autopsy on her former lover, but she'd also wished to keep her affair with Millbank a secret, especially at work, so she'd really had no option as the coroner but to do her job. She had been convinced he'd died of some bizarre natural cause until she'd had the fateful discussion with her counterpart in Basel.

"You know, the way he died is just so weird. I have been really bothered by it, and I've been trying to piece things together myself, but I just can't figure it out," Carmichael said.

"Well, that makes two of us, because we are kind of stuck, too."

"Wish I could help out, but I don't think I have any useful information."

"I do have one other question about the café, if that's okay."

"Sure, go ahead," Carmichael replied.

Andy was surprised how amicable the discussion had become; he'd been so concerned it was going to be confrontational. They had even resorted to calling each other by their first names. At this point, he no longer viewed Carmichael as his prey. He did, however, still occasionally wonder if this was some kind of ploy to throw him off the scent.

"The girl you were with that day, who is she?"

"She's just a medical student doing a rotation in pathology, that's all. It was a slow day, and we were bored, so we decided to get some coffee and pastries at the café."

"What's her name?" Andy probed.

"Taylor … something. I don't remember her last name."

"What happened when Millbank came in?"

"Uh, we discussed that already, Andy."

"I mean with Taylor."

"Oh, I don't know. She just took off," Carmichael stated bluntly. "I'm sure it was awkward for her to see me arguing with some older man."

"Did you talk to Taylor about the incident since then, or did she ask you about the confrontation with Millbank?" Andy continued in his interrogation.

"No. Not at all."

"Are you sure, Jennifer? I can't say why, but it's important for me to know," Andy said.

"Honestly, she didn't ask, and I didn't say anything. What's going on?"

"I really can't say, sorry. Anyway, you've been really helpful. Thank you."

"No problem. I am curious to know what happened too."

"You're making me think I shouldn't consider you a suspect anymore," Andy stated boldly and smiled.

"I shouldn't be. I told you several times I had nothing to do with Creighton's death. You'd be wasting valuable time and resources if you focused on me. Good luck, and let me know if you think I can help."

The Metropolitan Museum of Art was a New York City landmark. It had hosted the works of the most famous artists that had ever lived, as well as historical treasures such as the riches of the tomb of the most famous pharaoh, Tutankhamun. New Yorkers loved their museums, and the Met, as they called it for short, was the most famous one of them all. With its famous staircase, rising like the steps of an Aztec pyramid up to its colossal columns, indicating the entrance to the magnificent building, it was both an artistic and architectural marvel. Leila was excited to see it despite the fact that she was not particularly knowledgeable about art or art history. Taylor had a spring in her step, like a child let out of school early to go to the park and spend the afternoon playing carefree. Leila had to keep reminding herself that Taylor was a suspect in a heinous crime and that the only reason she was with her was to gather information to determine whether she was involved in a murder. After paying the entrance fee, they headed for the hall displaying famous paintings from the Impressionist period. As they walked, Taylor told her how she'd used to come here as a child with her parents. Leila sensed an opening.

"I hate to pry, Taylor, but you seem to have such nice memories of this place when you were a child, yet you also said you had many old wounds. You don't need to tell me anything you don't want to, but I have to admit that I am curious," Leila asked, ensuring her tone was innocent, with no suggestion of pressure.

"Well, that's a long story, and I'm not sure you really want to hear it," Taylor replied.

"You know, I had a really traumatic childhood in Iraq because of all the violence and the bigotry against Kurds, so I always wonder how other kids cope with childhood traumas," Leila added.

"Childhood trauma, huh! What were your parents like?"

"My parents? They're amazing people. My dad had a good life in Iraq, despite the violence and bigotry. He had a business selling electronics, and we were reasonable well off. He had lots of friends and loved his home, but he left it all behind to start all over again in the US for his children."

"Wow. That's impressive," Taylor replied.

"He sacrificed a lot for his family, I have to say."

Leila thought to ask Taylor about her father but was afraid to press that button again. She hoped it would come out naturally. *What are these old wounds*, she wondered.

"My mom did her best, though she was more consumed with herself than me."

"Do you have brothers or sisters?"

"No," Taylor responded. "You would think that would make it easier to give me some attention, but no—shopping for clothes, shoes, jewelry, and hanging out with her friends were her priorities."

"So, who took care of you when you were little?"

"A parade of nannies—the most expensive ones my parents could find. You know, to ease the guilt," Taylor replied, not caring to hide her sarcasm.

Leila couldn't resist asking Taylor once more about her father at this point. "What about your dad, then? Did he contribute to your upbringing at all?"

"Interesting question. Contributed to my upbringing?" Taylor repeated the question in a cynical tone. "Yes, I would say that he contributed to my upbringing, but probably not in the way you think."

"Well, I was curious about what you said before about old wounds, and now I'm that much more curious, but, again, you don't need to tell me anything you don't want to." Leila didn't want Taylor to even remotely suspect that she was in a sense interrogating her.

"I like you, Leila. Maybe I should come out to LA and do a rotation in hematology with you. Would that be possible?"

"Absolutely. I would love to have you come. It's much warmer there in winter, as you know."

"Let's have a look at some of the exhibits, and then we'll get some lunch somewhere. Uh, you don't have plans, I hope?" Taylor asked.

"No, none."

"Great. I'll tell you about my father over lunch—it would be easier to have a chat over lunch."

"Sure."

Taylor guided Leila through the vast array of Impressionist paintings—Monets, Manets, Toulouse-Lautrecs, and others. They also went to the large atrium that hosted numerous sculptures from various periods in history. Leila truly enjoyed herself and was growing to like Taylor—a lot. They were similar in many ways. They were both women in medicine in a field that, despite having more and more women, was still often led by old white men with gray or white hair. They joked about the various older male doctors they'd met, commenting that the Viagra business was so good because of the many rich old men in medicine and business. Taylor commented that there was a reason why a month's worth of birth control pills cost about thirty dollars while each Viagra pill cost fifteen dollars, and more if you got them on the black market without a prescription. She claimed it was because dirty old men could afford to pay that much for one erection, while the women they slept with couldn't afford to pay a proportionate amount for thirty days of pills. Leila agreed; she sensed that, for a young woman, Taylor had an excellent sense of where society put its priorities. They spent a couple more hours at the Met, getting to know each other and continuing to joke about old doctors. Taylor added that many of the doctors were probably nerds, based on their looks and mannerisms, and suggested that that achieving high positions of power and influence was the ultimate "revenge of the nerds."

Andy left the hospital after his hour-long conversation with Jennifer. He was more convinced than ever that she had not killed Mr. Millbank. Sure, she was very smart, but her calm and cool demeanor left him with a sense that no killer could be that calm and that cold—especially considering that the dead man had been her lover. He texted Leila that he was leaving the hospital, but she didn't reply. He thought about calling but then decided not to. Maybe she was making progress with Taylor Davis. He thought about the pictures from the café again, projecting the scene in his mind. Taylor's reaction had been so unexpected, while they had been focusing on Jennifer's reaction to the appearance of Mr. Millbank. And then, the image of Bryan popped into his head. What the hell had he been doing there? What was he up to? Tromsø, Basel, New York—and now Aberdeen. Andy couldn't piece it all together, except to think that Bryan was obviously involved in some way in these murders. But how? He called Detective Alvarez, who told him that there was nothing to do at the station and suggested he just take the afternoon off and relax. Andy was in the mood for a New York deli sandwich, so he headed to Times Square to the Stage Deli for one of his favorite, though rare, treats—a tongue sandwich on rye and a dill pickle.

Taylor chose a quiet Italian restaurant, Angelo's, not far from the Met, for lunch. She asked the maître d' for a table in a quiet corner, and as the restaurant was quite empty, he was happy to oblige. They continued their social-commentary discussion in the restaurant.

"We think we live in such an advanced and civil society here in the United States, yet I would bet we are going to be one of the last countries to elect a woman to lead the country, don't you think?" Taylor said.

"I don't know; I have a feeling the country is ready for a woman president now," Leila said optimistically.

"I'm not so sure. Besides, it would be nothing to be proud of at that point. Let's see—England, Chile, Brazil, Argentina, Australia, Israel, India, Germany, South Korea ... for God's sake, even Pakistan," Taylor listed all the countries she could remember that had or have women as prime ministers or presidents.

"Okay. I get it," Leila replied.

"We're not talking about some small or unimportant countries. The most important countries economically in Europe, the second-most populous country in the world, the biggest countries in South America, a country that is almost constantly at war. You see what I mean?"

"Maybe the women in this country are so smart that they know better than to go into politics," Leila said in a half-hearted attempt to support her adopted country's lack of women presidents.

"If only."

Leila was waiting for the right moment to return the conversation to the reason they were having lunch in the first place—Taylor's father, but again, she didn't want to seem overanxious. *Patience*, she said to herself. The waiter brought them some bread and offered a choice of wines. Leila motioned to Taylor with her hand to make the decision regarding wine and was quietly pleased when Taylor ordered a bottle of a fine Italian white wine. *In vino veritas*, Leila hoped, invoking the famous Latin phrase and hoping that the truth about Taylor's father would indeed come to light.

"How much longer are you going to stay in New York?" Taylor asked.

At first Leila was concerned as to how she would answer the question, but her lightning-fast brain sparked an idea.

"Not sure yet, but I sure miss my family. I see my parents at least once a week. My dad always wants updates on my love life," Leila laughed. "You see, I'm considered an old maid as a thirty-three-year-old single woman in my culture."

"Your dad sounds like a really nice man."

"He is," Leila said, deciding to keep her answer short in hopes that Taylor would initiate the discussion about her own dad.

"Not mine. He was a total asshole to me and my mom."

"I'm sorry. Is he dead now?" Leila asked, jumping on the opportunity when she noted Taylor described her dad in the past tense.

"No. Whatever gave you that idea?"

"Oh, because you said your dad *was* an asshole," Leila replied emphasizing the word *was*.

"Well, the truth is I don't know and I don't care what my dad is up to now, nor do I even know if he's alive, to be honest."

"I'm so sorry. What happened, if you don't mind me asking?"

Taylor's demeanor changed. Her face looked down for a moment and then back up at Leila. She swallowed and the edge of her mouth's usual slight upward turn flattened out. She pouted her lips and closed her eyelids for a couple of seconds. When she opened them again, a single tear that had formed in each eye was released and trickled down each of her cheeks symmetrically like droplets of condensed water on the outside of a cold glass. Taylor stared straight ahead now, looking intently at Leila, probing for signs of empathy. Leila stared back, mouth slightly agape and then, closing her lips, let out a gentle, ever-so-slightly audible sigh through her nostrils. Apparently, that was enough of a sign for Taylor to proceed.

Taylor shook her head slowly from side to side. "Leila, it sounds like you went through hell as a child in Iraq, but can I ask you something?"

"Of course. Anything."

"Did you go through it alone?"

"No. My whole family suffered, and we supported each other."

"Not me. I had no one. No siblings. A useless mother. No friends I could trust. I thought about telling one of my nannies once, but at the last moment, I didn't say anything."

"That's very sad, and I'm so sorry to hear that, but I don't fully understand."

"It's not easy. You see, I have never told anyone about this. Ever. No one.

You'll be the first to know. I can't believe it—you know, it's the first day I know you," Taylor said and let out an uncomfortable chuckle.

Leila remained silent, in part to encourage Taylor to continue but also in part because she didn't know what to say. Taylor stared into Leila's eyes. The tears had stopped, and her eyes squinted slightly, and then she began.

"My dad molested me. And not once. Over and over again. For years," Taylor said haltingly.

"Oh, Taylor," Leila said sympathetically, reaching her right hand across the table and wrapping it around Taylor's left hand. "I, uh, I don't know what to say."

"That's okay. What can you say?"

"How old were you?"

"It started when I was nine and it didn't end until I was thirteen."

"That is just awful—Taylor. I … I'm so sorry," Leila said, truly at a loss for words.

"It only ended when he left us. He was having an affair and ultimately left us for another woman. Thank God. How many kids can say that?" Taylor let out another uncomfortable laugh.

"Say what?"

"Thank God my dad had an affair. That's when it ended—the molestation, that is. I only saw my father once or twice after he left, and both times it was pretty soon after he moved out."

"Taylor, that is just so awful. I don't know how you got through it with no support. You were just a child. Your mom didn't do *anything*?"

"Nothing. She was powerless against my dad."

"Did he abuse her, too?"

"Not as far as I could tell, but I don't think they ever had sex—they were not a loving couple, that's for sure. Apparently, he likes his girls young … really young. You know, he touched me …" Taylor started and then paused for a moment before continuing. "He touched me everywhere."

"Oh, God," Leila said. She put a hand in front of her mouth, feeling as if she were going to vomit.

She stared down at the plate with her lunch salad untouched and felt even more nauseous. It seemed as if now that Taylor had begun, this was her opportunity to finally unleash the burden that had been kept inside her mind for thirteen years. She proceeded to describe in graphic detail all of the places and the manner in which her father had touched her. Leila became more and more nauseous. *How could any human being do such things to a child?* she wondered. But then, when she thought that this was the young girl's own father who had done this, a veritable cascade of emotions gripped her. Anger. Hatred. Sympathy. Pain. In spite of Leila's obvious discomfort with the discussion, Taylor pressed on as if she had just opened a can of soda she had shaken, spewing out all of the pressure that had built up inside her mind until it was exhausted. She described what had happened when she started puberty and began developing breasts, describing how her father had treated them like a new toy he had just received. Leila, now barely able to contain her emotions, needed to interject.

"Taylor, that is the most awful story I have ever heard, and remember, I am a witness to genocide. But somehow this feels worse. More visceral. More appalling. I don't even know what to say."

"There is nothing, really, you need to say. I appreciate that you are listening to me and letting me get it all out. You are the first person I have ever told about this."

"Really! You never told anyone?"

"No," Taylor replied.

"Did you tell him to stop?" Leila asked innocently.

"Stop? I'm his little girl. I couldn't do that. At least that's what my immature mind thought. When he left my room, I would go to the bathroom and throw up and then cry myself to sleep."

"I ... uh, I ..." Leila started to respond but couldn't continue. She was shaken, and the shock and sadness were visible on her face.

"It's okay. You don't need to say anything. Your face is speaking for you. I know this might sound weird, but it feels good to finally tell someone about this. It feels less lonely suddenly."

"You never got counseling?"

"Ha," Taylor laughed sarcastically. "Counseling. No. Who was going to take me to a shrink? Who was going to pay for it?"

"I mean, like, now ... now that you're an adult."

"Well, true. Now I can take myself, but who's going to pay for it? You know what a good New York shrink goes for these days? If I didn't hate my psychiatry rotation so much, I would have actually considered it as a career. You know, psychiatrists are considered the second-biggest thieves in New York—after the lawyers."

Leila laughed. A healthy dose of cynicism and biting sarcasm were clearly two of Taylor's coping mechanisms.

"What about someone at the medial school?"

"Forget it. You know, the truth is I counseled myself through this. When I got old enough, I took long walks in the park, and I would talk to myself for hours on end. People would stare at me when they realized I was talking to myself. It's funny, but today, with Bluetooth, I could talk to myself, only no one would realize it so long as I had an earpiece in."

"This doesn't sound like something you can counsel yourself out of, Taylor.

You know, I just am worried about you," Leila said.

"That's sweet. You're really nice. I wish you didn't live in LA. We could become great friends."

"We still could," Leila said, forgetting for the moment that until the investigation was over that would not be possible, and that if Taylor had anything to do with the murder of Mr. Millbank, it would be impossible afterward, as well.

"Yeah. I suppose you're right. Anyway, I think I did a pretty good job of counseling myself. It really was therapeutic, you know, talking to myself about the abuse. I just kept saying to myself that it was over now, and that I have my whole life ahead of me, and I need to make the best of it. I say to myself over and over again, 'Make good choices, Taylor, make good choices,' and since I was about fifteen years old, I have made mostly good choices."

"Do you ever think about the abuse?"

"Yes. From time to time, but not as much as I used to."

"Was it frequent? Did he touch you frequently, I meant."

"Is every day considered frequent?" came the sarcastic reply. "He came to my room like clockwork, pretty much every night, unless he was on some business trip. Well, until he started fucking that other woman. He waited for my mom to go to sleep, as if that way she wouldn't know. What an idiot. He would knock on the door, and—"

"Knock on the door!" Leila said in surprise. "Yeah, I think it was part of his sick fantasy."

"Why didn't you say 'No, don't come in.'?"

"I did a few times at the beginning, but that didn't stop him. I was a just a kid, and he was my dad. What the hell did I know?" Taylor continued. "So, he would come in and sit beside me on the bed, put his hand under my chin, and stare at me. I looked at him at first but then just looked down. I just wanted him to get it started and be done with it, so I could get on with my homework or TV or whatever I was doing."

"How long did he stay each time? I'm sorry—I shouldn't keep asking, but I have this, I know it's awful, this morbid curiosity. Please, we can stop this conversation any time, okay?"

"Yeah, I know," Taylor said assuredly, but then she continued, "It varied. Usually about twenty to thirty minutes. I now realize that this is the amount of time he needed to get aroused, and then I assume he went somewhere to jerk off."

Leila swallowed and gagged. She was going to throw up soon, she sensed. Taylor noticed how uncomfortable she was getting. Neither one of them had touched their food. "Maybe we should stop," Taylor suggested, "or you might need counseling—or a long walk in the park, at least."

"I think you're right. Maybe we should stop ... unless you want to continue, that is."

"I feel much better. We can stop now," Taylor said, smiling.

Leila couldn't help but notice that Taylor really did seem to be in better spirits. She thought that this lunch had, in fact, been her first counseling session, at least the first one with another person. But she did have one question she felt she needed to ask.

"Taylor, can I ask just one last question about this. Did—" Leila hesitated, not knowing how or whether to finish the question.

"Did he rape me, you're wondering?" Taylor interrupted, anticipating Leila's next question perfectly

"Yes," Leila said, hesitating and anxious.

"No. Mind you, I'm sure he would have if he had stayed with us longer. I know girls as young as thirteen get raped, but I think he was waiting for me to sexually mature more—it would have played out better in his fantasy. You know, I just thought of something funny ... and weird. I actually found the woman he left us for—I don't know why I did it, but I tracked her down to talk her recently. I likely should have thanked her—she probably prevented me from being raped by my own father."

Leila couldn't help but think that she knew exactly who this was—Mrs. Millbank. In the meantime, it had been a morning full of surprises. Some had been good ones—the Met, and getting to know a young a woman she genuinely was growing to like—yet the awful story Taylor had reported would consume her mind for a long time to come. She thought of her own dad and what an amazing and wonderful man he was, and she couldn't help but wonder how a father could do such awful things, the most awful things, to his own young daughter. *Surely, killing your child is not as bad as abusing your child*, she thought. Or was it? She wasn't sure.

Leila paid for lunch, and the two got up from the table and headed back out to the brisk January air. The waiter arrived at the table a moment later and looked up at the two women walking toward the door. He was curious and somewhat disappointed, since it was apparent that neither one of them had even lifted a fork off the place; they'd left their food untouched. The sky had cleared of its blanket of clouds, and the sun was shining brightly. Taylor said she had better be getting back to the hospital, though she was quite sure no one would have noticed she was gone. With that, she and Leila parted company and promised to stay in touch, exchanging phone numbers and e-mail addresses.

Leila stood and watched as Taylor expertly hailed a cab and disappeared into the back of the bright-yellow vehicle. Leila walked south along Fifth Avenue and at the first chance turned west into Central Park. As soon as she walked into the park, she pulled off the path onto the grass, walked up to the base of a tree, and threw up—not once but three times. She stayed hunched over, and a young woman walked up to her after noticing that she was not well. Leila lied and told her she must have eaten something that her stomach had chosen to reject. The woman offered her a bottle of water and a pack of gum, which Leila gladly accepted. She filled her mouth with the ice-cold water, swished it around her rancid mouth, and spit. She opened the pack of gum, took out four pieces, and quickly shoved them all into her mouth. She began her walk through the park back to the hotel. Then she stopped and looked to the north, the bare trees allowing her to see far into the distance, and then to the south, wondering just where Taylor had conducted her self-counseling sessions.

Then she started crying—a few tears at first and then a veritable cascade. She had lost herself in the thoughts of what it must be like for a nine-year-old girl to have a father who sexually abused her. She kept walking but continued to cry uncontrollably. The empty park, her brisk walk, and her hood ensured no one would take notice. She didn't want anyone to notice. She needed to shed the four years of tears Taylor must have shed before she could face the world again, no matter how long it took.

CHAPTER 33

Detectives Alvarez and O'Reilly were seated in the police station conference room, along with Evan, going through the remainder of the pictures. They had spent a few hours the day before and were now down to the last several hundred. They had become quite adept at quickly recognizing whether a set of pictures from a specific location would yield any fruitful information. Their goal was to complete this task prior to Andy and Leila's arrival, which they'd scheduled for 1:00 p.m. Alvarez had suggested that going through the pictures without the two doctors would make the process go faster, as they could quite quickly and easily weed out the pictures that did not clearly offer any useful information. They did, however, make notes of those pictures they wished to review with Andy and Leila.

The evening before, Leila had explained to Andy that she wished to be on her own after the difficult conversation with Taylor. She'd offered no explanation other than that she was tired and needed to catch up on some sleep. She was mentally spent from the revelations that had emerged from her morning with the young medical student, and she needed some time to digest it all—as well as to conduct some self-counseling of her own. Leila spent nearly three hours walking around Central Park, crying on and off throughout. She couldn't help but visualize the disgusting and depraved acts Mr. Millbank had committed. She even let herself feel happy he was dead, thinking that if any human deserved to die, he most certainly did, although she also thought that even in death, he had gotten off too easily for what he had done to his little girl. Her self-guided therapy was cathartic, and by the time the sun had eased itself toward the horizon, Leila, felt a bit better. She also felt cold and hungry, so she found her way to a Starbucks for a latte and a muffin. Then she returned to her room, emotionally exhausted, and fell asleep in her clothes.

Andy's text message chime interrupted the Wallflowers song "6th Avenue Heartache" with a message from Leila. *How fitting*, he thought.

Leila: Meet me in the lobby in 30 minutes. Andy: Okay.

"Hi, Andy," Leila said, kissing him on the cheek.

Andy's perpetual confusion regarding Leila's feelings came to the surface rapidly, like a submerged ball rising to the surface of a pool. He nonetheless submerged his feelings again.

"So, what happened yesterday?" Andy asked. "We went to the hospital together, you meet Taylor, and then I don't see you the rest of the day."

"You're not going to like this, but because I only want to tell the story once, you'll just have to wait until later. What time are we supposed to meet O'Reilly and Alvarez?" Leila replied.

"Remember, it's Sean and Jose now. One o'clock. In an hour or so. Are you hungry?"

"Starving. I, uh, didn't each much yesterday."

"Why?" Andy wondered.

"Please be patient. You'll know soon enough. Right now, I'm in the mood for something warm and comforting. Can we go back to the Soup Nazi?" Leila said, and she smiled, knowing Andy couldn't say no.

They headed back out, bundled especially well. Yesterday's clearing skies had been the manifestation of a cold front that had worked its way from Canada to the northeast. It was a frigid eighteen degrees. Leila got one large bowl of chicken noodle soup and followed that up with a tomato-based tortilla soup, complete with slices of avocado and tortilla strips, to which she added a generous amount of Tapatio hot sauce. She felt satisfied both with the soup and Andy's company. She hoped yesterday's catharsis had been sufficient so that she wouldn't cry again in front of the four men she would be seated with in the conference room when she revealed the bombshell of information locked away in her mind.

"Good afternoon. I am guessing you are both well rested, considering we gave you the morning off," O'Reilly said.

"Yes, thanks. I needed it," Leila replied, without revealing why.

"Very well, let's get started," Alvarez began. "Evan, Sean, and I combed through the rest of the pictures—we figured we could sift through them and weed out all the ones that didn't lead to any new information. I hope that's okay with you."

"Oh, it's more than okay with me," Andy said. "Me, too. Did you find anything new?" Leila asked.

"In fact we did, though we can't quite figure out what to make of it. How about you tell us about your day at the hospital yesterday first, and then we'll have a look at the pictures?" Alvarez said.

"Fine with me," Andy said. "Leila?"

Leila was momentarily silent, took a deep breath as if she were about to say something, and then stopped. She gazed out at each of the men seated around her, wondering how they would react to the shocking news currently locked in her brain waiting to be freed. She gathered her thoughts, deemed that her emotions were in check, and felt ready to reveal the discovery she'd made that would add yet another wrinkle to the case.

"Sure, why don't you go first?" Leila suggested.

"Okay," Andy said. "Well, I met with Jennifer Carmichael in her office and she was … what can I say, very straightforward and open, and I think honest, too. Either that or she's one hell of an actress."

"What do you mean?" O'Reilly asked.

"What I mean is that if she really were the killer or involved in the murder, you would think she would act aloof, defensive, or at least show some signs of stress, but my conversation with her was just the opposite. It was open and very matter-of-fact."

"Did you tell her about all of our pictures—with Mr. Millbank, the hotels, café, etc.?" Alvarez asked.

"Yes. I told her we had all these pictures of her with Mr. Millbank, and she just owned up to the affair and told me details that only she could know, and they fit in with the pictures. That's what I am saying— she wasn't trying to hide anything," Andy went on.

"What about the wig, then?"

"That was simply to maintain better discretion and prevent Mrs. Millbank from finding out who Carmichael really was. Makes sense, doesn't it?"

"Go on," O'Reilly requested.

"So, then we discussed the café incident, and she basically stated exactly what we had suspected from the pictures and the frequent calls and texts between her and Millbank. She said that she gave Millbank an ultimatum, but Millbank wanted to meet with her to discuss it, and she refused and cut off all contact until he met her demand. So he confronted her at the café. She said that he had been looking for her around the hospital and someone suggested he check out the café."

"Well, I guess that makes her less of a suspect, then," Leila said.

"Don't be so sure," O'Reilly disagreed. "Some of these cold, calculated killers can act cool and calm when being questioned—they are masters at throwing investigators off the scent."

"Sean, Jennifer is a doctor, not a cold, calculating killer," Andy said. "Look, I'm just saying she could still be involved," O'Reilly replied.

"If I may," Leila interrupted, "let me tell you about my discussion with Taylor. I think it may change your view of Jennifer, and—it will definitely change your view of Taylor."

"Oh!" Andy said. "Sounds like your conversation was more interesting than mine."

"That's, uh, quite an understatement."

"All right, Leila, go on," Alvarez said.

Leila paused and looked up as the four men once again gazed at her intently and expectantly. She gathered her thoughts; she'd rehearsed how she would express the horrific story of Taylor Davis to the group multiple times during the morning, and she felt ready to convey the shocking and awful revelation without getting emotional. Despite all that preparation, she nevertheless felt a lump in her throat and an uneasy fluttering in her stomach. She promised herself that she would not display any emotion or at least only a limited amount. She gazed over at Alvarez, and his kind face demonstrated patience. She then turned her eyes to O'Reilly; he was nervously tapping his pen on the table, evoking his usual impatience. Finally she glanced at Andy, but only for a fleeting moment—holding his gaze would only fire up her emotions more. Andy sensed this and looked down toward the table. Leila took one last breath and proceeded.

"I would like to start by asking the detectives a question, if I may?"

"Go ahead," said Alvarez.

"Now, I'm not saying that I think Jennifer or Taylor had anything to do with killing Millbank, but hypothetically speaking, are there instances when a person did kill someone not in self-defense yet it can still be considered legally justifiable?"

"Uh, no, not really," O'Reilly answered curtly.

"Well, it's not that simple, Sean," Alvarez said. "There is something lawyers call mitigating circumstances, which while they don't often completely exonerate someone, could affect aspects of the overall legal outcome, such as, for example, the sentencing. Why are you asking?"

"Because—you know what? Mr. Millbank deserved to die, that's why," Leila stated firmly.

The four men each expressed varying degrees of shock at what Leila, a physician sworn to protect human life, had just said. She continued. "For the first time in my entire life, I have to honestly say that I am glad someone is dead. That says a lot for someone who lived under Saddam Hussein for a while. Sure, the former ruler of Iraq was an awful man, and he killed many of my people, but the visceral hatred I feel for Mr.

Millbank now is like nothing I have ever felt before," Leila stated firmly and without hiding her anger.

"Leila," Andy said with a worried tone in his voice, followed by a pause. "What the hell are you talking about?"

"Taylor and I spent the morning together. First in the hospital and then, at her suggestion, we went to the Met and walked through the French Impressionism exhibits. I got to know her a bit there but mostly superficial stuff.

I was trying to earn her trust, and well, I definitely succeeded. I … I …" Leila hesitated. "It's just so awful. I hope you are all prepared to hear something horrific. Especially you, Andy. The detectives are probably used to this."

The four men were now practically out of their seats, leaning over toward Leila like children at a magic show waiting for the final stage of an elaborate trick. Alvarez's face had lost the kind, warm look it had had and now showed an expression of concern, while Andy's mouth was slightly open, practically expecting to be shocked.

"Okay, here goes," Leila began. "Taylor confirmed that Mr. Millbank was her father. She said that he had left her and her mother when she was thirteen years old."

Leila paused again and, knowing that her next line would deliver the information she needed to convey, took one last look at each of the men in the room.

"Taylor told me that from the time she was about nine years old until her father left them for Mrs. Millbank, he repeatedly sexually abused her. And that—" Leila interrupted her next thought as she peered at Andy, Evan, and the detectives for their reactions.

O'Reilly had stood up and was walking around the room nervously. Alvarez sat back in his chair and covered his face with his hands, and when a moment or two later he removed his hands from his face, Leila could see the tears welling up in his eyes. She remembered that he had his own young daughters. Andy sat far back in his chair and looked back and forth from Leila to the ceiling. Evan had the most dramatic reaction. He simply got up and walked out of the room.

"Should I go on?" Leila said, keeping her feelings in check. After all, she had had her catharsis yesterday. Alvarez, regaining his composure, sat up in his chair and nodded as O'Reilly turned back toward the table.

"Millbank started abusing his daughter when she was just nine years old. It began innocently, with him seating her on his lap, but then, as Taylor describes it, his hands began roaming. I am too disgusted to even describe the details to you, but trust me, it is absolutely horrific. At first, he would come to her room once or twice a month but the frequency slowly increased until it was nightly."

"Leila, this is just ... just awful," Alvarez said disconsolately.

"Oh, there's more. At the age of twelve, she started puberty. As you can probably tell from Jennifer Carmichael, Mr. Millbank is a breast man, so I am sure you can imagine what happened then. It's so disgusting to do something like that to any twelve-year-old girl, let alone to your own daughter," Leila continued, not attempting to hide her sarcasm or revulsion for Mr. Millbank.

"What a fuckin' pig!" Andy blurted out with what for him was a rare expletive.

"See, I told you he deserves to be dead. An incestuous pedophile. Does it get any worse than that?" Leila added.

O'Reilly was pacing rapidly. He was clearly not comfortable with this revelation. He stopped pacing, placed his hands on the front of the conference room table, and gazed at the others.

"Look, everyone, I am not denying he's a disgusting pig and all that, but our job is to solve this crime. The justice system will decide who is or isn't guilty," O'Reilly said.

Alvarez, now back to his usual calm self, continued. "Sean is right. We need to find out what happened. That is our job. The judge and the jury will ultimately pass judgment. That is what the justice system is for. Can we agree on that?"

"I'm sorry, but I can't agree on that part. I don't trust the justice system. Too many criminals go unpunished, and too many innocent people get punished," Leila said.

"Fair enough. Can we at least agree that we all want to find out what actually happened and how? That means not just to Mr. Millbank, but Mr. Stern, as well. Let's not forget about him," Alvarez pressed.

"Let me get this straight. We are trying to find out who killed a child molester and a serial rapist?" Leila said without hiding the cynicism she felt.

Alvarez looked at Leila and then Andy and then back at Leila. They all nodded in agreement that they were indeed all interested in solving the case. At that point, Alvarez was ready to reveal the new information that he, O'Reilly, and Evan had found out earlier in the day, which they initially hadn't been able to explain but which could now tie together the story of Mr. Millbank's murder.

"We have our own surprise, and all morning we were trying to come up with explanations, yet we couldn't. But Leila, with what you have now told us, I am afraid we may now know who killed Mr. Millbank, though I have to confess we still don't quite know how," Alvarez said.

"What is it?" Leila asked anxiously.

Alvarez motioned to Evan, who had returned to the room after a brief hiatus. He switched on his computer and the monitor that had featured so prominently in the days before. He tapped feverishly on the keys until an image appeared on the monitor. At first, neither Andy nor Leila noticed anything other than the outside of a Starbucks, but then Evan moved through the sequence. Leila asked what day this sequence of pictures was from, and Evan responded that it was November 18, just four days before Mr. Millbank was found dead in his room. The next picture showed the inside of the Starbucks, where the photographer had taken up a prime position from which he could see the entire seating area and the front where orders were placed. Evan tapped a key, and the next picture came up. Andy squinted, trying to see what Alvarez meant by their own surprise. Evan tapped a key again. A new picture appeared. Leila got up from her chair and leaned forward toward the monitor. She saw Mr. Millbank, but this was no surprise, since the photographer had been ordered to follow him and document his comings and goings. Another key was tapped. Still no reaction from Andy or Leila. They looked at each other, confused. Evan looked at Alvarez before tapping the key again, knowing that the next picture was the revealing one. Alvarez looked at Andy and Leila. He then nodded his head toward Evan. Evan tapped the key again. Leila let out a loud shriek. Andy shot out of his chair in disbelief. He approached the monitor, looked at it intently, and then turned to Leila. Her mouth was wide open, her hands on either side holding her face as if her mouth would continue expanding otherwise. The realization had sunk in for both of them.

"Oh no! You've got to be kidding me!" Leila cried out angrily.

CHAPTER 34

It had been more than a week since they had been in contact with de Ville. In their last conversation, he had been planning to try to find a connection between Bryan and Karina Hummels or Angelina Costa. It was odd that he had not been in contact, and O'Reilly and Alvarez figured he had no new information. While on the one hand they were concerned about the lack of progress, the fact was that their responsibility was solely to find Mr. Millbank's killer, and it was de Ville's responsibility to find Mr. Stern's killer. Selfishly, they agreed that if any information de Ville uncovered could help them in New York, they would gladly take it, but they also were confident they could solve the grisly crime without his assistance. It was only at Leila's insistence that the subject of Mr. Stern had even been brought up, and although neither O'Reilly nor Alvarez was keen to spend much time reviewing the situation in Basel, they ultimately relented.

"So, no one has heard from Detective de Ville?" Leila inquired. "As we said, no, nothing," Alvarez replied.

"Are you planning on getting in touch with him?" Leila persisted.

"Look, Leila, to be honest, our job is to solve the murder here in New York. We have neither the jurisdiction nor the time to deal with the other case," O'Reilly stated frankly.

"Well, Andy and I do care, and we want to solve both cases. Let's remember why you called us in the first place—for our hematology expertise—and as physicians, we are interested in solving the whole case, not part of it," Leila said, more irritated now. She fixed her gaze on Andy, and he took the hint.

"I agree with Leila. So, if you're not going to call de Ville, or are not interested, or don't have the time, or whatever, that's fine. Just tell us, so we can decide our next step," Andy said.

"We don't disagree with you. We just can't help you with that," O'Reilly replied.

"Well, you can—sort of," Leila said. "What do you mean?" Alvarez asked.

"Who has access to the account Mrs. Millbank established— remember, for the trip we took to Europe?" Leila asked.

"That would be me," O'Reilly answered. "Listen, you two have been incredibly helpful, and we'd be nowhere in this case without you. So, of course I will support whatever it is you would like to do. In fact, to make things easier, I'll tell the financial office that you are both authorized to draw from that account. I know Mrs. Millbank would support it."

"Thank you. That's all we need," Leila said.

"Uh, are we taking another trip to Europe, Leila? Is that what you're saying?" Andy asked.

"Let's see, our prime suspect's last known whereabouts is Aberdeen, Scotland. We have no idea whether de Ville connected Bryan to Karina or Angelina, and I want another shot at interviewing Bergeland—this time on our terms. Is that enough reason to go for you, Andy?" Leila stated with a confident and defiant tone.

"Sounds pretty convincing." Alvarez smiled as he looked at Andy.

At that point, they turned their attention back to the New York case. It was now clear that Taylor Davis had a motive—probably the clearest motive of all. Combined with the incredible revelation on the final pictures from Mrs. Millbank's trove, collected by her energetic and detail-oriented private investigator, they all agreed now on who the prime suspects were. What was left to figure out was just how the killers had perpetrated the murders. They reviewed the fact that Bryan had apparently gotten his hands on what they called the super-Lyzanda and that it could indeed cause severe bleeding, as it had for his sister. It wasn't yet clear how someone could have gotten Mr. Millbank—or Mr. Stern, for that matter—to ingest it, but the photographs offered a possible solution to that enigma.

Leila insisted that they review the last set of pictures one final time. Thus, back at police headquarters with Evan at the controls, Leila, Andy, and the detectives took one last look at the damning evidence. Evan began the sequence as he had done the day before. At first, the set of pictures just showed Mr. Millbank at the Starbucks near his office—they had seen many of these pictures in the months leading up to his murder. Evan scrolled quickly through the series of pictures until he once again brought up the incriminating image. Andy and Leila came to the same realization that Alvarez and O'Reilly had come to earlier even without knowing Taylor's history of abuse. There really was no other way to explain it. After all, why would Bryan and Taylor be seated together at a Starbucks? They didn't know each other and had no connection—other than the fact that both had a motive to kill Mr. Millbank.

When pieced together, all the photos; Bryan's travels to Norway, Basel, and New York; the accidental near-death of Diana Vasquez; and Mr. Millbank's sexual abuse of Taylor painted a clear picture. Bryan, distraught due to the death of his older sister, blamed Empire Health and Terrapharma for her death. He then, through his work, learned about Sami Innovations and their modifications of medications to be used for the offshore oil workers. He met with Erik Bergeland in Tromsø. It just so happened that Bergeland was also upset with Terrapharma's CEO over their business dealings, and thus he agreed to develop and produce a batch of super-Lyzanda for Bryan, who then went to Basel and somehow got Mr. Stern to ingest the drug. Then he flew to New York to do the same to Mr. Millbank.

While this offered a nice complete picture, Andy and Leila each punched holes in this theory. First, Andy stated, there was no way Bryan could know what the super-Lyzanda would do, as he had not to their knowledge experimented with it at all. Second, despite the fact that both men had bled to death, they still had no evidence suggesting how either man had come to ingest the poisonous medication. Along those lines, Leila reminded the detectives that Bryan had left Basel days before Mr. Stern was killed. With the knowledge gained about the effects of the super-Lyzanda from Diana Vasquez's accidental ingestion, they knew it was not possible that he was responsible for directly poisoning Mr. Stern. Leila also reminded everyone that Bryan had recently returned to Europe, and while this may have been work related, it remained unclear why he would go to Scotland. Furthermore, Andy reminded them that Bryan's superiors had stated they hadn't sent him to Scotland.

"Andy, most of what's left to be discovered in this case is in Europe—that's why we have to go," Leila said.

Andy nodded in agreement. Forgetting about the various twists in the case momentarily, he also thought that a trip back to Europe, where he had fallen in love with Leila, would give him the opportunity to explore Leila's feelings for him once again. Although he had given up on the idea of having a relationship with her, she seemed to be dropping a number of hints that perhaps there was still a glimmer of hope. While Leila seemed to be most interested in returning to Europe to answer the remaining questions surrounding the case, Andy was, in fact, equally excited to find out whether Leila's flirtations were just that or whether it was her way to send Andy a subtle signal. After all, it had been in Europe that they'd first kissed.

"I am actually really excited to go back, all of sudden," Andy said, offering no subtlety whatsoever.

"That sounds like the best next step to me. Sean, I hope you'll agree," Alvarez said, and he received an affirmative nod from Detective O'Reilly. "In the meantime, we will get a warrant to look at Taylor's cell-phone records and see if we can make a connection between her and Mr. Millbank, either that way or some other way. She must be the person who got Mr. Millbank to ingest the super-Lyzanda."

For their last evening in New York and after all their hard work, Andy and Leila decided that they deserved a night out. They elected to head to one of the city's more trendy spots. One of the younger (and supposedly hipper) detectives recommended Bar Boulud, a restaurant belonging to the famous chef Daniel Boulud. It was too cold to walk, so they hopped into a taxi and headed uptown. This would be their first social night out since the big blowup, as Andy thought of it; that had occurred just before New Year's two weeks ago. In the taxi, Andy wondered whether he should ask Leila about some of her flirtatious comments and actions since New Year's, but then he couldn't even convince himself that Leila had acted that way. He seemed to be in a permanent state of confusion when it came to his relationship with Leila. He knew that he loved her, and he felt he was indeed ready for a serious relationship—he was forty, after all—but Leila's behavior over the past two months had thoroughly confused him. The taxi pulled up to the front of Bar Boulud, and Andy decided he would play it by ear. Maybe some alcohol would help—but then he remembered the incident at the Olive Tree a couple of months back, when they'd overdone the arak, and he thought that perhaps that wouldn't be wise.

The menu was interesting and complicated. Leila suggested the waiter put together a tasting menu for them, and she let him pick the wines as well. When Andy pondered how expensive that could wind up being, Leila expressed her desire to pay for a really nice and expensive dinner for the two of them to share. Andy resisted.

"Leila, this is going to be at least a few hundred dollars. There's really no need."

"Of course there's no *need*," she replied sarcastically, "but I really want to. I haven't had a nice romantic dinner in quite a while. When was the last time we had a nice dinner?"

Here we go again, Andy thought to himself. *I can't figure this girl out.*

"You know, this whole case has been such an adventure that I can't even remember all the places we've had dinner," Andy said, purposely choosing to avoid escalating the discussion.

"Me, too. You know, it's been such a whirlwind, I can barely recall which cities we had fun in and which ones we had our little fights in," Leila said, smiling her broad Julia Roberts smile.

That beautiful smile was a double-edged sword—it brought out both his love for Leila and the dread that this feeling only flowed in one direction. Andy decided to take a chance.

"You know, Leila, you have the most beautiful smile I have ever seen."

"Andy, thank you. That is really sweet," Leila's face flushed with happy embarrassment.

"Whatever happens, I want you to know that I have really enjoyed all this time we have gotten to spend together."

"What do you mean 'whatever happens'?" Leila's happy tone suddenly changed, seemingly in response to this statement. Andy was taken aback and decided not to pursue that angle of conversation. He thought of a good way out.

"No, you misunderstood me. I meant however the case turns out, you know, whoever is guilty or not guilty. It has been fun working on it with you."

"Oh," Leila said, and her smile returned. "I did misunderstand you. I thought—well, never mind."

That was Andy's signal to start talking about the food, the décor, or anything else, but not their relationship. He figured he *would* find out where he stood eventually. Their dinner was truly delicious. Andy and Leila talked about their last trip to Europe. They recalled the many different people they'd met in Tromsø, Basel, Gstaad, and Lugano, all the hotels they'd stayed in, and the various restaurants in which they'd sampled the local flavors. All that reminiscing made them more excited to go back, though they also spent time discussing the reason they were going back and the concern they felt for all those involved in the case. Was Bryan really the mastermind behind the double murder? Had

Taylor, the seemingly lovely young medical student, actually exacted revenge on her abusive father, whom she hadn't seen in years? Who, if anyone, had helped Bryan in Basel to get Mr. Stern to ingest the super-Lyzanda? They were convinced that is how the two men had been killed.

After dinner, they returned to their hotel, reviewed their itinerary, and went back to their own rooms. They decided that their first step would be to try to track down Bryan. So they booked a flight to Edinburgh, Scotland, and from there, they would drive to Aberdeen. They weren't sure what they would find there, but their backup plan was to head back to Tromsø and take another crack at Mr. Bergeland. Now that they knew about the existence of the super-Lyzanda, they knew he must have been the one to produce it. They felt confident they would succeed in extracting this critical piece of information from him. Andy was so excited he could barely sleep. He was sure that when he returned from Europe this time he would have achieved his ultimate goal; he and Leila would have the information they needed to solve the case. He put the "sleep time" playlist on his iPhone, which started with Genesis's bizarre dreamlike song "Me and Sarah Jan," but he fell asleep to Norah Jones's mellow jazzy piano on "Don't Know Why."

CHAPTER 35

For two individuals who didn't live in New York, Andy and Leila had gotten really good at getting from Manhattan to JFK expeditiously. Their mastery could only be matched by native city dwellers who made that very trip regularly. Since avoiding New York's legendary traffic jams, especially the dreaded Van Wyck Expressway, was paramount, they quickly learned the reliable public transportation route, which included a short ride on the Long Island Railroad to the Jamaica station, followed by an even shorter trip aboard the AirTrain to JFK.

They disembarked at Terminal 7 and were shortly aboard an evening flight to London on British Airways, preferentially avoiding the American carriers. Their overnight flight arrived in the morning at London's massive Heathrow Airport and the impressive British Airways Terminal 5. The terminal's enormous concave roof collected the rainwater, of which there was no shortage in London, diverting it to storage tanks, to be reused within the terminal. Its huge ground-to-roof windows offered great views of the airport. The 747 pulled up to the B satellite terminal, from which a short train ride took them to immigration. After clearing immigration, they followed the signs for domestic departures for their next flight to Edinburgh, the beautiful and magical capital of Scotland. It was an unusually sunny winter day in London, and Andy was looking forward to the flight over the English countryside. Though neither had slept well on the overnight flight, they felt energized by the thought of being back in Europe and the possibility of tracking down Bryan and solving the case.

Neither Andy nor Leila brought up any discussion of the case or the status of their relationship during the trip to London. There was an understanding that, until they were in Europe, both subjects were off-limits. Andy did wonder, though, if and when the time would be right to finally resolve the issue most burning in his heart and mind—which had nothing to do with Bryan, Mr. Stern, or any aspect of the case.

The flight to Edinburgh was less interesting than Andy had hoped for. As the Airbus A320 made its northward sweeping turn, the almost-perpetual winter blanket of clouds made its appearance far below the plane's altitude, and the view of the British landscape was completely obscured. The descent through the clouds seemed to take forever, before the plane finally broke through the gray ceiling to reveal a stunningly green landscape that looked more manmade than natural. The rolling hills were reminiscent of a rumpled bed comforter in need of a tug from one end to smooth out the undulations. As the plane approached the ground, horizontal rivulets of water formed on the window, indicating that it was raining.

Andy and Leila gathered their luggage from baggage claim and rented a Vauxhall Astra sedan. The British-made car was popular with Scots and made up more than half of Avis's local fleet. Unlike other British-made cars, like the Rover brand of sport-utility vehicles, the luxurious Bentleys, or the sporty Aston Martins, the Vauxhall name never made a splash outside of the United Kingdom. Leila particularly liked the car's logo, a modern-looking griffin encircled by chrome handsomely adorning the grill plate.

The next step on Andy's meticulously planned itinerary was a drive into the heart of Edinburgh for some rest in their hotel, and as neither Andy nor Leila had ever been to this beautiful city, they planned a few hours of sightseeing for the end of the day. The city boasted the classically beautiful Royal Mile, starting at the House of Holyrood, the British Queen's Scottish headquarters, on the lower end and leading to the magnificent Edinburgh Castle, perched like a giant fortress in the sky, at the elevated end of the road. It was clear to see how this castle was easy to defend, as it was set atop black cliffs of volcanic rock that fell away on three sides and had only a narrow isthmus connecting the front gate with the rest of the city. After getting lost several times, Andy finally agreed to ask for directions, at Leila's insistence, and they finally found their way to the SAS Radisson in the heart of the Royal Mile.

After their short rest, they met in the lobby and headed out to see Edinburgh Castle. The sky had cleared, and it was surprisingly mild, with a temperature of fifty-five degrees—quite a contrast to frigid New York, and this despite the fact that their latitude was more aligned to central Canada. The warm waters of the Gulf Stream kept Scotland's winters relatively mild—just as they kept the winters of Norway more like those of New York than those of the equal latitudes in North America.

Following their tour of the castle and dinner at Ondine, one of Edinburgh's fine restaurants, they retired to their own rooms and their own thoughts for the night, in preparation for their pursuit of Bryan the next day. Andy decided this was the perfect place to listen to the enchanting music of Mike Scott and his Waterboys band, given that this city was Mike Scott's birthplace. He put on the solo album *Bring 'em All In*, with its salute to this magical city and historic country. It even had a song called "Edinburgh Castle," which Andy played over and over again, reveling in the thought that he was just steps away from the song's object. The music made him think about Edinburgh and Scotland rather than what tended to occupy his mind most during the lonely nights in hotel rooms. Now ready for much-needed sleep, Andy switched on the Waterboys' spiritual *Universal Hall* album and dozed off to the hauntingly beautiful fiddle melody of the song "Peace of Iona," an ode to one of Scotland's most mystical places, the island of Iona in the Inner Hebrides off the west coast.

For her part, Leila preferred listening to love songs and was listening to Maroon 5's *Songs About Jane* while studying a map of Scotland and Norway. She was exhausted as well and fell asleep to "She Will Be Loved." Her last vision before dozing off was of her and Andy driving through the Alps. *Will she be loved?* she wondered about herself.

With their bags packed and stowed in the trunk, and with Andy now serving as the navigator and Leila as the driver, they headed out of Edinburgh toward the northeast coast of Scotland. Leila had insisted on taking the wheel, so she could experience the odd sensation of sitting on the right side of the car as the driver—a feeling and responsibility Andy was more than happy to pass on to her. Clearly she was the more adventurous half of this duo. Despite a few wrong turns through Edinburgh's confusing maze of streets, they eventually found their way to and drove over the majestic, long Forth Road Bridge spanning the Firth of Forth toward Aberdeen, in search of the elusive Bryan Vasquez. They had no doubt he held the key information they needed to solve the mystery of the bleeders once and for all. The ever-changing Scottish weather at first cooperated with their journey, but as they approached Dundee, near the famous town of St. Andrews (home to the very first golf course) it had begun to rain. At first the rain was light and even welcome, adding to the atmosphere of the rugged terrain. However, as they drove further north, the winds off the North Sea began to gust more and more vigorously, eventually making the rain fall horizontally and buffeting the car, leading Leila to grab the steering wheel with both hands.

"Why on earth would Bryan come here?" Leila asked, peering intently through the windshield of the Vauxhall.

"I have no idea. This seems so far removed from anything related to the bleeders," Andy replied.

"How much further to *Aberdeen*?" Leila asked, voicing her emphasis on Aberdeen; she was clearly hoping it wouldn't be much further.

"Looks like about thirty miles. Do you want me to drive?"

"No. I'm fine. I just wish the rain would let up."

"I wouldn't count on it," Andy replied.

After another forty minutes of driving rain, they approached the outskirts of Aberdeen, a city of over two hundred thousand and the main gateway to numerous Scottish castles. Fortunately, Aberdeen was small enough that Andy and Leila were confident they would find someone who had noticed Bryan Vasquez. Their plan was to check the relatively few hotels in the downtown area, as well as the airport and seaport. Detective Kupfer, with his Interpol connections, had also arranged for the doctors to meet with Sergeant Ian Ferguson, from the Grampian Police Headquarters. As they approached downtown, they parked the car near the town square, not far from the seaport, and followed their plan to flash a picture of Bryan Vasquez at each of the hotels, which were all within short walking distance. Andy and Leila split up to make the tedious process move twice as fast. Their cover story was that Bryan was a friend of theirs from Los Angeles who had travelled to Aberdeen but had not been heard from in several weeks. After all, it wasn't that far from the truth.

As Andy hopped from hotel to hotel, he made no progress. While the hotel managers he spoke with were extraordinarily kind and helpful, not one of them could recall seeing Bryan, nor was there any record of a Bryan Vasquez checking in to their hotels. Leila's results were equally disappointing. After having consumed numerous cups of tea, thanks to the graciousness of their hosts, they were no closer to finding Bryan. Their final hope rested with Sergeant Ferguson, who agreed to meet with them just as his shift ended at 5:00 p.m. Late afternoon had quickly turned to night in the middle of winter at this high-latitude city, and the relative warmth of Edinburgh had turned to raw cold. It was dark, and the clothes-piercing wind chilled Andy and Leila's skin as they walked to their visit with Sergeant Ferguson.

"Good afternoon, doctors." Sergeant Ferguson greeted Andy and Leila with a heavy Scottish accent that required an especially acute ear to fully comprehend.

"Thank you so much for agreeing to meet with us—and so late in the day for you," Leila responded.

"No prroblem. When Simon Kupferr calls, I am always eagerr to help. So, I underrstand you are looking for an American man that you say came to Aberrdeen some days ago; is that rright?" Ferguson asked, rolling each of the many r's he uttered.

"Yes, his name is Bryan Vasquez, and he is a suspect in two murders—one in Basel and one in New York," Andy replied matter-of-factly.

"You're from Los Angeles, and the murders were in Basel and New York, you say. Why the hell are you here in Aberdeen, then?" Ferguson inquired, making no effort to hide his sarcasm.

"The last contact we had with anyone who knew his whereabouts was his employer, who said he'd booked a flight to Aberdeen. So that's why we're here."

"Does he know anyone here?"

"Not that we know of," Leila answered.

"We know he works for ExxonMobil and that he had some business in Norway. In fact, we know that he was in Norway last November," Andy added.

"Interesting. You see, some of the platform employees actually come from Aberdeen. Apparently there are not enough Norwegians for the tough work at sea, but we Scots love being out at sea," Ferguson said.

"Okay," Leila said slowly, "but how might that tie in to our suspect?"

"Oh, well, some of their transport ships dock here daily and take employees to and from the platforms. Perhaps—" Ferguson started, "but that doesn't make sense. I mean, why wouldn't he—"

"What?" Andy asked impatiently.

"Why wouldn't he just fly into Norway—it's not any easier to fly into Aberdeen, I imagine, than to Oslo or Stavanger."

"We think he knows he's a suspect, so perhaps he's trying to hide his comings and goings," Andy said.

Sergeant Ferguson suggested they head down to the docks and show the picture of Bryan around. He informed them that he knew most of the dockmasters and that if Bryan had been there, one of them surely would have spotted him. Andy and Leila agreed. They walked briskly to the docks and showed Bryan's picture to anyone they could find who worked in the area, but alas, no one had seen him.

"I'll tell ya, if he were here, one of the lads would have seen him," Ferguson stated confidently.

"Then why else would he be here?" Andy wondered aloud, clearly frustrated.

The three of them headed to one of the pubs not far from the docks and sat down to a dinner of fish and chips and, at Sergeant Ferguson's insistence, a pint of beer from his brother's microbrewery, which was situated not far away. It became clear that Sergeant Ferguson was known by many of Aberdeen's citizens, as many of the pub's patrons waved, winked, or stopped by to say hello. It was just such an encounter that led to the breakthrough Andy and Leila so desperately needed. It began with one of the men coming by to say hello to Sergeant Ferguson, like so many of the others before, only Colin McFadden's conversation took long enough that he ended up sitting down at the table with Andy and Leila. At first the conversation was all about the most recent results of the football matches in the Scottish Premier League. Then McFadden stated that he'd had to miss the recent derby, as the heated intra-city rivalries were known, between Dundee and Dundee United, because he'd had to fly an American businessman to Norway on short notice. Leila, sensing a break, pounced like a reporter sensing a scoop after a politician has inadvertently revealed a crucial fact.

"Did you say an American businessman?" Leila asked, leaning hard toward McFadden.

"Yes, why so excited, lassie?"

"We happen to be here looking for an American businessman whose last known location was Aberdeen," Leila said as she pulled up Bryan's photo on her iPhone. "Does this person look familiar?"

McFadden, looking decidedly uncomfortable, glanced at Sergeant Ferguson, who held his hands up, claiming he had nothing to do with the question. McFadden glanced at the photograph and then looked up at Ferguson as if to ask for permission to provide the answer.

Ferguson simply waved his hand, palm up, across the table toward his American guests, basically telling McFadden to come forward with the information.

"Look, he gave me a tip of five hundred pounds and told me not to tell anyone that I met him or where I took him. I, uh, I don't know what to do," McFadden said, looking to Ferguson for advice.

"Colin, this is a serious matter—there are two dead men, murdered—and these are two physicians from Los Angeles who are trying to solve the case. Tip or no tip, I think you need to own up to what you know."

"Very well. The lad in the photo is indeed the person who I flew to Norway. He paid me in cash in advance and then gave me the tip and asked me not to record the flight in the plane's log. I told him I could do that but that the Norwegian Civil Flight Authority would still record that this plane had landed in Bodø," McFadden admitted.

"Bodø? Why Bodø? Where is Bodø, if that's even the name of a city?" Andy asked, while Leila was already punching keys on her phone to look up the name.

"Well, he asked that I take him to Tromsø, but I told him that I was not approved for night flying in Norway and that this time of year it's always night in Tromsø."

"So why Bodø?" Andy asked.

Leila interrupted. "Let me guess. It's as far north or as close to Tromsø as you could take him?"

"Yeah, that's right," McFadden answered. "Am I in some trouble here, Sergeant?"

"No, mate, you're not. You just need to tell these investigators what you know."

"Well, that's pretty much it."

"Do you know what he did after you dropped him off in Bodø?" Andy asked. "Well, I needed to fill out some paperwork, so I had to go into the terminal—have you ever been to Bodø?"

"No," Andy and Leila answered in unison.

"Well, it's a very small terminal—just one small room, really. So, as I was filling out the paperwork, he went to the gate agent and asked when the next flight to Tromsø was," McFadden continued.

"Anything else?"

"No, that's it. Honest."

"Thank you so much, Mr. McFadden—you've been very helpful," Andy said.

After the bemused and befuddled Scotsman had left the table, Ferguson bought another round of beers, and Andy and Leila drank in celebration. They knew where they were heading next.

Detective Alvarez was staring at his computer screen, looking at the cell-phone records of Taylor Davis on one screen and those of Mr. Millbank on the other screen. Evan, seated by his side, was furiously banging on the keyboard, commanding the program to interpret the mountain of data in front of them. Evan would highlight one set of numbers after another and move from one window on the computer to another with such speed that Alvarez couldn't follow his actions. After about twenty minutes, Evan pulled up an Excel spreadsheet he'd created, and at this point Alvarez could see the results clearly. In the months leading up to Mr. Millbank's death, there had been numerous calls and text messages between him and Jennifer Carmichael, but only after the encounter at the Café de Bon Salud had there been there any calls between Taylor Davis's phone and Mr. Millbank's phone. All in all, there had been just three calls, all of them from Ms. Davis to Mr. Millbank.

The last one had been about fourteen hours before Mr. Millbank's body was found. It was a text message, but unfortunately, cellular carriers were not required to save the content of such messages, and most deleted them within days. Alvarez reminded Evan that they had been able to access the complete texts of the messages between Mr. Millbank and Jennifer Carmichael, even though months had passed. Evan responded by telling Detective Alvarez that if the messages were between phones with the same cellular provider, they were more likely to be saved for a longer period of time, but if they were between providers, they were often discarded quickly. Even so, Alvarez surmised that this bit of data was quite incriminating, even if he didn't have access to the actual exchange of words. As it was, the evidence against Ms. Davis was obviously mounting. Alvarez put out a call for her arrest and circulated her photo the next day during the morning report to all the officers of their precinct.

The thought of heading back to Tromsø filled Leila with both excitement and determination as she lay on her hotel-room bed. She recalled that she and Andy had been intimidated and belittled by Erik Bergeland during their last visit, and she wanted another opportunity to interview him. She had felt sure his aloofness at the time meant he was involved in the murders, but how many suspects could one case have? she wondered. After all, there was Bryan Vasquez, the primary suspect, who seemed to have been aided by Taylor Davis in killing Mr. Millbank. However, sorting out who killed Mr. Stern remained problematic. For one thing, neither Bryan nor Bergeland had been in Basel at the time of the murder, and it was highly unlikely (though not yet disproven) that Ms. Davis had made her way to Basel. Even so, she couldn't have participated in two essentially simultaneous murders across two continents. While they had potential suspects for Mr. Stern's murder in Switzerland in Karina Hummels and Angelina Costa, it remained unclear as to how Bergeland could be connected—was he connected? Leila knew the only way to find out was to head back to the blackness of Tromsø. *Does the sun even make an appearance in January?* she wondered aloud to herself.

What she couldn't understand was why Bryan had headed back to Tromsø, and why at this time. It must be to meet with Bergeland again, but why? Was he planning more victims? Tromsø. The city troubled her, what with its foreboding darkness, the arrogant and intimidating Bergeland, and now with the possibility of encountering Bryan. What would she say to him if she saw him? After all, he was the brother of one of her patients. What could she say? She lay on the pillow staring at the ceiling, looking at the patterns in the swirls of paint of this old hotel room. In her tired state, she imagined one of the patterns looked like

Bryan and another looked like Bergeland. She mock-interviewed each of them. She became more and more tired. The beers she had drunk had loosened her thoughts and opened her mind like a complicated knot being untangled. She looked up again and saw a pattern that reminded her of Andy. She knew that she would need to speak to him soon too. It was inevitable. She needed to tell him about the conversation she'd had with her parents over New Year's weekend. But what would she say? She fell asleep.

Neither Andy nor Leila would have guessed it would take three flights and over twelve hours to get to Tromsø. Although it was just over a thousand miles from Aberdeen to Tromsø as the crow flies, there were no direct flights, and the fastest path was to fly first back to London, then to Oslo, and finally to Tromsø, forming a giant J shape of nearly two thousand miles. Much to their surprise, as the plane was descending for its landing in Tromsø just past 12:00 noon, not only was it daylight but the sun was clearly visible just a few degrees above the southern horizon. As it turned out, the sun had reappeared above the horizon on January 15 after its fifty-day hibernation, though it would not be visible directly from the city, owing to the mountains, until January 21. Although sunrise to sunset was just under an hour, there was a much more prolonged twilight, so that the complete darkness only occupied about fourteen hours each day this time of year. The site of daylight in Tromsø was not only surprising but even invigorating, particularly given it was so unexpected. Although it was cold, just twenty degrees, the sun's light infused the two sleuths with strength and renewed purpose as if they were spring flowers unfurling and turning toward the welcoming energy of the sun.

Leila looked at Andy with a sparkling smile as the low sun shone through the plane's window onto her face, throwing her dark hair into sharp relief against the indigo sky behind her. Her look was one of poise and determination. After a smooth landing, they gathered their bags, hopped into a taxi, and headed to the same hotel, the Radisson SAS, that they'd previously stayed in. During their long journey, they'd discussed their objectives for the trip and formulated a plan they felt confident would be successful. After checking in, they embarked on the first part of that plan.

"Sami Innovations Headquarters, please," Andy said to the taxi driver as he and Leila settled into the back seat of the Audi sedan. In order to ensure that Erik Bergeland would be in his office, they'd had Simon Kupfer arrange a sham meeting with a prospective new client. Bergeland wouldn't turn down an opportunity to expand his business—and influence.

While the sun had set, a bright twilight had settled over this island city, with a light-blue dome of color overhead flanked by an intense navy-blue rim to the north and a soft-pink horizon to the south. As the taxi left the central downtown area and headed north, the road became narrower, and the neat rows of building lining the street gave way at first to houses flanked by snow-covered yards and then to a forest of tall pine trees. The same trees that had seemed to stand like guardians in the dark, protecting Sami Innovations, during their last visit seemed less intimidating in the twilight, with their dark and pointed crowns silhouetted beautifully against the light-blue sky. As the taxi approached, Leila pointed without speaking to the small parking area near the main entrance. Andy, who had been looking in the opposite direction at the fjord toward the east, turned his head in the direction Leila suggested and then quickly turned back to her, shrugging his shoulders. Neither understood the significance of the other taxi parked adjacent to the steps leading to the entrance.

"Where would you like me to stop?" asked the genial taxi driver in perfect English.

"This would be fine, thank you," Leila said forking over a hundred Norwegian kroner to the driver and asking for his mobile number so they could call him when they were ready to return.

They clambered out of the taxi across the street from the main entrance, on the side of the otherwise-deserted road. As they began walking across, a light came on in the foyer near the front door, and the silhouettes of three figures could be seen through the window. Leila grabbed Andy and instinctively pulled him back across the street and into the forest next to the road. At first Andy was confused, but he soon realized Leila's intentions. They found two of the larger trees and each took up a position behind one. Leila pulled out her iPhone and prepared to record video. They were about forty feet from the front door, hidden in the dark shadows of the tall trees. Carefully glancing around the sides of the trees, like children playing hide and seek, they waited patiently and silently.

As the minutes passed, the figures in the foyer were immersed in conversation, while the two sleuths, unprepared to weather a late-afternoon winter's day outside, grew colder. Two of the figures seemed to have short hair cropped close to their heads, while the third head had a rather odd contour, including a nearly perfect elongated dome shape with a tapered edge on the back of the head. Finally, the figures could be seen heading toward the door, and two of the figures exited. Leila began videotaping from her phone and prayed there would be enough light to capture the events. Andy looked intently at the door and recognized Erik Bergeland standing in the lit entranceway. The other two figures had their backs to him, but he was able to discern that one was a male and the other a female wearing a ski hat, which explained the odd-shaped silhouette they had seen moments earlier. Finally the two figures turned away from the door and momentarily faced Andy and Leila before hopping into the waiting taxi. Andy glanced at Leila, and they nodded to each other, asserting that they'd recognized one of the figures. It was Bryan Vasquez. The taxi reversed out from its parking space as Andy and Leila ducked fully behind the trees and headed back in the direction of downtown.

"Coast is clear; let's go before Bergeland heads out," Andy said.
"Wait!" Leila exclaimed.

"What—why? Time to confront Bergeland."

"Hold on a second," Leila said, tapping away on her phone while pleading for patience. Andy waited. Then Leila continued, "I have a suggestion."

"All right," Andy said hesitatingly. "Quickly though; I'm freezing."

"Who was the woman with Bryan?" Leila asked.

"I don't know," Andy said with a shrug.

"Don't you think we should find out before confronting Bergeland?"

"I'm not following, Leila."

"Andy, we have an edge now. We know where Bergeland is, and we know where Bryan is, but they don't know we're here. I think we should use that to our advantage. As soon as Bergeland knows we're here, that advantage is gone, and who knows what he'll do?"

"What do you expect to find out, though?" Andy asked.

"For one thing, I'd like to know who Bryan was with and why."

"Fine," Andy said, though clearly he was not fully in agreement. He was itching to get at Bergeland. "But we need to get out of the cold—we're not dressed for this, and we can't walk—"

Andy stopped talking as Leila motioned him to follow her. She led him through the snow-covered ground of the forest in the direction of the downtown, paralleling the street. Barely a minute had passed, and they had moved about a hundred yards away from the parking area of Sami Innovations, when Leila grabbed Andy by the hand and yanked him toward the street just as a taxi pulled up. Andy was amazed to be stepping into the same taxi they had climbed out of less than thirty minutes earlier. Once again, Leila had been a step ahead; she had called the driver to return to pick them up.

After returning to the downtown area, Leila led Andy to a sporting-goods store, where they bought ski hats and balaclavas. When Andy asked why the balaclavas, it only took Leila putting hers on for Andy to realize that this particular specialized cold-weather gear would serve a dual purpose. With the hat and the balaclava on, Leila was barely recognizable. A fitting disguise, indeed. Tromsø was a small city, with all the hotels and most of the restaurants and bars concentrated in an area that would barely cover two city blocks in New York. The proximity served as a double-edged sword. It offered an opportunity to find Bryan and the mystery woman relatively easily, yet it did not provide sufficient cover to do so without being spotted themselves. Hence the disguises. With their new gear on, they elected to go back to their hotel to pick up a map and make a plan for canvassing the city. Afternoon twilight had slowly darkened, and the navy-blue sky blackened as if a dimmer switch was being engaged and turned slowly.

Andy and Leila found a quiet corner in the lobby to warm up, have some coffee and hot chocolate, and look at the video Leila had shot in front of Bergeland's office. Unfortunately, the combination of their distance and the darkness had resulted in a grainy video from which neither could discern the features of Bryan's female colleague. Leila retreated to her room briefly to download the video from her phone and e-mail it to Alvarez and de Ville, in order to have each of their experts work on improving the resolution of the video. Upon returning to the lobby, Leila, with her winter gear on save for the gloves, hat, and balaclava, motioned to Andy to suit up as well, and they emerged into the frigid night air comfortably warm and perfectly incognito. Night had taken its rightful place, and the sky was now pitch-black, save for the incredible number of stars that were visible. Without the light pollution of New York or Los Angeles, and aided by the dry air, Andy and Leila were treated to an astronomical spectacle such as neither had ever seen.

"Oh wow!" Leila exclaimed as she looked up at the sky.

"What is it?" Andy asked noting Leila's upward gaze. "Oh, I see. Amazing."

"I've never seen anything like this. It's so beautiful. Have you ever seen this many stars in the sky, Andy?"

"No. I can't say I have. My only similar memory was the time I spent summers in the Adirondack Mountains of upstate New York. There were nights when I was out in woods on a hiking trip and the sky was this black and the stars this visible."

"As weird as this place is and despite our previous experience here, I have to say it is growing on me," Leila added.

"Yeah, me too, so long as I can tolerate the freezing cold," Andy replied.

The temperature was forecast to drop to minus two Fahrenheit, which on the one hand worried the two Californians who had never experienced such cold but on the other hand provided the excuse they needed for donning the balaclavas. They left the hotel lobby and walked south toward the aquarium and brewery, both of which were situated at one end of the downtown area. Their plan was to walk into each and every pub and restaurant. They figured that Bryan would be at one of them, given that happy hour had begun and dinnertime was upcoming. They assumed Bryan felt confident enough to leave his hotel room; he would think his brief stay and stealthy escape from Aberdeen would throw off any would-be pursuers. Andy also pointed out the fact that, as he was with a lady, it would be more likely he would be going out for a drink and/or dinner.

They agreed to enter each pub and restaurant separately, make a sweep while heading to the bathroom, and then exit if neither one found anything. They timed their sweeps and bathroom forays so that they could be in eye contact with one another the entire time except for precisely thirty seconds in the bathrooms. The pubs at first were not crowded; however, as the evening progressed, they became more and more crowded. Andy suggested they take more time in the crowded places to ensure they wouldn't miss Bryan or the mystery woman. They went through five pubs and four restaurants without spotting Bryan before they entered Thor's Hammer, a pub and restaurant dedicated to the famous Norse god. Clearly, this was the place to be. Upon entering the foyer and greeting the hostess, Andy pointed to the bar, and she smiled and spoke to them in Norsk. At least they recognized one phrase—"happy hour"—to which they nodded affirmatively without saying a word. As they passed the hostess, they saw a large dining area with a vaulted ceiling to their right. They headed in that direction and swept through the dining area quickly with no sighting. They went to their respective bathrooms and emerged almost simultaneously. As Andy was heading back to the bar, Leila pointed to a set of stairs, where a waiter could be seen carrying a tray of food up. They followed him and emerged on a large landing, where another hostess was standing. This dining room, with large glass windows overlooking the fjord, was smaller; a quick glance was all they needed to realize that Bryan was not here. They headed back down the stairs. Leila, who was leading the way, stopped abruptly, stretching out her hand behind her to stop Andy from toppling over her.

"What is it?" Andy whispered, now with the balaclava pulled under his chin. "The woman. I think that was her entering the bathroom."

"Are you sure?"

"No, she's not wearing the ski hat, and I only got a quick glance."

"Why don't you go in? I'll go into the men's bathroom, and we can meet in a minute by the hostess at the entrance," Andy suggested.

"Okay," Leila said, pulling Andy's balaclava over his face first and then hers.

Leila entered the bathroom and saw feet wearing black boots in one of the stalls. She headed for the sink and turned on the water. She waited there for what felt like hours but was only seconds. She heard the click of the lock on the stall move and heard the heels of the boots heading toward her. *Thank God for the large wall-to-wall mirror*, she thought. She only needed to glance at the mirror and use her peripheral vision to see the woman. It *was* the same woman—she was sure now, but she didn't recognize her. She waited for her to leave and then headed back out. Andy was already waiting for her. There were no men in the bathroom, he relayed to Leila. She told him that she was quite sure that the woman who had just left the bathroom was indeed the same woman they had seen leaving Sami Innovations earlier. Leila looked at Andy and pointed to the bar, and they marched with purpose and optimism in that direction. After turning the corner at the edge of the dining room, they were facing the large bar area. There were so many people, it was hard to discern whether there were cocktail tables between them or it was just a large mass of humanity. It reminded Andy of the documentary *March of the Penguins*, where thousands of penguins huddled together to provide community warmth. Perhaps this was the human version in another cold environment. He and Leila found a pocket of space in the corner, where they could see the open area connecting the dining room, bar, and exit. From this vantage point, they would be able to survey the whole bar area as well as watch people going to the bathroom or exiting the building. A man came up to them and starting speaking Norsk, to which they both just held their hands up, indicating that they couldn't understand him.

"There's a coat check behind the bar," he said in English, gulping from a large mug of beer, to which Leila nodded politely and said thanks.

"Who needs coats if they all drink this much?" Leila said as she turned toward Andy.

"I think we found the cure for dealing with the cold, dark nights around here," Andy chimed in, making a drinking motion with his hand toward his mouth.

Although they'd lowered the balaclavas' face-covering segments below their chins, they chose to keep their coats on, as well as their ski hats. Maintaining some sense of disguise was more important than committing a Tromsø fashion faux pas. Andy headed to the bar to get them drinks—after all, they couldn't stand in the bar without a drink, lest they draw some suspicion. As he wriggled through the crowd, he came to a sudden stop and, realizing what he was seeing, rapidly turned back to Leila.

"Where's my drink?" Leila asked, smiling.

"Holy shit, Leila—you're not going to believe this!"

"What? What is it!"

"We need to leave now. I'll tell you when we get outside."

Replacing their balaclavas over their faces, they made their way to the door and headed back to the hotel.

CHAPTER 36

JANUARY 18
TROMSØ,
BASEL,
NEW YORK

F elix de Ville arrived at his office and opened his e-mail. After the usual e-mails from the various cantons on the latest criminal activity and open arrest warrants, he was both surprised and definitely intrigued to see an e-mail from Leila Baker. She had never e-mailed him, and it had been some time since he had even received a phone call from her. The e-mail simply read:

Felix, do you know who the woman is in the video?

Thanks.
Leila

Felix clicked on the file to download the video. After thirty seconds, the file opened. The video was dark and grainy. He could make out a building, with a blond-haired man standing in a lit doorway and two figures facing the man. Then the figures turned, and de Ville could barely make out two faces, that of a man and a woman with a ski hat.

He looked intently. The figures entered a taxi, and the video stream stopped. He replayed it and paused it when the woman's face was at its most visible. He felt a flutter in his chest and a lump in his throat when he came to the realization that he, indeed, recognized the woman. *Where in God's name is this video from, and who is the man?* he wondered. He hit the Reply to All button, ensuring that Detective Alvarez would be included in the virtual discussion, and he began to type.

> *Leila, I hope you are well and that Andy is also okay. I can tell you who the woman is, but I have a few questions of my own that I'd like answered. Where was this video taken? Who is the man? The woman is Angelina Costa. I'm surprised you didn't recognize her, but now that I think about it, I don't know that you ever met her. Please let me know what is going on. So far, no progress on Karina Hummels. She hired a lawyer and is refusing to talk to anyone.*

Detective Alvarez and O'Reilly gathered in the conference room to discuss the case and review the progress with the commissioner of the NYPD. As each day passed, more and more pressure was being heaped upon him, which he paid forward to Alvarez and O'Reilly.

"Well, Jose, Sean, what's the latest? The mayor is making me report to him daily now. He's getting impatient. Actually, he's past impatient."

"Our doctor detectives are back in Europe, following up on a lead that Bryan Vasquez is back there again. We have an arrest warrant out for both him and Taylor Davis, and we think once we find them and bring them in for questioning, we'll get the answers we need," O'Reilly stated plainly.

"Sounds promising, but it's not good enough. I need an arrest today," the commissioner insisted.

"We are confident that we'll track down Ms. Davis today, sir," Alvarez said. "Let me know as soon as you've found her," the commissioner demanded as he strode out of the conference room while pulling out his cell phone to call the mayor.

"Jose, what the fuck! You shouldn't have promised him that! You know he just told the mayor that Ms. Davis will be arrested today," O'Reilly said.

"She will be arrested today, I am sure of it. Where the hell could she be, anyway? She's a native New Yorker who goes to medical school here, and we know her friends and her hangouts. I don't understand why we haven't found her yet," Alvarez replied.

"That's exactly the goddamn point. Maybe she went into hiding. Got a whiff that we're onto her and just fuckin' vanished. She hasn't been to any of the places she should be. Not her apartment, not to the hospital or medical school, the student union, the library. We even checked the café, and no one has seen her. For fuck's sake, I even tracked Carmichael down to see if she knew anything and, well ... nothing!"

"Shit. Shit!" Alvarez yelled out.

The expletives continued to fly out of the detectives' mouths, and while those coming from O'Reilly's curse-laden vocabulary were not surprising, the fact that Alvarez was demonstrating less restraint over his tongue suggested his anxiety level was mounting by the moment.

"I can tell you're feeling the pressure. I never heard you curse this much. You're saying 'shit' and 'fuck' even more than your foul-mouthed Irish partner!"

"What are we going to do, Sean?" Alvarez asked in exasperation.

"Let's pray Andy and Leila find something. Something big. When was the last time you checked your e-mail?" To answer that question, they ran over to Alvarez's office and sat together expectantly at the computer, like teenage girls hoping for messages from prospective boyfriends. As soon as he opened his Outlook e-mail, his eyes zoomed in on four messages—the first one from Leila at 8:37 a.m., one from Detective de Ville timed at 9:37 a.m. (which were 2:37 p.m. in Norway and 3:37 p.m. in Basel, respectively), followed by two more from Leila, one at 12:52 p.m. and a second one at 1:04 p.m. (6:52 p.m. and 7:04 p.m. in Norway). He looked at O'Reilly, who motioned to open them sequentially. They read with anticipation the first e-mail from Leila and opened the video. While they recognized that the man was Bryan Vasquez, whose face they now knew well from the pictures they'd recently reviewed, it was quite clear to them that they did not know who the woman was. They proceeded to read the next e-mail, which was from de Ville, indicating that Angelina Costa was the mystery woman in the video, and though they realized that she must be in Tromsø, since that is where Leila was, they were at a loss to comprehend what she would be doing there. Then they opened the next e-mail from Leila:

> *Felix, we're in Tromsø tracking down Bryan Vasquez. That is where the video was taken. The man is Bryan Vasquez. Thanks for your quick reply. Finally, a connection between Bryan and Angelina. Yeah! But why in Tromsø? We don't know. Any idea? Please stay on your e-mail— more messages to come.*

"Yes!" Alvarez said exuberantly. "Bryan and Angelina together—we needed that connection to support our theories."

"Except that doesn't really help our case here, Jose. Open the next one. The one with the subject line 'Big breakthrough.'"

Alvarez and O'Reilly, practically giddy with anticipation, sat huddled in front of the monitor of Alvarez's computer. They were desperate for information that would help appease the commissioner and the mayor and that could signal an imminent arrest in the bleeder case. Alvarez looked over to O'Reilly, who nodded and held up crossed fingers. Then Detective Alvarez clicked on the Open Mail button, opening a window with the short paragraph Leila had recently sent.

> *Big breakthrough. We think. We hope. Andy and I went to Bergeland's office today, and as we were about to go in, we saw Bryan and a woman talking to Bergeland. Turns out the woman is Angelina Costa, as you read from Felix's e-mail. We decided to stay incognito and look for*

Bryan and Angelina rather than talking to Bergeland.
Well, you're not going to believe this. We found them in a
bar called Thor's Hammer, having drinks with—are you
ready? Taylor Davis. What the hell is she doing in Norway!
I thought you guys were going to arrest her. Let us know
what you want us to do.

"Fuck!" O'Reilly yelled out loud. "Fuck, fuck, fuck! What the hell are we going to do now?"

There was only silence.

O'Reilly continued, now with a decidedly nervous tone to his voice, "Well, what are we going to tell them, Jose?"

"Who, Andy and Leila or the commissioner?"

"The fuckin' commissioner, man. You told him we were going to arrest Taylor Davis today. Today, Jose. Shit! We are fuckin' screwed, partner," O'Reilly said in resignation.

"I know. We'll figure something out, but for the moment, what should we tell Andy and Leila to do—they need some guidance. Read the last line in the e-mail again."

"I don't know. I, uh … well, they obviously have a good rapport with Bryan, right?" O'Reilly surmised.

"And Leila seemed to hit it off really well with Taylor, right? So-o-o," Alvarez said and then thought for a moment, "maybe they can convince them to come back to the US and turn themselves in."

"Yeah, right! There is no fuckin' way that's gonna happen. What do you think—they're just going to walk in here and admit they killed Millbank?" O'Reilly replied.

"You know, the funny thing is, even though all the suspects are in one city all at the same time, we still don't really know what happened. That's the part that bugs me the most. I would almost trade that for them all not being prosecuted."

"Are you crazy?" O'Reilly shouted. "Two men were killed, and these people somehow killed them, and you're suggesting they don't get punished?"

"They've all been punished already," Alvarez said quietly.

"No, Jose, they have not been punished. They had bad things happen to them, and if they are guilty, they exacted revenge—vigilante style. We are enforcers of the law! We can't let people take the law into their own hands. No way."

"A victim of rape, a mourning brother whose sister is dead because of a fraudulent insurance company and a greedy pharmaceutical company, and a child molested repeatedly by her own father. Those are the three people Leila and Andy found in the bar today. That's all I'm saying."

"Look, I understand that, but first things first. We need to know who did what to whom, and then we let the justice system decide what the outcome will be," O'Reilly replied more calmly.

"I'll tell Andy and Leila to try to meet with the three of them—or even the four of them, including Bergeland—if they can and find out what actually happened," Alvarez said to conclude the conversation.

He typed a detailed e-mail to Leila, asking her and Andy to find Bryan, Angelina, Taylor, and Bergeland and find out the truth once and for all and then to report back.

Leila and Andy were sitting in the lobby of the SAS Radisson having dinner, with Leila's computer on the table as if it were the third diner. Andy had the reindeer steak, the local Sami specialty he'd enjoyed previously, while Leila had grilled salmon over cabbage. They sat silently, each one thinking about what might have brought the three suspects together in, of all places, Tromsø, Norway, in the middle of winter. Finally the e-mail from Alvarez came through, and they knew what their next step was. As they were completing their dinner, their waiter came by, recognizing that they were not locals, and told them to get outside as quickly as they could, though he didn't explain why. Looking around the restaurant and through the glass into the hotel lobby, they could see a steady stream of people walking outside. It was now past nine in the evening, and neither could understand what could draw people out into the frigid Arctic night in the middle of winter. Naturally curious, they replaced their cold-weather gear, balaclavas and all, paid the bill, and walked outside.

As they exited the lobby, they followed the crowd around to the back of the hotel to the shore of the fjord. Noting that everyone's head was tilted skyward, they did the same, and it instantly dawned upon them what the attraction was. The night sky was filled with thin wisps of red and green rising high above Storsteinen, the hill opposite the city. It was as if Storsteinen were a stage, and a ghost-like curtain was draped above it, rising high into the atmosphere as far as the eye could see. Aurora borealis. The Northern lights. Though they had both heard about the phenomenon, they never quite imagined just how beautiful and spectacular it was. It was clear that even many locals were impressed by this particular display. It was truly magnificent. The winter sky in Tromsø was usually cloudy, thus frequently blocking aurora sightings, but this night the sky was crystal clear, and Mother Nature gave Andy and Leila and those around them a lifetime memory. After twenty minutes, the lights began to fade, as if the curtain had been drawn to reveal the star-filled black night.

Andy and Leila, both freezing cold despite their attire, were headed back to the hotel when suddenly Andy stopped in his tracks and grabbed Leila's arm. He pointed straight ahead, and they both picked up the pace of their walk to the point that they were no longer walking yet not quite running. As they approached the front entrance of their hotel, they were amazed to see Bryan, Angelina, and Taylor walk into the lobby of the SAS Radisson. They slowed just enough to keep some distance between themselves and their prey, and as they walked through the lobby entrance and saw the three suspects sit down at a table, they were pleasantly surprised and unable to believe their good fortune. Bryan, Angelina, and Taylor were sitting in the lobby bar at a cocktail table with none other than Erik Bergeland. They knew what they had to do.

"How do you want to handle this, Andy?" Leila asked.

"I say we play dumb. Let's go in and join them and ask them what they are doing in Norway," Andy replied.

"And when they ask us the same, what do we say?"

"That we have always wanted to see the Northern Lights and we heard that Tromsø is one of the best places on earth to see them," Andy suggested.

"Uh, Andy, they're not going to buy that," Leila said. "Why not? We have an advantage."

"Oh yeah—what advantage?" Leila wondered.

"We work together, and we're friends, so it is perfectly reasonable that we would take a vacation together. The four of them are supposed to be strangers, right? We can, without raising suspicion, ask them how they know each other. What do you think?"

"I suppose that makes sense, but—"

"But what? That's our opening, and then we see where the conversation goes from there," Andy said.

"It's not going to be that easy. Bergeland and Taylor know we are investigating the murders, and they're sure to say something, at which point Bryan will probably shut up," Leila said, continuing her vein of skepticism.

"Leila, I'm just looking for an opening, that's all. I don't know where the conversation will go from there, but I'll tell you one thing—it will be interesting, that's for sure."

"You're forgetting one other thing. If we are here on vacation together, then we must be more than just friends, right?" Leila purposely put Andy on the spot.

"I don't think that's what's going to be on their mind, Leila."

"Perhaps, but you should be prepared to answer that question, and, uh … I'd like to know what you are going to tell them if they ask," Leila pressed.

Andy could not believe that, of all times to bring up their relationship, Leila chose to do it at this most critical time of the investigation. Was this a test, he wondered? On the other hand, Leila had a good point. Certainly Bryan, who had known them both for some time now, would be wondering what they were doing on vacation together. He thought, and then he thought some more.

"Are you asking me to tell you how I plan on answering any questions they bring up about our relationship ... or are you asking me to answer the question for you?" Andy replied, reversing the discussion and putting Leila on the spot.

"What's the difference?" Leila responded.

Andy nearly chuckled out loud, but he kept it to himself. Just when he'd thought he had the perfect response, Leila had turned the tables back on him. Though Andy should no longer be surprised by Leila's intuitiveness and resourcefulness, this reply was spectacularly brilliant. Despite the awkward timing, Andy decided to come clean—finally.

"Leila, we really need to get in there before Bryan and company leave, but I'm happy to tell you briefly what I would say."

"Let's hear it, then."

"Leila is my girlfriend. I know it sounds crazy, but I have fallen madly in love with her, and she told me she was always fascinated by the Northern Lights, yet never got to see them, so I brought her here as a surprise for a vacation."

"That's pretty good, I must say. I think they'll buy that even though it's not true. I have to say you really said it convincingly, too, so make sure you say it the same way, okay?" Leila said innocently.

Andy laughed to himself. He couldn't believe that Leila still didn't realize that he was, indeed, madly in love with her. There will be time for that later, he figured.

"Shall we, then?" he said. And with that they strode confidently into the lobby to confront the quartet.

With balaclavas and hats hiding their identities, they walked into the lobby bar of the SAS Radisson, and pretending not to see Bryan and company, they sat at a table just yards away. They casually peeled their outer garments off, revealing their identities just as a birthday gift is revealed when the wrapping paper is removed. With their faces clearly visible, Andy purposely glanced over at the table of interest and willfully made full eye contact with Bryan Vasquez for the first time since Diana's last clinic visit. Bryan's eyebrows arched high, and his unblinking eyes stared straight back at Andy. His mouth opened in a combination of surprise and confusion—clearly he was shocked to see the doctor he knew from LA in this faraway corner of the world. Andy tilted his head gently forward and squinted as he brought his eyebrows down over his eyelids, feigning bemusement, while Leila simply looked at Andy, sensing some embarrassment and feeling that her facial expression couldn't quite live up to the sham surprise she needed to display. Andy waited to see what Bryan would do next and was pleased to see his face morph from surprise to recognition and then quickly to a wide smile. Bryan leapt from the chair at the table he was sharing with Taylor, Angelina, and Bergeland, and ran over to Andy to greet him. As he approached, he came to a full stop and threw his head back in further amazement to see Leila seated at the bar with Andy.

"Oh my God, Dr. Friedman, Dr. Baker. What the hell are you guys doing in Norway?"

"Well, Leila and I are actually dating, if you would believe that, and I surprised her with a trip to Norway for a vacation," Andy replied.

"In the winter, in Tromsø—you've got to be kidding me! If you came to Norway in the winter to ski, that's one thing, but why Tromsø?"

"It turns out Leila has always wanted to see the Northern Lights—she told me that once a while back, and well, I wanted her to experience it. We feel so fortunate that we actually got to see it," Andy replied.

"Wait, you and Dr. Baker are a … a couple?"

"Sure, I know it seems weird, but—"

"It's more than weird. You work together, and well, I don't know, I just never pictured that you two would be together. And Dr. Friedman, I thought you were Jewish, and well, Leila, you told me you were from Iraq, so aren't you Muslim?" Bryan asked, first looking at Andy and then at Leila.

Why did he have to bring that up now? Andy thought to himself.

"So what, Bryan?" Leila protested. "You think that religion should keep people apart? If things don't work out for me and Andy, is it okay with you if I date a Christian or a Buddhist?"

"Dr. Baker, I'm sorry. I didn't mean it like that. But you know it's not exactly like Jews and Muslims get along in the world," Bryan persisted.

"That's where you're wrong. First of all, Judaism and Islam are religions with more similarities than differences. Second, all the problems between the religions are political and not religious, and they haven't been solved because the idiot politicians in the Middle East care more about their political power than about their people. Oh, and Bryan, by the way, Jews and Muslims have lived side by side for thousands of years—it's only in the last seventy or so years that they've been at war. Besides, it's not like Andy and I are part of that world, anyway. We're Americans," Leila responded with conviction.

Andy was amazed at the great act Leila put on in order to maintain their cover as investigators. It was so good, he thought, that she must really believe what she'd said. At least he hoped so. Either that or she had a future in Hollywood. Despite having convinced Bryan that they were in Tromsø for a vacation, Andy knew the same argument would not work on Erik Bergeland, who would surely recall that Andy and Leila were investigating the murders. Nevertheless, building some trust with Bryan was an important first step in getting the answers they were seeking. They were far enough away and it was dark enough in the bar that the others in Bryan's party hadn't recognized them as yet. Leila pushed a bar chair back from their table in Bryan's direction, inviting him to sit down. When Bryan politely refused, indicating he needed to return to his friends, Leila glanced at Andy, and when he nodded affirmatively, she knew what to do.

"Bryan, we need to talk to you, so please have a seat," Leila said firmly. "About what?" he replied, motioning to the table he had left to suggest he needed to return to them.

"It actually has to do with the people you are here with, so won't you have a seat, please?" Leila insisted.

"Uh, I ... I'm confused. You don't even know those people."

"Actually, Bryan, we do," Andy said.

"What the *hell* are you talking about, Dr. Friedman?" Bryan said, and the tone of his voice shifted from bewilderment to alarm.

"This may take a while, and frankly, it would be more productive if we sat with Bergeland, Angelina, and Taylor, and all spoke together," Leila said catching both Andy and Bryan totally off guard by the sudden admission.

Bryan stared at each of them, shifting his eyes from one to the other in stunned silence. His mouth pouted, and he exhaled audibly through his nostrils. Then he looked up at the ceiling, his face pensive as he weighed his next move. A full ten seconds passed. Then, "Stay the fuck away from me!" he told them. "You got that? I'm not talking to you, and neither will my friends over there. Is that clear?" Bryan was shaking.

He gave one final look each at Andy and Leila before walking back to the other table.

"Leila, why did you let on so quickly that we knew the others? Not a good idea," Andy said.

"He was going to find out as soon as we confronted the group, and there's no point just talking to Bryan—we need to hear from all of them, and we need to hear everything. This was the only way, by my calculation."

"You know he's telling them all about us right now. They're going to know that we're onto them," Andy said.

"I'm not so sure. Seriously, what is he going to tell them? Remember that Taylor and Bergeland already know us. Let's just watch and see what happens," Leila suggested.

Bryan walked briskly over to Bergeland, Angelina, and Taylor. From their vantage point, Leila and Andy could see Bryan speaking rapidly, gesticulating, and finally pointing over at their table. Andy looked at Leila, who steadily put both hands, palms down, just above the table and slowly moved them downward, suggesting that they stay calm and stay put. As they continued to watch, Bryan took his seat. Bergeland was now speaking. Angelina and Taylor nodded affirmatively. Then Bergeland got up and walked over toward Leila and Andy.

"Dr. Friedman," Bergeland began, "Dr. Baker, it's a pleasure, and well …quite a surprise to see you here in my hometown again. I take it you're not on holiday here this time of year, despite what you told Bryan. I recall recommending you come back in the summer—it's not quite summer yet, as I am sure you can tell."

"Mr. Bergeland, since you suggest visiting Tromsø in the summer, I wonder what drew your colleagues to come in midwinter," Leila asked.

"The Northern lights, of course," Bergeland responded tersely.

"Look, let's cut the bullshit," Leila responded. "We're here investigating the deaths of Mr. Stern and Mr. Millbank, just as we were the first time we visited you. You know it and we know it, but I don't think your colleagues know it."

"Yes, you caught Mr. Vasquez quite by surprise with your presence here. He's still shaking," Bergeland responded.

"I feel bad about that—after all he's the brother of one of our patients," Andy said, still lamenting Leila's earlier candor.

"I need to ask you something, though, and I would like an honest answer, please," Bergeland replied. "What do you really want from me or Bryan or any of us? You're not law enforcement, and even if you were, you'd be way out of your jurisdiction. Certainly you can't arrest us."

"To put it simply, we want to know everything," Leila said. "Everything about what?" Bergeland chuckled as he replied.

"Mr. Bergeland, don't play dumb with us—we know you're quite brilliant, and you are a terrible actor. We want to know how four completely unrelated people from three countries, with completely different backgrounds, managed to, how shall I put this—?" Andy began.

"Kill two people," Leila finished Andy's sentence. "Who said we killed anyone? Do you have any proof?"

"We have a lot, and I mean a lot, of circumstantial evidence," Leila said firmly.

"You know, I never quite figured out your role in all this. You are physicians—not enforcers of the law. Why are you so involved?" Bergeland asked.

"We were asked to help because of the way the victims were found. Do you know that they kept bleeding for a while after they died?" Andy said.

"Yes, so I heard," Bergeland said, not hiding his sense of pride at the grisly accomplishment.

An awkward silence ensued. They glanced at each other and then at the other table, where Bryan, Angelina, and Taylor were looking at the three of them intently.

Bergeland resumed. "I have another question. What authority do you have in this case? We've already established that you are not law enforcement and even if you were, that you are out of your jurisdiction."

"You are right. We have no authority as law enforcement—obviously not here in Norway, but not in the US either," Leila said.

"We are merely consultants—unpaid consultants, at that," Andy followed up. "Very well, then. That makes things much easier," Bergeland replied.

"Easier for what? Leila asked curiously.

"Since you don't have any law-enforcement capacity, we can speak to you, how do you say, 'off the record,' right?"

"Yes, that's accurate, though we will tell the authorities what you tell us," Andy said.

"Fine, but legally it carries no weight—for sure not here in Norway, and probably not in the US, either," Bergeland said.

"I suppose you're right," Leila said.

"In that case, why don't you join us for the meal I had planned to share with my three friends? I am sure I can convince them to not only have you join us but to provide you with the information you are so interested in knowing. Dr. Baker, I believe you said you wanted to know everything, correct?"

"Yes, *we* want to know everything," Leila replied.

"Very well, then. Please wait here for a moment while I speak with the other three," Bergeland said.

Bergeland walked back to the table where Bryan, Angelina, and Taylor were seated. As he spoke, the other three nodded affirmatively one by one. Bergeland motioned to Andy and Leila to head over to their table. Andy and Leila were introduced to the only member of the quartet they didn't know, Angelina Costa. Pleasantries were exchanged with the others, including a warm embrace between Taylor Davis and Leila. The irony of the embrace was not lost on either Leila or Taylor. Bergeland led the group to the main dining area, where the hostess swiftly led them to a private room beautifully adorned from floor to ceiling in dark-wood square panels, each with a rim of ornate molding. Bergeland was speaking in Norsk to the hostess, apparently giving her instructions. The table was a large and unimaginably thick brown wooden plank with beautiful yet natural markings as if painted by an artist. The waiters swiftly set up six place settings, with several plates and glasses in front of each chair. Andy and Leila looked at each other and shrugged, not sure what to make of it all. Bergeland standing at the head of the table, looked over at Andy and Leila to one side, then to Bryan and Taylor on the other side, and finally toward Angelina at the foot of the table, and began to speak.

"I would like to welcome you all to my home city of Tromsø. While I can't say that I expected Dr. Friedman and Dr. Baker to be joining us for this celebratory meal, I am delighted that they are here and that they will be celebrating with us."

"Celebratory meal—are you out of your mind? Two people are dead because of you—that is not a cause for celebration," Leila blurted out.

Taylor's lips whimpered, and she was nearly ready to cry as she stared at Leila, her gaze like a laser aimed at Leila's head.

"You know, I thought at least *you* would understand, Leila," she said through the tears.

Bergeland, sensing the tension, walked around to where Taylor was seated and put his hand on Taylor's, as a father would to a daughter—a good father, that is. The gesture was meant to inspire confidence.

"Yes, Leila, if I may call you that, a celebration. We all have something to celebrate—including you and Dr. Friedman."

"Oh really? What are Leila and I celebrating, Bergeland?" Andy asked.

"Call me Erik, please. What have you been doing for much of the past two months?" Bergeland asked rhetorically. "You've been investigating the deaths of one Creighton Millbank and one Andreas Stern, have you not?"

"Yes, of course, but—" Andy began.

"Well, tonight, you will achieve your goal—you will have all of your questions answered, and you can return home victorious, knowing that you have solved the mystery."

"You mean find out how the four of you managed to murder two men," Leila continued defiantly.

"Why don't you let us tell you, and then you can pass judgment on us—isn't that fair?" Bergeland responded.

Leila didn't answer but nodded affirmatively. Her upbringing ingrained in her an abhorrence of intolerance and a prerequisite to intolerance is prejudice—prejudging, in other words, and so she convinced herself to allow the four suspects to tell their story and only afterward would she consider whether their actions were justified or not.

"Excellent. Thank you, Leila," Bergeland said triumphantly. "Now, before we start, let's have a drink and a toast."

The waiters quickly walked around the table pouring red wine into large goblets for each guest.

"I have spared no expense to provide you with one of the finest wines in the world, a Mouton Rothschild, 1983. To my guests from the US and Switzerland, I welcome you to the Paris of the North, as Tromsø is known. It's the most cultured city—by far, I would add—north of the Arctic Circle in the world. *Skøl,*" Bergeland announced with the traditional Scandinavian pre-drink salute.

"Skøl," added Taylor, having fully regained her composure.

"*In vino veritas,*" Bergeland added, clearly understanding the meaning of the Latin phrase and how it had particular meaning for tonight's meal. "I have asked the chef, whom I know personally, to prepare us a fine Scandinavian feast, so I hope you are all ready to eat a lot."

The waiters scurried in and out of their private room. The first course was a small plate consisting of smoked salmon with a dollop of crème fraiche and capers, seated in a cup of butter lettuce. A basket of fresh whole-grain breads and butter in porcelain holders shaped like Viking ships were placed on the table.

"Please enjoy the first of our dishes," Bergeland stated proudly.

He proceeded to explain how the process of smoking fish began in Norway and how proud he was to travel to nearly every corner of the earth and see smoked salmon in so many supermarkets. This line of the discussion lasted several minutes, after which Bergeland looked over at Bryan, who nodded.

"Well, then, shall we get started with providing Leila and Andy the answers they seek? Remember that anything you tell them cannot be used against you—not here in Norway, nor the US, nor in Switzerland. It would all be hearsay and hence inadmissible. So, while they will likely report what they hear to the authorities in your respective countries, that shouldn't keep you from telling them the truth. Oh, and by the way, Norway will not extradite anyone to a country that has the death penalty, so Bryan, Taylor, you need not be concerned. Angelina, I can't say the same for you, though."

Andy felt compelled to say something in this unusual and highly awkward setting. "Leila and I desperately do want to know what happened. Just so you know, we have found out quite a bit about the four of you through our investigation, but we certainly are missing some key pieces, and our goal has always been to simply find out the truth. We are neither your judge nor your jury—we are simply two doctors who were asked some advice about two bizarre deaths, and one thing led to another to the point that we became the key investigators in the case."

Leila also sensed a need to make a comment, especially given her earlier reaction.

"I, too, would like to say something before you start. While I stated earlier that Mr. Millbank and Mr. Stern were murdered, and nothing you say will convince me otherwise, I will be open-minded as you tell us what happened and will reserve my personal judgment of you until later," Leila stated sincerely.

"Thank you," Taylor said. "That's all I am asking."

"Well then, Bryan, the story starts with you," Bergeland said.

Bryan looked at Bergeland and then slowly around the table to Angelina, Taylor, and finally to Andy and Leila. Then he began.

"Dr. Friedman, Dr. Baker, you know that I have the utmost respect for both of you. You have been such important people in my life and the lives of my family, especially my sisters." He paused and looked admiringly at Andy and Leila. "When Vanessa died, I, along with my whole family, was devastated—crushed. You don't know this, but we even discussed a group suicide—that is how distraught we were. It was only our faith in God and our religious beliefs that kept us from acting on that urge."

"Bryan, I, I ..." Leila said hesitatingly, tears forming in her eyes.

"I know. I know you and Dr. Friedman did everything you could. I don't fault either one of you in any way, and neither does my family. But you have to understand that we did feel that Vanessa's death could have been prevented and was not justified. You yourself said," he continued, looking at Andy, "that had she been able to get the Lyzanda, she would not have died. Am I right?"

"Well, yes, but—" Andy replied.

"Yes, I know, you could not be sure, but doctor, I remember those visits with Vanessa and my parents in the clinic as if it were yesterday, and I know you won't or can't be sure, but I also know that you believed that obtaining the Lyzanda was critical," Bryan continued.

"Yes, I did believe that, and you know how hard we tried to get it for Vanessa," Andy said.

"I know you did, believe me, but at the end, we never did get it, and Vanessa is dead. Let me ask you something. If you believe that Vanessa would be alive if she got the Lyzanda and that her death was preventable, then surely someone or something is to blame, no?"

"Bryan, you have always had my sympathy, but it is not that simple," Leila said. "Bad things happen in medicine all the time, and even preventable problems don't automatically mean that someone or something is to blame."

"Fair enough, but then can you tell me why Vanessa, living in the richest country on earth, which has the best medical care in the world, couldn't get Lyzanda?" Bryan asked.

"I'm sorry, but as a proud Norwegian, I just need to point out that here in Norway we have the highest per capita GDP, making us the richest country on earth," Bergeland interjected.

Angelina chuckled at Bergeland's arrogance—which was seemingly never in short supply.

"I think we are second," she said, referring to Switzerland's high standard of living.

"Well, excuse me, my dear friends. I didn't mean to insult your nationalistic pride," Bryan replied, and they all laughed. "May I continue now?"

"Please do," Bergeland said.

"Well, Dr. Baker, Dr. Friedman, how would you answer my question?"

"I understand what you're saying. Continue?" Andy said.

"Uh, that wasn't a rhetorical question. I'd like one of you to actually take a crack at answering it," Bryan persisted.

"I'll try," Leila said. "Despite the fact that the US can provide incredibly advanced medical care, that care is not distributed equitably, and just as there are tremendous economic inequalities in American society, there are also medical inequalities. It is not a perfect system—not even close."

"And ..." Bryan cajoled Leila to finish her thought to the conclusion he wanted to hear.

"And Vanessa died as a result of that inequality."

"Thank you, Dr. Baker. Well said," Bryan said, now satisfied.

"And you blamed Vanessa's insurance company for her death?" Leila asked. "Yes, and ultimately the CEO is responsible for his company's conduct." Bryan went on to explain that he had taken it upon himself to go to New York and attempt to meet with Mr. Millbank. His goal had not been to harm him in any way—not at first—but merely to be able to tell him what had happened to Vanessa. His goal, he explained, had been to at the very least make him feel guilty and at best to win some financial consideration for his family's suffering. He went on to say that he'd flown to New York several times and made numerous attempts to meet with Millbank, only to be snubbed over and over again. He was able on one occasion to reach the vestibule of his office, where his secretary sat, and plead with her to let him see Mr. Millbank, but he had been escorted out by security. Bryan said he had made one final attempt over the summer but to no avail.

"You see, I tried over and over again to simply have a ten-minute conversation with Mr. Millbank. His blatant disregard for me, and in my view, Vanessa's death, enraged me. I went from just wanting to make him feel guilty to wanting to kill him. It was as if he were spitting on Vanessa's grave."

"So, what did you do next?" Leila asked, now fully engrossed in Bryan's story. "Truth is, I didn't know what I was going to do. For sure, I wasn't just going to get a gun and try to kill him. First of all, I hate guns—they frighten me—and second, I obviously didn't want to get caught. So, I just fantasized about how I would exact revenge—but they were just that, fantasies—until I met Erik, that is."

"Perhaps, I'll take over here, so Bryan can enjoy the appetizer," Bergeland said.

"Please go ahead, Erik," Bryan replied.

"First of all, I need to tell you a bit about myself and my company," Bergeland began. "Sami Innovations is not per se a pharmaceutical company, but we work with those companies to enhance the properties of their drugs."

Bergeland went on to explain how he'd gotten involved in this type of work by noting the need for a variety of medications by oil workers stationed for weeks or months on the vast Norwegian rigs in the North Sea. After some early successes with relatively inexpensive medications, such as antibiotics, anti-nausea medications, and others, Sami Innovations' reputation had grown in the world of "pharma," the moniker the largest pharmaceutical companies in the world were known by. It was at a pharmaceutical-company conference, Bergeland told them, that he'd first met Andreas Stern. They had discussed several of Terrapharma's best-selling medications and how Sami Innovations' technology could improve upon them. Their discussions eventually led to an agreement to take Terrapharma's erectile dysfunction drug, Vitax, and try to enhance it by making its effects last longer. At the time, Vitax was vying for market share with Viagra and Cialis but was not nearly as successful as its competitors. Bergeland now told them that his company had developed what became Provitax, a much-improved version of Vitax that eventually conquered the erectile dysfunction market and earned Terrapharma tens of billions of dollars.

"Well, believe it or not, Erik, we know quite a bit about that from the numerous e-mails you sent to Stern trying to extort more money from Terrapharma," Leila said.

"*Extort*, that's a very strong word, and I take offense to that. In business, we call that renegotiating a deal," Bergeland replied firmly.

"The e-mails were rather threatening, wouldn't you agree?" Leila pressed. "You are not a businesswoman, young lady," Bergeland responded in a patronizing tone. "This is how big business is conducted."

"Can we get back on track, please?" Andy requested. "So far, I don't see where this connects to Bryan."

"Patience, I'll get there, Andy," Bergeland responded.

Bergeland described how he had been on one of his many trips to Stavanger, Norway's oil hub city, when he'd met Bryan. It had been during a meeting with ExxonMobil executives regarding some unusual health problems their workers had exhibited on one of their rigs. Bryan was present at the meeting so he could get a sense of whether the problem might be related to the location or particular geology of the area where the rig was located. After the meeting, the two had struck up a conversation, during which Bergeland had enlightened Bryan about his company and their products.

"Bryan, I think it's best that you take over at this point," Bergeland said as Andy and Leila intently listened.

"Keep in mind that this conversation took place just a few months after Vanessa died. I had returned to work, but I was still hurting. After the conversation with Erik, I returned to my hotel room, and as I was lying in bed, I had an epiphany," Bryan said, and he paused.

"Yes, go on, then," Leila implored.

"I thought that if Bergeland could make drugs more powerful than their parent compound, perhaps he could make me something that I could use to hurt Creighton Millbank, who as I have already told you, I held responsible for Vanessa's death. I swear that the thought of killing him didn't cross my mind."

"Well, what were you thinking, then?" Andy asked. "Do you enjoy being nauseous, Dr. Friedman?"

"What kind of question is that?" Andy replied with a question of his own. "Just answer the question, please," Bryan responded politely.

"Of course not," Andy said.

"So, I thought if Bergeland could make me a drug that, for example, would cause severe and prolonged nausea, I would hurt Millbank that way."

"But that's not what you did," Leila said.

Bergeland took over the discussion. "That's correct, Leila. When Bryan approached me some weeks later asking me if I could make him a drug that could make Mr. Millbank sick, I asked him why he wanted to do such a foolish thing."

There was a short pause as Bryan looked over at Bergeland and then back toward Andy and Leila. Bergeland motioned with his hand, encouraging Bryan to explain, but Bryan held his hand up and then pointed toward Bergeland, implying that *he* should continue.

"Bryan told me what had happened to his sister. I was sickened. I have two sisters myself and couldn't imagine losing one, let alone in the manner in which Vanessa died. So I decided to let Bryan know about my predicament with Terrapharma and Mr. Stern and how I felt they had taken advantage of me and essentially robbed me and my company of perhaps a billion dollars or more. Keep in mind that Sami Innovations reinvests a lot of its money in advancing science, in the form of grants to medical research as well as its own research, and I felt that the greedy Mr. Stern was stealing from the future of medical research."

"In addition to stealing from you personally, let's not forget," Leila added. "Yes, from me, too."

"So, what did you come up with, then?" Andy asked, though he already knew the answer based on their prior research into the super-Lyzanda.

"First, I asked Bryan why he didn't also hold Mr. Stern responsible for Vanessa's death. After all, it was his company that charged the exorbitant price for such a vital and potentially life-saving drug," Bergeland continued.

"To be honest, I didn't think about that until Erik brought it up, but I agreed that the only reason Empire Health didn't pay for the Lyzanda was because it was so expensive," Bryan stated.

"So, right or wrong, you blamed both Empire Health's CEO, Mr. Millbank, and Terrapharma's CEO, Mr. Stern for your sister's death. Is that what you're saying?" Andy asked.

"Yes, and I am right to blame those two greedy men specifically. In my view, they killed Vanessa," Bryan retorted.

"So, you decided to kill them?" Leila asked. "No, I, uh …" Bryan hesitated.

"Bryan couldn't possibly know the outcome of what we decided to do—neither did I, for that matter," Bergeland interjected.

"Well, get on with it, then. What did you decide to do?" Andy demanded.

"It was my idea," Bergeland continued. "I told Bryan that we should hurt them with the same drug they'd denied Vanessa. It would be— what's the expression?—poetic justice."

"So, you came up with a powerful version of Lyzanda, just as you had done for other drugs," Leila said, jumping into the conversation. She was becoming annoyed at the deliberate pace of the unfolding story.

"Yes, you see, we know all about that on account of the fact that Bryan nearly killed his remaining living sister with it—presumably by mistake," Andy added.

"I figured you'd find out about that," Bryan said ruefully. "I can assure you I did not intend for Diana to take the Lyzanda that Bergeland had prepared for me. I was horrified and scared. I know you both helped her, and I can't thank you enough for that, but I assure you it was a mistake. I still honestly don't know exactly how that happened."

"So, Leila, why are you stringing us along if you already know about my special version of Lyzanda?" Bergeland asked, annoyed.

"We'd like to hear how you concocted this crazy plan—that's why!" Leila replied emphatically.

"Poetic justice," Bergeland replied.

During this discussion, Taylor and Angelina had been listening quietly. They knew their part would come soon. Taylor was fidgeting in her seat—she was nervous. She couldn't help but feel that Leila, one of the few people she'd ever trusted with her horrible secret and someone she'd quickly grown to admire, would be disappointed in her actions. In fact, she was neither anxious nor concerned about what judicial consequences might befall her when she returned to the United States, and she felt no guilt about her contribution to the murder of her father. Angelina, on the other hand, sat confidently in her chair and was following the conversation intently. She was looking forward to revealing her role in the complicated scheme.

"Well, go on. then. We still only have a small part of the story so far, Erik," Andy said.

"Very well. After further discussions with Bryan, I agreed to develop a small stockpile of potent Lyzanda. It took my chemists a few weeks to come up with some prototypes, which we then tested in animals to gauge the effect. Based on that research, which we conducted over several weeks, I offered Bryan two options. I had one version that I was sure would be potent enough to kill a human within minutes—again, that was based on the animal research—and one version that I was confident would cause significant bleeding but I was not sure if it would actually kill a man. Bryan, the good man that he is, chose the less potent version."

"I guess it doesn't matter now, but I never intended for either man to die. I just wanted them to suffer," Bryan stated.

"So, the two of you decided to somehow get Mr. Millbank and Mr. Stern to ingest these, well—poisons, shall we say, in order to what, make them suffer, with no intent to kill them. Is that what you're saying?" Leila inquired.

"Yes," Bryan said succinctly. "Agreed," Bergeland added.

"But you had no plan for how you were actually going to poison them, right?

Leila continued her interrogation.

"Correct," Bergeland said. "That's where the two lovely young ladies come into the story."

"Can I ask first, did either one of you know Angelina or Taylor at this point?" Leila went on.

"No," Bergeland said, laughing. "As smart as we thought we were, we were suddenly faced with the notion that while we planned to make the two men ingest the medication, we actually had no way of getting close enough to either one of them to actually pull this off."

"I remember speaking to Erik on the phone and basically giving up on the idea. I told him that I had tried to simply meet Mr. Millbank, to speak to him, and I could never even get close enough to shout at him. How would I ever get close enough to drop a medication in his drink or food?" Bryan added.

"I told Bryan that he needed to find someone who could get close to Millbank—someone he could fully trust," Bergeland stated.

"And Mr. Stern, as well. You didn't think you could find one person who could poison both, considering they lived in two different countries," Andy said.

"To be honest, the thought of finding one person who could get close enough to both men actually did cross our minds. We wanted to keep this secret to the fewest people possible, of course. You never know who might turn on you," Bergeland added.

"I know you'll find this absurd, but we actually thought about hiring a high-class prostitute to deliver the medication," Bryan said.

"So, how did you find Angelina and Taylor?" Andy asked.

Bergeland held his index finger up and then motioned for the waiters to come in with the main course. He was careful to ensure that their discussions were held out of earshot of any of the restaurant staff. The waiters at Bergeland's command came into the room, refilled everyone's wine, and set down plates with slices of brown meat with red centers at one side and a small piece of very dark, almost black, meat on the other side of each plate. An orange puree over a white puree sat in the center of each plate, with a sprig of rosemary jutting out as if it were growing from the side dish. The waiters poured some water for each of the guests and then departed. Bergeland gave them further instructions in Norsk.

He announced to his table guests, "So, in front of you, you have sliced reindeer filet—the most tender cut of meat from our main source of protein. In addition, and I suggest you really enjoy it, because this is a rare treat, we have a piece of whale meat—"

"Whale!" Leila exclaimed in protest.

"Now, now, please understand that it is legal for Norway to harvest several whales per year, according to the international treaty, since whales are used for subsistence by the native Sami," Bergeland explained.

"That's for the Sami, though, and not for us," Leila said.

"I am Sami, and you are my guests, so please relax and enjoy. It is a unique opportunity, so I suggest you give it a try. In the center of your plate you have a turnip puree on the bottom and a carrot puree sitting above it. Bon appétit."

Andy, never shy to try something new, cut a small piece of the whale meat, inspected it carefully, and slowly placed it in his mouth. He let it sit in his mouth momentarily and then chewed it, nodding his head at Leila to indicate that it was good and that she should try it. Leila shook her head in disappointment at Andy, then smiled, and cut a piece of her whale meat. She held the fork in front of her face briefly, and then placed it in her mouth, keeping her fork inside her mouth as if she might at any moment withdraw it with the fork still attached. She chewed the dense meat, swallowed, and thought for a minute. Then she impaled the piece left on her plate, picked it up, and put it on Andy's plate. One bite was enough for her.

"Well, Erik, let's get on with the story—or should I ask Angelina or Taylor to chime in? They haven't said a thing yet," Leila said.

"Actually, it's Bryan who should inform you of how he found them," Bergeland replied.

Bryan sipped more wine. By Leila's calculation, he had already downed three glasses. Perhaps, she thought, it would loosen his tongue even more than he had already done himself. *In vino veritas*, indeed.

"At Erik's suggestion, I flew to Switzerland and made my way to Basel. I decided I would follow in Mr. Stern's footsteps daily and hoped I would be able to figure out how to get close enough to get the medication into him myself. I followed him for a week, watching his every move. It turns out he went to the same pub after work each day and had a beer with another man, a friend, I figured. I inquired about getting a job at the pub, thinking I could easily slip the medication into his drink."

"Bryan called me to make sure that alcohol wouldn't inactivate the drug. I actually didn't know, but I had one of my scientists run a virtual experiment—a computer simulation—and found out that alcohol might even enhance the effect," Bergeland added.

"So, you didn't get a job, obviously," Andy said.

"No, Switzerland's labor laws are quite strict, and upon my inquiry, the pub manager asked for my Swiss passport. When I told him I was American, he just laughed and gave me a pint on the house."

"So, how did you find Angelina?"

"I kept going to the pub and began to notice that Angelina was there every day also—alone. I decided to strike up a conversation," Bryan continued. "I think it's time for Angelina to tell you her side."

"Very well," she began in accented English, "but first I need some information from our physician investigators."

"Uh, what do you want to know from us?" Andy said.

"Well, I know that you spoke to my friend and colleague, Jennifer Carmichael. She told me you were investigating the 'bleeders' case, as you call it, and that you have been to Switzerland—to Basel. So, before I just tell you," Angelina paused to think of the right word, *"everything,* I need to know what you know."

Andy glanced at Leila, and she nodded affirmatively and began.

"Angelina, we know a lot. About you. About Mr. Stern. Detective de Ville shared what he knew with us, including some cryptic e-mails. Before I tell you—and I am happy to tell you—I just need to know if I can be completely open in front of everyone here."

"Yes, you can," Angelina said.

The women made eye contact and had an immediate understanding.

"Andy and I spent quite a bit of time in Switzerland, and not only in Basel. We've been to Gstaad and to Lugano," Leila said, pausing and locking eyes with Angelina.

"Go on," Angelina encouraged her.

"We found out about a woman named Karina Hummels and that she and Stern met at a pharmaceutical conference in Gstaad. And, well, we have no proof, but I am quite certain that he raped her." Again Leila paused.

Angelina, sensing her hesitation, urged her to continue.

"We then went to Lugano and met a wonderful man named Massimo D'Antoni. He was a big help. In short, we found out that in 1999 you were a student at the University of Lugano, and Mr. Stern gave a lecture there, and ..." Leila continued to hesitate, as she was about to broach the subject of the rape.

"You can just say it, it's okay," Angelina said as she looked intensely at Leila. "He raped you," Leila finally got to the point.

"Yes, he raped me ... several times that night. You see, what you don't know is that he drugged me with a rag over my face and then tied me to the bed with fishing wire. I still have the scars on my wrists and ankles, as I tried to escape," Angelina completed the story.

"Oh my God! I am so sorry, Angelina—I had no idea," Leila said as tears formed in her eyes.

"That's not all. He had to gag my mouth so no one would hear my screams. He penetrated me vaginally a few times and, as that apparently was not enough, he raped me anally, too, the sick bastard."

Leila glanced at Bergeland and Bryan, who sat quietly, pensively. She then looked over at Taylor, who was seated directly across from her, and noted the rivulets of tears cascading down her face.

"Of course you didn't know—you couldn't know." Angelina went on, "I could never bring myself to tell anyone—not the police, not the university administration, and not my family. Definitely not my family. My father would have hunted Stern down and killed him with his bare hands. So, I kept the whole incident to myself."

"Until you met Karina Hummels," Andy said.

"Yes. While I learned to live with this horrific part of my life, when I learned that he had done the same thing—fishing wire and multiple rapes—to another woman, I could no longer remain silent. I knew I had to do something. I just didn't know what. I thought about it for months. Then Bryan sat beside me at the pub," Angelina said, raising her eyebrows, tilting her head slightly, and stretching her mouth into a closed-lips smile.

"What a ... *ahem* ... wonderful coincidence for you both," Andy said.

"Well, not a complete coincidence, Dr. Friedman," Bryan stated. "After all, we were both tracking Mr. Stern."

"I understand why you were doing it, Bryan, but Angelina, why were you following Stern—did you actually have a plan to do something to him?" Leila asked.

"No, no plan, but I knew I had to do something. When I thought about what Stern had done to me in 1999 and to Karina more than ten years later, I wondered how many more women he might have raped in the years in between. Part of my reason for following him was to see if he was still hunting women."

"So, I would say Bryan meeting Angelina was fortuitous but not a coincidence," Bergeland chimed in.

"Okay; then what happened?" Leila asked. "Bryan would you like to—" Angelina started. "No, please, you go ahead."

"Well, of course, we started with some getting-to-know-you talk, and after a while, I asked Bryan what he was doing in Basel. So, first he said it's for work, but then when I told him there were no oil nor oil companies based in Switzerland, he said he was sightseeing. Then I knew he was lying, because no one comes to Basel for vacation."

"Angelina read right through that—I'm actually not a good liar, which would, of course, make me a terrible criminal," Bryan said.

"Are you sure you're not a criminal?" Andy asked.

"I suppose that is for you or the criminal-justice system to decide—but why don't you wait for us to tell you the entire story?" Bryan suggested.

"Well, then I asked Bryan what he was really doing in Basel, and I told him that if he lies one more time, I will get up and leave," Angelina continued.

"Since I had a feeling that she could help me, I decided that I had better be honest, and so I was."

"Bryan told me the horrible story about his sister that you, of course, all know, but I resisted telling him my story—after all, it is very personal and very painful. So I asked him what he had in mind," Angelina said.

"Well, I didn't know if I could trust her—I was about to tell her that I was planning on trying to hurt someone—but I really had no option, so I told her about Bergeland, though I didn't use his real name, and I told her about the plan to poison Stern."

"At first I thought Bryan was crazy, and I wasn't sure whether to believe him or not, but he showed me the pills and even pulled up some of Bergeland's data on his computer. I was rather shocked to hear this—and while I hated Stern with every ounce of my being, I wasn't sure I was ready to participate in hurting him."

"Angelina, can I ask if you thought the Lyzanda could kill Stern?" Leila said. "I didn't know, of course, but I also didn't know how they could be sure he *wouldn't* die. So I told Bryan I would think about it and asked him to meet me the next day at a different pub."

Angelina went on to describe the events of the following days. First, she'd told Bryan that she needed to speak to Bergeland—after all, she was a physician and although pathologists didn't prescribe medication, they did know the effects of drugs on the body. In the discussions with Bergeland, she'd learned about the varying potencies of the Lyzanda he'd made. She'd then asked Bryan why he had chosen the less-potent version. While she accepted his explanation, she'd had another idea. She requested a meeting with Bergeland.

"I agreed to come to Basel and discuss the plan with Angelina—" Bergeland began.

"We knew you had come to Basel, and we always thought it was suspicious, but I guess now we now know why," Andy said. "So, what was this meeting about?"

"Well, it's quite interesting, actually. Angelina, please," Bergeland said.

"I wondered why Bryan chose the less-potent version of the Lyzanda—I mean if he wanted to cause Mr. Stern harm—I just didn't get it," Angelina explained.

"So, what did you all decide?" Leila asked.

"Ha," Bryan laughed, "*us* decide? Angelina made it plain and clear."

"I told them that I would find a way to get close enough to Stern to poison him but only if it was with a lethal dose of Lyzanda. I mean, why go through all the trouble and risk if the goal wasn't to kill him? Do you not think he deserved to die, the serial violent rapist that he was?" Angelina stated without a hint of hesitation.

"Angelina, please don't take this the wrong way, and certainly one rape is horrible enough, but when you say serial rapist, you only know of two, is that right?" Leila asked.

"At the time, yes," Angelina answered.

"I'm confused. What do you mean, 'at the time'?" Leila followed up her previous question with another.

"Let me proceed with the story, and you'll see, okay?"

"Sure, go on."

"I got Bergeland and Bryan to agree on providing me with the most potent form of Lyzanda Sami Innovations made—"

"A dose I was sure would be lethal, based on our animal studies," Bergeland interjected.

"One day at the pub, I went up and sat next to Stern and his friend. I wasn't sure whether Stern would remember me—twelve years had passed, and my hair was a different length and color, and well, he wasn't exactly focused on my face when he raped me. In any case, he didn't recognize me. I decided to chat him up and see how far that would get me. Since I was paying Stern all the attention and filling his head with flattering remarks, his friend took the hint and left."

Angelina explained that in the first conversation she had just become friendly with Stern, earning his trust so she could get close to him. After a few weeks, she got herself invited to Stern's office in Terrapharma by saying that she was very interested in pharmacology as a pathologist. Of course, Stern couldn't resist. After a few visits to the office, Angelina became friendly with Stern's secretary, eventually earning her trust as well. Then, one day, she went to Stern's office when she knew he was away; however, playing dumb, she was able to get into his office. She was able to distract his secretary by sending her on a meaningless errand.

"So, I found myself in his office by myself, and I began searching through his papers, not knowing what I was looking for nor what I might find. It just felt right to try to learn more about this sick, misogynistic man. To make a long story short, I found a safe behind a panel in the wall by pressing a button I found under his desk. After some searching, I found a key and opened it." Angelina paused.

"What was in there?" Andy asked.

"A small spiral notebook with a slim pen tucked in the spirals, and a small wooden box. I opened the box first ..." Angelina hesitated momentarily, "and I found a spool of fishing wire held together by tape. I examined it—remember, I am a pathologist—and I could see a brownish coating. I am sure it was blood. Perhaps even mine."

"Oh my God!" Leila cried out. "And the notebook—what was in the notebook?"

"Each page had a date on the top, and then three lines of text: a place, a name, and a number," Angelina continued. "At first I couldn't figure it out, since I didn't recognize the names—just dates going back to 1992 and cities all over Europe, many in Switzerland. Then I got to 1999. I found Lugano, Angelina Costa, and the number 9."

"Oh Angelina, I ... I ..." Leila again agonized.

"What was the number 9 for—did you figure that out?" Andy asked. Angelina was amazingly composed. "Oh, I am quite sure I figured that out, too," she said with a hint of sarcasm. "It was his, well, rating, shall we say—you know—of the girl or the experience."

"Rating?" Leila asked.

"Yes, you see, all the numbers were between 0 and 10. There were a lot of 4s, 5s, and 6s and only one 10. In between, there were a handful of 9s and 8s. So, in some bizarre sense, I should be rather proud of myself, don't you think?" she said, making no effort to hide her sarcasm.

"I'm afraid to ask, but I just have to know, Angelina—how many names did you find?"

"Fifty-seven."

The room was silent, save for soft whimpers coming from Taylor Davis. Leila wondered how they would ever get through her story, which was as horrific as Angelina's—perhaps worse, considering that she had been a child and had been victimized by her own father.

Angelina described the ensuing events more succinctly. Bryan had left for New York and promised to stay in close contact. Several weeks later, in mid-November, he'd phoned Angelina and asked her if she could poison Stern on a specific date. At first, Angelina couldn't understand why Bryan was insisting on a specific date. He then explained that he was planning the same fate for Mr. Millbank, and he wanted them to suffer the same fate on the same day. And thus a date was set.

It was now time to hear Taylor's story. The emotional toll of Angelina's story had weighed on the group, and they decided to take a break. Bergeland shouted instructions in Norsk, and within minutes dessert was served.

"What you have before you, my friends, is a true Norwegian delicacy called *multekrem*—it is composed of whipped cream, sugar, and the most ephemeral of all berries, the cloudberry. These berries are only found in high-latitude regions, mostly in Scandinavia, and only grow in the wild. Just don't ask me how I have some for you in the middle of winter. Enjoy!" Bergeland exclaimed.

CHAPTER 37

Late afternoon had settled over New York. A spectacular winter sunset was unfolding over the western sky, a bright-orange background punctuated by lines of thin gray clouds. Detectives Alvarez and O'Reilly had been summoned to police headquarters for an abruptly arranged meeting with the commissioner and, this time, the mayor himself. They desperately needed an update from Andy and Leila. Alvarez glanced at his watch and noted that it was 5:30 p.m., meaning it was 11:30 p.m. in Norway. O'Reilly insisted he call Andy.

"I don't care if he's sleeping. We need an update, and we need it now."

Reluctantly, Alvarez dialed Andy's mobile phone and was pleased to discover that Andy was awake. Andy told Alvarez that they were having dinner with Bergeland, Bryan, Angelina, and Taylor, to which Alvarez responded with frustration and anger. "How can you have dinner with these killers?" he demanded.

Andy explained that the dinner was, in fact, a tell-all discussion in which each of the players was recounting his or her role in the deaths of the bleeders. Alvarez stated that he and O'Reilly had been summoned by no less than the mayor of New York to provide an update, so he needed as much information as possible. At first Andy was reluctant to provide any details, as they had yet to hear the entire story, but at Alvarez's plea, he told him about the portion involving Bryan and Bergeland. He refrained from revealing Angelina's horror story—he felt he would be violating her privacy and that it was not his place to discuss it. After all, Angelina was not involved in the death of Mr. Millbank, which was the only death the New York detectives were really interested in. Alvarez thanked him and requested an update the next day.

Minutes later, Detectives Alvarez and O'Reilly were in front of the commissioner and the mayor. O'Reilly being the senior detective took on the role of spokesperson, and relayed to them the bad news that Taylor Davis was out of the country and the good news that Bryan had confessed to conspiring to kill Mr. Millbank. The mayor asked for details regarding the murder of Mr. Millbank, and he was intensely irritated when Alvarez told him that they hadn't yet figured that part out, but he also stated that Andy and Leila were getting closer and closer to that answer. The mayor left, and the commissioner told the detectives that they had one more day before he called the FBI for help. O'Reilly hated working with the Feds—they were condescending as all hell, and bringing them in was a validation of his and Alvarez's failure. He knew, though, that this was not an idle threat. They would need the answers by tomorrow. O'Reilly had Alvarez called Andy to relay that message.

After dessert and after-dinner drinks consisting of very expensive Canadian ice wine from the Inniskillin winery, Bergeland thanked his guests for a most enjoyable dinner. He was jubilant, in a rather bizarre way, considering how much suffering had been discussed throughout the evening by three people he claimed were his friends. While Leila had found his triumphant attitude disgusting earlier in the evening, she had significantly softened her stance after hearing Angelina's story. As it was now past midnight, Bergeland suggested they continue their conversation in the morning. Andy quickly calculated the time difference and, considering Alvarez's request, agreed—but only if they could start early. Bergeland informed them that "early" in Tromsø, in the winter, was not before 10:00 a.m. Andy said that would be too late and insisted they start at 8:00 a.m. In the end, they agreed to meet at 9:00 a.m. Bergeland suggested meeting at his office in order to provide the privacy the group needed, but Leila objected, recalling the wholly unpleasant experience during her first visit there. Bergeland made a phone call and spoke briefly in Norsk. He then told them to meet at the Arctic Cathedral, situated just across the bridge, on the other side of the fjord. He said they would have privacy there. And with not another word, the group dispersed. The lobby was empty at this point. Bergeland left, while the others all headed for the elevator. Taylor got off on the second floor, Angelina on the third floor, and Leila on the fourth floor, leaving Bryan and Andy alone in the elevator. Bryan looked quizzically at Andy and asked why he was getting off on a different floor from Leila.

"None of your business," Andy said and marched quickly out of the elevator and down the hall.

Andy met Leila in the lobby at 8:00 for a quick breakfast before heading toward the cathedral.

"I'm getting sick of smoked and pickled fish and cheese, you know. I miss my mom's cooking," Leila said.

Andy, for his part, was perfectly happy to eat pickled herring and smoked salmon every morning. After breakfast, they agreed to walk to the cathedral. It was about a twenty-minute walk, and they decided to use this opportunity to get some exercise. It was pitch black, save for the streetlights, and although the sun would eventually make a cameo appearance later in the day, it wouldn't do so until nearly noon and then only for about an hour. They walked briskly, both to stay warm and to make the walk feel more like real exercise. As they reached the crest of the bridge, the Arctic Cathedral's triangular shape was immediately visible, as it was front-lit by numerous lights. Its pure-white color made it stand out so unbelievably brilliantly against the black background that it looked like a mirage. They arrived precisely on time, and as they walked in, they were escorted by a young boy to the back of the building and then to a room behind the altar, where they found the quartet seated in the same arrangement as they had been the previous evening. Andy and Leila took their assigned seats.

Bergeland started. "Shall we begin then, since our doctors seem to be in a bit of a hurry?"

It was clear to Leila, given the half-empty coffee cups, that the quartet had been there for some time prior to their arrival. Clearly they had met to review their strategy for revealing the next phase of the story—the death of Mr. Millbank.

"I'll begin," Bryan said. "So, I had found someone to help me poison Mr. Stern, and now I needed to find someone to do the same for Mr. Millbank, since I couldn't get close to him myself, despite numerous prior attempts to just meet him. I elected to take the same strategy I had taken in Basel—follow Millbank around until I found someone who might be able to get close to him. Unfortunately, it was not so easy. Unlike Mr. Stern, Millbank did not have a regular happy-hour meeting with any friends. I got really frustrated, but I was driven, so I kept going, until one day, a breakthrough."

"You met Taylor," Andy said.

"No, actually. Mr. Millbank started spending time with a very attractive woman. I didn't know who she was, and it took several of these encounters before I found her alone at the bar after the rendezvous. I didn't want to approach her before Millbank left, for fear he would then recognize me."

"Who was she?" Andy asked.

"She told me her name was Alexa, though I suspected it was an alias."

"Jennifer Carmichael!" Leila said.

"Eventually I would find out her real name, but never from her. As I was growing impatient, I quickly dove into a discussion regarding Millbank and her relationship with him. Unlike with Angelina, I didn't trust Alexa, but as I had no other leads, I decided to make up a story about investments I had in the insurance industry without even saying anything about health insurance. I purposely kept it very vague. Then, well, I just said I was very upset with the man she was with, and I asked her if she would help me."

"Weren't you afraid, she would tell Millbank?" Andy said.

"Yes, but I had an idea. If she agreed to help, I would turn the story from insurance to health insurance and tie it together that way, and if not, I would misidentify Millbank," Bryan said.

"*Misidentify?* I don't understand," Andy said.

"So, here's what happened. She vehemently disagreed, said I was crazy and that she was going to call Millbank and tell him immediately. I then realized I needed to put plan B into place."

"And what was plan B?" Leila asked.

"I got extremely upset, raising my voice and telling her how the man she was with—I called him Arthur Goldsmith—had lost my family fortune that I'd invested with him, because he'd told me he would double my money in less than a year."

"So you never told her about Vanessa?" Andy asked.

"No, I told you I didn't trust her, so I needed a way out in case she didn't agree," Bryan said.

"And did you get any reassurance that she wouldn't say something to Millbank?" Leila asked.

"Yes. She called me a 'fucking loser idiot'—fucking idiot wasn't enough, apparently—and said that I had the wrong man," Bryan said. "She then got up and walked away."

"How can you be sure she didn't say anything to Millbank?" Andy asked. "I can't be certain, but if she told him, why would he even believe it?"

"Well, it's a moot point now, anyway," Leila offered.

"Quite brilliant, don't you think?" Bergeland said with such pride he could have been Bryan's father.

"That's interesting, actually, because Dr. Carmichael was a prime suspect for a while," Leila said. "So, Bryan, you were back to square one. What did you do next?"

"Yes, square one. Nevertheless, I was persistent. I hadn't come this far in the plan to not poison the man I held responsible for Vanessa's death. Then, one day, I followed Millbank to the Café de Bon Salud. It wasn't easy, as he took his car service and I had to quickly catch a taxi to follow him. Thank God New York is the easiest place on earth to find a taxi quickly, and I managed. I followed him into the café carefully—it was cold, so I was very well covered, with a scarf across my face. I had no idea what he was doing there, but it became apparent when I walked in and saw Alexa seated at a table with another younger woman."

"Taylor," Andy said.

"Well, yes—but how are you so sure?" Bryan asked.

"Bryan, we've been investigating this crime for quite some time, and we made a lot of headway, as we told you," Andy followed up.

"I understand, but I am curious to know how you came about this information. Millbank's visit to the café was totally spontaneous … unless … Were you following him, too?"

"Not us, but a private investigator who was working for Mrs. Millbank. He took many—and I mean many—pictures, including quite a few of the encounter at the café," Andy confessed.

Leila added, "We also know you were there—that's, in fact, what led us to track you down. It was the final piece of evidence that confirmed to us that you were involved in the murders."

"How did you know that?"

"The photographer shot a series of pictures of Taylor leaving the café, and in one of them, we saw you. Imagine how surprised we were to see you in the same café as Mr. Millbank and one of our prime suspects at the time, Jennifer Carmichael," Andy said.

"The one thing we didn't understand, though, was Taylor's reaction. We put together why Jennifer reacted the way she did when Millbank showed up, but how Taylor even recognized Millbank remained a mystery," Leila stated.

"Until you lured me to reveal my darkest secret to you," Taylor said. These were the first words Andy and Leila had heard her say in Norway.

"You know, Leila, if I didn't look up to you the way I do, I would never have even agreed to be in your presence right now. I still can't believe that I opened up to you and told you what my father had done to me. After all, it was the first time I ever spent any time with you."

"Taylor, I ..." Leila couldn't think of what to say.

"It's fine. I'm here, aren't I?" she said in a resigned tone. "That should tell you something. I don't regret opening up to you. It was the first time in my life I'd told anyone, and it was actually very therapeutic. So, even though I had no idea that you had me under investigation and that you were taking advantage of my trust in you, I still benefited from that discussion."

"If it's any consolation, I am really glad you left New York to come here, because if you were still there, you'd have been arrested by now," Leila said with a half-smile.

"Are you saying you're happy I got away with killing my father? Because that wasn't your feeling last night," Taylor pressed.

"Yes, I am happy you are here, but you haven't gotten away with anything yet. I can assure you that if Detective Alvarez and O'Reilly have their way, you will be arrested," Leila said.

"I still want to hear the end of this crazy story," Andy said.

Bryan took over again, leading the next phase of the tale. He described how he had followed Taylor out of the café and when he'd caught up to her, she'd been clearly distraught, crying uncontrollably. He'd eventually been able to calm her down, at which point she'd asked him if he would walk her home. When they got to Taylor's apartment, she'd asked him to come up with her. He'd hesitated, realizing he had just met her and not being sure what she had in mind. Taylor insisted, and Bryan relented. After a brief introduction, Taylor had made up a story about why she'd been crying. She hadn't been about to tell Bryan her life story, yet she was comforted by his presence.

"It was weird, I'll tell you. I thought she was mentally ill and decided I would keep my eye on her," Bryan said.

"I was going to tell him, you know, about my dad and all that he had done to me, but I just couldn't do it. I decided to change the story a bit," Taylor said. "I told Bryan that the man was my estranged father and that he had abused my mom and I hated him for it. The part I revealed that *was* true was that I hadn't seen my father in years, and it was quite a shock to see him."

"As you might imagine, that was my opening. I decided to tell Taylor about Vanessa—in fact, I trusted her enough at that point to tell her about Bergeland and my plan to kill Millbank. I also told her that another man was going to be poisoned in Switzerland, but I didn't tell her about Angelina. I didn't feel it was my place," Bryan said.

"So, then what?" Leila asked.

"Taylor immediately lit up and said she wanted to help," Bryan said.

"The hatred I had for my father was such that despite trying to live my life in a highly moral and ethical manner, it was a no-brainer," Taylor added. "I was still suffering from nightmares and attachment issues—I've never had a boyfriend—and I felt that killing him would cure all that."

"Has it?" Leila asked.

"Leila, that wouldn't justify what—" Andy said.

"I didn't ask you, Andy, and I don't give a shit what you think. You can't possibly put yourself in Taylor's shoes. Taylor, I am just curious. Has killing your father helped you … honestly? It's okay if the answer is no."

"It's helped a lot. I swear to you. I stopped having nightmares about my abuse—it's like I closed a chapter of my life and I am starting, well, not only a new chapter but a new book."

A silence followed. Bryan put his hand on Taylor's shoulder in a comforting and reassuring gesture. Andy looked down, not knowing what to think. Leila looked over at Taylor and gave her a half-smile.

"Shall I continue?" Bryan asked. "Please do," Bergeland said.

"I selected the date, communicated it to Angelina, and asked Taylor if that would work for her. They both agreed."

"One thing I don't get, though, is how Taylor would meet Millbank, and how you could be so sure she could poison him on a specific date," Leila asked.

"Ah, well, there is one more accomplice, though her part was small, and she didn't really know what was going to happen—so please don't plan on arresting her," Bryan continued.

"Carmichael?" Andy queried.

"No, Andy. Mrs. Millbank, right?" Leila stated. "Very good, Leila," Bergeland announced.

"Mrs. Millbank? But, why would she—" Andy began.

"Dr. Friedman, she didn't know what we were planning, though even if she did, it wouldn't surprise me if she still would have helped," Taylor said. "I swear that Mrs. Millbank had no idea that we were going to poison her husband. For one thing, we didn't know her at all and couldn't really trust her, and for another, we didn't want to her to be part of the plot, not knowingly."

"So, what did she do for you?" Leila asked.

"I'm not sure what you know, but basically, she was aware of who I was—I mean, she knew her husband had an estranged daughter. So I called her out of the blue and told her I wanted to surprise him. I even used the word *dad*, so she wouldn't suspect anything—I otherwise would never call that bastard my dad," Taylor explained. "So, she agreed to tell me where they were going to have dinner on November 21."

"And that was all we needed to know," Bryan said. "We showed up to dinner and sat at table not far away, yet not visible from the table where Mr. and Mrs. Millbank were eating," Bryan said.

"Then, at an opportune moment, with the two pills in hand," Taylor continued, "I went over to my father's table and shocked the hell out of him. He was so taken aback, he got up after a minute to go to the bathroom to gather himself. I figured he would do something like that. Mrs. Millbank got up and followed him, unsure of why her self-confident husband would react that way—after all, she didn't know he'd molested me. Why would he ever tell her that? And that's when I dumped the pills into his wine."

"How did you know he would drink all of it?" Andy asked.

"That's where the pill potency comes in, Andy," Bergeland said. "One pill would most likely be lethal and two doubly so. So we didn't need Mr. Milbank to finish the wine."

"As it happened, he did finish it after he sat back down," Taylor said.

"Uh, what did you tell him, and how did you keep your composure, knowing you were probably poisoning him to death?" Leila asked.

"Obviously, we had planned for this evening, and I knew I needed to do it for myself and, well, for Bryan too, after he'd told me about his sister. My father was both a child molester—bad enough—and a ruthless businessman who took others' lives for granted."

"Ask yourself this question, Dr. Friedman, Dr. Baker," Bryan continued. "How many other people do you think died as a result of Millbank putting profits ahead of human lives? Dozens? Hundreds? Thousands? You know that his company insured millions of people, and their policy was to deny as many expensive services as they could. Think about it."

"What about Stern?"

"I can simply say," Angelina stated, "that I had no difficulties placing the Lyzanda in Mr. Stern's drink. I agreed to have dinner with him at one of Basel's finest restaurants, and I had to force myself to eat because I was so nauseated sitting with this disgusting person. He got up to use the restroom, and I dropped the crushed pills into his wine. It was very expensive wine, so I knew he would finish it, and he did."

"And how did you, uh ... get rid of him at the end of the night? I am sure he had some expectations," Leila asked.

"I started throwing up—and not in the bathroom, but right at the table. I figured that would work, and it did. I told him I was sick, and I left."

"Can I ask how you got yourself to throw up?" Andy asked.

"I just looked at him, my rapist, in the face, and it just came naturally," Angelina said with a wry smile.

Leila puffed her cheeks and took a deep breath. Thinking about Bryan's loss and Angelina and Taylor's sad and dreadful accounts was truly quite exhausting. Andy just sat at the table silently, not knowing what to say. The silence, which lasted for nearly two minutes, spoke volumes. During that time, Leila kept glancing at Bryan and then Angelina and then Taylor, her eyes communicating the deep sense of sorrow she felt for all of them.

Then she glanced at Bergeland, but she didn't know what to think. Was he a co-conspirator, aiding and abetting three emotionally fragile people into committing murder? Two murders. Or was he merely playing the part of the caring uncle who could offer his counterparts an opportunity to oblige their darkest wishes? As she observed Bergeland, his face beamed like that of a proud parent, and while on the one hand it gave her pause, she also sensed that he truly had grown to care about these three afflicted souls to whom life had dealt severe and unfair atrocities. Leila also realized that Bergeland had merely provided the ammunition and had never appeared to coax any of them into using it. It had been Bryan, after all, who had orchestrated the events leading up to the murders, and Angelina and Taylor who had pulled the trigger.

"So, yes, Leila and Andy, it is true that my colleagues and I did conspire to and succeed in killing two men," Bergeland stated proudly. "But what kind of men were they? One was a serial rapist who brutalized more than fifty women, doubtless causing degrees of emotional pain and distress that cannot even be measured, and whose drug company priced life-saving drugs out of the reach of millions of people. The other was a child molester of the worst kind, if there could even be degrees of child molesters—one who preyed on his own flesh and blood and not once or twice but for years. He, too, put his company's profits ahead of the lives of yet more millions. And so seated before you are a victim of horrific child abuse, a victim of a dastardly and cowardly rape, and a devoted and loving brother whose sister, as you know well, died needlessly. I am quite curious to hear your thoughts."

Andy called Alvarez and O'Reilly, as he'd promised. They spoke briefly—Andy provided a general overview of what had transpired throughout the long and detailed discussion in Tromsø and promised a full report when he and Leila returned to New York. Andy was sure to deliver the gist of the discussion solely with facts and without passing any judgment. Both Alvarez and O'Reilly insisted that Bryan and Taylor fly back to New York and turn themselves in to the police. Alvarez assured him that he would find them outstanding lawyers and that the justice system would consider all of the mitigating circumstances.

Andy told the detectives that he would pass the message along, but that he, of course, had no authority over them and could not force them to return—not in Norway and not anywhere. And with that the call ended.

Bergeland suggested they take the cable car up to Storsteinen and have lunch at the restaurant at the top of the magnificent hill. He told them they would be able to see the sunrise from the restaurant while enjoying lunch.

"How many places on earth can you have lunch and watch the sun rise?" he said. "It's relatively clear except for a few high clouds, so I expect a quite spectacularly colorful sunrise. Shall we?"

The tense, icy atmosphere melted into the fjord below them. The silence turned to smiles and the discussion to how they were all coping with Nordic cuisine. It was clear no one wanted another Norwegian feast. Bergeland told them that the restaurant on Storsteinen only served hamburgers, hot dogs, and French fries. When Leila challenged him, Bergeland smiled and said that he was telling the truth, but that for those who preferred something else, there would be smoked salmon sandwiches, as well. They all laughed and left the cathedral like longtime friends. Neither Andy nor Leila responded to Bergeland's earlier request for their 'thoughts.' Neither one had quite come to grips with all that had happened in the last two months, let alone the last two days, and neither one had yet processed it all. Their thoughts would remain their own—at least for some time.

Chapter 38

Andy and Leila spent several more days in Tromsø, catching up on much-needed sleep, debriefing each other, and decompressing from the horrific revelations they had heard from Angelina Costa and Taylor Davis. They spent their mornings sleeping; their afternoons conversing, in an attempt to make sense of the entire story; and their evenings negotiating with each other, and with their own hearts and minds, regarding the meaning of justice, both in general and, more specifically, for the quartet. What would constitute justice for the willful and planned killing of two men? What should ultimately be the fate for Bryan Vasquez, the mastermind and organizer, Jan Erik Bergeland, the provider of the impressively elegant weapon, and Angelina Costa and Taylor Davis, the stealthy and eager executioners?

Leila and Andy also discussed how they would present what they'd heard to Alvarez and O'Reilly when they returned to New York to complete the mission the two detectives had set before them two months ago. It was hard to believe all this had taken place in just two months—it seemed like much more than that. They reasoned that this was why it had taken them the additional days to review all the details and to discuss their feelings. Through their discussions, they came to the realization that it would take them more time to digest all the details and, most importantly, to explore their inner feelings, before they could pass judgment on the quartet. At one point Leila stated that it would likely take weeks, if not months, for her to come to a sense of closure regarding how she felt about Bergeland and Costa—and especially how she felt about Bryan and Taylor. She was most concerned about Taylor, with whom she'd formed a rather sudden, yet powerful, relationship.

In order to relieve some of the tension the discussions generated, they took time off each evening to visit Thor's Hammer, where they became fast friends with the bartenders and staff. The mass of people and the alcohol lightened the mood, and they engaged in many a conversation with the locals, discussing everything from living in such an unusual environment, where your relationship with the sun was, for much of the year, an all-or-nothing type of interaction, to the cuisine, to what people did for fun and excitement. The locals answered by stating that, like the rest of humanity, they adapted to their environment, spending their winters indoors in lit environments, working, playing sports in enclosed soccer fields and tennis courts and, of course, going to the pubs in the evenings. They spent their summers outdoors: hiking, biking, boating, and playing sports—and drinking at the pub's outdoor gardens. No doubt the Norwegians liked sports and liked drinking, the two activities that continued throughout the year regardless of how much or how little daylight the sun had to offer. Andy and Leila rarely ever saw an overweight person, and when they did, they figured it was a tourist.

It was at Thor's Hammer that they parted company with the quartet of conspirators. Bergeland would, of course, stay in Norway, this being his home, and would continue his work at Sami Innovations. He did not need to fear prosecution, as no crime had been committed in Norway, and it was very unlikely such a case would rise to the level of the International Criminal Court. He was proud—too proud, in Andy's opinion—to have taken part in such a complex and successful conspiracy, and he was proud of Bryan, Angelina, and Taylor as well, for having managed to concoct and complete the operation. He was like a general proud of his troops for securing a vital piece of land. Angelina was heading back to Switzerland—back to her job and her life there, without the slightest worry of being prosecuted for her part in the murder of Mr. Stern. She was either supremely confident she wouldn't be prosecuted, or she didn't care—regardless, she was not staying in Tromsø.

As for Bryan and Taylor, the situation was much more complicated. Andy and Leila informed them that the NYPD was adamant about arresting the perpetrators of Mr. Millbank's murder, despite the mitigating circumstances. As far as the mayor and commissioner were concerned, Taylor and Bryan had killed Mr. Millbank, and they must be arrested. They were satisfied to let the district attorney's office and the justice system decide their fate following their arrest. Bergeland informed Bryan and Taylor that extradition from Norway to the United States was quite complicated, with the major issue being the death penalty. Norway did not have the death penalty and, in general, would not extradite persons to countries that did. Since in the United States the death penalty was a state issue, and New York State did not have the death penalty, he wasn't completely sure how Norwegian authorities would handle this specific case. He had already contacted a well-versed lawyer in Oslo to provide counsel.

Andy and Leila parted company with the quartet on their last night in Tromsø. They'd requested a private conversation with Bryan and Taylor, which Bergeland not only obliged but, using his ever-present connections, was even able to find the four of them a quiet place for in the raucous pub. Following that final discussion, they bid their good-byes, not knowing if or when they would ever see each other again.

Back in a Tromsø taxi for the last time, Andy and Leila were returning to the airport for what would be their final journey of this investigation. Their early-morning flight in the dark Arctic sky left Tromsø airport at 7:30 a.m. and arrived at Gardermoen Airport shortly past 9:00 a.m. as dawn had finally crept its way to the far reaches of the northern hemisphere. From there, they flew nonstop to JFK, and two short train rides later, they were back in Manhattan. After all their discussions the previous days, they reserved the flight home solely for rest and entertainment. Andy watched the original Norwegian version of *Insomnia*, a murder mystery that, ironically, took place in northern Norway during the summer, in which an outsider detective who couldn't sleep, due to the incessant daylight, went a bit crazy. Leila needed a romantic comedy, and fortunately for her, the flight had a special on the career of Drew Barrymore. She watched *The Wedding Singer* and *50 First Dates*. It might as well have been an Adam Sandler retrospective.

Upon settling in to their hotel in Manhattan, they had a light dinner at the restaurant, and went to sleep early—the jetlag taking hold and forcing their eyes shut just as they hit the pillow in their respective rooms.

At 5:00 a.m., Andy was wide awake. *Why can't Bergeland invent a cure for jetlag?* he wondered. *Is the mind's biological clock so entrenched that a bit of chemistry couldn't tweak it in just the right direction?* He had tried Ambien and Melatonin, as his colleagues had recommended, but never found either one that helpful. He decided to head down to the hotel's pool and go for a swim. Upon arriving at the pool, through the glass partition between the pool and the gym he saw Leila exercising. He waved. She laughed. And on they went with their exercise.

They arrived at police headquarters downtown at 9:30 and were warmly greeted by the security agents, who recognized them and asked them where they had been. Leila chuckled and said, "Everywhere and nowhere." Then she and Andy were escorted by one of the young officers back to the conference room in which so many of the key revelations in the case had taken place. Detective Alvarez made sure that the familiar spread of bagels, donuts, and beverages was already present. Andy pointed out to Leila the bagels, lox, and cream cheese, to which she responded by poking a finger into her open mouth. She was sure she would need at least year to regain the taste for smoked fish! Andy, of course, dug in.

Leila and Andy had to wait an unusually long period of time, which made both of them a bit nervous. In the past, the detectives had always arrived within minutes of their being seated in the conference room. After forty minutes, Andy got up and headed to the door. The moment before he grabbed the doorknob, the door swung open, and four men and one woman entered the room. They motioned to Andy to have a seat next to Leila, which he quickly did, feeling a bit intimidated not only by the people who were present but by their body language, which spoke to the seriousness of what was about to happen. It reminded Andy of a war movie in which the top-ranking officers walked in with a tall, imposing posture, intent on imposing their will simply by their stature and stance. The introductions began.

"Dr. Friedman, Dr. Baker, thank you very much for coming in to speak with us today. We know you've had a long journey, and we appreciate that you are anxious to get back home to Los Angeles. My name is Commissioner Garret Williams, and I am in charge of the New York Police Department. I am not sure you recognize Mayor Gary Steinberg, but he has become so intrigued about the case that he wanted to meet you and be here in person to get the debrief. You of course know Detectives Alvarez and O'Reilly. On the mayor's left is Rosa Colon; she is the mayor's spokesperson and media liaison. I hope it's okay with you that we are all here together to be debriefed?"

"Yes, no problem," Andy replied quietly. He was surprised by the presence of the leader of one of the largest cities in the world.

Leila got up and shook each person's hand. Andy followed suit.

The mayor explained that the public in New York, as tough as they were known to be, were particularly sensitive about terrorism, given the events of 9/11 and other more recent attempts to cause mass deaths and mass hysteria. He told them that the media has gotten into a frenzy about some kind of bioterrorism as the cause of Mr. Millbank's death. He further stated that the nightly news shows simply wouldn't let that angle of the story go—though there was not an iota of truth to it— until they got an explanation. While he was concerned about finding, arresting, and prosecuting the culprits, his main focus and reason for attending this meeting was to get sufficient information to dispel the notion that what had happened to Mr. Millbank had anything to do with terrorism. Commissioner Williams, in an effort to ensure that Andy and Leila would be completely forthcoming, assured them that anything they reported regarding conversations they'd had with the alleged perpetrators that could not otherwise be proven could not be used in court. He did stress that any other evidence they'd uncovered, such as the pictures, could be used but reiterated that their conversations could not be used.

"So, please, we are asking you to report everything you know and how you came to acquire that information," the commissioner said, "as it will undoubtedly help the mayor and his staff—that's why his spokesperson is here—to relieve the public and the media regarding this being in any way related to bioterrorism. Okay?"

"Sure. We'll tell you what we know. We have nothing to hide, and anyway, we told Bryan and Taylor that we would be reporting back to the NYPD," Andy said.

The rest of the morning was spent painstakingly reviewing the entirety of Andy and Leila's investigation, with occasional help from the detectives in filling in certain gaps, such as O'Reilly's conversations with Mrs. Millbank and any information that they might have forgotten. The mayor and his spokesperson were repeatedly astonished, not only at the effectiveness of the two doctors' investigative skills but also at some of the information they were hearing. The mayor had not yet been briefed about the sexual abuse suffered by Taylor Davis, and while the murder of Mr. Stern was less of a concern for him, he was no less horrified at Angelina Costa's story of the serial rapist she'd helped kill. This was the first time that the detectives had heard this part of the story. After nearly three hours of discussion, the group took a break for lunch, after which the mayor was going to consult with Andy and Leila regarding how best to explain the poisoning of Mr. Millbank to the public.

Andy and Leila took one last walk around downtown New York, knowing that first thing the next day they would be headed back to Los

Angeles and their regular routine. They discussed how, in part, they were happy this adventure was coming to an end and how they missed being at work with their team, but they also lamented that nothing as exciting as what they had just been through might ever happen again.

"A once-in-a-lifetime adventure," Leila said.

Andy just smiled and nodded his head. There was really no better way of saying it.

They returned to the conference room at the requested time and assumed the same seats they had been situated in earlier.

"I must say," the mayor began, "that I am of two minds regarding Mr. Vasquez and Ms. Taylor—well … and Dr. Costa, as well. They did plan and commit first-degree murder, but …"

The mayor hesitated. He glanced slowly around the room and made eye contact with each of the individuals surrounding him. Detective Alvarez and O'Reilly gazed back stoically, while Andy's facial response was one of acknowledgment. When the mayor's eyes met Leila's, she returned a rueful expression as if to say, "Can you blame them?"

"Anyway, it is a difficult moral dilemma, and I don't envy the prosecutor who will handle the case," the mayor said, completing his thought.

"Uh, what do you mean, the prosecutor?" Leila asked.

"Are you going to extradite them?" Andy asked.

"Well, we can't extradite them—the Norwegians will have to do that at the request of the State Department. I have already reached out to the undersecretary who handles such requests—"

"So, you are going to try to prosecute Bryan and Taylor?" Leila asked, the slight raise in her voice signaling her concern.

"Listen, I appreciate what your feelings for them might be, but we will have to follow the law. I am not above the law—even as the mayor."

"That hardly seems fair," Leila replied.

"What if the Norwegians won't extradite them?" Andy asked.

"Well, then they can be prosecuted in absentia or not at all—that is up to the district attorney," the mayor replied.

"So, they either stay in Norway, if they are even allowed to, or they will be sent to prison," Leila stated.

"Or they will get acquitted, Leila," Alvarez added.

"That's not very likely, is it?" Andy asked.

"You never know how juries will decide. Bryan and Taylor will certainly have a sympathetic story to tell," Alvarez replied.

"If their lawyer lets them take the stand," O'Reilly chimed in.

"Is there any way they can come back to the United States and not have to face the justice system?" Leila asked.

"The only option is for the governor to pardon them, and then they'll be free, but I am pretty sure he can only do that after they are convicted—if they are convicted," the mayor said.

"I see," Leila said. She whispered something to Andy.

"So, one last question, and then we will let you go. Can you advise us on how to explain the death of Mr. Millbank to the public?" the mayor requested.

"And the media," Ms. Colon added.

"Yes, of course, the media—that is who the public listens to anyway," the mayor said.

Ms. Colon added, "Doctors, we need to explain the bizarre way he died in a way the public will accept and understand, one that alleviates any concern that his death had anything to do with bioterrorism or some contagious disease. And we need Anderson Cooper to be able to explain it too."

"Are we going to get to meet Anderson Cooper?" Leila asked excitedly.

The meeting attendees all laughed, though they could not be sure whether Leila meant it as a joke to break the tension or if she was serious.

"No, no, that's not the plan—you don't need to do that. We need to put out a press release, and then he and that doctor on his show, what's his name—?" Ms. Colon continued.

"Sanjay Gupta," Leila and Andy answered simultaneously.

"Yeah, Sanjay Gupta. He can explain it to the world. You understand what I mean, right?"

"Ms. Colon," Andy began, "we explain complicated medical issues to patients all the time—some of whom have little to no education—so we are used to giving explanations to lay people."

"Great! Well then, let's hear it," Ms. Colon continued. "How would you explain it if Anderson Cooper were sitting here?"

"Leila, go ahead," Andy said in an encouraging tone.

"Okay. Let me think for a second," Leila began, and she took a moment to gather her thoughts. "How about this? 'Anderson, let me be crystal clear about one thing. The death of Mr. Millbank was not an act of terrorism. It was a simple poisoning. That's it. Shall I elaborate?'"

"Yes, Dr. Baker, please do," Ms. Colon replied, as if she were Anderson Cooper.

"Blood clots are one of the most common conditions in the United States and, in fact, are one of the most common causes of death. In order to prevent and treat blood clots, doctors prescribe medicines called blood thinners. Warfarin, the most commonly used blood thinner, is one of the most prescribed medicines throughout the world. Unfortunately, warfarin is not easy to work with—you need to get regular blood tests, and it has many interactions with food and medications, which could result in serious consequences. So, drug companies have made new blood thinners—they are safer and easier to manage—and Mr. Millbank was poisoned with one of those and bled to death. It's really that simple," Leila said to complete her explanation.

"Where can someone get this medicine to poison someone?" Ms. Colon continued, still pretending to be Anderson Cooper.

"Blood thinners require a doctor's prescription, but once a patient has that in hand, any pharmacy could fill it, and then they would have it."

"So, they're not hard to get, then."

"Well, not if you can get a doctor to prescribe them, but no reasonable doctor would give a prescription unless a patient had a blood clot or needed a blood thinner for some other reason," Leila replied.

"If you have the pills, then, you could conceivably poison someone—is that right?" Ms. Colon continued her Anderson Cooper impersonation.

"Well, yes, if you can get them to take it," Leila said. "Of course, I understand. Thank you, Leila."

"Hold on a second," O'Reilly interjected. "You said nothing about the super-Lyzanda."

"Right, Sean. That was on purpose. It would only confuse things. I didn't say anything that wasn't true," Leila said.

"I like that, actually. Leila is right—it would make it too confusing to discuss Bergeland's special concoction, and it really doesn't make much difference," Ms. Colon said.

"You don't think someone will find out about it?" Alvarez asked, playing devil's advocate.

"If they do, we will explain it, but as a first pass, I like Leila's approach," Ms. Colon replied.

Ms. Colon looked at the mayor with a satisfied look on her face, and he understood that they'd gotten the advice they'd been seeking. Leila offered to speak directly to Sanjay Gupta if that would help.

"Well, on behalf of the citizens of New York City, I would like to thank you both immensely for all your work, and while I can't offer much, I am putting together a letter of commendation from my office for all your efforts," the mayor said.

"Thank you, Mr. Mayor. That will help us explain our prolonged absence to our boss. He is always looking for publicity for our hospital and our division," Andy said.

With that, Andy and Leila's role in the case of the bleeders was over.

CHAPTER 39

JUNE 30–JULY 4
LOS ANGELES,
NEW YORK,
TROMSØ

The marine layer of fog burned off by eighty thirty, and a spectacular summer Saturday was on tap for Los Angeles. Andy met Leila at Café Bonaparte in the Hermosa Beach pier plaza; it was Andy's favorite local hangout. He brought Leila her usual vanilla latte, though not from the usual source, for Café Bonaparte served the world-renowned Italian coffee, Lavazza, which Leila enjoyed even more than Starbucks'. Andy decided on a cappuccino. He placed them on the table out in the glorious morning sunshine and then returned to the bar and brought back a chocolate croissant and a chocolate-chip-and-raspberry muffin. The pastries were freshly made and among the best he'd ever had.

After they'd solved the mystery of the bleeders and returned to their routine, yet busy, life in Los Angeles in late January, Leila had finally revealed to Andy what had transpired over the New Year's weekend when she had refused to talk to him. Leila had spent that whole weekend with her parents, talking about her life, her goals, and her dreams. Her mother had expressed concern that she was getting too old to start a family, reminding her repeatedly that all of their relatives of similar age were already married and had families. Leila pointedly reminded her mother that the women were all housewives, and while she made sure to state that she wasn't being judgmental, she also made sure to highlight the fact that she was a physician—the first one in her family, male or female. As her mother had become more and more frustrated, she'd reassured both her parents that she did want to get married and start a family. However, she'd also affirmed that she wouldn't marry just anyone in order to appease them—or anyone else. Her parents had asked Leila whether she was at least making an effort to meet men and asked her specifically about when her last date had occurred. As Leila was getting ready to answer the question, her parents had each in turn interrupted her and offered to arrange dates for her from the small, but tightknit, Kurdish community in Los Angeles.

In no uncertain terms Leila let her parents know that she had no interest in being set up, and she used the opportunity to ask them whether it was more important to find someone she loved, regardless of his background and religion, or whether it was more important to marry a Kurd. Her father told her that he expected her to at least marry a Muslim, and preferably a Kurd. Her mother disagreed, simply stating that Leila needed to find the right man and get married and start a family, regardless of his religion. At that point her father became upset, got up, and left the conversation. Leila then took the opportunity to tell her mother about Andy.

She decided to just come out with it and reveal everything. First she explained how she'd met Andy and what a wonderful working relationship they had. Then she told her about how they had become close over the course of the many trips they had taken together while working on the case of the bleeders. She went on to say that she had fallen in love with him, and he with her, during those weeks when they'd spent so much time together. Leila explained to her mother that it had been like having a long date, every day, for numerous days on end. Only when her mother became convinced that Andy was a good person for Leila did Leila disclose to her that he was Jewish. At first her mother was taken aback, more by surprise than by anguish. When Leila pressed her mother to reveal her thoughts about this, she posed two questions to her daughter: "Is he a good man?" and "Does he love you?" Leila was able to respond affirmatively to both. Her mother smiled and said that she was happy for her. She went even further and expressed relief that her daughter was finally in a serious relationship. It was quite a gesture for her to say she was "relieved" that Leila was in love with a Jewish man.

Leila then asked for some advice, specifically wondering what she should tell her father. Her mother reassured her that though her father would be upset at first, he would come around. She suggested that it would be best if she, his wife of forty years, delivered that piece of information—at an opportune moment. Leila agreed.

By the time Andy and Leila returned to Los Angeles, it was late January, and Leila's mother had already had several conversations with her husband about Leila and Andy. Her father's initial and firm recalcitrance melted like snow on a mountaintop in the spring, retreating ever so slowly day by day, until almost imperceptibly, it had vanished completely. Then he eventually agreed to meet Andy. An early March barbecue was arranged at the Baker household in El Segundo. Mr. Baker, at first skeptical, spent a lot of time talking to Andy. They talked about Andy's background and upbringing, his religion, politics, and sports. Mr. Baker and Andy noted similarities in Kurdish and Jewish history and culture. After all, both ethnic groups had been persecuted throughout history, and while Israel had become a Jewish state and the Kurds had yet to realize the dream of having their own state, they nevertheless found that they had more in common than either one would have thought.

Andy and Leila "officially" became a couple after the barbecue. Although they had kept their relationship a secret at work—at least for a while—over time it became more and more difficult to keep it hidden, and by the time they decided to let their team in on their supposed secret at one of their weekly meetings, knowing smiles formed on all the faces. Their nurse, Andrea, took great joy in telling them both, to a chorus of giggling, that everyone in the division already knew. Nevertheless, a round of cheerful applause ensued.

Now here they were, enjoying a quiet weekend morning in Hermosa Beach. The crowd of tourists—inland Los Angeles beach seekers and beach-volleyball players—had yet to arrive. Besides the other early birds, the surfers and bikers, the Pier Plaza was largely empty.

"So, after all those trips to all those places, it's hard to believe we haven't gone anywhere in—what, five months?" Leila said, sipping her coffee.

"I know. I'm excited to go back, actually. You've never been to New York in the summer, have you?" Andy asked.

"No—is it different?"

"Well, yes and no. I mean, the city itself looks mostly the same. It's the park that looks completely different, and of course, it's much warmer—hot, in fact," Andy replied.

They were heading to New York for a vacation and to meet up with their old friends Detectives O'Reilly and Alvarez. And from there, at the advice of one Erik Bergeland, they would head back to Tromsø. He'd so enticed them with what they could see and do there in the summer, aside from mentioning that they would get to view the midnight sun, that they simply couldn't resist. Bergeland had offered to host them and cover all their expenses, but Leila had politely refused, and Andy agreed. They finished their breakfast and headed to the airport. There would be no awkward airport greeting this time.

It was a warm, humid evening in New York City. Andy and Leila hopped out of the taxi in Greenwich Village and headed to the Olive Tree Café. It had been Leila's idea to go back there; she felt that, in order to tackle any remaining demons from that fateful night eight months ago, they needed to go back and have an enjoyable meal there. Andy appreciated the sentiment, and he realized that much of this vacation would be about retracing their steps, albeit in a much more relaxed and warm atmosphere. They were looking forward to seeing Detectives O'Reilly and Alvarez once again.

"I miss those guys," Leila said.

"Me, too. They've made me think of police officers in a different light," Andy replied.

"What do you mean?" Leila wondered.

"You need to understand that pretty much all of my interactions with police officers have been getting traffic tickets."

"That's lame, Andy. The police protect us—which includes giving *you* traffic tickets."

Andy laughed. He appreciated that he had found his match when it came to a biting, sarcastic sense of humor.

After ten minutes, Jose and Sean arrived and greeted Andy and Leila with broad smiles and warm hugs. Although their time together had been all in all very short, it had been intense, and their bond of friendship had remained strong over the interceding months. Jose remarked that he had always wondered whether there was more to Andy and Leila's relationship than they'd had let on.

"So, when's the wedding?" he asked, laughing.

"Hey, not so fast. I'm still figuring this guy out," Leila said, pointing at Andy, who proceeded to blush.

"So, Sean, why don't you tell them *your* news," Alvarez said. O'Reilly was embarrassed, and now he turned red in the face. "

Go on," Alvarez coaxed him.

"Well, uh, after the case, I became friendly with Mrs. Millbank," he said haltingly.

"What the—are you kidding me?" Andy said.

"Sean is too embarrassed, but I'll say it for him. They are more than just friends, trust me," Alvarez added.

"How sweet, Sean. I was always amazed how much information and help she gave us during the investigation. Now I see why. She apparently had an ulterior motive," Leila said.

They all laughed and then headed to their table for dinner. This was their first face-to-face meeting since the investigation had ended. They had managed to keep in touch over the months, though they hadn't discussed the case further. This was an opportunity to revisit the case and for both pairs to obtain some follow-up in an exchange of information. Andy and Leila agreed that they would honestly answer any remaining questions the detectives might have.

"Is it okay if we discuss the case now?" Alvarez asked. "Sure," Andy said.

"So, you know that neither Bryan nor Taylor have turned themselves in, right?"

"If you say so. I mean, we don't have any independent knowledge, honest.

Right, Andy?" Leila said.

"Yeah, I haven't heard from either one of them, and Bryan's family will not discuss his situation with us. I thought that they were going to be extradited from Norway," Andy said.

"We tried—that's not going to happen. Norway is pretty strict about who and where they will extradite people to," Alvarez replied.

"So you have no idea at all where they are now?" O'Reilly followed.

"No. Honestly, we don't. The last time we saw them was in Tromsø in the middle of January, during those days when they finished telling us about, you know, how they pulled it off—killing Stern and Millbank," Andy replied.

"I'm sorry for the two of you, as I know that it's your job to catch them," Leila stated. "But do you really expect them to turn themselves in? After all, they did admit to killing Mr. Millbank, not to mention Mr. Stern."

"Leila, do you think it's right that they got away with premeditated murder? Do you think they should be able to hand out justice on their own?" Alvarez asked.

"I understand what you're saying, Jose, and I am not going to answer those questions. I'm just asking if you are really expecting them to ever show up here."

"Immigration is aware that they are fugitives, so if they ever attempt to return to the US, they'll be apprehended immediately."

"Well, that doesn't answer the question," Leila said.

"Then we're even, Leila, because you didn't answer mine," Alvarez replied with a smile.

"Let me say something about this as the veteran police officer," O'Reilly said. "Look, Jose and I, we're not trying to be insensitive to what happened to Bryan and Taylor. It's—sorry, I don't know how else to say it—fuckin' horrible, but you need to put yourself in our shoes for a minute. We are enforcers of the law, and we take an oath to do that, and as part of that oath we investigate and apprehend people who commit crimes. And we have a justice system that we believe in, and while it's not perfect, it works very well. So I honestly think it would be in their best interest to return to the US and face a trial. Obviously, there are major mitigating circumstances—and very sympathetic ones, too—and all that would be taken into account."

"Come on, Sean, is there any way they would be found not guilty?" Leila wondered.

"You never know. The case is all circumstantial, and with a sympathetic jury, they could easily get acquitted," O'Reilly responded.

"And don't forget what the mayor said—if they got convicted, the governor could pardon them," Alvarez added.

"Well, there's no guarantee of that. What if they get convicted and don't get pardoned? They'd go to prison for many years, if not for life," Andy said firmly.

"Speaking of going to prison or not—do you ever speak to Detective de Ville?" Leila asked.

"Not anymore, but we did in the weeks following the meeting we all had here in New York—you remember, the one with the mayor," Alvarez said.

"And ... do you know what happened with Angelina?" Leila asked cautiously.

"Yes," O'Reilly said. "When de Ville presented the case to the prosecutor, he decided to conduct his own investigation of Mr. Stern's alleged rapes, and well, it's pretty incredible, actually."

"What? What is it?"

"The prosecutor, with Dr. Costa and Ms. Hummel's help, was able to locate forty-six of the fifty-seven women that Angelina thought Stern had raped. He got a statement from all of them under oath, and then he met with Angelina," O'Reilly said.

"And, what did he decide to do?" Leila asked.

"He reviewed all the evidence he had, which was basically circumstantial and incomplete, and decided there was not enough evidence to try Dr. Costa—so, she's a free woman," O'Reilly concluded.

"A free woman, indeed," Leila said pensively. "In more ways than one."

There was a brief silence as the four exchanged glances, each wondering what the others were thinking with regard to that outcome. They finished their dinners and at O'Reilly's insistence headed to an Irish pub—Foley's on Thirty-Third Street. Leila had had enough of the serious discussion regarding the case, and as they settled near the bar, she quickly got the attention of the bartender and ordered a round of Guinness.

"Well, enough about the bleeders. Let me tell you what I'd really like to know more about," Leila said.

"Yeah, what's that?" O'Reilly said.

"Well, Sean, what I am most interested in you telling me is, well … I want to hear all about Mrs. Millbank. What is she like? How long have you been dating? You know—everything."

They all laughed, further embarrassing detective O'Reilly. He was reticent at first, and the discussion wandered over to a review of the plight of Detective Alvarez's children. But eventually, following a second round of Guinness, the vault slowly opened, and O'Reilly provided Leila with the details she was seeking. The rest of the evening was enjoyable and uneventful, with no further discussion of the whereabouts of Bryan or Taylor.

Following their overnight flight from JFK back to Oslo's Gardermoen airport, Andy and Leila found themselves back in Norway for the first time in over five months. They had been in the beautiful high-arched terminal before; only this time, the view through the large windows revealed a landscape remarkably different from the gray and white of clouds and snow. It was, in fact, so different and so green that it seemed like a different country. The sun was shining brightly and already quite high over the eastern sky, despite the fact that it was only 6:00 a.m. They filed through passport control quickly despite the immigration officer questioning them on their repeated trips to Norway. Then they headed to the domestic terminal, where they boarded an SAS flight to Tromsø. They had a definite feeling of déjà vu. Andy and Leila had researched the various places they could go and the many activities they could pursue in Norway, but they knew they had to start in Tromsø. Unlike their rendezvous with Alvarez and O'Reilly in New York, they had no reunion plans in Tromsø—not with Bergeland, despite his overtures, and not with Bryan or Taylor, neither of whom had been in communication since they'd left Tromsø last January.

It was a spectacular day to fly. Summer had overtaken Norway, and the sky was an unimaginable deep and clear blue color. Peering out the window, Andy could see the famous glacier-carved fjords of Norway. It still amazed him that they had been formed during the last ice age by the crushing weight of the ice literally forcing the earth downward below sea level. Much of Norway's scenic beauty could be attributed to the lasting effects of the massive glaciers which, upon receding over a hundred thousand years ago, had allowed the Atlantic Ocean to pour in, unimpeded, deep into the coastal landscape. Andy could almost imagine the fingers of ice long ago filling in the space between the coastal mountains. The view was spectacular, and Andy had Leila leaning over him in order to share the view. Andy offered to trade seats, but she just smiled and said she preferred to lean on and over him in order to see. As the plane descended, they could easily make out Tromsø, the island floating like a giant tapered leaf on the calm waters of the fjord. Andy pointed out Storsteinen and the bridge connecting Tromsø to Tromsdalen on the mainland. The plane landed gently, and once outside, Andy and Leila were stunned at how warm it was. Following the numerous frigid days and nights they'd experienced, to be able to stand on the sidewalk wearing a short-sleeve shirt and jeans was quite unexpected, even odd. It was noon, and the sun hung like a jewel in the southeast sky a full sixty degrees above the horizon. The only bit of sun they had previously seen here had been a distant orange orb just over the horizon as they'd had their final meal on Storsteinen with the quartet.

Andy had made a to-do list for their time in Tromsø, consisting mostly of retracing their steps and reliving their often-bizarre adventure. They arrived at the SAS Radisson, the same hotel where they had stayed before and where they had found the quartet together for the first time. There was one difference this time though—Andy and Leila needed only one hotel room. Despite the long journey, they felt energized and were ready to explore the city, which hardly resembled the one they had seen before. For one thing, it had essentially been dark during their previous visits, yet now the city was bathed in warm sunlight. They ate a quick lunch at the hotel and headed south down the main street to the Aquarium. It was fronted by a large sign boasting that it was the northernmost aquarium in the world. Nearly every tourist attraction (and even many non-tourist attractions) made the same proud claim. The aquarium had many exhibits of fish and crustaceans, but the main attraction was the large pool in an icy-cold room, where many seals of several types playfully moved from the water to their rocky platforms.

After leaving the aquarium, they strode through the center of the city, where the hotels and most of the restaurants were located. As they moved among the people, mostly locals by their estimation, Leila wondered if they might run into Bryan or Taylor. Andy suggested they be extra vigilant, on the chance that either one was still in Tromsø. *Where are you, Taylor Davis?* Leila asked inwardly. She also wondered about Bryan's whereabouts. At the last visit of the Vasquez family in the clinic, neither Jessica nor her parents admitted to knowing where Bryan was. The obvious lack of any signs of concern left Andy and Leila convinced that they had been in contact with him, knew where he was, and were not telling, but the doctors elected not to pry.

As the day wore on, the toll of their trip began to wear on them. Thus, in preparation for experiencing the midnight sun, Andy and Leila elected to take a nap. Amazingly, the curtains in their room couldn't be closed completely, leaving a ray of sunlight beaming across the room like a laser. Nevertheless, their fatigue overcame the inescapable sunlight, and they fell asleep lying on their sides with Andy's arm across Leila's midriff.

Andy rolled over, his hands stretching across the bed. After a few seconds, he came to the realization that Leila was not in the bed with him. He called out for her, but there was no answer. She wasn't in the room. It was 9:00 p.m., and he'd been sleeping for four hours. He reached for his iPhone and dialed Leila's number.

"Hi, babe—whatchya doing?" came Leila's voice.

"Me? What are you doing?" Andy replied, a bit annoyed.

"You were sleeping, and I had woken up, so I came down to the lobby to get a drink," Leila replied.

"Why didn't you wake me up?"

"Why should I have woken you up?" Leila replied playfully.

Andy realized he wasn't going to get anywhere continuing this line of conversation. He agreed to meet Leila in the lobby following a shower.

"Hey, there. Do you feel refreshed?" Leila asked cheerily.

"Yes. When did you wake up?" Andy asked.

"About an hour before you. I started reading but got bored, so I came down here. You should go out and see the sun, by the way."

"What do you mean?" Andy asked.

"Just go look, and tell me what you think."

Andy obliged by heading out of the lobby and walking to the edge of the fjord. He looked up and noted that the sun was still sixty degrees above the horizon, only it had shifted to the western sky. It was odd. He was used to the sun rising, arcing overhead, and angling back to the horizon. Here the sun was just circling over the city like a bird surveying the ground below.

"So, isn't that weird?" Leila asked Andy upon his return to the lobby.

Andy acknowledged that the sun's motion was not what he had expected. Then he decided that he was hungry. They found their way to the Arctandria Restaurant, the same restaurant they'd eaten at on their first night in Tromsø. After they were seated, Andy noticed Leila was acting a bit strange.

"Leila, what's going on? You're acting all weird," Andy asked.

"What are you talking about?" she said, though the Cheshire grin she couldn't contain belied her response.

"Don't pull that shit on me. I know you well enough by now that I know you're hiding something," Andy stated purposefully.

"Andy, come on. I'm not hiding anything," Leila said, painfully trying to contain her smile.

"I don't know what you're up to, but I know you're up to something. I know it."

Leila offered no further clues to her mischievous behavior during dinner. Andy resigned himself to finding out what Leila was up to on her own terms. By the time they'd finished eating, it was nearly eleven in the evening. It was time to head to Storsteinen, Tromsø's best vantage point to see the midnight sun. As they walked out, expecting some semblance of twilight, both Andy and Leila were surprised to note just how bright it still was outside. The sun continued its meander overhead, only slightly lowering its angle over the horizon but now hovering over the northwestern sky. From the time they had landed in Tromsø and first stepped outside at the airport earlier in the day, the sun had made a 270° arc overhead, with hardly any change of its angle above the horizon. The temperature had dropped from a comfortable sixty-eight to a slightly cooler sixty degrees. They each donned a light jacket as they began the walk across the bridge to Tromsdalen. As they reached the top of the bridge, once again the remarkable sight of the Arctic Cathedral stood before them, only this time illuminated by soft, yellow sunlight. Once in Tromsdalen, they followed the path toward the cable car that would take them up to Storsteinen. It was 11:45 p.m., yet children were playing on the streets while their parents watched them from their porches. Despite the fact that it was still daylight, Andy found it odd. *Surely, they must go to sleep at some point*, he thought.

Finally reaching the bottom of the cable car, Andy and Leila both felt a sense of excitement. Between their nap and the ongoing daylight, they felt no weariness at all, not in their bodies and not in their minds. As they reached the cable-car entrance gate, they were dismayed to see a rather long line of people waiting. It was strangely comforting.

"I guess we're not the only crazy ones," Andy said.

"Uh, excuse me. We're not crazy, and they're not crazy. If we were in New York, we'd be out at some bar or club," Leila responded.

"And if we were in Los Angeles, we'd be sleeping."

"Not necessarily," Leila said.

As they reached the back end of the line, the couple in front of them asked them in English where they were from.

"Is it that obvious that we're tourists?" Andy asked.

"No, but Tromsø is a small city, and we know most of the couples our age," the woman replied.

"How come there are so many people here? Are they all tourists?" Leila asked.

"No. Mostly locals."

"So, why is there such a line then, if you all live here and can do this any time?" Leila followed up.

"This is the first really nice day this summer. It's been quite rainy for the past few weeks. You're lucky. It's not like this very often," the man replied.

Within fifteen minutes, Andy and Leila were in the cable car with the couple that had been in front of them and several others. They reached the top in five minutes, climbed out of the cable car, and headed over to the viewpoint area. It was indeed a spectacular sight. It was now 12:30 a.m., and the sun was still shining. It had dropped a fair bit toward the horizon since earlier in the evening but still was a good twenty degrees above the horizon. Andy and Leila snapped numerous pictures, ensuring the clock in their camera was set properly so it would accurately time-stamp each picture. After walking around taking in the spectacular views of the island city far below, the bridges connecting the two shores to the mainland, and the Arctic Cathedral, they found an unoccupied picnic table and had a seat. They were happy.

"Andy, isn't so strange to be back here? After all, this is where we came when the investigation ended, to have lunch with Bergeland, Bryan, Taylor, and Angelina."

"Yes, a strangely triumphant meal, wasn't it?" Andy said.

"Why do you say *strangely* triumphant?" Leila asked.

"Leila, they were celebrating the deaths of two people—two people they murdered, I might remind you."

"That isn't fair. You know that they don't view it that way. They weren't celebrating the deaths of Stern and Millbank but rather their own liberation from the private hell those men caused them," Leila replied. "To them it was all about getting closure for all the suffering they'd gone through. You and I will never understand that. At least, let's hope not."

"That's not how Alvarez and O'Reilly see it."

"Two different views," Leila said.

"Two different views of the same thing," Andy said, thinking of a song he liked, called "Two Different Views," by the band The Fixx. *There will always be two different views of the same thing, baby, too many views that can collide*, he sang to himself.

"So, what *do* you think, Andy? You know, with all of our many discussions about the case, I don't recall that you ever told me your final thoughts. Last time we were here, Bergeland threw that question out, remember?"

"Yeah, what did he say, exactly? 'I am curious to hear your thoughts,' was it?

"Yes, something like that," Leila said slowly.

Andy remained silent and pensive. "Well?" Leila demanded.

"Do you really want to have this conversation now—haven't we talked about it enough?" Andy stated, clearly feeling uncomfortable.

"But Andy, you never told me what you would actually do if you were the judge or juror," Leila said.

"Really. We are on vacation. You want to have this conversation right here and right now?" Andy asked, hoping not to receive an affirmative answer.

"Yes. Yes, I do. Andy, we need to talk about it, and we need to get our own sense of closure. With all of our discussions, I still don't have that," Leila said. "Trust me, we'll enjoy the rest of the trip much more without this hanging over us. Why the hell do you think I agreed to come back here?"

"I thought you wanted to see the midnight sun and enjoy Tromsø in the summer, as Bergeland suggested."

"Yes, that's part of it, but Andy, we need to exorcise the ghosts of this whole experience too," Leila said as her tone turned more somber. "Do you know I've been thinking about Bryan and Taylor and Angelina every day?"

"No, why didn't you tell me?" Andy asked, suddenly alarmed.

"So, you mean to tell me you don't think about the case or think about Taylor and Bryan and Angelina? Did you feel like you have closure?" Leila asked firmly.

"Of course I've thought about it, but I guess not as much as you," Andy replied.

"You've probably just suppressed it all," Leila said.

"Are you psychoanalyzing me?" Andy asked wistfully.

"No, I'm ..." Leila hesitated. "Look, I want us to get closure. I want us to talk about our feelings about Bryan and Taylor. I, uh, I need to talk about it, and I need to hear your view, okay?"

"What if we don't agree?" Andy wondered.

"Oh, Andy. We don't have to agree. For me to put the case behind me, I need to come to some conclusions about my feelings, and you know, honestly... I need to know your feelings, too."

"Okay," Andy said as the minor chords of the acoustic guitar playing the melody and thought-provoking lyrics of "Two Different Views" filled his head:

> *Big ideas I can't suppress*
> *Little lies I do detect*
> *Through pleasure, pain, delight, and wonder*

There's the rub of irony
When indecision slices me
From high of highs, it pulls me under

There will always be two different views of the same thing,
baby
Too many views that can collide
There will always be two different views
Too many views we're loaded by

Andy looked at Leila and smiled, his heart warmed by her presence. He wondered if Leila had purposely chosen this spot with ever-present light to ask him to shed light on his own feelings. It was somehow appropriate, he thought to himself.

"Leila, it has been difficult for me to come to any conclusions. I think that's why I don't like to talk about Bryan and the rest of them, because I am truly conflicted."

"That's why we need to talk about it," Leila answered in a reassuring tone. "At first glance, it's so obvious that what they did was wrong—and I know this will sound crazy—but I actually feel guilty that I can't feel any anger toward them, especially Bryan. He's such a great young man. Full of spirit and full of love for his family. I admire his devotion to his sisters and parents."

"Don't you see, though? It's precisely that devotion that you admire that led him to do what he did, you know," Leila said.

"That's what makes it so hard," Andy said and he paused.

"Go on," Leila encouraged him.

"How could I admire him for the very quality that led him to kill two men?"

"Do you think it matters who he killed ... or why?"

"It shouldn't. It's not like it was self-defense. It was, in a sense, the opposite—instead of just a gut reaction, he actually took months to think about it."

"You said it *shouldn't* matter, but that means you are leaving an opening for saying it *does* matter," Leila continued.

"I don't know," Andy said.

"What if he'd killed two strangers for no reason—he didn't even rob them?"

"Well, sure, that would be different," Andy replied.

"Then it does matter. You just answered it for yourself."

"Okay, yes, it does matter. He killed two of the most disgusting, repulsive men that have ever lived."

"So, does that absolve him, then?" Leila continued the interrogation.

"Not in a court of law," Andy replied.

"That's a copout answer. I want to know what *you* think, Andy."

"Why are you being so persistent—are you judging me or something? Does this have to do with us? Is that why you were acting so strange earlier?"

"Easy there, Andy. Don't get all defensive. I'm not judging you. I love you, and this has nothing to do with us. It does have to do with you and me getting our feelings out about the people who told us straight to our faces that they killed two men."

"Okay, sorry. I overreacted."

Andy thought for a moment while gazing at the sun; it had seemingly reached its nadir and started to climb further above the horizon.

"Leila, I would really like to forgive them all for what they did, except they won't apologize, will they?"

"Do they need to apologize? They all knew exactly what they were doing. An apology under such circumstances would ring a bit hollow, in my view."

"Speaking of your view—ahem—what *is* your view?"

"Let's finish with you, first," Leila insisted.

"Fine. I am coming to the realization that I am truly caught with two different views. On the one hand, they are all premeditated murderers. On the other hand, they are all victims whose lives were shattered by the two men they killed. I suppose if they could honestly tell me that killing Millbank and Stern gave them closure for the horrors they lived through and would help them in the long futures they have ahead of them, I could sit down with them face to face again. Having said that, though, I think I will always have two different views."

"Well thought and well said, Andy. I know it wasn't easy, but I appreciate you telling me all that. I think this catharsis will help you," Leila said, and she smiled adoringly at her man.

"I hope so."

"I know so," Leila said.

"So, what about you, then? You've obviously spent a lot of time thinking about it. Where do you stand?" Andy asked.

"I have thought about it a lot. Every day," Leila began somberly. "And it is difficult. You and I are doctors. We care for people's health, and we work toward preventing harm and, in a manner of speaking, preventing death. We are indoctrinated that every life is precious. I remember taking care of a hemophilia patient who was a gang member, who'd been in jail, and who'd confessed to me to doing some really bad things to others. I just took care of his medical needs—without judgment. Trust me, this guy was a scoundrel."

"Did he kill anyone?"

"Not to my knowledge, but he did assault people," Leila replied.

"So, if you see every life as precious, then you must view Bryan, Taylor, and Angelina as murderers."

"It's not that easy, and it's not that simple," Leila continued. "I feel bad for Bryan, don't get me wrong, but he was not himself a direct victim of the brutal and disgusting acts of Mr. Stern and Mr. Millbank. They were, as you said, the scum of the earth. Part of me feels strongly that people like that have no right to live, but then, another part of me does feel that every life is precious, and no one has the right—no matter what—to take another person's life."

"Two different views," Andy said.

"Two different views. At least we can agree on that."

They took a brief hiatus from their discussion, getting up to walk around. The sun was now rising, however not in its usual waking direction in the east but rather in the northern sky. It was the one direction in which the sun was never visible in Los Angeles. Leila grabbed Andy's hand and smiled again the Cheshire grin that had made Andy suspicious of what she might be up to.

"What is it, Leila? You're up to something, I know it."

"One last question about Bryan, Angelina, Taylor, and Bergeland, okay?"

"Sure, what is it?"

"Would you ever want to see them again?"

Andy thought for a moment and looked at Leila.

"Yes, of course. As strange as this will sound, I will forever cherish the memories of you and I investigating this case and, well … Bryan and Taylor and Angelina, and even Bergeland, the bastard." They laughed, and Andy continued, "You know, who knows if our relationship would be what is now without them?"

Still laughing, Leila led him to the far southern end of Storsteinen. As they approached the precipice on this part of the mountain, he could make out four figures—two men and two women.

Two different views, he thought to himself. He decided that at this moment he would take the more benign view.

ABOUT THE AUTHOR

G uy Young is a physician who was raised on Long Island, New York, and lives in Los Angeles. He cares for children with blood disorders at Children's Hospital Los Angeles. This, his first novel, is a medical mystery. Young is married and has two boys.